MW01035297

Also by Kali Wallace

Shallow Graves

THE

MEMORY

TREES

KALI WALLACE

To Heather —

Wishing you
Happy Reading!
on your
cold.
Maine nights!

KATHERINE TEGEN BOOKS
An Imprint of HarperCollins Publishers

Katherine Tegen Books is an imprint of HarperCollins Publishers.

The Memory Trees
Copyright © 2017 by Kali Wallace
All rights reserved. Printed in the United States of America.
No part of this book may be used or reproduced in any manner whatsoever without written
permission except in the case of brief quotations embodied in critical articles and reviews.
For information address HarperCollins Children's Books, a division of HarperCollins
Publishers, 195 Broadway, New York, NY 10007.
www.epicreads.com

Library of Congress Control Number: 2017932868
ISBN 978-0-06-236623-8

Typography by Heather Daugherty
17 18 19 20 21 PC/LSCH 10 9 8 7 6 5 4 3 2 1
❖
First Edition

FOR MY SISTERS, SARAH, ALIA, AND LILY

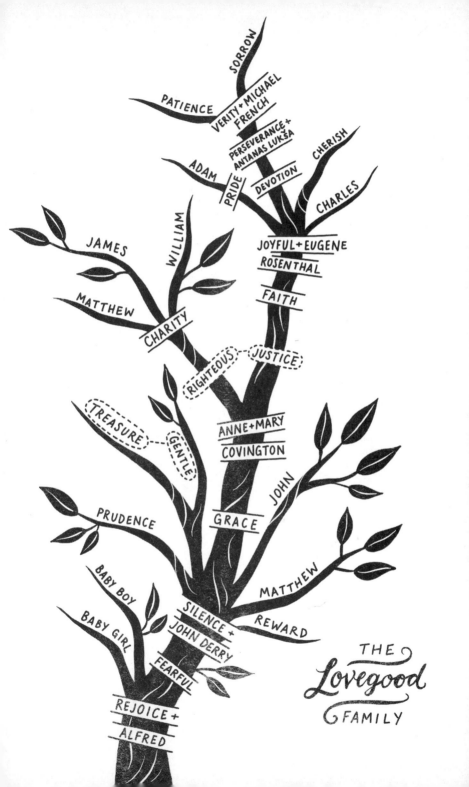

1

BEYOND THE WINDOW the morning was bright and glittering, the sky a breathless blue, and the hotels on Miami Beach jutted like broken teeth across the water, but all Sorrow could see was the orchard. There were trees whispering behind the walls of the office, and she almost believed if she turned—if she was quick—she would glimpse their sturdy thick trunks and rustling dead leaves from the corner of her eye.

"Your father is very worried about you," Dr. Silva said.

Sorrow rubbed her arms and looked away from the window. That cool breeze touching the back of her neck, that was only the air conditioner.

Dr. Silva was, as ever, perfectly composed in a pencil skirt, a cream blouse that complemented her dark skin, and heels so high Sorrow wondered how anybody could walk in them without risking ankle damage. Sorrow had seen Dr. Silva regularly when she first moved to Florida, but it had been two years since her last appointment, and the doctor had moved her practice from a hospital in Coral Gables to a Brickell skyscraper overlooking Biscayne Bay. Boats crawled through the no-wake zone far below, and cars glinted like jewels on the bridges.

Sorrow was leaning in the corner of the leather sofa, her legs sticking painfully to the seat. Dad was in the waiting room, probably paging through a glossy travel magazine, checking his email, checking the time. He had made the appointment, gotten Sorrow out of bed, fixed her breakfast, taken a day off work to come with her even though she was perfectly capable of driving herself. Sorrow's stepmother, Sonia, had watched it all with worried eyes and a concerned pinch to her lips, but she hadn't argued or interfered. She hadn't offered any opinion at all except to say, "I think that's a good idea."

Dr. Silva was waiting for an answer. Sorrow thought about rolling her eyes, didn't. Thought about giving an unimpressed snort. Didn't. The silence stretched. There wasn't a trace of impatience on Dr. Silva's face.

Finally Sorrow said, "I can't stop thinking about my sister."

It was the first time Sorrow had admitted it out loud since the party, and once she started, the words were tumbling out: she had been thinking about Patience when she disappeared that evening from her grandparents' house on the edge of the Everglades, and she had been thinking about her day and night since then. She thought about Patience when she woke in the morning and when she tossed and turned in bed at night, when she went to school and when she came home, when she hugged her stepsister, Andi, good-bye at the airport, when Sonia asked about her day, when she shrugged away from her father's concern. She had been thinking about Patience when she was blowing off meeting her friends, when she was supposed to be doing her homework, taking a trigonometry exam, writing an English essay, and she had been thinking about Patience when her teachers had called Dad and Sonia into the school to discuss the recent decline in her already unimpressive academic performance.

Every day, every moment, she was thinking about Patience in their mother's orchard in Vermont, her long brown hair and soft hazel eyes, how she had loved racing playfully through the apple trees while Sorrow tagged along, always smaller, always slower. In her thoughts the seasons turned around them in a film-reel flicker of color—winter brown to pale spring green, summer's deep mossy shadows to autumn's blaze of red and gold—and no matter how hard Sorrow tried, no matter how desperately she reached, Patience was always just beyond her grasp.

She had been thinking about who Patience would have been, if she had lived.

There were blank spaces in Sorrow's memory surrounding the day Patience died. Where before she had always let her thoughts skitter away from those days like roaches fleeing a sudden light, now she turned in to them, examined them, unflinching, and all she found was a thicket of shadows obscuring her view, a tangled wall of branches between her and the past. Nothing she did helped her push through. All she had were questions and the long-ago echo of nightmares tinged with fire.

"Why can't I remember what happened?" she asked.

Dr. Silva, her voice as calm and deep as the cloudless sky, said, "Memory is imperfect, Sorrow, even in the best circumstances. Your sister's death was a terrible trauma, and the effects of such a trauma, especially at such a young age, they last a long time. You might never remember everything."

"It's been eight years," Sorrow said, and there it was again, the whisper of wind through remembered trees all around her, the imagined shadows reaching up the walls and bending onto the ceiling. "I don't have nightmares anymore."

"Why is it so important to you?" Dr. Silva asked. "What do you think will change if you remember?"

It wasn't enough to sketch in those terrible days with what others had told her. Dad hadn't even been there when Patience died; he had visited only a few times a year throughout her childhood. She could never talk about it with her mother; their phone conversations were carefully light, deliberately casual, and they never, ever mentioned Patience. A girl who couldn't remember, a man who had been hundreds of miles away, a woman who would not even say her daughter's name. A few lines of empty fact: unexplained fire, unexpected tragedy. It wasn't enough.

Dr. Silva was speaking, but her words were a murmur at the

edge of Sorrow's awareness. Sorrow was staring out the window again at beaches and bridges and keys, and what she was seeing was the orchard not as it would be now, in the first blush of spring with apple blossoms opening pink and white, but as it had been before Patience died. It had been winter-gray and barren, the naked branches of the trees silver in the moonlight, the nights so bitterly cold she felt it still as an ache in her chest.

The Lovegoods of Abrams Valley, the family of her mother and grandmother and the long unbroken braid of women before them, they had always lived and died by stories they told, their remembrances held dear long after most families would have let old names and old deeds disappear into history.

"I want to go back," Sorrow said. "I need to go back to the orchard."

Patience deserved that. She deserved to be remembered.

2

REJOICE LOVEGOOD

?–1790

DAWN CREPT OVER the mountains, and the land breathed. She felt it beneath her, a living thing, as she climbed the hill away from the cabin. The newest saplings, one year old, were knee-high now on the cusp of summer. The hills were mottled brown and green, shapes indistinguishable in the murky half-light before sunrise, but the sky was an extravagant smear of pink and orange and gold, such glorious colors they felt like fire in her eyes, embers beneath her skin.

At the summit of the hill waited the gnarled old oak. It was a magnificent tree, so broad and so towering she had thought it might have a story, a history, some weighty reverence due to its great age and imposing height, but the villagers had laughed when she asked. It was only a tree, they said. A tree in a sea of trees, a world of trees, but even so, she had not the heart to cut it down. It would stay here. She would clear the hill around it, bring her apple trees up the south-facing slope in clean curving rows, over the top and down the northern side. By the end of this summer she would have this hill ready for her rootstock. The land was stubborn, the roots hard as iron and the stones plentiful, but her stubbornness, she had learned, was greater.

Last year's planting had the look of spindly sticks, offering a shy spattering of leaves as they broke from their winter dormancy. Those from the year before, no longer saplings but still skinny as colt legs, were branching into proper little trees. The oldest, the first she had planted, they were three years old, and their branches were innumerable, their early-summer leaves lush and supple, and their blossoms as shy and pink as a smile.

Four years now she had toiled alone in these dark woods. That first winter, after she had cleared the land and planted her precious roots, but before she had known if even a single apple tree would take, she had huddled in her cabin as the wind snaked through chinks in the mud. She had been barely more than a girl when she crossed the sea, spring-fresh and unformed, not yet twenty years of age, and though she felt ancient in her heart as the cold closed around her, old as the mountains in her bones, she had wept like a child when the storms wailed. Wept for the girl she had been and the misty green hills she had left behind, wept for the family across the sea that would never again speak her name except in shame and, someday, perhaps, regret. She had wept until she was scraped raw inside, empty but for the leaden weight of every memory of the life she had left, the grasping thorns of every choice that had brought her to this bleak and howling place. When darkness fell she poured rivers of tears into the wood and soil and stone beneath her, a well of loneliness that felt as though it would never run dry.

But slowly, slowly, winter had broken its hold on the mountains. Gray skies cracked apart to reveal searing blue, and the call of songbirds and drone of insects chased away the mourning wind. Spring came with a crush of green, a blush of pink, and she did not have time to weep anymore. She had work to do. The tears she spilled had nourished the land, softened it for her ax and spade, flowed through the earth, feeding her trees both wild and tame. Her sweat sank to join it, her blood as well, so much through that first year, so often, the land might have been an extension of her own body, flesh and stone, water and blood.

The wind turned, a gentle breeze tugging at wisps of unbound hair. The work never stopped, but she allowed herself this small luxury of watching the sun rise. Today the dawn was joined by a hint of smoke in the air. It had become a familiar scent these past few days, and she wasn't yet sure how to feel about neighbors planting themselves so close. She had met them yesterday. A man and his family, grim stern-faced folk lately of a plantation in Massachusetts. The boys were strapping and strong, the wife unsmiling and silent; one of the sons, a child of about ten, had spat on the ground and glowered, mumbling *witch* to the earth before his mother herded him away. The man had asked to speak to her husband, her father,

her brother, each question lifting his voice and brow with increasing disbelief that he had come so far into the mountains to find a woman alone on a piece of land she had cultivated with her own hands, and no man to rule her.

She had told him she was a widow—handily dispatching the imaginary husband she had invented to secure the land—and she had watched the calculating spark appear in his eyes. Her land was rich, the soil good, and most of all it was already cleared. Her apple trees were young but thriving. His own land promised years of toil to come.

She patted the trunk of the magnificent oak and felt its warmth beneath her fingers, its welcoming strength. She had acres to tend, and the sun was rising. The smoke of the neighbors' fire was as delicate as spider silk against the brilliant dawn. The man would be waking with avarice in his heart and deception in his eyes. As the summer bloomed he would try to clear her along with the shrubs and stones and snags, as though a woman were no more than another obstacle on the landscape.

But she had shed tears and blood to make this land a part of herself. She was not so easily frightened away.

3

SORROW RESTED HER forehead against the window as the plane descended. Lake Champlain glittered in the sun, deep blue dotted with small boats like scattered toys. Burlington at its shore barely looked like a city. No skyscrapers, no lanes of highway glinting with traffic, no suburban sprawl stretching to the horizon. She had looked it up: the entire state of Vermont had roughly one-quarter the population of Miami-Dade County.

Everything was small and strange and unfamiliar. She hadn't been sitting by the window when she flew away eight years ago. All she remembered of the day she left were tree-lined roads blurred through tears, her father a stiff and quiet stranger beside her, a hollow ache in her chest that felt like something had been torn away, and not understanding, not really, that she wouldn't be coming back for a very long time.

Her eyes were hot, her head heavy, but her insides were an electric tangle of nerves. For three months she'd been pushing and planning for this trip. Telling Dad and Sonia that letting her go was the only way they could help. Enlisting Dr. Silva to argue on her behalf. Reassuring herself, over and over again, in every way she knew how, that it was what she needed to do, that when she was standing on the ground in Abrams Valley, breathing the summer mountain air beneath a clear blue sky, the gaps in her childhood memories, all those empty spaces edged with thorns, would collapse on themselves, and she would remember. She scarcely dared think about what she would do if it didn't work, if her month in Vermont passed and nothing changed.

She had left Miami in the muggy darkness before dawn, after managing barely an hour of restless sleep. Right up until she passed through security she had been expecting Dad to change his mind. All through the days leading up to her leaving, through the drive to the airport in the morning darkness, the walk through the terminal, there had been words perched on the tip of his tongue, a single breath from being spoken, but in the end he'd only said, "You don't have to stay if it's not what you expect."

Sorrow had hugged him good-bye, told him she would be fine, and fled into the security line.

The pilot advised the flight attendants to prepare for landing. A few rows up a toddler shrieked excitedly. Trees gave way to open fields, open fields to an expanse of asphalt. The plane landed with a jolt and a rumble. When it rolled to a stop and the clatter of seat belts filled the cabin, Sorrow pulled out her phone, texted a single word to her father—*landed*—because he would call if she didn't. After a moment, she texted the same to her stepmother, Sonia; she couldn't be sure anymore that what she told one of them would reach the other.

She scrolled through messages from her stepsister, Andi, from her friends, from her cousins, but she didn't want to go through a dozen *have a safe trip!* and *don't get eaten by a moose!* texts right now, not from the same people who had reacted to her trip with varying degrees of skepticism and doubt, peppering her with invasive questions: "But your mother, is she okay now? Is she seeing a doctor? Is she medicated?"

Sorrow's Florida family had always treated her family in Vermont as an artifact of ancient history, a distant, troubled past to be occasionally puzzled over, mostly ignored. They thought it charming that Sorrow could name her ancestors back twelve generations—but only the women, rarely the men—and didn't that tell you what you needed to know about her mother's side of the family? They knew her parents had never been married, hadn't even lived together for more than a few months around the birth of each daughter, but they didn't like to judge, that wasn't what they were saying, sometimes these things happened. None of it was important anyway. It was all so long ago. There was nothing there worth going back to.

They had never known Patience.

To them, she was a concept veiled in tragedy more than a person, a sad story to be shared when Sorrow was out of the room. Heads shaking, voices low: She had an older sister once, you know, up in Vermont, but the poor girl died. Sixteen years old. There was a fire.

The airport was small, so it was only a few minutes before Sorrow was standing beside the baggage claim, tapping her fingers against her leg, waiting for the belt to move.

She looked around the room, the milling people, the families and reunion hugs.

She didn't see her mother. She looked again.

The flight was on time, even a few minutes early. Maybe Verity hadn't gotten to the airport yet. The baggage belt chugged to life, and the passengers crowded closer. Maybe she was parking. Maybe Sorrow was supposed to meet her outside. Verity had only said she would pick her up; they hadn't decided on a meeting place. Maybe it was a longer drive than Sorrow remembered—she wasn't even sure what she remembered. Narrow roads, green mountains, blue sky, an ache in her throat that had taken weeks to fade, but no sense of time, no sense of distance.

She spotted her bag, bright blue, and wrestled it off the belt.

"Sorrow."

She turned, and there was Verity.

In Sorrow's memories of her childhood in Vermont, she could not recall her mother ever wearing anything other than a skirt or a dress. Even when she was working in the orchard or garden, Verity had worn long skirts, usually handmade, often patched so many times they looked like one of Grandma Perseverance's quilts. She had never even owned a pair of jeans, as far as Sorrow knew. None of them had. It was one of the things that had earned Sorrow and Patience relentless mockery from kids in town. The adults hadn't been much better, wondering aloud if the Lovegoods were Amish or Mennonite or their own particular brand of backwoods weird, and what was their mother thinking, dressing them like that? If their father was around she wouldn't get away with that, but the Lovegood women, they didn't have much use for men, did they? Sorrow had never known how to respond. The women in their family did things their own way. That was all she had known when she was a child.

But now, eight years later, Verity was wearing jeans and a T-shirt. Her hair was shorter, a stylish cut that wouldn't have been out of place at Sonia's investment banking job, with threads of gray lightening the dark brown. Sorrow had looked past her twice while searching the room. She hadn't recognized her own mother.

"Hi," Sorrow said.

She didn't let go of her suitcase or step forward. She tried a smile, wasn't sure it worked. Her face was warm, her heart beating too fast. She thought about saying *hi* again. She thought about saying *Mom*, but her mind stuttered over the word. She hadn't called Verity *Mom* in years, since the first time they spoke on the phone after Sorrow left Vermont. That first conversation had been painfully brief. Sorrow had barely been able to choke out a single word, and Verity had sounded like a stranger, eerily calm in a way that Sorrow now knew was an effect of the medication she had been on at the time. Later conversations had been smoother, easier, as Verity got better and Sorrow adjusted to her new life in Florida, but at some point, without Sorrow even noticing, the word *Mom* had withered to dust.

"It's good to see you," Verity said. She started forward, paused when a man with a toddler on his shoulders pushed between them. Her lips twitched. "It's really good to see you."

She held out her arms, and Sorrow hesitated only a second before stepping into the hug. It didn't feel right; she was taller than her mother now. Sorrow had shot up to five foot eleven in the summer between fifth and sixth grade, giving her one wretched year of being the tallest person in her class. She had never realized it would translate into gaining inches over her mother too.

"How was your flight?" Verity asked after she stepped back.

"It was good. It was fine. Long, but okay." Sorrow didn't know what else to say. She couldn't carve any thoughts from the nerves muddling her mind. She pulled out the handle on her suitcase. "This is all my stuff."

"All right, then." That twitch of the lips again, not quite lifting into a smile. "Let's go."

They walked side by side out of the airport. Verity stopped next to a green car, a Subaru station wagon. Sorrow's memories of her childhood were foggy, often more vague than specific, but she remembered a car much like this one, older, dirtier.

New car, new clothes, new hair. A lot could change in eight years.

"Grandma is really excited to see you," Verity said. "I hope you're ready to let her feed you. She's been baking all week. I tried to tell her that you're just one girl and one girl doesn't need five pies, but you know how she is."

Sorrow dug into her backpack for her sunglasses, mostly to have something to look at, something to do with her hands. It was easier to gaze out the window at the landscape than to stop herself from staring at Verity's profile, at once familiar and strange.

"I can probably eat five of Grandma's pies," she said. "Just give me a fork and show me where to start."

Grandma Perseverance never spoke—she had been mute since long before Sorrow was born—so there were no phone calls between them, only letters, actual letters written in pen on paper. Grandma's tended to be full of news about the garden and the orchard, the weather and the wildlife, but little about herself. Sorrow remembered her grandmother as a prolific writer, filling journal after journal with her slanting script, often sitting up late into the night to write by lamplight, but she had never shared what she wrote with anybody.

"Maybe you can convince her to take it easy while you're here," Verity said. "I certainly can't get her to take a day off, or even sleep past six o'clock."

"I can try," Sorrow said. "I'm looking forward to helping her in the garden."

"She'll love that," Verity said.

"But you should probably be warned that last year I ran over Sonia's hibiscus bush the one and only time I tried to mow the lawn, so I might be kinda useless."

She forced a light laugh, but Verity didn't join her. She didn't say anything, and Sorrow's face warmed. She didn't know if it was okay to talk about her stepmother with her mother, to joke about Florida while winding through Vermont, to mention that the garden at home was largely decorative, not functional, and that the only food they grew was basil and cilantro in pots on the porch. The two halves of her life had been separate for so long she didn't know how to move from one world to the other, how to choose what to bring and what to leave behind. She didn't know if Verity's silence meant she had already chosen wrong.

She cleared her throat. "You said you were thinking of hiring somebody to help out?"

"Just for some of the extra work we have in the spring and summer." A pause, a sidelong glance. "You remember the Abramses?"

Verity's voice was even, her tone casual, but still Sorrow felt something shift between them, as though the air had grown heavier in an instant. Her first reaction was a hum of fear: Verity had noticed. She had noticed Sorrow's patchy memory.

But in this, at least, Sorrow had an answer. She did remember. Many of her childhood memories were as frail as morning mist, but she could have been away eighty years instead of eight and she would remember the Abramses.

The Abramses and the Lovegoods were the founding families of the town of Abrams Valley. They had lived side by side since the eighteenth century, two families bound by mutual suspicion and animosity for two hundred and fifty years, ever since the preacher Clement Abrams had accused Rejoice Lovegood of witchcraft.

Sorrow knew that history the same way she knew the sun rose in the east and set in the west, a truth so unshakable she wouldn't have been able to forget it even if she had wanted to.

The Abrams family had occupied such a large part of her childhood it felt like they had been a cloud over the Lovegood orchard, a creeping gloom where there should have been sunshine. Don't talk to the Abramses. Don't trespass on their land. Don't even cross the fence, and if you must, don't get caught. Come tell me right away if you see an Abrams in the orchard. Those were the rules that governed Sorrow's childhood. Those she had never forgotten.

Mr. and Mrs. Abrams had worn country club clothes and looked down their noses at the half-feral Lovegood girls. Their daughters had shiny blond hair and prep school uniforms; Sorrow and Patience hadn't been allowed to play with them. They were the only other children nearby, but their mother's rule was absolute.

"Yeah, I do," Sorrow said. "Sure. They have two daughters?"

Verity wasn't looking at her now. "Julie and Cassie. Cassie is about your age."

And Julie was the age Patience would have been, had she lived. Sorrow's thoughts quivered around their names, like rippling water in a pond. Blond hair, bright spots of color. Red coat, pink boots. Cassie, the younger, she recalled mainly as sneering insults behind her back, glares from across the street. She could not summon the details of their faces, but she remembered cold, and she remembered shadows, and she didn't know why. She shook herself, focused on what Verity was saying.

"You hired one of them?" she asked doubtfully. "Really?"

"Oh, goodness, no," Verity said. "Their cousin. He's barely an Abrams at all. Only in name, really." At Sorrow's questioning glance, she explained, "Ethan is Paul's brother's son. Paul and Hannah, our neighbors?"

"If you say so. They were only ever Mr. and Mrs. Abrams to me. I sort of remember there was another Mr. Abrams."

"Dean," Verity said. "Dean Abrams is Ethan's father, but he and Jody are divorced. They have been for years."

The other Mr. Abrams. That was what Patience had called him, and Sorrow had thought, for a long time, that was his proper name. He and his family had lived in town. Pretty redheaded wife with a sad smile, and a little blond boy who had once checked out the library's copy of *My Father's Dragon* when Sorrow wanted it. She didn't remember anything else about them.

"I'm going to need a flowchart to keep everybody straight. I can't believe you hired an Abrams. What about the whole . . . thing?" Sorrow waved her hand, accidentally knocking her knuckles into the window. She tried for a teasing tone, didn't think she quite managed it. "Fight? Everything? Pitchforks and torches and all that?"

Verity smiled. "Well, now, I know we're not as cosmopolitan as Miami, but we only bring out the pitchforks for special occasions these days."

Sorrow gave her a skeptical look. "So nobody cares? That you've got an Abrams working for you?"

"I didn't say that," Verity said. "But Ethan's a good kid. If he would rather make his own way than rely on his family's money like the rest of them, they've only got themselves to blame."

Sorrow shifted in her seat, tugged at the seat belt digging into her collarbone. Verity's words ought to have been comforting. She was saying all the right things. She was calm, rational. She was smiling, joking even, about a topic that had been so fraught before.

But she always had been able to smile when she had to. When the police came by, when the social worker visited, Verity had been able to put on a mask and become a woman who was a little odd, a little eccentric, but ultimately harmless. They had all worn masks for the world—for strangers. Patience had been so much better at it than Sorrow. Everything Sorrow had known about keeping their family's secrets she had learned from her sister, but poorly, a clumsy imitation.

Sorrow had been afraid, before she came back to Vermont, that she would look at her mother and see her sister. They had the same dark hair, the same long nose, the same sharp face. But Verity didn't look anything like Patience. Sitting at the wheel of her Subaru, carefully signaling to pass a slow-moving truck, she looked only like herself, a middle-aged woman from rural Vermont. If her mood was a mask, Sorrow no longer knew how to see through it.

"It's going to be weird being in a town that has a population smaller than my high school," she said.

Verity's smile was so genuine that Sorrow felt she was balanced on a precipice, toes curling over the edge.

"I'm glad you're here," Verity said.

Sorrow looked away. "Me too," she said.

The farther south they traveled, the more familiar the landscape became: rolling mountains and green forests, small towns surrounded by fields, old farmhouses in various stages of decay, horses and cows grazing in pastures. Later in the summer, after a month or two of riotous growth, the forests would become impenetrable walls of green, the heat suffocating, the air oppressive and hazy. Dust would hang above country roads in clinging yellow clouds, and everybody would yearn with sluggish impatience for the first crackling cool day of fall. But now, on the second Saturday in June, the summer was fresh and new.

The sun slanted bright and blinding over the mountains, and it was late afternoon when they passed the sign at the edge of town. Welcome to Abrams Valley. Bold white letters on a green board. Heart of the Green Mountains.

"Not much has changed," Verity said softly. "We've got the same problems as most small towns, I guess. More people commuting to Boston. They laid off about half the workers at the quarry last year. But mostly things just kind of go on."

Along Main Street there was a handful of bakeries and restaurants, souvenir shops with T-shirt racks and postcard displays on the sidewalks, outdoor-gear stores with window signs welcoming Appalachian and Long Trail thru-hikers. A scattering of tourists wandered aimlessly. The quilting and knitting store was in the same spot, with the same carved wooden sign over the door offering Yarn & Fabrics.

Sorrow swallowed, took a breath. "Does Ms. Cheek still own that place?"

"She's mostly retired now, but she still shows up to boss the new manager around a couple times a week," Verity said.

Ms. Cheek and her employees—all old ladies just like her, gray-haired and grinning—had always greeted Grandma with hugs and kisses on the cheek, opened a bottle of Abrams Valley cider before sitting down to haggle over prices and invent quaint names for Grandma's colorful quilts.

The library in its old Victorian house hadn't moved, but it had been repainted a cheery bright blue. In the flat square park at the center of town a banner spanning two trees announced a festival celebrating the 253rd anniversary of the Battle of Ebenezer Smith's Stockade, the town's one and only claim to historical semi-fame. Below the banner a smaller sign advertised a twice-weekly farmers' market.

The grocery store was in the same place, with the same produce bins on the sidewalk, but the original sign had been replaced by a corporate chain.

"I have to stop in for a few things, if you don't mind." Verity put on her signal to turn in to the parking lot. "I'll only be a minute, if you want to wait. Or you can come in?"

"I think I'll wait out here," Sorrow said. "My head is still all *ugh* from the traveling."

Verity nodded. "Get your first taste of mountain air. It'll help."

When she was gone, Sorrow stepped out of the car and leaned against it. She closed her eyes to feel the sunlight on her face, to take in the sounds of the town. All she wanted was a few minutes of quiet to let the thoughts rattling around her mind settle. She had known this valley once. She had known this town and these streets. The people who owned these stores. The shape of these mountains, and the scent of these trees. She should know it still. She had been gone only eight years. That wasn't long enough to forget.

But forget she had. There were shadows in her memories, like low clouds casting swaths of landscape into darkness, and the biggest of these, the darkest, hid the cold late winter days when Patience had died. Dr. Silva said it was normal, but it didn't feel normal. It felt like a black hole inside her, sometimes centered in her mind, sometimes in her heart, a well of impossible gravity distorting everything around it, slowly stripping the light and color from all the rest of her childhood memories, even the good ones, so gradually Sorrow hadn't noticed it happening until it was too late.

A shopping cart rattled and shoes scuffed on asphalt. Sorrow's eyes snapped open, but it wasn't Verity who stood before her. It was Mrs. Abrams.

For all that she hadn't been able to remember the woman's name twenty minutes ago, Sorrow recognized her immediately, like a puzzle piece snapping into a scene that hadn't made sense before. Sleek blond hair, tailored clothes, makeup tasteful and perfectly applied, Hannah Abrams was dressed for an uptown lunch, not a trip to the grocery store—but she seemed absolutely comfortable with it, as though she was the one who fit and the rest of the town failed to measure up.

"You're the Lovegood girl," Mrs. Abrams said.

Sorrow had heard *you're the Lovegood girl* more times than she could count when she was a child, usually right after some stranger had looked over her homemade clothes and ill-fitting shoes and wrinkled a nose in disapproval.

It didn't sound any better now that she was sixteen, but she pulled up a smile and her best talking-to-adults voice. "Yeah, I'm Sorrow. It's nice to see you again, Mrs. Abrams."

Hannah Abrams smiled too, more reflex than intent. "I'm surprised you remember me."

It was so close to what Sorrow had been thinking about she felt momentarily thrown, and she fumbled for a reply that wasn't a defensive *of course I do*. "I, uh, yeah, it's all starting to feel familiar, now that I'm here. I didn't realize until just now how much I missed the mountains."

"It's beautiful here in the summer," Hannah said. "I've always loved the long sunsets in particular. Are you in town for long?"

"A month," Sorrow said. Across the parking lot Verity emerged from the store with a reusable grocery bag in each hand. "There's my mom."

She didn't mean it as a warning, only a polite way to extract herself from awkward small talk, but Hannah's expression changed abruptly. Sorrow hadn't even realized there was a softness in her face until it was gone. Her eyes narrowed, her lips thinned, and she squared her shoulders as she turned.

"Hannah," Verity said.

"Verity," Hannah replied.

"Are you bothering my daughter?"

Sorrow began, "She was only—"

"I was only surprised to see her," Hannah said. "I didn't know she was coming to visit."

"That's because it's none of your business," Verity said.

She tugged at the handle of the car's hatchback, then remembered it was locked and clicked it open. She shoved the bags into the back; Sorrow darted forward to catch a jar of olives before it crashed to the ground.

"What?" Verity snapped. Sorrow flinched, but it wasn't directed at her. Verity was glaring at Hannah Abrams, who hadn't moved her cart out of the way. "What do you want? Are you going to make a list of what I'm buying? Do you want me to prove I'm feeding my child?"

"Don't be ridiculous," Hannah said.

"Then what do you want?" Verity's voice rose to a shout, and an elderly couple pushing a cart nearby turned to stare. "What do you want? Why can't you just leave us alone?"

Hannah looked at Verity, her lips parting with the beginning of a word, but she changed her mind and turned to Sorrow instead. "I hope you enjoy your visit," she said shortly. "You've been gone a long time. A lot has changed."

Sorrow darted a nervous glance toward her mother and did not answer.

Verity slammed the hatchback. "Get in the car, Sorrow. We're leaving."

Sorrow twisted in her seat as Verity pulled the car out of the lot. Hannah Abrams was still standing beside her red shopping cart, watching them drive away.

4

SORROW DEBATED FOR a full minute whether to say anything, but she couldn't keep quiet.

"What was *that* all about?"

Verity adjusted her grip on the steering wheel, twisting both hands over the vinyl with a soft creak. "It's none of her business what you're doing here."

"She was only saying hi. It was no big deal."

"Why are you defending her?"

"What? I'm not—I'm not defending anybody."

Sorrow pressed her hands to the seat beneath her legs to keep them from shaking. She hadn't even been back in Vermont for a couple of hours, and already she'd said something that had pushed Verity's mood from warm and cheerful to prickly and dark. She didn't know what she had said that was so wrong, and not knowing gave her a sickly, despairing knot in her stomach. She needed to know. She couldn't let herself fall into this cycle again. She used to know how to navigate her mother's mercurial moods, the pitfalls and traps of life with a woman who could tumble into a black spiral of despair at the merest push, but she didn't know anymore. She had always followed Patience's lead, but Patience was eight years gone and Sorrow was alone now, grasping desperately for reminders of everything she had once known about keeping the peace.

"I wasn't even talking to her," she said slowly. Cautiously. Calm voice, no anger. She could do this. "I was just—should I have ignored her? Not even said hi?"

A long pause, then Verity said, "You've been gone a long time."

It was exactly what Hannah Abrams had said not five minutes ago.

"You don't remember." Verity's voice was suddenly quiet, a drop that felt like the earth opening up beneath them. "You don't remember the kind of trouble they used to make for us. For our family."

The words felt like a barbed accusation. Sorrow wanted to deny it, refute it, spit out a defense. She did remember. She remembered police coming to the farm sometimes. A social worker as well, a round woman with an unflattering pageboy haircut, and she recalled clearly how thin-lipped and pale Patience would be when the woman left, how Verity would vanish to her bedroom and close the door, and how Grandma, forever silent, would sit in the kitchen by the woodstove for long hours through the night. She remembered whispers following her and Patience around town, and Patience tugging her away before she could hear what was being said—she remembered that so clearly she felt the phantom sensation of Patience's fingers grasping hers, warmth and pressure and comfort, the aching deep certainty lodged somewhere beneath her heart that her sister would keep her safe.

"I guess there's a lot I didn't understand," she said slowly. It felt like half trembling confession, half desperate apology, but it was as far as she was willing to go.

"You were a child," Verity said. She took a breath, let it out slowly. "I never wanted you to worry. There were times I was so afraid they would . . . The right person would listen to them, to the things they said. I was so afraid of losing you."

Sorrow looked away, a flush creeping over her skin. It wasn't the Abramses who had taken her away in the end.

"They can't do anything now," she said.

"It's not that simple, Sorrow."

They fell into silence as they left the town behind. Houses on the outskirts gave way to run-down trailers and weathered barns, unwelcoming wooden fences and pickup trucks with political bumper stickers, road signs marred by bullet holes. Those things had always been there; there was unhappiness and hardship everywhere. But as a child Sorrow had rarely paid attention to life outside the orchard, and until she left she had never traveled anywhere beyond Abrams Valley. Her world had been so small, her understanding of it even smaller.

They passed the turn to the property that used to be the Roche farm; there was a new mailbox with no name on it. The sight of it brought back a memory, sudden and clear: Mrs. Roche, in their kitchen, scolding Verity about how irresponsible it was to let her daughters run wild. She should send them to the public school in town and buy them nice clothes and shoes. She should let them make friends. It wasn't right, said Mrs. Roche, to dwell too much in the past. Verity had barely said a word, but Mrs. Roche hadn't noticed. Patience and Sorrow eavesdropped from the stairs, their shoulders pressed together, and when Mrs. Roche was gone, Patience had fanned herself and swanned around the house mimicking Mrs. Roche's Southern accent until Sorrow was doubling over with laughter and Verity's stony silence cracked into a watery smile.

After the Roche property was the Abrams farm. The long driveway was paved and lined with flowering shrubs and short lampposts. The house looked the same—huge, rebuilt and remodeled so many times the original farmhouse was barely visible—but the detached garage hadn't been there before.

What Sorrow remembered standing in its place was an old barn, deep red and looming, the door into its hayloft gaping like a Cyclops's watchful dark eye.

"They used to have a barn, right?" she asked.

"They tore it down," Verity said. "The fire, remember? The first fire."

There it was again, the prickly flush of embarrassment, almost shame. She hadn't forgotten. Not that. Not *that*. She might not remember the weeks before her move to Florida, the days surrounding her sister's death, but she knew the recitation of facts her father and therapist had given to her, and what she knew was this: There had been two fires that March eight years ago, one in the Abrams barn, the other in the abandoned Lovegood cider house. The first fire had damaged the barn but had not harmed any people or animals.

The second had killed Patience.

When she was little, Sorrow had suffered nightmares every night for months, always about the same thing: falling into a bottomless pit while fire raged around her. Her father assured her she hadn't been present for either of the fires, she had been safe at home in bed, but she imagined her sister's last moments so vividly, so many times, she believed could feel the crackling heat and taste the smoke. The nightmares had faded, become a reminder more like a toothache than a terror. It had been years since Sorrow had woken in a panic, screaming for help.

Dad said the police believed Patience must have seen the fire or smelled the smoke—even though the cider house was far from the house, and it had been the middle of the night—and was trapped when she went to investigate. Nobody had ever been blamed or arrested.

When Sorrow had begun to realize how little she remembered, she had tried to research it, look up articles and information online. Abrams Valley had a weekly newspaper that mostly reported on trail clean-up volunteer days and high school football games, and the fires had been in the news—the sudden death of a teenage girl was a shocking tragedy for so small a town—but all Sorrow learned was that the police believed both fires had been started by a drifter or an addict trying to keep warm. There had been a meth lab bust on Mill Run Road a few months before, and locals were convinced big city outsiders were bringing trouble into their quiet little town. It had been a bitterly cold winter. Nobody in Abrams Valley locked their outbuilding doors. Who knew what somebody off their head on meth or heroin would do if they were caught out?

Sorrow had hoped, when she started looking, there would be something Dad had neglected to mention, something that explained why Patience had been outside, why she hadn't called for help, why she hadn't woken their mother or grandmother. But nothing she found filled in those blanks.

There had been a fire. Patience died. It was maddening, simplistic, and hollow, but that was what Sorrow knew.

The Abrams house and garage passed out of sight. On the opposite side of the road was the stretch of land that had once belonged to the Johnsons. They had moved a few years ago—gotten tired of the winters, Verity had reported during a phone conversation, and the property had passed through a couple of different owners since then. There were two horses grazing in the field, a big gray and a smaller bay, both flicking their ears and tails at flies.

"Who lives there now?" Sorrow asked, grasping for something to fill the silence.

"The Ghosh family," Verity said. "Jana and Helen. They moved here from New York last August. They have two kids about your age. Jana wants you to give her a call if you're interested in working a little. I know you're only here for a month, but they've got an opening for a few shifts a week while one of their regulars is traveling."

"Yeah, maybe," Sorrow said, but she was barely listening. She hadn't remembered how long the seven miles between town and the orchard could feel. It was as though the mountains were closing around her, the valley deepening, the trees crowding the road.

"They bought one of the outdoors stores, and they've been doing pretty well with it. If you want . . ." Verity trailed off, the words fading into a soft ending.

Sorrow's heart began to beat faster. She sat up straighter. She wanted to tell Verity to stop the car. She needed a moment to catch up. A chance to breathe. She wasn't ready. Eight years was barely a blink for the town, less than a flicker for the mountains, but it was half of her life, and she wasn't ready.

The road bent around a curve, and there was the orchard.

Long lines of trees passed in a flicker of light and shadow. The pink and white flowers were gone and the apples hadn't yet swelled, so there were only the green summer leaves in endless rows. Before the road dipped again, Sorrow saw the ragged crown of the black oak, sitting like a watchtower atop the hill. At its base would be the grave of their ancestor Silence Lovegood, who had murdered her own children two hundred years ago and been hanged as a witch. The tree's massive shape was so etched in Sorrow's memory she could have drawn it with her eyes closed, needing nothing but fingers and feel to re-create branches she and Patience had climbed countless times on summer days that had seemed to last forever.

Sorrow couldn't see around the shoulder of the hill to the remains of the cider house. It was hidden from the road. Once a ramshackle wreck, now a charred ruin. Verity had never mentioned tearing it down. Sorrow had never asked.

Verity turned in to the driveway. The wooden fence was unpainted and crooked, as it had always been, and there was no gate. There was no name on the leaning mailbox; everybody knew whose farm this was. The drive was unpaved and rutted, a narrow track through a green tunnel of sugar maples.

In Sorrow's memories, through all the years she had been away, the little white farmhouse had faded, seeped into the gray rain of that last cold spring, leached of warmth and color. She expected it to be smaller, shabbier too, the paint peeled away, the front lawn patchy and brown.

But the house was in better shape than it had ever been during her childhood. The white paint was fresh, the shutters robin's-egg blue. The lawn was rich deep green, a little high, but not choked with weeds. Flowering bushes grew along the front of the porch in bright bursts of breathtaking color. She had known Verity and Grandma were fixing up the place, but she felt a pinch of betrayal to see how neat it was now, how clean, how colorful. The farm hadn't spent the past eight years sinking into dilapidated disrepair in her absence, crumbling in reality as it was in her memory.

It didn't look like a place where a family could have been so easily broken apart.

Verity turned off the engine. "Well. Here we are."

The car was too small, the air too thin. Sorrow fumbled with her seat belt, pushed the door open. The moment her feet touched the ground, a wave of dizziness washed over her, as though the earth itself were recoiling from her touch. She clung to the car, squeezed her eyes shut, and swallowed back sudden nausea. She waited for the ground to settle.

"Sorrow?"

She opened her eyes. The sky was blue and clear, the trees so green it hurt to look at them. The day was hot and muggy and everything smelled of grass, of earth, of living, thriving things. Leaves rustled in a gentle breeze. The sun was sinking toward the horizon, pressing long shadows into the ground. The orchard was beautiful. She had forgotten that, somehow, lost the loveliness in all her memories sharp with killing frost, murky with mud and matted dead leaves. It was beautiful.

The storm door squeaked open. Eight years and nobody had oiled the hinges. Grandma Perseverance stepped onto the front porch.

"Sorrow," Verity said again. She was at the back of the car, tugging at Sorrow's suitcase. "Okay?"

Sorrow took a deep breath. "Yeah." Another breath. "Fine." The words came from the top of her lungs, high and shaky.

Verity dragged her suitcase toward the house. Grandma was smiling. She was smaller than Sorrow remembered, fragile as an autumn leaf, but she was smiling.

Sorrow closed the car door. The air was warm and sweet. She

could do this. This had been home once. This had been her entire world.

She went to the porch and hugged her grandmother gently, so gently, afraid of holding too tight, and she exhaled.

5

THEY ATE DINNER at the kitchen table, the three of them and an empty fourth chair. Their plates were full of roast chicken, potatoes, early greens from the garden, a meal so familiar the scent of it made Sorrow's heart ache.

The room around her didn't have the same effect at all. The kitchen had been completely remodeled: new cabinets, new appliances, new flooring, new paint. The woodstove was in the same place, but it was sitting on an expanse of colorful tiles rather than crooked, soot-stained boards. The kitchen was in what had been the first building on the property, a small, dark log cabin that hoarded warmth like a dragon. Their ancestor Rejoice Lovegood had built it when she was first planting the orchard, but those carefully hand-hewn logs were exposed on only one wall now. The rest had been plastered and painted the color of daffodils.

Verity listed all the changes to the house with unmistakable pride, as though she were introducing Sorrow to a new friend. The house did look good, Sorrow couldn't deny that, but still she felt a pang of discomfort. She didn't know where Verity's remodeling urge had come from; she didn't remember her mother ever replacing or improving anything in their home. But that had obviously changed, and changed drastically. They had made everything new in Sorrow's absence. It didn't feel like her childhood home anymore.

"We're just about done inside," Verity said. "What do you think?"

"I like the tile especially." Sorrow pointed with her fork, feeling a bit ridiculous, but it was all she could think to say. She couldn't get away with silently nodding forever. "It looks like a flower bed."

"It was a pain in the butt, but I guess it was worth it." Verity was smiling when she said it. She had barely stopped smiling since they had arrived. "I had to learn how not to accidentally cement myself to the floor."

"It barely even looks like the old cabin anymore," Sorrow said.

It was the wrong thing to say. Verity's smile faltered, and Grandma's hand curled into a half-formed gesture.

"But you can still tell it used to be," she added hurriedly. "This was always my favorite room. Remember how we used to . . ."

They used to pass long winter days when the snow was high and the temperature low here in the kitchen, always the warmest room in the house. Sorrow and Patience would play Pioneers: baking inedible bread in the woodstove, rearranging the cabinets to count supplies, darting outside for firewood, gasping in the cold and hurrying back inside. They had taken turns sitting at the window with a rolling pin, pretending it was a flintlock rifle and calling out warnings when an imaginary Abrams emerged from the snowy orchard. When there was nothing else to do, Patience had been happy to indulge Sorrow in games that were far too young for her. They were good memories, full of laughter and warmth and light.

But Verity was largely absent from them. She had spent most winter days up in her room, with the door closed and the curtains drawn.

Sorrow took a sip of cider, felt the soft burn in her throat. She looked from her mother to her grandmother, back to her mother. It wasn't Verity's fault she had colored so many of Sorrow's good memories dark with her illness. Sorrow knew that. She could march through all of the rational, responsible, mature explanations in her mind, her own thoughts blending with Dr. Silva's calm voice. But right now, sitting in the kitchen of her childhood home, which looked nothing like she remembered, too afraid to even speak her sister's name lest it drop into a well of silence, none of it helped.

"I like it," she said weakly. "It's cozy. Are you about done? Or is there more to do?"

With a barely concealed look of relief, Verity began to tell Sorrow about the changes they had been making around the property—replacing the roof of the barn, fixing the fences, planning a new chicken coop—her description of every project peppered with praise for the unfailingly helpful Ethan Abrams. Sorrow wanted to ask, but didn't, how they were able to afford all of the improvements and hiring help to do them. She was certainly no expert in the economics of running a farm, but she knew they had canned food obsessively when she was a kid, mended clothes as though fabric were spun from gold, saved every nail and board for reuse. There had been nights she had gone to sleep with a pit of hunger in her stomach, and days when neighbors had dropped by unannounced with homemade muffins or hot soup. It seemed impossible now, with a bounty of food spread before them and home improvement plans stretching into the future, but growing up as the poorest family in town—or at least the most visibly lacking by modern standards, rich only in history and land and old apple trees—with one of the wealthiest families right next door, that wasn't something Sorrow had ever forgotten.

Grandma contributed in her own way to Verity's chatter over dinner, nodding and pointing, scribbling a few words on the notebook she carried for that purpose. Sorrow had once been able to follow her grandmother's manner of speaking easily, but she had lost the knack. She found it disorienting to keep up, and dismaying for how little she understood.

They talked about the garden, they talked about the fences, they talked about the trees, they cleaned their plates and emptied their glasses. Verity smiled again; Grandma laughed her silent laugh. Sorrow felt her way into a rhythm of asking questions and letting the answers fill her vague recollections with color and light.

They did not talk about Patience.

Verity didn't say her name, not once, and Sorrow couldn't bring herself to say it first. Every time the word crept toward the end of her tongue, she caught herself and stopped, frustrated and uncertain. And, every time, she felt guilty for her own reaction. She had been here only a couple of hours. They were getting to know each other again. There would be time enough to talk about Patience later.

After dinner was finished and the dishes washed, Verity said, "You should call your father."

Sorrow made a face. "I texted him earlier."

Landed when the plane touched down, and *yes* in response to him asking if Verity had picked her up. She had hoped she could get away with that, at least for this evening. She wanted to feel like she was *here*, feet solidly on this once-familiar ground, before the fishing-line tug of home pulled at her again.

"Call your father," Verity said, unimpressed. "He'll be worried about you."

"Yeah, whatever." Verity just kept looking at her, so Sorrow gave in. "Fine. Fine! I'll call."

Verity assured her the only place on the property she would get a cell signal was the end of the driveway, so Sorrow fetched her phone and went outside. The farmhouse had a landline now—they had never had a phone when she was a kid—but there was no way she was having a conversation with her father where Verity and Grandma could overhear.

The sun had set, and the sky was streaked with wispy clouds lit from below in hues of pink and orange and red, a brilliant palette above the shadowed humps of the mountains. The evening was warm, but it would cool off overnight. The green closed around Sorrow as she started down the driveway between the rows of sugar maples. Like all the trees on the farm, the maples were old, so old they should have stopped producing syrup long ago, but somehow they endured.

In the autumn the maples would turn a brilliant blazing red, but for now they were as green as everything else in the valley, a deep, deep green fading into black with the encroaching twilight. Sorrow felt a nervous flutter in her chest thinking about how dark it would be when the last sunlight was gone. It was never dark in Miami, not even when a storm knocked out the power, and it was never quiet.

She stopped at the bottom of the driveway to check her phone. No service. Took a few more steps, past the fence, right up to the edge of the asphalt. The road smelled of tar and oil, still radiating the heat of the day. There, at last, a weak signal appeared. Sorrow called her father.

Dad answered right away. "Sorrow! I was just about to call you."

He might have been telling the truth, or he might have been just about to call the same way he was just about to stop traveling so much for work, or just about to plan a trip with Sorrow to visit her stepsister, Andi, at Stanford. During one of the rare times when Dad and Sonia's recent coldness had erupted into yelling, Sonia had shouted, "You're never where you need to be! You're never here!" Sorrow, hiding in her room and pretending to do homework, had felt a crushing mix of embarrassment and anger and hurt. He was her *dad*, and he wasn't a bad person, but Sonia was his wife, and she was right, and Sorrow hated knowing she was right almost as much as she hated all of the petty disappointments.

"I just wanted to let you know I'm here," Sorrow said. "At the farm. I made it just fine."

"Good. That's good."

A pause. The television was on in the background: the gentle roar of commentators speaking over a cheering crowd, a sound so familiar Sorrow felt a pang of homesickness. Phillies hosting the Giants at home. Sorrow strained to hear, but if Sonia was home, she wasn't saying anything—and Sonia wouldn't be watching a Phillies game without saying anything, usually several anythings, many of which could not be repeated in polite company. A year ago it would have been a Saturday night date for Sorrow and Sonia, to watch the game and eat takeout and curse the players for their many mistakes.

But by the time the season had started this year, Sorrow had been so wrapped up in her own worries she hadn't noticed until it was too late that Sonia hadn't said a word about spring training or games in months. The few times she had wanted to approach Sonia with takeout menus on game night, she had stopped herself, cringing with uncertainty. She didn't know if they did that anymore. Sonia didn't make a point of being home for games. She didn't offer up tickets as a way to have a girls' night when Dad was out of town. Everything had changed, and neither of them had said a single word about it.

"So everything is okay?" Dad asked. "What have you been up to?"

"Nothing," Sorrow said. "Just dinner. I haven't even unpacked.

I've only been here a couple hours."

"Well, I know, but—it's okay?"

"It's *fine*," Sorrow said. "Why wouldn't it be fine? I'm in Vermont, not Syria."

"Sorrow."

Sorrow squirmed at the scolding note in his voice. "Really. It's fine."

"And how's—"

Don't ask, Sorrow thought urgently. Don't ask.

"How's your mother doing?"

"She's doing great," Sorrow said, a shade too loud. "Really good. Everything looks great around here. You wouldn't believe the renovations they've done. It looks like something out of a magazine."

She winced, fully aware she was laying it on thick and Dad would see right through it. But it wasn't just that he was asking. It was the way he was asking: cautiously, almost hopefully, like he was fully expecting Sorrow to beg to come home tomorrow.

"You'll have to send me pictures," Dad said.

"Yeah," Sorrow said. "Where's Sonia? Is she there?"

"She's out at dinner with friends," Dad said.

"Oh. Okay. Sounds fun." Sorrow wanted to believe Sonia was out with her friends. She didn't want to think Dad was covering up that she had gone to stay with her sister, finally giving up the happy-couple pretense now that Sorrow and Andi were away. She wanted to believe it so desperately it hurt, but she didn't dare ask for fear of what her father's answer would be. "Tell her I said hi."

"You should call her tomorrow," Dad said.

"Yeah."

"And let me know right away if there are any problems."

"Really, Dad?" Sorrow said, exasperated. "Come on. There aren't going to be any problems. It's going to be *fine*."

"But if you need anything—"

"I know! I know." Sorrow craned her head to look up at the sky. "I've got to get back in to help clean up."

"Okay. Enjoy your visit, sweetie. I love you."

"Yeah. Dad, do you—"

The words caught behind Sorrow's teeth.

Do you even remember her? That's what she wanted to ask. It was unfair. It was the wrong time. She'd spent three months pushing her father and his concern away; she couldn't spring the past on him now like none of that had happened, however much she needed to know: Do you remember Patience? Am I allowed to talk about her? Verity won't even say her name. We've talked about a hundred things and she hasn't once said her name.

The words were there, behind her lips and on her tongue, but she said nothing.

"Sorrow? What is it?"

It wasn't her father she wanted to ask anyway.

"Nothing," she said. "Love you too. Talk to you later, okay?"

They exchanged good-byes and good nights, and Sorrow stared at her phone until her father's picture blinked away.

The long tunnel of trees along the driveway was barely green anymore, and the first stars were coming out, bright pricks of light twinkling in the restless air. An engine rumbled, and headlights shone around a bend in the road. Sorrow stepped farther from the asphalt as the car passed. Somebody was heading down from the mountains, probably hikers whose day had run long. The car was gone in moments, and the road was dark again. A mosquito nipped at her arm. She slapped it flat, wiped the smudge on her jeans.

It wasn't that she didn't know what her father was worried about. She knew exactly what he was worried about. She knew exactly why he and Sonia had been so stiff with each other lately. She knew why Andi hadn't come back from California for the summer. She knew why all of their conversations now turned into awkward exchanges of questions and avoidance. She knew why her father had become more overbearing and Sonia more distant. For months Sorrow had been making herself smaller and smaller, trying to duck between them like she was dodging raindrops, and she knew exactly who was to blame.

She knew it was her fault.

It had started the day she had accidentally gone missing. It hadn't been intentional, no matter what anybody believed. She hadn't meant to make them worry.

They had been at Sonia's parents' house for a spring break party. Mima and Abu lived way out on the outskirts of Miami's metro area, at the fringe where suburban sprawl gave way to the Everglades. They had moved out there after decades in Little Havana, when Mima finally convinced Abu that she would be happier in her retirement with a piece of land to tend and a pair of binoculars for bird-watching. The party had been a noisy, crowded affair: music blaring, coolers packed with ice and beer, food-laden tables sinking into the soft grass, adults barking out warnings every time the kids tumbled too close to Mima's garden, and Andi, home from college for the week, basking at the center of it all like a queen on a throne.

Sorrow had wandered around with a Solo cup of Diet Coke gone flat, ignoring the cousins who tried to pull her into a soccer game, letting aunts and uncles and friends stop and ask her about school, ask her if she had a boyfriend or maybe a girlfriend, ask her if she was proud of Andi, if she was thinking of going to Stanford too, after she graduated, wouldn't that be fun, both of them out in California? Smiles, nods, murmurs of agreement, but what Sorrow was thinking was that she had two more years of high school ahead of her, and even then she would never be Stanford material. She was an average student, never having quite recovered from a rocky start to her formal education. Thanks to Verity's homeschooling, she had begun school in Florida capable enough in reading, writing, and arithmetic, but while she'd had an encyclopedic knowledge of the history, geology, and ecology of the Green Mountains, and the uncanny ability to name every one of her maternal ancestors stretching back to the middle of the eighteenth century, her awareness of other topics had been somewhat lacking. Even worse, she'd had no idea how to sit in a classroom when she would rather be outside, or how to take a test when she would rather be collecting beetles and flowers. She hadn't even known she was supposed to come back inside after recess. She had learned how school worked, reluctantly, begrudgingly, and when she was older she found biology and environmental science classes she enjoyed, but she would never be a top student like Andi.

And that afternoon at the party, after her face started hurting from being prodded into stiff smiles for hours and there was no sign anything would be winding down, Sorrow had slipped away. She'd rolled a bike out of the garage—the one Abu was supposed to be using for exercise, doctor's orders—and rode away down the tree-lined road to where the pavement ended and the dirt began and she couldn't hear the music and laughter anymore. She hadn't meant to go far or stay away long, but there was always a tantalizing glimmer of water through the cypress trees, and all she could hear was birds singing and insects humming. At the end of one dirt road she found the remains of an old orange grove—a small one on a few soggy, ill-chosen acres—and she leaned the bike against a tree to look around. The property was abandoned, the trees draped with Spanish moss. She didn't see any Trespassers Will Be Shot on Sight signs warning her away, so she took her chances and spent some time exploring the old grove, breathing in the rich scents of greenery and decay.

Daylight faded, and the shadows around her grew deep and dark, but she didn't leave, and into that breathing silence came a thought she hadn't let herself think in years: Patience would have loved this.

The unfamiliar trees, the dark water, the chattering bugs, the flat ground unwrinkled by even the slightest hill, and seeping from it a sense of history both vivid and alien: it was like nothing Patience had ever known, nothing she had ever had a chance to see. She would be twenty-four now—no longer a girl but a young woman—and that had stopped Sorrow in her tracks. All the questions everybody had been asking her all afternoon, they were things Patience had never even been allowed to contemplate, every one of them a path she had never been able to follow. Sorrow was two months past her own sixteenth birthday and already venturing into territory Patience had never had a chance to explore. She had been doing it all along, ever since she left Vermont, but it had never taken her breath away as it did that evening, when she realized her own life now stretched longer than Patience's ever would.

She didn't know what Patience would be doing now, had she lived. She didn't know what she would be like, what choices she would have made. If she would have stayed in the orchard in Vermont like their mother and grandmother, or if she would have fled for college, travel, adventures elsewhere in the world. If they would be friends as well as sisters, or if they would be such different people they would have no point of connection. She didn't know. There were days when she could barely remember Patience, when her entire childhood in the orchard had the feel of a dream slipping away after waking, fading into a blur of unfamiliar colors. She feared someday her memories would be gone for good.

Sorrow hadn't realized anybody would miss her from her grandparents' party until she heard the whelp of a police siren and saw blue and white lights flashing through the trees. Shouts echoed: her name, called over and over again. The party had broken up to search for her. Andi was furious, Sonia confused and annoyed, but Dad, he was the worst, because between hugging Sorrow and saying, "We were so worried," and "Don't you ever do that again," he looked at Sorrow and saw the tears on her face and heard the stammer in her voice, and it was as though she had gone into the Everglades a daughter he knew and come out a stranger, and she had looked right back at him and seen a man as unfamiliar as he had been the day he took her away from Vermont.

No matter what she said after, however she reassured him, the damage was done. Her parents were looking at Sorrow but they were seeing Verity's illness, with her bottle of pills and her hospital stays and a long, long family tree of twisted and diseased branches. Dad made therapy appointments for her and called every day when he was traveling. He began to check her homework, worried anew over her usual academic disinterest, and when Sorrow complained to Sonia, Sonia only said she wasn't going to get between Sorrow and her father. Sorrow quickly learned that answering "Fine" when either of them asked how she was doing would only invite more questions, more digging, cautious looks and careful smiles, and it was all so overwhelming she caught herself thinking maybe Dad was right. Maybe there was something to find, if she cracked herself open and peered inside. Maybe there was a time bomb ticking away behind her heart, buried in that black hole of her memories, the ones edged with nightmares of fire. What kind of person couldn't even remember her own sister's death? Had to learn it instead like a lesson in school, a recitation of facts, because her own truth of it was gone?

Something crunched on the road's gravel shoulder to the left, down the hill toward the Abrams farm. Sorrow's heart skipped, and she turned, stared hard into the shadows. There was a shape in the distance, a few hundred feet away. Her breath caught. There had always been bears wandering through the orchard in the summer and autumn, chomping happily on fallen apples before waddling away. Patience had given them names: Sir Scruff, Lady Furrington. Plump lazy creatures who never bothered anybody. Nothing to be afraid of. Still, Sorrow's heart was hammering.

Then the shape moved, and a pale light sliced through the dusk.

Not a bear, then, unless the bears had taken to carrying phones on their forest rambles. Sorrow pressed her fingers to her sternum, willing her heart to slow down.

From this distance, in the twilight, she couldn't make out anything about the person on the roadside, but she saw when they turned. A stillness fell between them. Her skin crawled. She had been spotted.

Headlights appeared on the road, and Sorrow took a step back, but the car lurched to a stop before it reached her. In the sudden blinding glow Sorrow saw a short skirt and bare legs, a shimmery shirt nearly translucent in the light, a flash of blond hair. Abrams hair, the same crown for every head all the way down their line. A car door opened, music spilled out with bright catches of voices and laughter, and the girl climbed in. The sound of the door snapping shut echoed through the valley. The car pulled a sharp U-turn and headed back toward town. The red taillights faded.

Sorrow started back up the driveway. The maples were dense with leaves now. They had been barren the day she left.

Her steps slowed. A cool breeze snaked through the trees, turning leaves in the arched branches overhead. She rubbed her arms to chase away a sudden chill.

Not even a week ago, at their last appointment before she'd left, she had told Dr. Silva that she couldn't even remember her sister's funeral. What kind of person did that make her, she had asked, that she couldn't remember putting her own sister in the ground? Dr. Silva had assured her there was no betrayal in not remembering, no failure on her part, but Sorrow had been unconvinced.

She was still unconvinced, and she grasped at this flicker of knowledge like a lifeline: the trees had been bare. It was only the vaguest shimmer of an image, more impression than thought, but the longer she held it, the more certain she became that she could feel the spring cold on her face, stinging and sharp, the sun too bright, offering too little warmth. Shoes that didn't fit right. A dress that itched. The earth soggy beneath her feet where snow had melted away.

The air stirred again, and a single leaf fluttered down from the maples. Sorrow bent to pick it up. In the evening gloom it might have been blazing autumn red rather than rich summer green. She twisted the stem, watched it turn, wondered if it would be supple or crackling dry if she closed it in her hand.

The breeze died. The night was heavy and humid again, and the orchestra of crickets surged all around. Sorrow dropped the leaf and swiped her hand on her shirt, brushing away the sensation of it pinched between her fingers. She was tired. Her nerves were overloaded. She was going to be eaten alive by mosquitoes if she stayed out any longer. She marched up the driveway through the tunnel of trees. Ahead the farmhouse shone like a lighthouse glimpsed across the ocean at night.

6

EIGHT YEARS AGO

THE DAY THEY buried Patience was cool, the sky a brilliant, aching blue. The apple trees in the Lovegood orchard still had not bloomed, and the ash trees in the cemetery grove remained leafless and brown. Nothing had been right since Patience had died. It was supposed to be spring, but there was no sign of it in the orchard.

Patience's grave was at the end of a row next to their great-grandmother Devotion Lovegood, a woman she had never known. That spot at the end of the row should have been Grandma's. Sorrow had always imagined it would be Grandma's.

There were only a few people at the funeral. There was no preacher. The gravedigger and his assistant stood a respectable distance away; the tires of their yellow backhoe had pressed muddy tracks into the earth. The men were quiet now, but before, as the small family had been gathering, Sorrow had heard the young man whisper to the older that the witch weather seemed to be breaking, and the older man had hushed him with an elbow to the side and a wary glance at the barren trees. It would have delighted Sorrow before, to hear men from town murmuring nervously about her orchard's strange weather, but now it only made her sick to her stomach. A man from the nursery had brought an ash sapling in a cloth sack. Dad and Grandma would plant it later, after Patience was in the ground.

Sorrow stood between Dad and Grandma. Nobody spoke. The Lovegood women did not bury their family members with empty words and meaningless prayers. Their only ceremony was giving the dead back to the earth and planting a new life to mark its passage. That was what Mom had said one day in town, when they saw a long funeral procession on the road. Sorrow had marveled at how a dead person could have known so many people, enough to fill all those cars.

Mom was there too, at Patience's graveside. She wore a plain gray dress Sorrow had never seen before. At her back was a man in white and a woman in a dark skirt. The woman was a doctor. Sorrow had overheard Dad saying to Grandma that Mom was only allowed to come to the funeral if she was supervised, and she would go back to the hospital after.

Later, when the funeral was over, Mom would say good-bye to Sorrow. Sorrow would reach for her, wanting a hug, but Mom would flinch away. Her voice would be flat and dull and tired. When she was gone Sorrow's stomach would cramp and her head would hurt and Dad would try to take her hand, but Sorrow would pull out of reach. She would walk back to the house behind Grandma, and she would notice how Grandma looked into the orchard, her eyes sad but her chin lifted in hope, as though she expected winter's grip to finally break now that their tears were shed and Patience was gone.

In the morning, Dad would put a suitcase full of Sorrow's things into the trunk of his rental car. Grandma would hug Sorrow, kiss her forehead, give her a quilt folded into a neat square, and only then would Sorrow understand that she was leaving. She didn't want to go. She couldn't leave Grandma alone. The garden wasn't sprouting. The orchard wasn't blossoming. She couldn't leave. She would shout and fight and kick, clawing at her father when he tried to wrestle her into the car, slapping her grandmother away when she tried to help. She would hurt both of them, and herself, when she fell to the ground and scraped her knees and wailed. Only when she had tired herself out with fighting and crying would Dad lift her into the car.

Grandma would stand by the driveway and watch as they drove away.

"Your mother is very sick," Dad would say as they left Abrams Valley.

It was what everybody had been saying for days. Doctors and police officers and the social worker in her pink suit as she sipped tea in the kitchen. They asked Sorrow if she was hungry, asked her if she had clean clothes, asked her how much her mother slept, how much she ate, how often she got out of bed. She didn't know what to tell them. Patience had always warned her not to talk to strangers, but Patience was gone and Sorrow didn't know what to do. It was easier not to say anything.

As they left Abrams Valley, Dad would say it again: "Your mother is very sick."

And he would say, "Your grandmother thinks it's best if you come stay with me for a while. Just until she gets better."

And Sorrow would feel cold and small and hollowed out inside. Grandma was sending her away.

Tomorrow Sorrow would stare out the car window and she would remember pictures of palm trees and alligators in a library book, Patience tracing her finger all the way down to where Dad lived, and she would be too afraid to speak. Lovegoods didn't leave the orchard. In all of Mom's stories, every tale she had shared of their family when they cuddled together by the fire on cold winter nights, nobody ever left. Sorrow hadn't even known they could. Mom had never said. Sorrow had never been to the airport before. She had never left Vermont, never ventured beyond the bounds of Abrams Valley. The orchard and the farm and the town were the only world she had ever known. She would remember Patience in the cemetery grove, not a shape in a white sheet but a living girl, her cheeks pink with cold beneath the spring green of her knit hat, and she would understand what she hadn't understood before, and it would feel like a tangle of branches and vines wrapped around her heart, growing through her veins and squeezing her lungs. With every mile the distance tore at the underside of her skin like soft grass roots ripped away, until there was nothing left in her father's rental car but a hollow shell of a girl, rigid with guilt and fear and a future looming over an unknown horizon, all of her warm, messy, pulsing, breathing insides left behind in the orchard.

Her father wouldn't look at her. He would be holding the steering wheel so tight his knuckles were white, and he would say, "If she gets better."

But that was tomorrow.

Now, in the Lovegood cemetery, Patience was wrapped up in a white sheet, and she was in the ground, and Dad was whispering that it was okay to cry, it was okay, but all Sorrow could feel was the sour ache at the back of her throat where a scream was gathering, growing like a summer storm, but instead of letting it loose she swallowed it down, down into the pit of her stomach, and locked it away beneath the fear and the suffocating sadness, buried it beneath the rich tumbling dirt, down with the roots and the worms and the darkness and the quiet.

7

ANNE LOVEGOOD

1836–1894

IT DIDN'T TAKE long for her mother to find her. Anne scrubbed the tears from her face; she didn't want Mother to know she had been crying. She was sitting against the big oak on the hill with her back pressed against the trunk, her knees hugged to her chest, the small wooden tiger Father had carved for her gripped in one hand. She was too old for toys, but she carried it everywhere with her now, a little piece of home tucked in her pocket like a talisman.

When she heard footsteps approaching she straightened her legs and lifted her chin. Mother stepped into the clearing around the oak. She spotted Anne, but before she approached she looked around, up into the branches of the massive old tree and down at the soil. She scuffed her shoe into the dirt and nudged a white stone, turned it over with her toe before bending to pick it up. The clearing around the oak was bare, without a single speck of grass, only a scattering of small white stones.

"I know you're not happy here," said Mother. "I know you miss your father. I know you miss your friend Mary too."

Anne, fourteen years old and ashamed of her tears, sniffled wetly. "I never wanted to leave. I *told* you I never wanted to leave."

It was not, perhaps, the truth, but Mother let the falsehood pass unremarked. Anne had believed it an adventure when her parents had first announced that Mother and Anne were leaving Mussoorie for America, while Father would stay behind to finish his work with the Survey of India. She had been so excited, and her dear friend Mary excited for her, even though it meant they would be so far apart from each other. Anne had bid farewell to her father and her home, and she and her mother had wound out of the Himalayan foothills, crossed the sweltering lowlands until the mountains were no more than a shadow of memory behind them, all the way to Bombay and a ship waiting there.

Only when they were aboard the ship and the continent was sliding from sight had Anne's breath caught, her heart stuttered, and she understood: She would never see India again. Her father would be continents away. Her best friend, Mary, would be on the other side of the world, and they would never again walk arm in arm through the gardens, never again share notes and secrets, whispers and laughter. Anne was leaving, and she would never return.

Whatever she had imagined of Vermont during the long

journey, it was nothing like the lumpy, tree-choked land around her. Mother had spoken of mountains, but these small, forested humps were disappointing compared to the towering pinnacles they had left behind. The town was dull, captured in the bottom of a valley rather than spread gloriously upon a ridge like her beloved Himalayan hill station, and its people were grim and suspicious. They all knew Mother—but her name was spat derisively from scorn-twisted lips, and the sight most presented to Anne was that of turned backs or scowling faces. Anne could have sworn she heard one woman mutter, *"Witch-spawn"*—so unexpected, so barbaric and provincial, she had nearly laughed. She would have laughed if she could have told Mary, if there hadn't been thousands of miles between them and nothing but ink and paper to span it, if she hadn't seen the pinched look on Mother's face and felt a seasick uncertainty about what to do.

The orchard itself was the worst of all, worse than the mountains that weren't mountains, worse than the townspeople who muttered and glared. The house was wrecked and filthy, having been claimed and abandoned by a succession of failed farmers since Mother's childhood, full of broken furniture and cobwebs and animal nests. The whole property was an ugly, overgrown place, its trees stuck in every season of the year from barren winter to leafy high summer—sometimes all on the same tree, pink blossoms hanging from the same branches as orange autumn leaves. Everywhere, the air stank of rotting apples. Mother had mentioned building a cider house for pressing cider, and the very thought made Anne gag.

Mother was right. Anne was not happy here.

Finally Mother said, "Your father and I thought you would like—"

Anne snorted, a rough unladylike sound. "You didn't even ask me. Father would never have sent me away if you had asked."

Mother sighed, and when Anne glanced up she was pinching the bridge of her nose. Her eyes had been bothering her more and more lately. Even with the eyeglasses she had bought in London, she still squinted over every page by candlelight, peering close to the letters and deeds that had dragged her on this long journey, back to a home she had not seen since she was a child. She looked tired now, aged ten years rather than mere months since they had left home.

Father was supposed to join them someday, when the British Army was done with him. Anne had walked the perimeter of the Lovegood land—Mother's land, she refused to think of it as hers—every day already, holding in her hand the magnetic compass given to her as a parting gift from Surveyor-General Waugh himself, who had tugged at her braid and chucked her chin and told her to practice her sums like a good girl. She promised herself she would fill dozens of notebooks with carefully collected angles and azimuths and calculations before Father arrived, even if she was the only one who understood what they meant. There was a school in town, but it was run by the pastor's wife and full of dim-witted farmers' children, all smaller than Anne by a head and not a one of them knowing the difference between a sine and a cosine if their lives depended on it.

But if Anne was expecting an apology, an admission of error

from Mother, she was to be disappointed.

"I know this is not what you are accustomed to," Mother said. She still wasn't looking at Anne as she spoke. Her gaze was fixed instead on the ground at her feet, where white stones lay half-concealed beneath fallen leaves. "To be quite honest, I had not thought I would ever come back. When the solicitor's letter arrived, I very nearly burned it."

Anne had read the letter Mother was talking about. She wasn't supposed to, but she had sneaked it from Mother's valise while they were aboard the ship. A lawyer in America had written to Mother to tell her that her property in Vermont was the subject of extensive legal challenges, and did she wish to appoint a representative or perhaps settle the matter by offering the land for sale?

Mother had not wanted to do either. She was going to deal with the matter herself.

"You should have burned it," Anne said miserably. "I want to go home. I hate it here."

Fresh tears rose in her eyes; she swiped them away. There was no sense hiding them now. She wanted Mother to see how afraid she was of forgetting the sound of Father's voice and the tickle of his whiskers against her cheek, the glimmer of sunlight on Mary's hair and how warm her hand felt clutched in Anne's, the way the mist crawled through the foothills to make an island of the hill station, as though the rest of the world had dropped away. There was a hole in Anne's heart, a raw wound, and she did not want to hide it anymore.

Mother lifted her eyes from the ground to the sky. Beyond the oak's broad branches, patchy clouds were gathering together to blot out the blue.

"My sister taught me to climb this tree," she said.

That was the very last thing Anne had expected her to say.

"You have a sister?" she asked.

"I did, once," Mother said. She pressed her palm against the trunk of the oak. "I had four sisters and two brothers."

"I never knew," Anne said quietly. Mother spoke so rarely of her family and her childhood that Anne imagined it as a forbidden puzzle box full of long-kept secrets, always locked away, hidden.

"I scarcely remember them," Mother admitted. "For many years I had thought I'd forgotten them, but I'm remembering more, being back here. I was the youngest. The last to learn to climb. Prudence was the eldest. She was the one who taught me."

A thousand questions trembled in Anne's chest, but she spoke only one: "Where is she?"

Instead of answering, Mother gathered her skirts and sat beside Anne on a large woody root. She took a breath as though steeling herself to speak—but that was nonsense; Mother was sharp and clever and stern, never unsteady, never uncertain—then another, and a third, and with every inhale Anne felt her expectation grow.

"They're gone," said Mother. "All of them. They died when I was young. For a long time I thought—I thought it better that I never speak of them. I thought it better to never say their names. To forget them."

Anne said nothing, too afraid of shattering the fragile stillness around them. She was holding her wooden tiger so tight her fingers trembled.

"I was wrong," Mother said. "I was wrong to let myself forget them. I know that now. It is better, I think, to tell their story—to remember who they were. To remember who they came from. Who they could have been, if they hadn't died that summer. It was the coldest summer anybody could remember—so cold there was frost in July, and none of the crops grew."

Anne drew her legs to her chest again and rested her chin on her knees to listen.

8

SORROW WOKE BEFORE dawn's first light crept over the farm. The morning was clear, the air cool on her bare arms. She blinked up at the dormer ceiling. The rooster crowed again—her unwelcome alarm clock—and downstairs the screen door squeaked opened and clattered shut.

At home on a Sunday morning nobody would be up before nine, but this was a farm. Verity and Grandma had always been early risers. Sorrow sat up and blearily rubbed the sleep from her eyes.

Her childhood bedroom hadn't changed much in eight years. Same bed, same dresser, same ladder-back chair in the corner with old wood showing through peeling blue paint. When she was little she had hung her dresses on a string stretched across the wall—there was no closet or wardrobe. The nails were still there, but the string was gone. The sheets on the bed were new, a little stiff, but the quilt was the same soft pink-and-green one that had been in Patience's room for years before she had noticed Sorrow coveting it. The pattern of green pinwheels and pink starbursts had made Sorrow feel like she was lying in a field of flowers.

She smoothed her hand over the faded cotton, the worn seams, the delicate stitches in intricate, curling designs. Grandma's handiwork. In a corner on the back side she would have stitched her artist's signature in white thread, the letters so small they were barely a bump: *Per.Love.* That was how she had always signed her work, because *Perseverance Lovegood* was too many letters. Tourists used to stop into the quilting shop looking for new Per Love designs. They probably still did.

Only after Sorrow had dressed did she notice her favors were gone.

Every year when she was a child, as the weather warmed and the last snow melted, she would begin to find little treasures throughout the orchard, nestled in the roots or tucked into the crooks of branches. She had found small animals carved from wood, fine pearl buttons that shone in the sun, scuffed glass beads on leather strings, and shiny pennies from long ago. A frail metal lady's fan with the finest filigree. Wire-framed eyeglasses with one lens broken out. One summer she had found a pocket watch with a cracked face and the words *To George, Love Forever, From Catherine* engraved on the inside. She had dug it from summer-dry dirt on a hot sunny day, but it had flung drops of dank water all over when she'd swung it on its chain. Months later it would still speckle the chest of drawers with gritty droplets. She had made a nightly ritual of wiping it clean.

She had told her father about the favors once when he was walking with her in the orchard. His visits had been brief and rare; he would drive a rental car up the driveway for a few days of stilted conversation and sleeping on the sofa, and he would leave again with a promise to return. That summer day in the orchard, listening to Sorrow chatter about buttons and bottles and Indian Head pennies, he had smiled an uncertain smile and told her she had a good eye. That night Sorrow had overhead her parents having a quiet conversation in the kitchen, Dad's unintelligible murmurs followed by Verity's sharp answer: "There is nothing wrong with our daughters, Michael."

After Dad went home that time, Verity told Sorrow not to tell anybody else about the favors.

"It's none of their business," she had said. Her voice was tired, not angry, but her disappointment was sharper for its weariness. "It's easier not to give them an excuse to ask questions. Let's keep our own secrets, okay?"

Sorrow had always known there was a line between their family and everybody else, a wire fence separating *us* and *them*, but she had never been entirely sure what side of the fence her father belonged on. Verity's answer was clear: Dad was *them*, an outsider. Sorrow had promised she would never tell anybody again, and the memory made her squirm now: how easily she had promised, how little she had questioned the boundaries her mother placed around their world.

The favors had been such little things, cherished but inconsequential, not worthy of secrets or fights. Sorrow was the only one who found them, because she was the only one who ever looked, making a game of it on the days when she was feeling most lonely and Patience refused to play with her. The top of the dresser was empty now, dusted and polished to a shine. They were all gone. She hadn't taken any of them with her when she left.

She checked the drawers of the dresser, then the nightstand. Looked under the bed. She found nothing.

It wasn't a big deal. They were only things. It would have been pointless for Verity and Grandma to leave so much clutter gathering dust for eight years. She looked in the top drawer again, fingers skittering expectantly into the corners. It didn't mean anything. It wasn't worth getting upset over.

But—she hated to admit this to herself, hated how childish it was—she *was* upset. The collection had been hers. As a child she had believed, fanciful as it was, that the orchard revealed the favors to her on purpose. When a gray spring day needed to be brightened by a flash of color, when a tiresome summer afternoon needed to be livened with a doll or figurine or handful of buttons, she could trudge into the acres of apple trees and search until she found something curious and new. She was never alone when she had the favors. She could always imagine girls from long ago sharing their treasures as they played together.

If she had been given a choice, she wouldn't have left them behind. But nobody had asked her. She didn't remember who had packed her things. Grandma, probably. Maybe Dad. Verity had been hospitalized by then.

Sorrow pressed the heels of her hands to her eyes to chase away the sudden sting of tears. They were only things. Trinkets and toys. She hadn't even remembered them until just now.

The light through the window had changed: the sun was rising in a burst of yellow over the mountains. Sorrow looked around the room one more time, at the empty dresser and narrow bed, the suitcase spilling clothes across the floor. She grabbed her shoes and her Phillies cap and headed downstairs.

The kitchen smelled of baking bread, and Grandma was standing at the sink, rinsing out a bowl. She gave Sorrow a smile and gestured to a teapot in the shape of a pumpkin. Sorrow had to check two cabinets before she found the mugs; everything had been rearranged, spices now residing where dishes had been, cups filling the space once occupied by canned goods.

"Hey, do you know . . ." Sorrow paused, sipped her tea. "Do you know what happened to my little favors?"

Grandma tilted her head slightly. Sorrow couldn't tell if it was a question or not.

"All those little things I used to collect from the orchard? I was just wondering if they got packed away somewhere."

Grandma's mouth curved in a thoughtful frown; she didn't reach for her pen and paper. It had been easy, once, to read Grandma's expressions and gestures, to carry on a conversation with only the quirks of her lips as replies—or so Sorrow had thought, when she was little. Looking at her grandmother now, not knowing what she was thinking, she realized that maybe those exchanges had never been conversations in the first place. She had chattered a lot, and Grandma had smiled and nodded in response, but that wasn't the same thing at all.

"You don't know?" she asked, to be sure she was interpreting the frown correctly.

Grandma shook her head.

"Okay. But you do remember—"

Sorrow set the too-strong tea on the table. She didn't know where Verity was. She couldn't remember if her mother's bedroom door had been open or closed—and how strange it was, to not have noticed what had once been her first warning of how a day might go.

"You do remember them, don't you? My collection?"

Grandma nodded slowly.

Sorrow looked away, uncomfortable under her grandmother's gaze, and embarrassed by her relief. "Okay. It's not a big deal. I can look for them later." She glanced around the kitchen, spotted the bowl of pancake batter, the pack of thawing bacon. "Is there anything I can do to help? Since I'm awake at this obscene hour, you might as well put me to work."

Grandma nodded and waved for Sorrow to follow her out to the back porch. She picked up a covered bucket, handed it to Sorrow, and pointed across the lawn at the chicken coop. A soft mist rose as the morning sun burned off the night's dew.

"Feed the chickens?" Sorrow guessed.

Grandma mimed reaching out and grabbing something.

"Collect the eggs too?"

Grandma patted her arm.

"Okay." Sorrow peeked under the towel; the bucket was half-filled with vegetables and grain. "I think I remember how."

The skin around Grandma's eyes crinkled with silent laughter. Sorrow decided to take that as a vote of confidence. The dewy grass dampened her sneakers and tickled her ankles as she crossed the lawn. Unlike the house, the chicken coop looked exactly as old and shabby as she remembered: the once-white paint gray and chipped away, the entire structure sinking into the ground at one corner.

The chickens clucked and jostled, and the rooster eyed her suspiciously as she unlatched the gate. "Shoo. Back up or you don't get anything."

She hadn't tended chickens since she was eight—at home all of their food came wrapped in plastic, thank you very much—and it had been her least favorite chore as a child. She had always wheedled and bartered to convince Patience to do it. But she remembered how to jam the vegetables into the wire and scatter the grain on the ground. The chickens set upon their breakfast with enthusiasm.

The sound of a car on the driveway caught her attention. Sorrow turned and watched a mud-splattered Jeep pull up and park beside Verity's Subaru. The driver was dressed in jeans and a T-shirt that were more grass stain than fabric: he had clearly come to work.

The way Verity had described her feud-breaking Abrams employee as so helpful, the *most helpful* person she knew, had made Sorrow picture somebody obnoxiously peppy and interfering, the kind of polo-shirt-and-combed-hair rich kid who enjoyed taking pity on women who couldn't handle their own farm. But he just looked like a guy. About her age, maybe a year or two older, with sandy blond hair beneath a battered Red Sox hat. He was yawning and heading toward the porch when he spotted her.

"Hi," Sorrow said, waving. "Good morning."

He hesitated a moment, then walked across the lawn to the coop. "Hi."

"Hi," Sorrow said again, but she was distracted when one of the chickens began pecking at her shoe; she had dropped the feed on her own feet. "Go away, go away, go *away*, creature."

When she looked up again he was smiling bemusedly, like he couldn't quite decide if it would be rude to laugh.

Sorrow said, "You can't turn your back on these ferocious beasts. They're shifty."

"You're a lot bigger than them, you know," he said.

"I know," Sorrow said. "But there are more of them than there are of me, and I've seen *Jurassic Park*. I know they're pack hunters. I don't trust their beady little dinosaur eyes." She nudged another hungry chicken away with her foot. "I'm Sorrow. Verity's daughter."

"I, uh, yeah," the guy said. "I thought so. I'm Ethan. I help your mom and grandma around the farm."

"She told me. She made it *very* clear that you're the reason the lawn actually looks like a lawn these days and not some kind of tropical jungle."

"Yeah, well, I try. Did you just get here?"

"Yesterday."

"And Miss P's already got you doing the chores she hates."

"I knew it!" Sorrow said. The chickens clucked angrily and swarmed away from her. "I knew she was being sneaky, but she looked so innocent when she asked."

She reached for the latch on the gate, then remembered that she was supposed to collect the eggs too. The henhouse had been stuffy and small even when she was little.

"I don't think I'm going to fit in there quite as well as I did when I was eight." She pulled open the henhouse door. "Wish me luck."

"Don't let them see the fear in your eyes," Ethan said.

Sorrow flipped him off before she ducked inside, which earned her a laugh.

When she emerged again, fresh eggs laid carefully in the bottom of the bucket, Ethan opened the gate for her. As they walked up to the porch, he pointed to her hat. "Phillies, huh? Not Marlins or Rays?"

"Oh, come on, now," Sorrow said. "There's no reason to be mean, not when we've just met."

"I thought you were from Florida? Morning, Miss P."

Grandma smiled at Ethan and patted his arm.

"I am, but it's Phillies all the way in my family. My stepmom's family," she said, stumbling over the clarification. "Her uncle used to play for them back in the seventies. He came over from Cuba to play."

"Wow, really? That's cool," Ethan said. He took plates from the shelves and set them out on the table; it was obviously habit for him. "Anybody I've heard of?"

"I doubt it. He was only a second-string outfielder for a few years—'76 to '79."

"Still cool," Ethan said. "So he wasn't with them when they won the series in 1980? Won against the Royals—"

"In six games," Sorrow finished. "I know that, trivia guy, but only because it's family legend for me. What's your excuse? Spend a lot of time on Wikipedia?"

"Sort of," Ethan admitted. "My grandfather really loved it. He and I used to make a game of memorizing all the series and championships. He liked to spring random quizzes on me every time I visited. I got candy for a prize, so I was pretty motivated."

Sorrow stopped in the middle of setting out forks and stared at Ethan. "Your grandfather? Eli Abrams?"

"Oh, god, no, not him," Ethan said, shaking his head. "This was my grandfather on my mom's side. Grandpa Eli wouldn't—I can't even imagine him going to a ball game. Or voluntarily talking to a kid."

"I remember him a little," Sorrow said. "We used to see him around town."

What she remembered of Eli Abrams was the click of his silver-tipped cane on the pavement, the stale scent of cigar smoke wafting after him, and the way he would scowl and spit when Grandma passed. She remembered, too, watching Patience twist up clusters of dried grass to mimic the hair he had growing from his ears, and laughing so hard her stomach hurt.

Eli Abrams had died when Sorrow was about seven. That night

Verity had opened a bottle of cider to raise a toast of good-bye and good riddance.

"So what happened? To your Phillies guy?" Ethan asked.

"It's kinda sad, actually," Sorrow said. "He died during spring training. Got in a fight."

Sonia's parents had a little shrine in their living room: photographs of a handsome young man with a wide boyish smile, a bat and a jersey and a hat, all kept meticulously dusted in a quiet corner. Sorrow knew all the stories about how his father had died in one of Castro's prisons, and that was when he decided to leave Cuba forever, how the family would still be there if he hadn't taken that boat and that chance, all the uncles and aunts and brothers and sisters left behind, and how after he died in a knife fight—drugs, women, baseball, politics; the story of that fight changed with whoever was telling it—the entire family left Philadelphia for Miami and never looked back.

Seeing that shrine, hearing those stories, that was the first time Sorrow had realized somebody else's family could have a history as strong as the one she had left behind—and she had no part in it. It was bad enough that there were so many people to keep track of, that their food didn't taste like her food, that the cousins had games and jokes she couldn't follow, that she couldn't understand half of what anybody was saying because every conversation slid effortlessly between English and Spanish. That shrine for a lost young man, those photographs and memories, they carried stories she would never fit into, a history she would never share.

There were footsteps on the porch and a few thumps as Verity stomped dirt from her shoes. Grandma waved them all to the table to eat when she came in, and over breakfast baseball talk gave way to small talk. Sorrow learned that Ethan had been doing work for Verity and Grandma for a few months; he also had a job at a restaurant in town, so he made it out to the farm only two or three times a week. He was trying to save up for college, he said, because his father would only help if Ethan went to the right kind of school.

"Define 'the right kind of school,'" Sorrow said.

"Harvard, obviously," Ethan said, "because as my dad loves to remind me, Abrams men have gone to Harvard for five generations, and I'm not going to be the one to screw that up. But if I can't quite swing that, he'd settle for any of the Ivies."

"You're better off making your own way," Verity said. "You don't need their help."

Sorrow glanced at her, eyebrows raised. That was easy to say if you weren't the one trading a legacy spot at Harvard for a lifetime of student loan debt, but she didn't know Ethan, didn't know his relationship with his father and the Abrams side of his family. It sounded like a conversation they'd had many times before.

Ethan shrugged, didn't agree or disagree, and changed the subject. Conversation turned to the work that needed to be done around the farm, the projects they had planned for the summer, Verity and Ethan deciding what to trim, what to paint, when and how, and Grandma filling a page of her notebook with her own suggestions in elegant, spidery handwriting.

Verity had never asked Sorrow about her own college plans.

Sorrow could not recall a single time when they had ever talked about what she would do after high school. She talked about school during their phone calls, mostly because she never knew what else to talk about it, but always carefully, choosing her words so that she wasn't complaining too much, but she wasn't too excited either. Verity had never gone to college—Sorrow wasn't even sure she had ever graduated from high school, and not knowing made her uneasy. Over the phone, from the safety of her bedroom in Florida with the air conditioner humming and palm trees swaying outside, Sorrow had always been wary of saying anything that would make her life in Florida sound so much better than the one Verity could have given her. It was easier to edit and elide than to risk saying the wrong thing at the wrong time.

Sorrow grew quieter and quieter as the meal went on. She barely even followed what they were talking about, much less had any idea how to help. She didn't know how to be a farm girl anymore. She hadn't even been able to feed the chickens without dropping half of their food on her shoes. She had forgotten so much in her years away, transformed into a girl who didn't fit the puzzle gap she had left behind, and she didn't know how to find her way back.

9

AFTER BREAKFAST VERITY asked, "What do you want to do this morning?"

They were alone in the kitchen. Grandma was in the garden, Ethan digging tools out of the barn.

Sorrow twisted a dish towel in her hands and took a breath. "I was thinking about bringing flowers to the cemetery."

Verity looked at her in surprise.

"I thought we could both go?" Sorrow said.

There was a long silence, and Sorrow's hope crumpled. Verity was going to refuse. She was going to say no. But it was fine. It wasn't the same as when Sorrow had been a child pleading for her mother to get dressed, to leave her bedroom, to eat lunch and walk through the orchard and lift her face to the sun. It wasn't the same thing at all, this small overture, however much Sorrow felt she was flickering between then and now, the dark old kitchen and the light new one, memories clouding around the sunny morning with sickly uncertainty.

"We can do that," Verity said after a long silence.

Sorrow's smile was shaky and relieved. She turned away quickly.

They gathered a bouquet from the beds around the house: Siberian iris, lily of the valley, peony. The last of the spring poppies were bursts of orange and yellow, now fading in the summer heat. She had known all of them once, the names of the flowers and trees, the shrubs and clover and grass. It hadn't been terribly useful when she moved away and teachers expected her to know things like state capitals and presidents, but growing up in the orchard it had been the only knowledge that mattered.

They walked down the hill and along the edge of the fallow field. The grass was high, and fat bees bounced lazily between flowers. The rusty iron skeleton of an ancient pickup truck was slowly being claimed by the earth; soil in its bed bloomed with wild daisies, and a whip-thin maple sapling was growing hopefully through the gap where the windshield had once been. There was a small bird's nest tucked between the doorframe and the side mirror.

Sorrow glanced into the nest as they passed: empty.

Verity said, "It turns out it's more trouble than it's worth to pay somebody to haul something like that away."

"It's been here forever anyway," Sorrow said. "It gives the meadow character."

"It was my father's. He got it from his father when it was already a classic—did I ever tell you about them?"

"I don't think so," Sorrow said. Verity's father had died when she was only a child. He was buried in the family graveyard, but Sorrow didn't know much more about him than his name, which had always stood out from the eccentric but thoroughly New England Lovegood names. "His name was . . . Anton? Where was he from again?"

"Close," Verity said, smiling. "Antanas. And he was born in upstate New York, but his family was Lithuanian. His parents came over after World War Two. That truck, it was the first real American thing they bought, their first big purchase, after they'd been working long enough to save up some money. My grandfather was absolutely meticulous about maintaining it. He gave it to my father for his eighteenth birthday, and it ran perfectly for another fifteen years until the day my grandfather died. According to my father, he was driving in from the orchard when the truck stopped and wouldn't start again, and he knew right away what that meant."

Sorrow looked back at the truck, a ruddy fossil in a rich green field. "I didn't know any of that."

"I wish I knew more about his family," Verity admitted. "I was only six when he died. Pancreatic cancer. It happened so fast we barely knew he was sick before he was gone. But I remember how much he loved that truck. And I remember . . ." Verity laughed a little, shaking her head. "He used to sing these old songs. I couldn't understand a word of them, but he had a lovely voice."

Verity's father and his family had never featured in any of the stories she'd told when Sorrow was a child. Verity had an encyclopedic knowledge of the Lovegoods, so extensive and detailed it had always made Sorrow's head spin to learn new pieces of it, but the more distant branches of their family tree had never gotten as much attention. She had always assumed it was because the Lovegoods were more important than everybody else. She hadn't realized until she moved away how thoroughly her mother's one-sided interest had skewed what she knew.

Past the truck, around the field, to the edge of the orchard. Steps Sorrow had walked a thousand times, barefoot and in stomping winter boots, in sunshine and rain and snow, sometimes skipping, sometimes dawdling, often with no particular destination in mind. The orchard had never been a place that invited hurry. It moved at the pace of the seasons, the change of the weather, the slow orbit of the earth. Their apple trees were the oldest in all of Abrams Valley. They weren't as bountiful as they had once been, but they still blossomed pink and white when the weather warmed, and in the fall Verity hired people from town for the harvest. The Abrams Valley variety was an old-fashioned apple: small and sour and hard, too bitter to eat, good only for cider.

It should be called the Lovegood variety. That was what Verity used to say, and Sorrow had always bobbed her head in agreement. The Abrams family had the town and the whole valley, with an Abrams Street and an Abrams House, a plaque on a church about its founding minister, Clement Abrams, and another in the park commemorating the day the town name had been officially changed from Cold Hollow. The Abrams name was stamped all over everything, touching every part of the valley. There was no reason for them to claim the apples too. The Lovegoods had been first to the valley, first to plant an orchard. The apples were rightfully theirs.

The scent of apples lingered even now. Sorrow tasted the air as they walked, their footsteps crunching softly on the dirt road, morning sun warm on their shoulders.

Sorrow was quiet for a minute, then said, "I think I saw one of the Abrams girls outside last night."

"Here?" Verity looked around, as though she expected an Abrams to leap from the trees. "In the orchard?"

"No, on the road, when I was calling Dad. I couldn't tell who it was. Are both of them living at home now?"

"They are. Cassie's back for the summer from that prep school of hers, and Julie finally managed to finish college at UVM."

"Finally?"

"She transferred out of a couple schools before she stuck with one."

"That sucks for her."

Verity raised her eyebrows. "Those girls have been given every opportunity, and more chances than most people get, and all they do is throw them away."

Sorrow slanted a glance toward her. "Didn't you just tell Ethan to throw away those same opportunities and make his own way?"

"That's different," Verity said. "He's more like us than he is like them."

Sorrow started to reply, stopped herself. She didn't like the judgmental tone in her mother's voice, the *us* and *them* and lines between traced in the air with an electric crackle. Eight years in Miami had shown her there was a much bigger spectrum of rich to poor than existed in Abrams Valley, and probably in the whole of Vermont. There were a lot of people in the world with problems bigger than anything the Abrams and Lovegood families could imagine. Sonia's parents hadn't even been able to stay in their own *country*, much less own and farm the same valuable parcel of land for twelve generations.

But she didn't know if she was allowed to say that. For all that this road was familiar to her feet, these trees in summer as comforting to her as an old blanket, she couldn't shake the feeling of being the stranger here, a visitor who hadn't quite learned all of the rules.

The Lovegood family cemetery was on the west side of the orchard, in a deep hollow at the bottom of a hill, far from the house and road. A little farther on was the property line, and beyond that a nature preserve popular with hikers and fishermen. The preserve had once been Lovegood land, long before Sorrow was born, but her great-grandmother Devotion had donated it to a public trust to keep the Abramses from getting their hands on it.

There were no big monuments in the Lovegood cemetery, no crosses, no stone angels on marble bases. The headstones were plain white rectangles: chips of marble, names and dates, nothing else. No words identified the interred as beloved mothers or fathers, cherished sisters or brothers. Verity used to say they didn't need words carved in stone to remind them where their family had come from.

What they had instead were the ash trees.

When a member of the Lovegood family died, before the earth had settled into a solemn depression over their body, before the mourners had walked the path back to the house, an ash sapling was planted over their grave. There was one for every person buried in the cemetery. Their family was old, but most generations had only one or two daughters, few had any sons, and many had died young. But there were trees enough to form an impressive grove, and their branches wove together in an arched canopy, and sunlight through the gaps cast a dappled pattern on the ground.

The oldest and grandest ash belonged to Rejoice Lovegood, their ancestor who had first planted the orchard. She had died in 1790, but there was no birth date on her gravestone, because nobody knew when she had been born. She had come to Vermont alone, before it was Vermont, a young woman without a family. Nobody knew where she had come from or what her name had been before she chose Lovegood for herself. She had eventually met and married a French trapper, but the women in their family never took their husbands' names.

Sorrow hadn't known that was unusual until Mrs. Roche, their neighbor down the road, had told her most families used their father's name, not their mother's. Mrs. Roche hadn't exactly said the Lovegoods were weird for doing it the wrong way around, but Sorrow had known she was thinking it. Mrs. Roche carried everything she was thinking in the climbing arches of her drawn-on eyebrows, and they climbed extra high, with more than the usual amount of arch, when she was disapproving of Sorrow's family.

Beyond the gray lines of the split-rail fence, splashes of yellow in the green revealed themselves to be plastic strips tied around the trunks of the ashes, and in a few high branches, dangling from ropes, were bright purple squares.

"What's all that stuff?" Sorrow asked.

"Some forestry students put them up," Verity said.

"Are the trees sick?"

"Not yet," Verity said. "They're trying to keep this bug called the emerald ash borer from getting established in Vermont, so they're teaching people how to recognize ash trees and look for the signs. I guess the bugs are attracted to purple, and the traps are supposed to catch them."

"Have they?" Sorrow looked up and down the trunks of the ashes, searching for signs of disease, infestation, rot. The trees were strong and healthy, as far as she could tell; a leaf she plucked from a low branch was soft and supple. But she didn't know what to look for, and so much of what could go wrong with trees wasn't visible from the outside.

"The beetles aren't here yet, if that's what you mean. You look like you expect one to crawl down your neck any second now."

Sorrow rolled her shoulders to relax. "I didn't know that was a thing you had to worry about. In Florida they've got this little bug called the psyllid that causes citrus greening, and it's killing orange trees all over. It's not the bugs that kill the trees, actually. It's a bacteria they carry. It does something to . . ." She trailed off. "It's really bad. I wrote a paper about it for my environmental science class."

Still Verity said nothing, and Sorrow's questions about the ash trees faltered in the silence. Dad and Sonia had seized on Sorrow's interest in biology and ecology with a fervor that embarrassed her, especially after she'd realized—with help from Dr. Silva—that they were only desperate for her to show some spark of academic inclination because that was the only way they knew how to relate to a teenage daughter. Thanks to Andi, with her valedictorian GPA and college applications and extracurriculars, the rubric their parents had for assessing how their daughters were doing was one on which Sorrow was never going to tick very many boxes.

She thought Verity might understand that, if she explained. Verity, who had never quite fit into what the world expected her to be, living according to the weather and seasons, measuring accomplishments in harvests and planting, she would be unimpressed by Dad and Sonia trying to fit Sorrow into a mold that hadn't been made for her.

But Verity didn't ask. She didn't seem to have noticed that Sorrow had spoken at all.

When they reached the corner of the cemetery fence, Sorrow kicked at a fallen rail before stepping over.

"I'm surprised you haven't taken this whole thing down." The fence post wobbled ominously when she nudged it. As a child she had walked the entire length of the cemetery fence as a balance beam, but barely half of it was still standing. "I think if I sneezed on it the whole thing would fall over."

She glanced back. Verity had stopped on the outside of the fence.

"Are you . . . ?" Sorrow gestured with the bouquet of flowers.

Verity looked at her, then looked into the orchard, away from the gravestones, away from the ash trees, and said nothing.

Sorrow waited, waited, stared and waited for an uncomfortably long time before she realized, in a crush of embarrassment, that Verity had no intention of crossing the fence.

Her face grew hot. Verity wasn't even looking at her. "I, uh. Okay. I'll just . . . Okay."

Sorrow left Verity at the fence and walked alone through the cemetery. The grass was long and untrimmed, and tangles of weeds choked each headstone, dotted here and there with plastic bags and scraps of trash. Every piece of rubbish she spotted tightened a knot in her throat. It wasn't supposed to look like this. It never had before. She used to play out here, climbing the trees and walking the fence. On summer nights they would come out as a family, all four of them, spread a blanket on the ground and look up at the stars. It wasn't right that Verity had neglected the graveyard, not when she was putting so much effort into cleaning up the rest of the property.

Sorrow's steps slowed as she reached the far corner.

She hadn't known, before that moment, how fast an ash tree could grow. The ashes of the cemetery were tall and sturdy, towering so high she had to crane her head back to glimpse their crowns, but the youngest ash had been a sapling when she last saw it, a whip of soft wood in a burlap sack of dirt. In her mind that was the way it had remained. But Patience's tree was well over ten feet tall now, tall enough that Sorrow had no proper scale for estimating its height. A single-story bungalow in a Miami suburb? A swaying palm in a postage-stamp yard? She looked up and up and she wondered—it hurt, to wonder, like a bee sting in her chest—if she would be taller than Patience now, as she was taller than Verity, herself sturdy and treelike where they had always been willowy and graceful.

The headstone at the base of the tree looked like all the others. *Patience Lovegood.* A name and a pair of dates.

Sorrow did the subtraction in her head, just in case—what? They wouldn't have gotten the numbers wrong. Patience had been sixteen when she died. That was all anybody would learn of her from her headstone. Five years from now, ten, a hundred or more, that was all any stranger walking through this grove of cemetery trees would see, pausing on their way to search for invasive beetles or an overgrown trail or a minute of peace and quiet. That was all they would ever know. They wouldn't know how Patience had smiled, how she had been so polite to people's faces but so mocking behind their backs, how she had made her little sister laugh with her impressions and her jokes. How she had been fine one day, dead the next. How pink her nose would turn in the cold, that one fierce spot of color in a snow-pale face and a scattering of freckles. How she loved to race Sorrow through the orchard and never, ever let her win.

There was a pressure growing in Sorrow's chest, a lump sitting at the top of her lungs. The insect chorus around her rose and rose and blended and hummed. She carried Patience in her thoughts, memories of washed-out color, fading echoes, but it had always been from far away, surrounded by people who hadn't known her, a landscape she had never walked. She remembered asking, long before Patience died, what happened to the dead when they were buried, and the softness in her mother's voice when she described the dismantling of a body, the natural cycle of decay, particles that had once been flesh and blood turning into roots and leaves, and no way of knowing if the things that made a body a person were transformed as well. Thoughts into flowing sap. Love into bark as impenetrable as armor. She remembered how her mother had found it comforting, the inevitable end, the joining of one to all who had passed before.

Patience hadn't found the promise of a quiet end in the orchard comforting.

The thought shivered over the surface of Sorrow's mind like a breath of winter wind.

They had come out here that day.

She remembered now, so clearly she didn't know how she could have forgotten.

She and Patience had walked through the orchard on the day before Patience died. It had been cold, the muddy gray end of winter in Vermont, and in her mind that gray took on a shimmering quality, as though she were glimpsing it reflected in a pond. The cold hadn't stopped them. It never did, not when they wanted to escape the oppressive silence their mother knit around the house on her bad days.

Sorrow remembered standing in this very spot, which had then been empty, a blank space beside a grave, and asking Patience if this was where their grandmother would be buried when she died.

She looked back. Verity was still waiting by the fence, and Sorrow felt a fleeting panic, that Patience wasn't here to tell her what to say, what to do with their mother's distance and her silence. They had once shared an elaborate sign language of expressions and gestures, a system for navigating the minefield of their mother's moods, but Sorrow had lived eight years without Patience's guidance, eight years in unfamiliar terrain, and she had never felt as lost as she did in that moment, looking across the neglected cemetery to Verity, with absolutely no idea what to do.

She leaned over to set the bouquet beside Patience's headstone. The flowers were already wilting in the heat.

As she straightened up, a spot of yellow in the green caught her eye. Somebody had left a ring of small yellow flowers draped over the corner of the headstone, a crown made from a braid of soft green stems. The name came back to her: hop clover. It grew along roadsides, at the edge of the woods. It was the kind of small, insignificant flower anybody could pluck while wandering around. She glanced to where Verity was lingering outside the fence—but she knew it hadn't been her mother, and Grandma would have left flowers from her own garden.

She reached for the ring of flowers, tugged at it with two fingers. It snagged in the grass. She let it go. Patience's life had been small, occupied by only a few people, but there was somebody outside their little family who remembered Patience, and missed her, and brought her flowers.

Sorrow closed her eyes until the sting faded. She had no idea who it could be, and she felt the presence of that unknown visitor as a shadow behind her, faceless, soundless, a hole in the morning light.

She left the braided clover on Patience's grave, and she walked back through the cemetery grove to where Verity was waiting. She pressed her palm to the trunks of the ash trees as she passed. They were solid and rough and strong.

10

GREEN MOUNTAIN GEAR was located on Main Street between a boutique clothing store and a real estate office with pictures of log cabins and ski resort condos plastered in the front window. Directly across the street was the Abrams Valley Post Office—which, in keeping with the regulations of the federal government, was supposed to close every weekday at 5:00 p.m. The curtains were drawn, the door closed, the flag lowered from its pole.

Sorrow was halfway through her first week in Vermont. It was Wednesday and, according to her phone, exactly 4:47 p.m.

"Drama," said Kavita, leaning on the counter to stare through the store's front window. "So much drama. It never ends."

Kavita's mothers, Helen and Jana Ghosh, owned the store. This was the second shift Sorrow had worked for them, after Verity had volunteered her labor to fill in for an employee who was backpacking through Nepal. Sorrow wondered, a little guiltily, if Verity was trying to shuffle Sorrow into town and away from the farm during her visit. She didn't think it was deliberate—didn't *want* to think it was deliberate—but that only meant it was something she couldn't even imagine asking about. She also didn't know the first thing about hiking or camping, but then neither did most of the people who came into the store. Kavita's older brother, Mahesh, was technically working too, but he had retreated to the back room to text his girlfriend, which was, as far as Sorrow could tell, how he spent 99 percent of his time.

Sorrow had a book open on the counter before her, a field guide to wildflowers of New England. She had been trying to remember all the plant names she used to know by heart—regional common names only, never any Latin designations—but she let the book fall closed to watch the scene across the street.

The postmaster was arguing with two women. He was the same man who had held the position eight years ago; Sorrow recognized his short stature and elfin ears but didn't think she had ever known his name. The women were stooped and sweaty, with bulging packs on their backs and bandannas over their hair. One of them was shaking a hiking pole. The postmaster crossed his arms resolutely. The hiking pole shook some more. A family of tourists in shorts and T-shirts scurried around the argument.

"They're mad because the post office closes?" Sorrow asked.

"Because it closes too early for the smelly trail crowd to hitch-hike their way into town for their resupply runs," Kavita said. "This happens at least twice a week. Somebody doesn't read the message boards and sends their stuff to General Delivery, and then they get here and realize Grumpy McAsshole over there has locked up already. Right now he's trying to tell them their phones have the wrong time. Look, they're pulling them out to compare."

"This is so exciting I don't think I can stand it," Sorrow said, and went back to her book.

She was midway through a page about wild trillium when her phone beeped. The incoming text was from her stepsister, Andi.

Hey, what's up, vermonster?

A burst of surprise, followed by a twinge of guilt. Sorrow hadn't texted Andi since she'd landed. She had been telling herself—for three days—that she would definitely get around to it before Andi noticed. Too late for that now. Sorrow stared at the words for a moment, then put her phone away without answering.

"Once the show is over, you can probably knock off," Kavita said. "The moms won't care. It's always slow once the day-trippers are gone for the night."

"I was hoping to get a ride home after close."

"That works too. Oh, look." The argument outside the post office was ending with the two hikers storming away and the post-master victoriously watching their retreat. Kavita twisted her long black hair up off her neck. "It always ends the same way. Postal goblin, one; Appalachian Trail hopefuls, zero. They never win. We tell them they should send their resupplies here instead, but there are always a few who don't listen."

"Sucks for them," Sorrow said, disinterested, and she went back to her wildflower book. She had picked it off the store's rack when the flow of customers slowed in late afternoon, thinking only that she wanted to remember, a half-formed idea telling her that if she could fill the hollow spaces in her mind where she had once kept the names of flowers and trees, the patterns of the weather and the rhythm of the seasons, the rest would come back too. Maybe not all at once, in a flash of revelation, but she had to start somewhere.

Kavita wasn't quiet for long. "Oh, hey, it's Mrs. Eyebrows."

Sorrow looked up again. There was an elderly woman standing outside the store, her crown of tight gray curls just visible above an array of North Face and Marmot decals on the glass. She moved a couple of inches to the side, revealing her face and the high-arched eyebrows that were more pencil line than hair.

"That's Mrs. Roche," Sorrow said. She would recognize those eyebrows anywhere. "She used to live down the road from us."

Kavita rolled her eyes. "Yeah, I know. Everybody still calls that place the Roche place, even though that couple from Texas owns it now. Same way they still call our place the Radcliffe place. It's like nobody in this town has ever heard of property changing hands."

Sorrow's phone beeped. Another text from Andi: *Give me a call when you get a chance. We need to talk about the shit going on at home.*

She once again put it away without answering. "They called it the Radcliffe place even when the Johnsons lived there. It would be easier if you just changed your name. Is she going to stand there all night?"

"Who knows? The only time she's ever come in was for our grand opening. She wanted to meet 'those nice lesbians from New York.' I doubt she—ooh, she is."

Mrs. Roche pulled open the door and stepped inside, and she looked around for a moment before her gaze settled on the counter.

"Sorrow Lovegood!" she exclaimed. "As I live and breathe!"

Sorrow smiled. "Hi, Mrs. Roche. It's good to see you again."

"Look at you," Mrs. Roche said. She looked a lot older than Sorrow remembered: her steel-gray hair was thinner, her skin sagging around her face, her shoulders stooped. She came forward with her hands held out but dropped them when Sorrow didn't move from behind the counter. "You look just like your sister."

The words struck Sorrow like a blow in the chest.

She had been expecting people to recognize her. Mrs. Abrams in the parking lot, others around town. She had been expecting *you're the Lovegood girl*, the looks and the whispers, the leading questions about why she had come back.

But she hadn't been expecting this. She wasn't prepared for somebody to look at her and see Patience.

"Thank you," she managed, and her smile was frozen on her face, brittle and tight. "How's Mr. Roche?"

"He passed a few years ago," Mrs. Roche said. "You're so kind to ask."

"I'm sorry to hear that." Sorrow only remembered Mr. Roche as a cardigan sweater and a puff of pipe tobacco; he had rarely joined his wife when she visited the Lovegoods.

"Is there something we can help you find, Mrs. Roche?" Kavita asked.

Mrs. Roche adjusted her purse strap on her shoulder. "Oh, no, I just wanted to stop in and say hello to Sorrow. We worried she might have forgotten all about us." She lowered her voice and leaned forward slightly. "You know about the fire, of course. It was a terrible tragedy."

Kavita glanced at Sorrow, as though confirming that Sorrow was, in fact, still standing right there and could hear Mrs. Roche just fine. She twitched one shoulder in an apologetic shrug. "Yeah, I've heard about it."

"Patience was just the sweetest girl," Mrs. Roche said. "I think about her every day. You must miss her so much."

"I do," Sorrow said, because what else could she say? *I think about her every day* was what people said about someone they hadn't thought about in years.

"It'll do your mom a world of good to have you around," Mrs. Roche said. "There's too much sadness in that old orchard. Maybe you'll even convince her and your grandma to come out for the battle this year."

Sorrow blinked. "The battle?"

"You know. The battle. You must remember." Mrs. Roche gave Sorrow a concerned look, and Sorrow's heart began to beat faster. It was bad enough to think Verity might notice gaps in her memory, but this was Mrs. Roche. If Mrs. Roche noticed, the whole town would be discussing Sorrow's post-traumatic amnesia by tomorrow. "We do it every year, right there in the park," Mrs. Roche went on, waving toward the store's front windows. "It's our best festival. Well, not as good as the harvest, but every town has a harvest."

"Oh. Right. I saw the sign," Sorrow said, with a rush of relief. Not something she had forgotten, then, only something she had never experienced in the first place. "We never went when we were kids."

Not to that festival or any others, May Day or the harvest, Thanksgiving or the holiday lights on Main Street. Sorrow had only known what they were missing when Patience tried to convince Verity to take them into town. Verity had always refused. She didn't need the town to tell her how to mark the passage of the seasons, she would say, and Patience would roll her eyes and huff and say that wasn't the point, the point was to *see* people, and not be stuck in the orchard alone all the time, and it wasn't fair that they didn't even get to *try*, not even for a little bit. Sorrow had always dreaded the times when Patience would ask to do something their mother would refuse. On a good day the refusal would come with stony silence. On a bad day it would end with a slamming door and a gaping dark stretch of time when they didn't know when Verity would emerge from her room again.

"There was really a battle here?" Kavita asked.

"Yes," said Mrs. Roche, but she added, "a very small one. It was really more of a disagreement between families."

"It was a bunch of farmers with pitchforks," Sorrow said.

Mrs. Roche conceded the point with a small nod. "But that's

where it all began, you know. The feud between the Lovegoods and the Abramses. You know all about that."

Kavita slanted a glance toward Sorrow. "I've heard a little. I didn't think it was a big deal, like, historically."

Mrs. Roche leaned forward eagerly. "Oh, it may not seem that way now, but I promise you us old folks remember when it was different. When we first moved to town back in—it must have been 1978, goodness, where do the years go—we weren't here a week before some of the ladies from church stopped by to warn us about walking through the woods after dark. They made sure we understood it wasn't safe, not with Devotion Lovegood prowling her property with that great big shotgun of hers, and Eli Abrams doing the same on his side of the fence, each looking for any excuse to shoot and call it a hunting accident."

Kavita laughed, but it had an uncertain edge to it. "Seriously?"

"As the grave," Mrs. Roche confirmed. "It did get a bit better when Devotion passed, God rest her soul, but then it got right nasty again when Henry Abrams had his accident. He was never as mean-spirited as the rest of them, and when he was alive he did what he could to keep his brother Eli from doing anything rash." She paused and gave Sorrow a thoughtful look. "I'm sure your mom's told you about all that. It wasn't an easy time."

"A bit," Sorrow hedged. She knew almost nothing about her great-grandmother Devotion, but she didn't know if it was because she had forgotten or because she had never known in the first place. "I was a little young for that kind of story when I left."

Mrs. Roche patted her hand. "Of course. And I expect it's

difficult for her to talk about, all things considered. She was such a trouper when your grandma needed help."

Sorrow only nodded, because Mrs. Roche was still giving her a look like Sorrow ought to know exactly what she was talking about, and the last thing Sorrow wanted to do was admit that Mrs. Roche knew more about her family than she did. It might not matter in a normal family or a normal town, but she was Verity Lovegood's daughter, and the one true thing everybody knew about Verity was her obsession with her own family history. Mrs. Roche would have a week's worth of gossip fuel if Sorrow let on there were big pieces she was missing.

"What's this festival like, anyway?" Kavita asked. "How do you celebrate a battle?"

"We reenact it every year," Mrs. Roche said.

Another laugh, this one less uncertain, and Kavita said, "Small towns are so weird."

Mrs. Roche poked her with a long, knobby finger. "Don't be like that. It's a great deal of fun. This year it's the kindergarten's turn. There's a pie contest too. I'll be looking forward to seeing both of you there." She pointed at each of them in turn. "And you bring that handsome brother of yours along."

"Please don't let him hear you say that," Kavita said. "His ego's big enough as it is."

"Give your mother my regards, Sorrow, and your grandma." Mrs. Roche hitched her purse on her shoulder and turned toward the door. "I've got to get going. I promised Barbie Rheingold twenty-five cupcakes for tomorrow and I'm out of wrappers."

She turned to leave, but she was only a few steps from the counter when the door opened and two girls came in. They were teenagers, maybe sixteen or seventeen, one white with her blond hair cropped into a spiky pixie cut, the other Asian with red streaks in her black hair. The blond stopped abruptly just inside the door; her friend bumped into her shoulder before stepping around and smiling brightly at Kavita.

"Hi, Kavita," she said.

"Hi, Ellie," Kavita said.

"Is—"

"He's not here."

"—Mahesh working today?"

Her blond friend snickered, and Ellie blushed. "Oh. Well. Okay. Tell him I said hi?" She offered a little wave to Mrs. Roche. "Sorry, I didn't mean to interrupt."

"That's quite all right," Mrs. Roche said. "How is your grandfather doing these days?"

"He's all right, I guess." Ellie shrugged, and a beat later she remembered to add, "Thanks for asking."

"Did you need something?" Kavita asked.

"No, I mean, we just came to say hi, so . . ." Ellie's face was furiously red now. She looked around for her friend, who was flipping idly through a rack of shirts. "Let's go. Cassie?"

The name, spoken so casually, felt like an electric spark. Sorrow had rarely thought about Cassie Abrams in the years since she'd left. She didn't think they had ever interacted much—they were forbidden from playing with each other—except for those few times their paths had crossed in town, and Cassie had snarled some insult about Sorrow's patched clothes or messy hair, and Sorrow had slunk away in shame. She remembered Cassie vividly as a little girl on a snowy day, a vision of pink and red, but the image had no context. Ribbons in her hair. Hands on her hips. Mrs. Abrams had always dressed her up like a doll, earning coos and compliments from ladies in town that had made Sorrow glower with envy.

Sometime during the intervening years, that little girl had evolved into a teenager with spiky hair and raccoon-like eye makeup and punk schoolgirl clothes. If Ellie hadn't said her name, Sorrow wouldn't have recognized her at all.

"Wait," Sorrow said. She stepped out from behind the counter, aware of Kavita and Mrs. Roche watching her curiously. "You're Cassie Abrams?"

At the door, Cassie turned. "Do I know you?"

"I'm Sorrow. I live next door—I mean, used to live—"

Cassie narrowed her eyes. "You're Sorrow Lovegood."

"Yeah. That's me."

"Why the fuck would you ever think I'd want to talk to you?" Cassie yanked the door open; the bell jangled cheerily.

"Wait, what?" Sorrow said. "What's that supposed to mean?"

Cassie looked back at her. "What are you doing here?"

"Uh, I work here," Sorrow said.

"Not *here*, god, I mean *here*. In town. What are you even doing back here?"

"I'm visiting my mother and grandmother," Sorrow said. Her heart was thudding painfully. She shouldn't have said anything. She didn't know why she had to say anything. "Not that it's any of your business. Why do you care?"

"Are you kidding me? After all the shit your family has done to mine?"

"I don't know what—" Sorrow's voice was shaking now, a tremble in her throat and in her lungs. "I don't know what you mean. What did I ever do to you?"

Cassie stepped forward so fast Sorrow stumbled backward, knocked her elbow into a clothing rack. Ellie said, "Cassie, come on," and reached for her sleeve, but Cassie twisted out of reach. Mrs. Roche was watching, wide-eyed, her lips shaped into a soft O. Sorrow didn't lose her balance, didn't fall, but still she felt a wash of vertigo, as though the floor were tilting beneath her and the walls changing around them, rippling like water, shifting from colorful to dark, from bright to shadowed.

She blinked rapidly, steadied herself, and Cassie was right in front of her.

"You know, it's almost been normal around here," Cassie said, jabbing her finger at Sorrow, stopping just short of touching her. "With you gone and your mom finally on some fucking meds—"

"Holy shit, Cass," Kavita said.

"But now you're back and everybody is all, oh, look at her, how brave she is to come back after such a terrible tragedy, boo-fucking-hoo, like they've all forgotten that there wouldn't have *been* a tragedy if your sister hadn't been a complete psycho going around setting shit on fire for fun."

The floor dropped from beneath Sorrow. There was a roar in her ears, thunderous as a storm, but every one of Cassie's words came through clearly.

"What?"

"Oh, please," Cassie said, rolling her eyes. "Like anybody believes that stupid story about a stranger setting those fires. Awfully convenient they could never find him."

"You don't—you don't know what you're talking about." Sorrow's hands were shaking; she clenched them into fists at her sides. "My sister didn't—she wasn't like that. Patience didn't do that."

"Oh my god, you're just as delusional as the rest of your family," Cassie said. "It must be nice to live so far fucking removed from reality. I just hope you don't like playing with matches too."

Cassie swept toward the door before Sorrow could respond. She dragged Ellie outside, and they were shapes beyond the glass, silhouetted against the evening sun, and they were gone.

Kavita let out a short breath. "I, um . . ."

Mrs. Roche said, "Oh, my goodness. That was—well."

Sorrow's head was pounding and her skin was prickling all over. It wasn't true. It couldn't be true. She had known Patience. That wasn't the kind of thing a person could forget. She might forget a day or a string of them, names and faces, but she hadn't forgotten the shape of who Patience had been. Sorrow had known her own sister.

"I don't know about that girl," Mrs. Roche said. She muttered something else, an excuse and a good-bye, and she was gone too.

Somewhere beneath the shock and embarrassment and creeping anger, Sorrow knew Mrs. Roche was probably racing away to tell everybody she knew what she had just seen. The Abrams girl and the Lovegood girl, right there in the store, you should have seen. The whole town would hear about it.

Kavita began, "So that was—"

Before she could finish, Mahesh stuck his head out from the back room. "What was that? Was somebody here?"

Kavita glared at him. "Wow, seriously, could you be more clueless?"

"What? I thought I heard somebody," he said.

"Your stalker was here, along with Cassie, who totally just flipped out on Sorrow here for . . . something." Kavita looked at Sorrow. "I take it you guys weren't friends back in the day."

She was striving for an easy tone, like Sorrow wasn't rigid as a statue beside her, still gaping at the door where Cassie had just left. Sorrow made herself take a breath, then another. She opened her hands, flexed her stiff fingers, imagined she heard them creaking like tree branches.

"No," she said. "We didn't even know each other." But that wasn't right. That wasn't how it worked between their families. They had been forbidden from speaking to each other, but they had known each other, the way trees on opposite sides of a fence could grow together for centuries, roots and branches intertwined. "We weren't friends. And what she said, it's not true."

A long pause. Kavita leaned against the counter.

"What?" Sorrow said. "Have you heard that from other people?"

"No," Kavita said quickly. "I mean, yeah, we've heard about the fire. And your sister. Ethan told us about it. But not what Cassie said."

"What did Cassie say?" Mahesh asked.

Kavita ignored him. "It must've been really hard," she went on, slowly, like she was giving Sorrow a chance to speak.

Sorrow looked down at the floor, stared unseeing at the carpet.

"I can—no." Kavita stopped herself. "No. I *can't* imagine what that was like. I can't imagine it at all. It must have been terrible."

Sorrow managed a nod, a faint "Yeah," scraped from her throat, but she didn't know what else to say. Since she had arrived in town she had been bracing herself for the recognition, for the moment when eyes lit up with understanding and lips pursed with unspoken words: *Oh, she's that girl, the other Lovegood girl, the one they sent away after—you know.* Mrs. Abrams, Mrs. Roche, they had both proved it true. They looked at Sorrow and saw not a sixteen-year-old girl visiting family for summer vacation, but the echo of a tragedy.

But she hadn't expected this. She wanted to run after Cassie and call her a liar, grab her and shake her and make her admit Patience could never have started the fire that killed her. She could refute what Cassie had said until she was blue in the face. She could shout it from the rooftops and prove true everybody's suspicions about the Lovegood family's lack of sanity.

But she had no proof. She didn't even remember the fire.

She wanted Cassie to be wrong. She wanted it to be a lie.

But she didn't know.

11

KAVITA AND MAHESH dropped Sorrow off at the end of the driveway, and she walked up to the house through the tunnel of maple trees. Ethan's Jeep was still parked in the driveway, and inside Grandma and Verity were fixing dinner.

"We got a bit of a late start," Verity said. "Chicken pot pie in about forty-five minutes. Go tell Ethan he's staying for dinner." She was scrubbing a cutting board in the sink, her hair drifting about her face in wisps.

Sorrow hesitated. She had been bracing for questions about her day, thinking of ways to answer without mentioning Mrs. Roche or Cassie Abrams.

But Verity only looked up and added, "I think he's in the barn. Okay?"

"Yeah." Sorrow pivoted back to the door. "Okay."

The barn was about a hundred yards from the house, across the broad expanse of lawn and beyond the tangle of Grandma's garden. The door was open a crack, a bar of yellow light slanting out. As Sorrow approached there was a rumble from inside: an engine, spluttering.

She pushed the barn door open wider; the wheels on the track loosed a rusty shriek. The barn was stuffy, still hot from the heat of the day, and dust tickled her nose. It had been decades since the building had housed animals, but the scent of hay lingered. Ethan was leaning over the engine of the old green John Deere tractor. He looked up when Sorrow came in.

"Hey." His Red Sox hat was pushed back and there was a smudge of grease on his forehead.

"Hi," Sorrow said. "I've been commanded to command you to stay for dinner. At least it sounded like a command."

"It's that late?" Ethan said. "I, uh, I didn't realize. I've been . . ." He gestured with a wrench, knocking it into the tractor with a loud metal clang. He had the radio on low: an AM sports station. Yankees versus Orioles. Yankees up by two. "Mostly not fixing this."

"Does it still run? It's been dying for years."

Ethan shrugged. "Sort of. I don't know. I don't really know what I'm doing."

He didn't particularly sound like he wanted company, and Sorrow had delivered her message, so she turned to leave. "Verity says it's forty-five minutes until the food is . . ."

There was a pile of cardboard boxes just inside the door.

She hadn't noticed. She had come into the barn to fetch this tool or that a few times since Monday, and she hadn't ever noticed the boxes just inside the door. The barn was full of junk, had always been full of junk. The floor and stalls and shelves were so packed Sorrow was used to looking over the clutter without seeing it.

Patience. Something in her heart thrummed like a plucked string. Grandma's handwriting in black marker on brown cardboard. *Patience, Patience, Patience.*

The boxes were sealed with cracking tape and darkened by water stains at the corners. Something had chewed through the side of one. A mouse, maybe, its entire family too. Patience would have laughed at that, mice living in her clothes like creatures from a fairy tale, nibbling apart the seams to make a nest.

Sorrow stepped around a rusty red wheelbarrow and reached for the top box. The tape came away easily, brittle as ashes. Beneath the cardboard flaps was a bulky gray sweater. Sorrow brushed her fingertips over the fat stitches. It had been Verity's before Patience claimed it. She would wear it on chilly mornings like a robe; its sleeves were so long they had covered her hands, except for the holes where her thumbs punched through. Sorrow inhaled, yearning for the scents of woodsmoke and cinnamon tea, but she smelled only engine oil and hay.

"Sorrow?" Ethan's voice, hesitant.

She wasn't going to search through Patience's things with an audience. She wasn't going to search at all, because she wasn't try-ing to find anything. A box of matches. A lighter. A helpful note detailing how much she loved starting fires. Sorrow hated that she was even considering it.

She folded the box closed and regarded Ethan thoughtfully. She didn't know anything about him except that he didn't like his family and he put up with her mother's eccentricities. The brief conversa-tions they'd had over the past few days had been about work around the farm, nothing more. If Andi were here she'd be rolling her eyes and dismissing Ethan as too quiet and boring to talk to, but Sorrow thought it more likely he just liked being left alone. That was fine with her. They didn't need to be friends. All Sorrow wanted was somebody who could answer a question.

"Can I ask you something?" she said.

"Sure," he said.

"It's kinda personal."

"Uh . . ."

"Not personal about you." Sorrow left the boxes by the door and wound her way through the clutter to stand beside the tractor. "It's more about my family. That kind of personal."

Ethan set the wrench down and wiped his hands on his jeans. "Okay."

"I know we don't know each other, but I can't ask Verity or—"

"It's okay," he said, laughing a little. "What is it?"

"It's about my sister. You know what happened to her."

Ethan leaned against the tractor's large front tire; the yellow paint on the wheel rim was almost completely rusted away. "Yeah. I do. I remember when it happened."

"What do you remember about it?"

"Not much," he said. "Just people talking about it. My aunt and uncle took Cass and Julie out of town for a while because they were so upset. Mostly Julie, I guess. She's the one who saw it from her window, and she was . . . not okay. She got really quiet after that and never really came back. That's mostly what I remember."

"Do people really think . . ." Sorrow swallowed, pressed on. "Do people think Patience started the fires herself?"

A few seconds passed before Ethan answered. "Where did you hear that?"

It wasn't quite the vehement denial Sorrow had been hoping for. "At the store today."

"Somebody just came up and said that to you?"

"Well. Not *somebody*. It was Cassie."

"Oh, god, of course it was." Ethan took off his hat, ran a hand through his hair, put it on again. "I should have guessed."

"Why? Has she said stuff like that before?"

"Not that I've ever heard, but she'll say whatever's going to stir up the most shit, whether or not it's true." Sorrow's skepticism must have shown on her face, because he added, "The last thing she said to me, right after I started working here a few months ago, was that I was a traitor to our family and should be disowned."

"That seems . . . extreme," Sorrow said. "Even for our families."

"It's not like we're close. I don't care what she says." But there was a bitter edge to his words, and Sorrow wondered if Cassie had upset him more than he wanted to admit.

"But is Cassie the only one who thinks that? About my sister?" she asked.

"I think most people figure the police were right about what happened," he said.

"You mean that it was some random drug addict or something."

"Yeah."

"But most people isn't everybody," Sorrow pressed. "Cassie must have gotten it from somewhere. What about Julie? What does she think?"

"Julie never talks about it," Ethan said. "Not ever. Cassie probably said it just because she knew it would bother you. And, honestly? If there was any chance my aunt and uncle thought your sister was responsible, the whole world would have heard about it."

"I guess that's true," Sorrow admitted. Mr. and Mrs. Abrams had once called the police because Grandma had been walking too close to the property line; they would never have let something like possible arson go, no matter how tragically it had ended.

"Why does it matter?" Ethan asked. "Do you—is that what you think happened?"

"No, nothing like that," Sorrow said quickly. "I was just wondering why she would say that. Wondering if that's what people think." She didn't like the way Ethan was looking at her, like he was trying to figure out what she wasn't saying. She took the coward's way out and promptly changed the subject. "So you working here really does upset your family?"

"Yeah, but I don't care," Ethan said. "It's still better than letting my dad think he can decide for me."

"You're doing it to piss off your dad?"

"It's working. He hasn't spoken to me in months."

"That's a good thing?" Sorrow said.

"You've clearly never met my dad if you have to ask that." Ethan didn't even try to hide the bitterness in his voice that time, and Sorrow had the uncomfortable realization that in trying to deflect the conversation from herself she had pushed it into territory that was painful for him.

"I don't think I ever have, actually." In Sorrow's mind one Mr. Abrams was indistinguishable from the other: blond hair, polo shirts, nice cars. "Does that mean working here was your idea? Not Verity's?"

"No, it was mine," Ethan said. "And I asked Miss P first. I mean, I sort of—she would never admit she needs help with anything, even though she's like seventy years old, so I kinda let her think she was doing me a favor. She's always been nice to me, even when I was a little kid. Verity took some convincing."

That wasn't how Verity had made it sound; she had talked about hiring an Abrams like it was some kind of coup. And Sorrow hadn't questioned Verity's version of events. She hadn't even wondered if she'd needed to.

"I think I sort of forgot what it was like," she said. "Our families. I mean, I remember, but it was always just . . . you know, stories. Ancient history."

"People don't really forget ancient history around here," Ethan said. "You know they still call it 'witch weather' when there's an early frost or a bad snowstorm."

The words whispered an echo in Sorrow's mind, a long-ago memory of bright colors and spice cake—the yarn and fabric shop where Grandma sold her quilts. Two women talking in low voices: *This chill in the air, it's witch weather.* Locals. Sorrow had seen them in the store before. They had shared a glance, a purse of the lips when they realized Sorrow was eavesdropping from behind a shelf, and the subject changed. She had known what they meant, and at the time it had made her feel proud, that those two women in the shop would blame the weather on her family.

There was a crunch of footsteps outside the barn. Verity appeared in the doorway. "There you are. I thought you'd gotten lost."

"Between here and the house?" Sorrow said.

"Well, you are a city girl now."

"No need for a search party." Sorrow glanced at Ethan. "We were talking tractor repairs."

"I thought I told you not to bother with that piece of junk," Verity said.

"It's only about fifty percent junk," Ethan said. "Maybe seventy-five. The rest still works."

"It's almost as old as I am." Verity stepped into the barn and rapped on the hood of the John Deere with her knuckles. "I remember when we got it. We had to replace the one my grandmother drove into the pond."

Sorrow was certain she had misheard. "She did what?"

"She drove the old tractor into the pond. The one over in the northwest corner?"

"I know which pond," Sorrow said. "I'm more interested in why your grandma drove a tractor into it. On purpose?"

"Absolutely. She was trying to make a point." Verity's smile was a flicker, gone far too quickly. "The pond is right on the property line, and she didn't like that Eli Abrams—that would be your grandfather." She nodded at Ethan. "She didn't like that he kept pulling up the fence posts to claim the whole pond for himself, so she got on her tractor and rode down there and plowed right over the new fence he'd put up."

"I think my grandfather told me about that when I was little," Ethan said. "Only in his version she tried to run him down first. He really didn't like her."

"Well, she might have killed his father, so he had his reasons," Verity said.

Sorrow laughed, a short startled sound, but Verity's expression didn't change, and Ethan only looked uncomfortable. The walls of the barn swallowed her laugh into an uneasy silence.

"Are you serious?" Sorrow looked between the two of them. "You're serious. Is that true? She *killed* him?"

Verity didn't answer right away, so Ethan said, "I don't know if it's true. I only know what Grandpa Eli used to say, and he was . . . you know. Not all there. Alzheimer's. He was always saying Devotion Lovegood drove his father to an early grave. He loved to blame a whole bunch of stuff on her and Miss P, like stupid stuff they obviously . . ."

Ethan trailed off. He ducked his head and rubbed the back of his neck, and he glanced at Verity with a look Sorrow understood all too well. That was the look of somebody who knew he had said the wrong thing but didn't know yet how Verity would react.

"But he said stuff like that all the time," he went on quickly. "He was blaming communism on your family too, in the end. All kinds of stuff. Nobody listened to him."

Verity's expression hadn't changed. It hadn't changed *at all*, and her stillness made the hair on Sorrow's neck stand up. Verity was looking at Ethan, her expression carefully blank, and his face was growing redder, and Sorrow almost felt sorry for him, definitely would have if her heart weren't racing, if there weren't a weight on her chest, if she could blink, if she could look away, if every muscle in her body weren't tense with waiting to see what Verity would do.

Verity moved her hand, turned slightly, and for a heartbeat Sorrow was absolutely certain she was going to storm out of the barn. She would return to the house and thump up the stairs to her room. Sorrow could already hear her door slamming, that angry clap echoing through the house, a sound she hadn't heard in years but had never, ever forgotten.

But Verity didn't leave. Slowly she unfroze, melting from a tense statue to a flesh-and-blood woman again, and she tapped her fingers idly on the tractor, a nervous, arrhythmic drumbeat. She said, "We can't claim responsibility for the communism, but he wasn't entirely wrong about George Abrams. He and my grandmother hated each other, and they had good reason for it."

"What kind of reason?" Ethan asked—too eagerly, Sorrow thought, too quickly, but she had believed the same once too, that asking Verity to delve into one of her cherished stories was the best way to smooth over an uncertain moment.

"Their parents," Verity said. "They were only little kids at the time, barely old enough to know what was going on, but their parents were once on opposite sides of a little small-scale war here in town."

Disappointment curdled in Sorrow's chest. Of course they were. March back through history to parents and grandparents and beyond, and all you would ever find were entire lifetimes of distrust and spite traded back and forth across the fence line.

But Verity was talking, and Ethan was listening, and if Sorrow interrupted or walked away now, she would be the one who tipped the moment from cautiously curious into more dangerous terrain.

"Devotion's mother—her name was Joyful—she grew up during World War One." Verity leaned against the tractor and hooked her thumbs into the pockets of her jeans. To Sorrow the motions seemed deliberate, a calculated picture of ease. "Before the war, there was a big family living here, a few generations all crammed in together. But then the influenza epidemic happened, and the war happened, and by the start of 1920 there was only Joyful and her grandmother Justice."

Sorrow walked along the cemetery rows in her mind. Justice's ash tree had been struck by lightning long ago, but it had survived; its trunk was split midway up by a thick black scar. At the base of Joyful's she had once found a rusty skeleton key for her favor collection.

"It was a terrible winter that year," Verity went on, "and not just for the Lovegoods. It was bad for the whole valley, although of course they blamed us, as usual."

"Witch weather," Sorrow said quietly. The words felt cold in her throat, like the first startled breath after stepping outside on a winter day. Ethan gave her a quick look, but Verity went on as though she hadn't spoken.

"Joyful was only about twenty years old, but she wanted to find a way to support herself and her grandmother besides apples, so they wouldn't have hard times like that again. It just so happened that was the winter Congress passed the Volstead Act. Prohibition," Verity explained, before Sorrow could admit she didn't pay nearly as much attention in history class as she should. "She became a bootlegger."

"No way," Sorrow said, surprised. "Really?"

Verity looked pleased. "She was very good at it. She and her husband—his name was Eugene Rosenthal. He was a musician more than a criminal, really. Trumpet player. Joyful was the brains behind the smuggling operation. For about ten years they had the fastest route for bringing Canadian liquor over Lake Champlain and down to Boston and New York. As you can imagine, not everybody around here was happy about that."

"No, wait, don't tell me," Sorrow said. "It was the Abramses."

"You don't get any points for guessing that," Ethan said, laughing.

"The Abramses—they were two brothers—they tried to shut her down, but nobody much listened, so they decided to take care of it themselves." Verity paused and tapped her fingers on the tractor again; Sorrow didn't think she knew she was doing it. "They knew Joyful stashed her goods up by Peddler's Creek when she moved them through town, and that's where they were going to hit her."

"That's in the preserve," Sorrow pointed out.

"It is now," Verity agreed. "It was Lovegood land then. There are those small caves up along the creek—where the trail forks to the lake?"

Crackling autumn leaves under her boots. Vibrant red and gold branches arching overhead. The cold bite of wind whistling along a steep granite face. She walked the path in her mind, and with every footstep the memory shimmered and rippled, as though the ground and trees and stones were made of water and she was moving through a reflection. There was a wooden sign at the trail junction. Left and up for Frenchman Peak, right and into the deeper, darker woods for Lily Lake. She stepped beneath the cool damp overhang of rock, where footprints scuffed the bare ground and the remains of a campfire had been carelessly scattered. She felt her sister at her back, a comforting presence, and remembered how Patience had grumbled about the litter, about the fire, about people ignoring the preserve rules. They had cleaned up the garbage, the two of them, and left it in a little pile to pick up on their way down from the lake. The day, in Sorrow's mind, was gold and red. The last autumn they had together.

"They're not very big caves," Sorrow said faintly. Cool air breathed through the open barn door. "Barely caves at all."

"Big enough to hide a few barrels of whisky," Verity said. "And one day Joyful's twins—they were nine years old—they were swimming up in the creek when the Abrams brothers found them.

Naturally there's some debate about what—"

In the cave Patience had taken off her gloves to press her hands to the overhanging granite, and Sorrow remembered how oddly her voice had echoed, not expansively but dully, as though the stone were swallowing her words, and she had said, *Do you think the mountains remember when terrible things happen?*

"They shot the little kids," Sorrow said.

Verity stopped. "Well—yes. That's what I was about to say."

Sorrow hadn't realized she'd interrupted. "Sorry. Yeah."

"One of the twins, Charles, he was killed immediately. The girl, Cherish, was injured, but she managed to get off a shot that hit one of the Abrams brothers before she got away." The look Verity gave her was considering. "Have I told you this before?"

Sorrow didn't have an answer, so she only said, "I don't remember. What happened?"

But she knew this story. Every word Verity spoke was a burr itching at the back of her mind. She didn't know the names, nor the details, but she knew the shape of it. She knew the way her sister's voice had risen and fallen when she stood in that slanting cave and told Sorrow to listen, *listen*, and she took Sorrow's hand in her own, peeled off her mitten, and pressed her fingers to the cold stone. *Listen.* Abramses and Lovegoods, parents and children, Prohibitionists and smugglers. Smashing bottles and hijacking wagons, burning fields and barns, setting stock loose and stalking the hills with guns in hand. Bodies dragged down from Peddler's Creek and hastily buried. Shots ringing in the woods all through the night.

Sorrow had never been able to hear what Patience wanted her to hear.

"The townspeople called it Bloody July," Verity was saying. "Something like twelve or fifteen people died altogether. They finally convinced the sheriff to do something, and he sent one of his deputies to arrest Joyful. Only the deputy was stupid enough to wait until dark, so nobody could see who was coming up the drive. Not that it would have made any difference—at that point they were shooting at anybody who came close."

"They killed him?" Ethan said.

Sorrow had almost forgotten he was there. She made a fist, released it. The sensation of Patience's hand covering hers faded. She missed it as soon as it was gone.

"Nobody knew who fired the shot but, yes, they killed him," Verity said. She pointed. "Right out there on the drive in front of the house. The sheriff called in the FBI to help, and they arrested Eugene Rosenthal for the murder."

"Why him?" Sorrow asked. "If they didn't know who actually fired?"

"Does it matter?" Verity said. She gestured broadly, sweeping her arm to take in the barn, the door open to the night, the land beyond. "Because he was Jewish. Because he was a jazz musician. Because he was from New Jersey and not from around here. Because it was right at the beginning of the Hoover years and the FBI wanted to prove itself. He was the one they decided to blame, but it never went to trial. He died in police custody." There was the faintest crack in Verity's voice. "They said it was suicide."

"He's not in our cemetery," Sorrow said.

"Joyful let his family take him back to New Jersey," Verity said. "And for the second time in her life, she went from being surrounded by family to having almost nobody. She had two surviving daughters—Pride and Devotion—but Pride left too, a few years later. She ran away. She came back as an old woman, but I don't think my grandmother ever forgave her for leaving. She definitely never forgave the Abramses for their part in it all. Grandma Devotion wasn't exactly the forgiving type."

Sorrow had been so lost in her memories of Patience in the cave by the creek she'd almost forgotten what had turned Verity down this story path to begin with. "Because she was the drive-a-tractor-into-the-pond type instead? Where does that come into it?"

"Simon Abrams had a few children, but the only one who stuck around was George. And George got it into his head that he could finish the fight his father had started," Verity explained. "He had this foolish idea that people might remember his father more kindly if Simon had been defending Peddler's Creek from criminal trespassers, not opening fire on little kids playing on their own land. So he tried to prove that our land ought to have been Abrams land all along."

"Is there any truth to that?" Sorrow asked.

"No," Verity said. "Not a shred. It was all jealous squabbling. It went to court a few times, but there was no point after my grandmother put the western acres into a trust. That only made George more bitter. The way Mom used to tell it—"

"Grandma?" Sorrow said. "You mean, when she was still—"

"When she was still talking, yes. She told me every time they met George Abrams in town he would take out this watch of his— the old-fashioned kind, on a chain—snap it open, and tell them he was counting down the minutes until the Lovegoods were gone for good."

Sorrow opened her mouth to say, But that's my watch. That's *mine*.

She stopped herself; she knew how ridiculous that sounded. She remembered the watch clearly, a prized favor unlike any other, and how happy she had been to find it, how proud she had been to add it to her collection. She could feel it beneath her fingers: the metal clasp, gritty dirt on the case, drops of stagnant water seeping through the edges even months after she'd plucked it from the orchard. She hadn't known who it belonged to. It hadn't occurred to her to ask, when she had believed so fervently the favors were the orchard's gifts to her and her alone.

Verity was saying, "It went on like that for a while, with George issuing threats nobody ever took seriously, until one day he was gone."

"What do you mean, gone?" Sorrow asked.

"I mean he disappeared," Verity said. "People looked, obviously. The police came here. Devotion claimed she had caught him dumping lye in one of our wells—the one down in the meadow—and she ran him off. She said he'd probably skipped town because he was too much of a coward to show his face after getting caught. She boarded up the well, and nobody ever saw George Abrams again."

The sensation of water on her fingers was so strong Sorrow

looked down. Her skin was dry. She shook her hand anyway, wiped it on her jeans.

"Nobody in my family ever believed that," Ethan said. "They're all convinced she killed him and buried him somewhere in the woods. My dad and uncle used to go looking for his body when they were kids, like it was a game. The way they talk about it now, I think they're still disappointed they never found a skull."

"They get that from their father, Eli," Verity said. "It's just venom and spite, passed down again and again. Pulling up fence posts around the pond was the least of what he did to get back at my grandmother—and my mother, after Devotion died."

"What did he do to Grandma?" Sorrow asked.

Verity started to answer, got so far as parting her lips to speak before the stillness came over her and her hand flattened on the tractor fender. The hair on Sorrow's arms prickled. It was only a question. Verity had been talking, she had been fine, telling a story in her rambling way, and Sorrow had only asked a question. She hadn't said anything wrong. She didn't know why those words would have dropped like lead weights, why Verity wasn't answering. If there had been a line she wasn't meant to cross, she hadn't seen it. She hadn't been looking.

"Nothing as exciting as a Prohibition-era shoot-out." Verity pushed away from the tractor and headed for the door. "Dinner will be ready soon. Come in and wash up."

Sorrow watched her go, a shadow moving between the barn and the house, the sound of her footsteps fading. She couldn't feel the long-ago autumn day anymore, nor the touch of cool stone beneath her palm. She couldn't feel the weight of the watch, and she missed it. She didn't want to chase after Verity and navigate dinnertime around a mistake she hadn't even known she was making. She wanted to take her memories somewhere quiet, turn them over in her mind, examine every shining facet. She wanted to remember again the feel of Patience's hand on hers. But she was firmly back in the barn, and Verity had walked away, and she could taste the scent of rust and old hay in the back of her throat.

A wrench clattered into a toolbox, and Ethan wiped his hands on a dirty rag. "Dinner?"

Sorrow turned toward the door, then paused. "What was it you stopped yourself saying before? About Grandma?"

He didn't have to ask her what she meant. "It's nothing. It's stupid. My grandfather was totally senile by the time I was old enough to listen to him. I think he was confused, you know?"

"About what?"

"His brother Henry died in a car accident. It was just an accident, but Grandpa Eli had this thing about how it was all that Lovegood woman's fault, everything was her fault, the Lovegoods had destroyed his father and now his brother and . . ." Ethan made a face and let out a short breath. "He was confusing your grandma with her mother. The same way he used to confuse the guy at the gas station with Richard Nixon. It was kinda sad, really. There was no reason to bring it up. I shouldn't have mentioned it."

The words rang with hollow familiarity in Sorrow's mind as they walked back to the house. Shouldn't have mentioned it. Shouldn't have said anything. How many times she had thought that to herself, always so cringingly aware of saying the wrong thing. She felt a petty sort of satisfaction to learn that Ethan ran into those same traps, but the feeling was gone almost immediately. It wasn't a contest. There was no prize for being the person who could run the obstacle course of Verity's moods without tripping.

12

EIGHT YEARS AGO

ON THE FIRST day of spring, Patience said, "Let's go for a walk in the orchard."

Sorrow scraped up a spoonful of oatmeal and considered the view through the kitchen window. The day was gray and overcast, threatening rain or even snow. Sheriff Moskowitz had come by earlier to tell them about a fire in the Abrams barn, but he was gone now, and the house was quiet. They were alone in the kitchen: Grandma was tucked into her chair on the porch with her quilting frame, and Mom had gone upstairs.

"It's too cold," she said.

Patience bumped her shoulder. "It's not that cold. Aren't you bored being cooped up here?"

"Maybe," Sorrow said. They were all tired of being stuck inside through the gray days and cold nights. Tired of the howling wind, tired of the mud, tired of sweaters and scarves and boots, tired of barren branches and brown hills. Sorrow was ready for winter to be over.

But she was nervous about going into the orchard. The sheriff had asked them about strangers lurking in the woods, about drifters and troublemakers. He had kind eyes but he'd fixed them on Sorrow when he asked some of the questions, almost like he could see right through her skin to her heart beating rabbit-fast underneath. He had only left after Mom told him they didn't know anything and Abrams problems weren't Lovegood problems and they didn't want to get involved anyway. But the scent of his cologne lingered in the kitchen, and Sorrow was afraid he would come back.

"Just a little walk," Patience said. "It's not raining yet. We can look for favors."

"I don't want to," Sorrow said, but Patience only laughed.

"Get your coat," she said. "You never know. We might find something."

When Sorrow was bundled up in her boots and coat, they tromped outside together. Sorrow skipped down the porch steps, saying, "Hi, Grandma. Bye, Grandma."

In her rocking chair, Grandma nodded and smiled. She was wearing fingerless gloves and a bulky sweater; one of her quilts was tucked over her knees, and on her lap was a journal, one of the many little books filled with words she never let anybody read. Another quilt, unfinished, was stretched over the frame, waiting for her careful stitching. The new quilt was a blush of soft spring colors: pink and green and blue, flowers and leaves and sky.

Patience bent to kiss Grandma's cheek. "We're going for a walk. We'll be back soon, okay?"

Sorrow ran ahead. She followed the path around the barren garden, past the coop where chickens pecked in the mud, over the split-rail fence, and down to the old dirt road where the rusty pickup truck sat abandoned in a fallow field. There had been horses and cows and goats on the farm when Mom was a little girl, but the only animals they had now were the chickens.

Sorrow stopped at the edge of the orchard to scrape mud from her boots. Drifts of snow lingered beneath the apple trees, slumped and dirty with a hard crust on top. Everything was brown and gray and still. The trees were naked, without a hint of their first buds, dusted with lacy frost from their massive trunks to their highest branches. She loved the orchard, but at the end of winter, in this cold, uneasy borderland between the stark white silence and the first waking whispers of spring, the quiet put an uneasy pinch in her chest.

"Is Mom okay?" she asked when Patience caught up.

"She's fine," Patience said.

"She won't come downstairs," Sorrow said.

"She was down earlier." Patience's breath misted in the cold. Beneath the brim of her green knitted hat, her hazel eyes were bright, her face pale. "She's worried, that's all."

"Because of the fire?"

"Because sometimes she worries," Patience said. "It'll be fine.

The fire has nothing to do with us. Race you to the graveyard?"

She was off before Sorrow could reply. Sorrow sprinted after her, jumping over fallen branches and sliding on icy snow. Patience was taller and faster and soon out of sight.

When she reached the cemetery in the western hollow, Sorrow skidded in a patch of snow and tumbled into the fence. She caught her balance and righted herself before climbing to join Patience on the other side.

"You won," Sorrow said, panting for breath.

"Someday you'll beat me," Patience told her, but she didn't mean it. Patience liked winning.

Patience wandered along the fence, looking up at the naked branches and the gray sky. Sorrow wound through the middle instead; she wove figure eights around the ash trees, starting with the oldest and tallest at the grave of Rejoice Lovegood and cutting diagonally through the grove to the youngest tree at the grave of their great-grandmother. At the base of Devotion's tree, Sorrow jumped for the lowest branches. Her mittened fingers caught briefly on the bark, her boots scrabbled on the trunk, and she dropped to the ground again.

Patience, moving at a more leisurely pace, took a few minutes to catch up.

"Is that where Grandma will be buried when she dies?" Sorrow asked, pointing to the space beside Devotion's grave.

Patience's green hat was a bright spot of color against the shades of brown and gray. "Don't say that. Grandma isn't going to die anytime soon."

"I was just wondering." Wondering, and imagining the whip-thin ash sapling they would plant above Grandma's grave. Her headstone would be white and clean, not yet greened by moss, and her name would be carved in neat block letters: *Perseverance Lovegood*. As the years passed the ash would grow straight and tall like the others, another sturdy sentinel for the grove.

"Someday she will be, I guess," Patience said. She looked up at the gray sky, into the gray orchard. "We'll all be here eventually. Let's not talk about that."

"I was just wondering," Sorrow said again. A tickle of guilt curled in her chest. Grandma would live for a long time yet.

"Well, stop wondering," Patience said. "And don't let Mom hear you talk that way. It'll upset her."

"I *know*," Sorrow said, and then, because she couldn't help herself, "I wasn't the one who upset her yesterday."

There was a flash of anger over Patience's face. "That's not the same thing. That's not even *close* to the same thing."

"She was really upset," Sorrow said.

Patience threw her hands up. "That's why it's so stupid! It shouldn't even be a big deal. It's just school. Everybody goes to school."

"We don't."

"That's the problem," Patience said. "Why does Mom get to decide that for us?"

"Because she's our mom." Sorrow's heart was beating quickly. She wished she hadn't said anything. She wanted to jump the fence and run into the orchard. Patience knew better. She knew not to ask about school, or to bring up what Dad said about how they lived, or to ask about anything that would upset Mom. She knew not to push and push until Mom fled the kitchen and closed herself in her room.

But that was exactly what she had done yesterday. Patience had broken all of her own rules.

"She says it's safer this way," Sorrow said.

"Safer than what?" Patience asked. "Safer than never doing anything? Never going anywhere? Maybe Mom and Grandma are happy to stay here forever doing the same things over and over again, but I feel like—" She made a frustrated noise and slapped at the trunk of an ash tree. "I feel like every time I want to do anything different this stupid orchard is reaching out to pull me back. Like I've got the roots all tangled up here"—she tapped her chest, right over her heart—"and I can't get away. Don't you ever feel that? How hard it is to breathe?"

Sorrow stared at her sister, too afraid to answer. She had never heard Patience talk like this before. She didn't sound like Patience at all, but Mom. If Sorrow closed her eyes, she wouldn't have known the difference, and that scared her as much as the sheriff in the kitchen, as much as the gaping darkness of the cider house, the dull echo of a door slamming closed, and the aching cold winter nights that made it feel like spring would never come.

Patience let out a frustrated sigh. "Never mind. You're too little to understand anything."

"I understand," Sorrow protested, although she didn't know what Patience meant.

"Don't you ever get tired of it? Being stuck here where we can't even talk to anybody?"

She was looking at Sorrow for an answer, but when Sorrow tried to imagine talking to strangers in town, or kids her own age, taunting words echoed in her ears and a door slammed shut in her mind. She squirmed under the weight of Patience's earnest gaze. She didn't know what Patience wanted her to say.

"They would be mean to me," she said finally, her voice small.

Patience's eyebrows lifted. "Is that what you're worried about?"

All the things Sorrow was worried about buzzed around her mind like bees. She couldn't even begin to name them all, so she didn't try, and only nodded.

"Well, I wouldn't let them," Patience said. "You would just tell me who was being mean, and I would stop them." Her voice softened with concern. "Is somebody being mean to you?"

Sorrow pressed her lips together and shook her head.

Patience's eyes narrowed. "Are you sure?"

"Yes," Sorrow mumbled, kicking at the base of Devotion's ash tree.

"Okay. But you know that if somebody is bothering you, you can tell me, right? I won't tell Mom. Are you sure there's nothing?"

"I'm *sure*," Sorrow said, letting the word drag out. "You don't have to keep *bothering*—oh!"

"What is it?" Patience asked.

Something glinted in the dormant brown grass at the base of the tree.

Sorrow bent to pick it up. It was a pair of wire-framed eyeglasses.

One of the round lenses was missing, and the other was split down the middle by a crack.

"Look," she said.

She held the glasses out to Patience, who looked at them for a moment, then glanced at the base of the tree where Sorrow had found them. "Did you just find those right there?"

"Yeah," Sorrow said. "In the grass."

Patience took the glasses from her gingerly, turned them in her hands, then hooked the arms over her ears and looked down her nose at Sorrow. "I say! I can see clearly now!" she exclaimed, her voice warbling with a fake accent. "Fetch me the mail, butler. I must know if the queen is inviting us for tea today."

Sorrow giggled. "The queen doesn't want to have tea with *you*."

"Here, you try." Patience took the glasses off and settled them gently onto Sorrow's nose. "Be careful. If that glass breaks it'll stab you in the eye."

"Ew, gross."

The glasses were too big for Sorrow; she tilted her head back to keep them from slipping down her face. "I say!" she said, mimicking Patience's accent. The one lens distorted the cemetery grove around them, making everything big and blurry. She took the glasses off. "I don't like them. Everything looks funny."

"That's because you don't need them to see, silly," Patience said. "Aren't you glad you came out here today? You found the first favor of the spring."

"No, it's—" Sorrow stopped herself. "Yeah. The first."

She unzipped her coat to tuck the glasses safely into the inside pocket, and as she did she pressed briefly, quickly, on the small lump of the favor she had found yesterday. The one she could feel tucked against her ribs like an ember. The one she was keeping secret. The puff of air she let in made her shiver before she got her coat zipped up again.

"Are you cold?" Patience asked.

"No." Sorrow's cheeks stung and her nose was running, but she wasn't ready to go back to the house, where Mom would still be in her room and the day would stretch long and quiet. "Can we go see the witch's grave?"

"You shouldn't call her that," Patience said.

"That's what everybody calls her."

"Everybody who? You don't even know that many people."

Sorrow shrugged and pretended Patience's words didn't sting. "I want to go to her grave."

Patience relented. "Fine, but only for a little bit. It's colder than I thought out here."

13

THE NEXT AFTERNOON Sorrow took her phone down to the end of the driveway. It was half past noon in California, which meant Andi would likely be in the middle of her lunch hour, and *that* meant the conversation would have a natural time limit.

She sat on the top rail of the fence and scrolled down to Andi's number. Then she stared at her phone until the screen went dark. She wished she had a way of knowing before she called what the problem was, and what Andi's mood would be, so she could prepare herself.

She and Andi had always gotten along well enough, once Sorrow had gotten used to the loud, chatty, know-it-all older girl who had crashed into her life after she moved to Florida. Dad and Sonia had only been dating when Sorrow first went to live with him, but somehow their fledgling relationship had survived the unexpected arrival of a grief-stricken little girl, and before long Sonia's family had welcomed Sorrow as one of their own. When she was feeling generous, she was grateful for that, how easily they had accepted a weird, quiet girl who was prone to disappearing into the backyard to hide under shrubs for hours on end.

When she wasn't feeling quite so generous, she wondered if it had been so easy for them because her arrival had been barely a blip in their lives, if the worst thing that had ever happened to her—something so huge and so terrible it had cracked her world right down the middle, opening a chasm she still didn't know how to bridge—had been nothing more than a minor adjustment for them.

She wasn't feeling particularly generous today. There was too much wriggling around in her mind already. Cassie's accusation and Verity's story and, most of all, her memories of Patience, those small rough gems offering proof that she had been right, that coming back here was the best way to remember, but she couldn't make sense of them yet. She needed more. She needed to hoard and polish and study every new memory, turn them over in her mind until the shape of what was missing made more sense. Talking to Andi wasn't going to help her do that. But she made the call anyway.

Andi answered right away. "Hey."

"Hey. I got your texts."

"Oh, I'm sorry, do I know you? This number belongs to somebody I used to know, but I haven't heard from her in a million years."

Sorrow was regretting the call already. "Very funny."

"Yeah, no, not really," Andi said. "I was beginning to think you'd been eaten by a bear."

"I was at work last night," Sorrow said.

"How can you have work? You're only there for a month." There was noise in the background on Andi's side of the call—a busy street, chattering voices—but Sorrow couldn't picture what kind of restaurant she might be in or what street she was walking down.

"I'm helping some neighbors at their store. Just a couple of shifts a week."

"So you're not actually that busy," Andi said.

Sorrow bristled. "This is a *farm*. I'm busy all the time."

"What, are they making you do manual labor?"

"Nobody's making me do anything." Sorrow closed her eyes. She was not going to let Andi under her skin. "What did you want?"

"Wow. Okay. So we're gonna be like that."

"No, I—" Sorrow let out a huff of breath. "I didn't mean it like that. I just meant—it sounded urgent?"

"But not urgent enough for you to answer right away."

Sorrow had been assuming that Andi was just being Andi, overly dramatic and self-centered. A year ago Sorrow would have known, but it was different now. Andi lived across the country, Dad and Sonia were barely tolerating each other, and everybody was expecting Sorrow to have some kind of breakdown before their eyes. Now, for the first time, she felt a genuine nudge of worry. "Did something happen?"

"How the hell am I supposed to know?" Andi answered. "That's what I want to ask you! What's going on at home?"

Sorrow's worry vanished like a burst bubble. "You want me to tell you what's going on at home."

"Well, Mom isn't telling me anything. She just keeps saying everything is fine, like she always does, but we know that's bullshit."

"You want me to tell you what's going on at home," Sorrow said again. "You mean the home that's like two thousand miles away from me."

"Yeah, but you were there last—"

"The home that you're so worried about you decided not to come back even for a visit this summer."

"I have work," Andi snapped. "It's *important.* I didn't just decide to go off and play in the woods for the summer."

"I'm with my family," Sorrow answered. "I know that's not important to you, but you could at least pretend it matters."

She didn't remember sliding down from the fence, but she was standing in the grass now, and her hands were trembling. She hadn't wanted to bring any of this with her to Vermont. She already felt like she was being split in half across miles and years, tugged both ways by families that would never understand each other. But Andi didn't care about any of that. She had never even asked why Sorrow was coming back to Vermont.

"You're not being fair," Andi said. She was always first to break the silence.

"*I'm* not being fair?"

"You were supposed to keep an eye on them."

"They're adults," Sorrow said. "What the hell could I do? They don't need a babysitter."

"Well, that's good, since you're not doing it anyway."

"You're just as far away."

"You can't expect me to drop everything in my entire life."

"But it's okay to expect me to do that."

"I expected you to at least make an effort," Andi said, exasperated.

"Right. I have to do it. Because what you're doing is *important*, but all I'm doing is playing in the woods."

"Yes! No! I don't know! I thought maybe you would try, since you're the whole reason they're—"

Andi broke off suddenly. Sorrow felt numb all over, numb and empty and too light, as though she would float away if she let herself.

"I'm the reason they're fighting," Sorrow said. "You can go ahead and say it."

"I don't mean—"

"Yes, you do. But it doesn't matter. They don't tell me anything. Not even when it's all my fault."

"Have you even *asked*?" Andi demanded. "Or did you just decide to fuck off to Vermont for the summer with no explanation and who cares what the rest of us think?"

"I'm not—"

"I don't care," Andi said. "I don't care! I don't know if you did something or your dad did something or you're just both being

selfish assholes, but I don't care about your stupid reasons. I just
hope you fucking fix it when you get around to it. I've got work
to do."

Andi hung up.

"What the *fuck*." Sorrow glared at the phone, but Andi didn't
call back.

Andi's accusation—suspicion, whatever it was—wasn't anything Sorrow hadn't been carrying for months already. It had been
there at the back of her mind since that day in March when they had
all surrounded her after the party, worried and angry and rightfully
unsatisfied by her explanations. It had been there every time her
father looked at her like he was afraid of what she would do next,
and every time Sonia looked at her like she no longer recognized
her. It had been there when she had told them both, ignoring the
hurt and fear in their eyes, that the only way they could help was to
let her leave.

Hands shaking, eyes stinging, Sorrow slipped her phone into
her back pocket and pressed the heels of her hands to her eyes, willing the tears not to fall. She couldn't stand here on the side of the
road all day, but if she went back to the house now, with red eyes
and a red face, she would look like she had been crying, and Verity
would know something was wrong. Sorrow didn't talk about her
Florida family with her mother, not about fights and problems. It
was simpler to keep her two families as separate as she could—or
it had been, when there had been little reason for their jagged, ill-
fitting edges to meet.

She kicked through the grass along the fence, making her way back to the driveway, but instead of heading to the house, she left the packed dirt and stepped into the trees.

This was the oldest part of the orchard. These few acres between the house and the road were where Rejoice Lovegood had planted her first trees and nurtured them through hot summers and frozen winters. She had been alone then, before she met her husband and bore their daughter, Fearful, before Clement Abrams or any of the other white neighbors had arrived. There had been an Abenaki village down at the far end of the valley, Rejoice alone at this end, and nothing but forest in between.

According to the old stories born in the feverish depths of puritanical imagination, Rejoice had fed these oldest apple trees her own blood when it looked like they might not survive, and that was why they had endured so long.

Sorrow breathed in the scents of soil and moss, mud and grass, and the ever-present memory of apples. She tried to let the orchard soothe her as she walked, tried to let the sunlight and the canopy of green draw out the ache in her chest like poison from a snakebite. Two squirrels chased each other up a tree in a chattering burst. It was a beautiful afternoon, hot enough to make the shadows welcoming.

The day couldn't be more different from the last time she and Patience had walked together in the orchard.

Sorrow's steps faltered, and she exhaled softly, let the memory settle like snowfall over her thoughts. That cold day at the clawing, blustery end of winter. She had been bundled up in boots and gloves, skidding on soggy patches of snow as she chased after

Patience with no hope of catching her. That girl she had been, not once suspecting how little time she had left with her sister, she had wanted to see the witch's grave.

Sorrow turned to the north, took a breath, and climbed the hill.

By the time she reached the summit, her heart was racing and her calves were burning. She stopped in the shade at the edge of the clearing.

The oak that grew atop the hill was a massive black-barked monster, towering over the whole of the orchard. Its leaves were as big as dinner plates, its branches as fat around as whole trees. Bulbous knots protruded from its lumpy, deformed trunk. It was ugly, misshapen, and had been struck by lightning more times than anybody could count. Verity had once told Sorrow the black oak looked as it did because it absorbed all the blights and diseases that threatened the orchard, gobbled them up like a ravenous beast and swallowed them down into the soil where they could do no harm, and Sorrow, wide-eyed and credulous, had believed it. It was the biggest tree in the orchard, the biggest in all of Abrams Valley. Nobody knew how old it was; it had been towering and ancient already when Rejoice Lovegood first came to the valley.

The oak was surrounded by a barren patch where no grass or shrubs ever grew, and in a curve around one side of the clearing were six ash trees. They were very old and very tall, all the exact same age: one for each of the children Silence Lovegood had slain. Their father's family had insisted the children be buried in town, far from their mother and the stain of her wickedness. Silence's daughter Grace, the only survivor, had planted the ash trees for her siblings years later.

Silence herself was buried at the base of the oak beneath an uneven rectangle of white stones. She had neither a headstone nor an ash tree. She had only the roots of the black oak wrapped around her in a tangled cage.

They had come up here together the day before Patience died. Sorrow remembered the dull, cold dread she had felt about going back to the house and how important it had been to convince Patience to walk a bit longer. She remembered leaving the cemetery and hurrying around the hill, both wanting and not wanting a glimpse across the meadow to the burned Abrams barn in the distance.

Sorrow walked the perimeter of the oak's clearing to the northern side. The apple trees were too tall, the orchard too lush for a view from this spot, so she picked her way down the slope until she met the orchard road. From there she could look along a wide gap between rows of apple trees and see the Abrams house on its hill: tall, white, a blinding spark on the landscape. The new garage stood beside it, the one that had replaced the old barn—it was whole, of course it was whole, but for the briefest flicker of a moment Sorrow saw a black wound in the corner where fire had eaten it away.

There, below, was the meadow on the property boundary between Lovegood and Abrams land, and there was the fence that separated them. From this distance the double strands of wire were no more than the merest pencil sketches. The Abrams side was mowed in long sweeping lines; on the Lovegood side the meadow was choked with grass and wildflowers so thick the leaning fence posts were half-hidden.

At the western end of the meadow was the old stone well where George Abrams might have died, and might still remain, rotted away to a skeleton. It was small and round and innocuous, its weathered lid a circle of silver wood.

And there was the cider house.

14

A MEMORY WAS a thing with no shape, no mass, but indescribable weight. Words spoken in cold winter air, secrets shared, a sprint, a chase, a smile, a favor, these things had their own gravity, distorting everything around them like the heaviest star, shaping time and space even when the heart remained hidden.

Sorrow and Patience had walked through the orchard together a hundred times, a thousand, in every season, in drizzling rain and blazing sun, howling wind and whipping snow. Every one of those walks was compressed to a single pinpoint of a single day: the last day of Patience's life.

But all Sorrow felt now, standing at the edge of the meadow, was a nervous tremble in her chest. She should have come down here sooner, to this quiet place where Patience had died.

The cider house was a black ruin cupped in a meadow of vibrant green. Eight years of wind and rain and snow had washed the stench of smoke away, stamped the ashes into dirt, polished the blackened boards to a sheen. Wildflowers bloomed in the rich tangle of grass around it, and a thicket of trees huddled at its back. It was about half the size of the barn, with one story above the ground and a cellar below. The fire had brought down one of the long walls and half of the roof, but the rest of the building remained, a crooked, leaning skeleton of blackened boards and beams. There was grass growing inside, reaching for sunlight through the tumbling walls. A few yellow and pink flowers stood out against the charred wood.

Verity hadn't had the building torn down, but the forest was slowly reclaiming it anyway.

There was a hole in the wooden floor; it had been there before the fire. At some point in the past the boards had rotted and the cider press had smashed through to the cellar. Sorrow and Patience had been forbidden from playing inside ever since Patience, a courageous thirteen years old, had decided to build a balance beam across that hole in the floor. She couldn't find one board long enough, so she had tried to nail two together and ended up sticking her hand on a protruding nail. It punched right through her palm, and Verity had had to take her to the urgent care clinic for stitches and a tetanus shot.

It would have been fine—Patience thought it was cool, having a hole in her hand; she kept shoving the bandage in Sorrow's face to show off—but Mrs. Roche had seen them going into the clinic, and she had mentioned it to their neighbors the Johnsons, and the Johnsons, who were newcomers to town, had carelessly told Mr. and Mrs. Abrams. After a visit from child services, questions from the social worker, and a tearful apology from Patience, Verity had put a padlock on the door and forbidden them from playing in the old ruin again.

The sheriff said Patience had fallen into the cellar.

Sorrow was never supposed to hear that. She had crept out of bed to listen from the stairs when the sheriff was talking to Verity and Grandma in the kitchen.

Patience must have fallen into the cellar through that gaping hole in the floor. She was knocked unconscious, and the roof collapsed. Julie Abrams had seen the fire from her bedroom window and woken her parents to call 911, but by the time the firemen arrived it was too late.

Sorrow had never questioned it, that story she'd overheard as a child, but she knew now the sheriff had probably made up the unconscious part to be kind. Patience would have been trapped in the cellar whether she was awake or not, whether she was injured or not. She could have been screaming for help. Nobody would have heard. The Abrams house was too far away, the road even farther. The cellar was at least ten feet deep. She wouldn't have been able to escape.

Sorrow looked up at the remains of the cider house roof, where rafters and beams were broken at burned, spiky ends. She brushed her fingertips over the wood, almost expecting—it was stupid—almost expecting to feel cold winter wind breathing through the gaps. She closed her fingers into a fist, squeezed her eyes shut to chase the sensation away.

Sorrow lifted a hand to scratch the side of her neck—brush a hair away, or a spiderweb—and she stilled, suddenly tense, nerves sparking. She turned. The meadow was empty. Grass rippled on both sides of the wire fence like the pelt of a slumbering creature, a gentle breeze caressing shades of green from light to dark to light again. Up the hill the Abrams house gleamed in the sun; its red-brick chimney was an artery on the side.

It was too hot to be wandering around out here in the orchard, collecting ticks and a sunburn in exchange for nothing but more questions, waiting for the kaleidoscope contents of her memories to shake into some kind of sense. There was nothing of Patience left in the cider house. Sorrow could stare into that patchwork of darkness and light for hours and it wouldn't tell her anything she didn't already know. It was only a ruin.

She strode away from the cider house, aiming for the shade of the apple trees, but just as she dipped from sunlight to shadow, something caught her eye. She stopped again, turned, cast her gaze over the meadow.

There was something on the well. A small object perched right on the rim.

She looked around, her skin prickling into goose bumps. She was alone in the meadow. She had been all along.

She kicked her way through the high grass, her shoes squelching in hidden pockets of mud. The well was about waist-high, and it had been boarded up for as long as Sorrow could remember, a double layer of solid hardwood planks bolted securely into the masonry and stone. She had never known before why it was covered. She didn't like knowing now. It had always seemed such a harmless thing, squatting there in a meadow of rich green, part of the landscape.

Perched on the edge of the cover was a single white rock.

Sorrow reached for it, but she stopped a few inches shy, curled her hand into a fist to steady it. It was one of the stones from Silence Lovegood's grave. There were no chalky white stones like that anywhere else in the orchard.

She remembered watching Patience's hands, thin and winter-pale, gloves stripped away in spite of the cold, her long fingers moving with nervous energy as she passed the stone back and forth between her hands, back and forth, back and forth, constant motion while the rest of her was so still, and her voice tight and unwelcoming—

There had been somebody else in the orchard that day.

15

EIGHT YEARS AGO

THERE HAD BEEN somebody else in the orchard that day, but when Sorrow followed Patience out of the cemetery grove, it was so quiet they might have been the only people in the world.

They skirted the hill in the center of the orchard, staying well above the meadow and the fence line. For that Sorrow was grateful. Patience didn't always heed their mother's warnings to stay as far from the Abrams property as they could, and normally Sorrow enjoyed the little thrill of disobedience she got from ducking through the wires past the No Trespassing signs or chasing frogs around to the forbidden side of the pond. But today, looking at the Abrams house across the wind-scalloped field of snow made

Sorrow's insides squirm like a knot of worms.

From this far away the burned corner of the Abrams barn didn't look like much, only a black bite chomped into the red. The sheriff had said nobody had been hurt; the Abrams didn't have any animals. All that had been damaged was the hayloft where Cassie Abrams had her playhouse.

"What are you staring at?" Patience asked. She was several steps ahead, already climbing the hill.

"Do you think they're going to catch who did it?" Sorrow asked.

"Probably," Patience said with a shrug. "You don't have to worry about it. It's nothing to do with us."

She started walking again. Sorrow sniffled, wiped her nose on her coat sleeve, and went after her. The snow was deep on the north-facing slope. Sorrow followed in her sister's footsteps, stretching her legs to reach each punched-through hole, until the ground leveled, the trees opened, and a whirl of wind bit at her face. They had reached the black oak.

The clearing around the oak was slick with hardened patches of ice, but the ground above Silence Lovegood's grave was bare and muddy. Patience picked her way over the ice, choosing each step carefully, but Sorrow ran past her and threw herself into the trunk of the oak. She climbed up onto the fat, knobby roots that curled from the ground like monstrous snakes and hopped her way around the tree, keeping one hand on the trunk for balance.

"Is this where she killed them?" Sorrow asked.

Patience knelt beside Silence Lovegood's grave to move the white stones back into tidy lines and pick away stray leaves and twigs. "You've heard this story a million times."

"I like it."

"Because you're a morbid kid," Patience said.

Sorrow didn't know what *morbid* meant. "Am not."

"You are too. You already know how it goes."

"This is where she killed them," Sorrow declared. "Her very own children, six of them. All but the littlest girl, Grace."

"She ran away and hid in a fox burrow until she heard the townspeople calling for her," Patience said.

"You just made that up," Sorrow said, laughing. "That's not part of the story."

But Patience didn't laugh. "It doesn't have to be part of the story to be true. Close your eyes. Try to imagine it."

Patience looked so serious and so earnest that Sorrow did as she said. With her eyes closed she wobbled on the tree root, put a hand out to steady herself.

"She had to hide *somewhere*," Patience said. "She was so scared. She ran and ran and ran until she was lost in the forest. She couldn't hear her mother shouting for her anymore. She found a little burrow and she crawled into it. It was quiet and dark and there were roots and dirt crumbling all around her."

Sorrow opened one eye to look at Patience. "How did she fit?"

Patience tossed a handful of matted leaf debris at Sorrow's shoes. "It was cozy," she said. She looked around, then lowered her voice. "You know, if you dig down deep enough, this dirt is still red and sticky. That's why nothing grows in this clearing."

A shiver chased down Sorrow's spine. "Nothing ever?"

"Nothing except this oak, because it drinks up the blood."

Sorrow plucked off her glove to touch the tree with her bare hand. She thought it might be warmer than it ought to be. She might feel red sap gulping through the wood. She snatched her hand away.

Silence Lovegood had been left alone when her husband, John Derry, died in 1816, during the coldest summer anybody could remember. It was so cold Enoch Abrams and his brothers Gideon and Zadock convinced the town Silence was using witchcraft to curse the whole valley. Only the Lovegoods, they claimed, had the power to manipulate the seasons with their unnatural command over life and death. The story was one of Sorrow's favorites. She especially liked to whack at the scarecrow in Grandma's garden, pretending to be little Grace Lovegood chasing the Abrams men away with a rake, shouting, "Za-*dock*, Za-*dock*!" with a *thwack* on the second syllable, over and over again.

Silence Lovegood had denied she was a witch, but the cold summer, the failed crops, the unseasonal frosts that crackled through the forests in June and July, it all scared the townspeople too much and nothing could change their minds.

"I think it's stupid," Sorrow said.

"What is?"

"She didn't have to kill them. She could have moved away."

Patience gave her a look that said she was deciding if what she had to say was too grown-up for her little sister. Sorrow hated that look.

"It wasn't that simple," Patience said. "As awful as it is, I think she thought she was protecting them."

"Yeah, but"—Sorrow made another loop around the tree, hopping faster this time—"she wasn't. That's stupid. You can't protect somebody by hurting them. She could have taken them to live somewhere else." Sorrow tried balancing and jumping to the next root on one leg. It was harder than using both, but she was sure she could do it. "Why didn't she just go somewhere?"

"Sorrow."

The warning in Patience's voice made her heart skip. When Sorrow rounded the tree again, Patience was on her feet, and there was somebody else in the clearing.

"Julie," Patience said.

A teenage girl stood between two ash trees. Julie was the older Abrams daughter. With her blond hair dyed in pink streaks, a puffy purple down coat, and red tights, she was a vibrant rainbow of color in the gray orchard. Julie was the same age as Patience, and until December she had been away at boarding school. Mrs. Abrams had told everybody Julie was taking a break because she had been working so hard. Mom said Julie had been kicked out.

Julie stepped out from between the ash trees. The wind curling through the clearing tugged at her pale hair. "Hey," she said.

"What are you doing here?" Patience asked.

Sorrow looked at her sister in surprise: she wasn't used to hearing such a sharp tone from her.

"Nothing," Julie said. She kicked at a clump of ice. "Walking. I saw you come up here."

"You're trespassing. You can't be here."

Julie rolled her eyes. "Seriously? You're going to be like that?"

"I'm not being like anything." Patience shifted her weight from one foot to the other and passed a small white rock quickly from hand to hand. "You can't be here. This is private property."

"Why do you care?" Julie snapped. "Are you gonna call the cops on me?"

"I might," Patience said. "You know they were already here."

"Yeah, our place too, looking for the dumbass who tried to burn our barn down. My parents are freaking out like they're going to find an arsonist lurking in the woods or something. It's so stupid."

"You need to leave," Patience said. She closed her fist around the white rock, and for a second Sorrow thought she was going to throw it at Julie.

Julie's face went through a complicated change, flashing from surprise to hurt to something harder. "You're serious."

"Yes. You have to go." There was a tremor in Patience's voice. "You shouldn't be here."

"I can't believe you. Do you treat all your friends like this?" Julie asked, then laughed, a harsh, ugly sound. "Oh, right, I forgot. You don't have any other friends."

Patience's face was pale, her lips pinched, and her voice tight when she said, "We're not friends."

Sorrow knew at once, with the certainty of a thunderclap, that Patience was lying. Julie was telling the truth. They were friends. They weren't even supposed to talk to each other. Mom didn't have many rules for Patience and Sorrow, but that one was absolute: they could not be friends with the Abrams girls. And Patience had broken it.

"That is so dumb." Julie rubbed at her nose; the tip was pink. "You want to let our stupid families dictate every fucking aspect of your life, you go right ahead."

"It's not like that," Patience said.

"It's exactly like that. You didn't care before. Why do you care now?"

"The police came to our house this morning." Patience was speaking quickly, her voice trembling. "The police came to our house because of *your* family and *your* problems. It doesn't have anything to do with us but now my mom is upset and—"

"Oh my god, so what? Your mom freaks out about everything."

"Why did the sheriff have to talk to us?" Patience was shaking with anger now, the white stone still clutched in one hand. "Did your parents tell him to? Did they tell him to bother us?"

"They wouldn't—"

"Why can't they mind their own fucking business?"

Patience's words rang through the trees, and in the silence that followed the wind rose, made the branches of the black oak creak and the last clinging dead leaves rustle. Sorrow scarcely dared to breathe. There was a hot dense ache under her ribs, right where the favors in her pockets were pressing into her side. She shivered and wiped at her nose with her mitten. The wool smelled like woodsmoke; the scent made her nauseous.

"You know what?" Julie said after a long, horrible silence. "That's exactly what I'm going to do."

"You—"

"I don't care." Julie took a step back and spread her arms wide, and she said it again, loud enough to echo through the orchard. "I don't care! I'll mind my own business. It's fine! I won't bother you again. Exactly what you want. You ever get over yourself and change your mind, you know how to find me."

She stomped into the orchard, slipping once on a lingering patch of snow. Patience watched until the bright purple of her coat disappeared into the trees.

She sniffled softly, scrubbed at her face, and said, "We're going home."

She held out her hand. Sorrow didn't take it.

"Come on. It's cold."

Sorrow stared at her sister. "Are you friends with Julie?"

"No. She's being—I'm not."

"She said you were."

"What do you care what she says?"

"Does Mom know?"

Patience stepped forward so quickly Sorrow stumbled backward, her boots skidding on the ice, but Patience caught the front of her coat before she fell.

"Don't you dare say a word to her about this," she said. Her voice was low and angry and unlike anything Sorrow had ever heard. She didn't sound like Patience at all. She sounded like a stranger.

Sorrow's heart was hammering. "But if you—"

"Don't you *dare*," Patience said, giving Sorrow a shake. "She's upset enough as it is. You don't say anything about the fire or the Abramses or *anything*, okay? Don't make it worse."

"I won't," Sorrow whispered.

"You have to promise. You're not going to say anything to upset Mom."

"I won't!" Sorrow said again. "I promise, I won't!"

Patience let her go and turned away. Her face was so pale and so hard it might have been carved from stone. She threw the white rock at the base of the oak. "We're going home now."

Sorrow followed without a word.

16

SILENCE LOVEGOOD

1782–1816

THE FROST HAD not broken. She knew before she opened her eyes.

Silence lay abed beside her husband. His breathing was slow and steady. The children snuffled softly in their blankets. Beyond the log walls of the cabin a single bird braved the cold to greet an unnatural dawn. Its voice rose and rose, spinning to shrill, impossible heights before falling quiet, and only when it was gone did Silence rise. She pushed the curtain aside, stoked a small fire in the woodstove, shed her nightdress for her day clothes. Her throat was tight, her mouth tinged with the metallic taste of fear. It was too cold. Spring was late in coming. The trees would not blossom. The wheat would not grow. It was too cold.

She moved without noise, stepping over her children. Seven small sleepers all in a row. Her mother had borne only one child that survived infancy, as had her grandmother before her, but what they had lacked in fertility Silence had made up and more. Her littlest, Grace, born five years ago in a flood of blood and pain, was curled like a kitten in a nest of blankets by the hearth.

It was May of 1816, but there were no leaves on the trees, no grass sprouting in fresh green shoots, no apple blossoms covering the hills with a delicate spring blush. There was only cold and frost and the eerie dry fog that sat upon the land like smoke, never washing away with the frequent rains. It was a wicked spring, a bitter spring. Yesterday her sons had come home with eyes blacked and lips bloodied by the fists of boys in town who blamed them—blamed *her*—for the ill-fortuned weather.

The townspeople remembered when this had happened before: during the summer of 1805, when her mother, Fearful, had died, and fifteen years before that, at the passing of her grandmother Rejoice. The apple trees had turned brown in mourning, the flowers withered, the grass dried: the entire Lovegood orchard cast into an unnatural autumn. It had not lasted—the wicked weather faded after the dead were buried and the living had shed their tears—but the memories endured.

This time, unlike before, the cold reached beyond the orchard and chilled the whole of the valley, the whole of Vermont, perhaps the whole of the world. Neighbors were packing their carts to move south. The Smith family had already gone to their cousins in Virginia. The Van Tassel brothers were looking even farther afield;

they planned to board a ship in Portsmouth that would take them to Charleston, where, it was said, snow never fell, and certainly not at the end of May.

John had asked her, two days ago, if they might consider leaving as well. He had asked with hunched shoulders and lowered eyes, knowing before he spoke what the answer would be, but Silence had allowed herself to consider the question. She had never been anywhere beyond the Hollow—they were calling it Abrams Valley these days, giving Enoch Abrams and his wretched family all the more reason to puff their chests as they strutted through field and town—and she could not even imagine what they might find outside this valley. The world, when she allowed herself the luxury of contemplating it, stretched forever in every direction as an endless expanse of trees, shadows as dark as night and twice as cold, and it took her breath away, the hugeness of it, how far a person might walk and never see home again.

"We will stay," John had said when Silence did not answer. "The weather will break soon."

Silence gathered her shawl around her shoulders and stepped outside. The morning was gray and still, trees and earth and sky the same color that was not a color, branches blending into clouds where the forest reached for the dawn. She knew with a certainty as solid as the mountain peaks that John was wrong. The weather would not break. The trees would not blossom. Her fingers itched to take up a knife as her grandmother was said to have done—long ago, when she was a woman alone in the wilderness—to slice her skin and drip blood over the trees starving for warmth, for life, to give of herself freely to wake the orchard from below.

But she could no more coax the apple trees to bud than John could force the sun to shine. Silence broke a thin layer of ice in the water pail. Fetching water was Prudence's task, but Silence was loath to wake her on so bleak a morning. The children would be hungry, and John's face would grow pinched with guilt as they grumbled, and he would check his mean stores of bullets and powder, offer an empty promise of fresh meat before vanishing into the mountains again. Dreams of crackling fatty venison sustained them no more than crops that did not sprout, apples that did not blossom, yet dream they did, as their bellies rumbled and their skin grew thin.

Every time John left, Silence believed he would never return. Her mother's voice, lost to her these eleven years but still clear in her memory, whispered in her mind in every idle moment, and most insistently in the quiet before she slept: *He was a good man once, but he will change. He will falter. He will leave. That's what men* do. *We haven't anybody but ourselves to trust.*

Silence shook away the echo of her mother's nervous prophecies. Fearful had chosen her husband poorly, a lazy man and a wastrel who mightn't have been Silence's father at all, if village tale-tellers were to be believed. But Silence was not her mother, for all that she could feel her like a wraith behind her shoulder or a poison in her blood. John was not clever, but he was steady, and right now, on this grim morning, there was work to be done that could not wait for the black cloud of her mother's memory to pass.

She picked up the water pail, flung the chips of ice over the ground. The earth around the cabin was hard and slick, frozen overnight into bumps and troughs. She chose her steps carefully, eyes on the ground. She could ill afford a fall.

When she looked up, the Abrams men were there.

Enoch Abrams and his brothers stood at the edge of the orchard, where the trees met the muddy track. Enoch was the eldest, the tallest and broadest and most imposing; Gideon and Zadock looked as though they had been cast in the same mold as their eldest brother, but more clumsily, with grittier clay and less care. Gideon carried a flintlock musket on his shoulder. Zadock, a pitchfork.

Enoch carried only his leather-bound Bible.

"Good morrow, Sister Derry," he said, and his voice, his booming preacher's voice, it trembled through the orchard with force enough to shake icicles from branches.

Silence straightened her shoulders and narrowed her eyes. "My name is Lovegood, Enoch Abrams, and you are trespassing without leave on my land."

Gideon Abrams snorted, loud as a horse. "The land is your husband's, as your name would be, if he were man enough to control his wife."

"How early you rose to carry these childish insults to me." Silence did not let her voice tremble. Men like Enoch Abrams craved the fear of others more than sustenance, more than water. "Does your good wife know you are about this morning?"

But shapes moved in the orchard behind the Abrams brothers,

and her bravado quailed. A dozen men or more emerged from the gray morning shadows. There was William Prewitt from across the Hollow, and his two grown sons. There was George Dobbes and his brother Eliot, both gaunt as skeletons from having survived the fever that took their parents. The Howe boys, all three of them; the youngest was no older than her girl Pru but wore a countenance of such twisted anger he might have been an old man. Many of them were armed, if not with guns then with spades and pitchforks. The Twisdon boy, no more than fourteen and motherless since autumn, carried a hatchet.

Silence had only a water pail, and an empty one at that.

The sharp metallic taste of fear was in her throat again, and with it the steady thumping drumbeat of her heart.

"We have not come to sow hardship where already too much has been sown," Enoch Abrams said. "We have come as friends and neighbors. We entreat you to hear us."

Silence marveled that the Bible did not burst into flames in his hands, so shameless were the lies spilling from his wormlike lips.

"The whole of the Hollow can hear you," she said, "yet you have said nothing worth hearing. What do you want?"

A murmur passed through the gathered men. It did not surprise them to hear a Lovegood woman speak so forthrightly—but if they had been strong men, able to hear a woman's voice and not quiver in cowardly disgust, they would not be following Enoch Abrams. They avoided her eyes, every man and boy. When Abrams took a breath to raise his voice, Silence knew what he was going to say before he said it.

"We want you to lift the curse you have set upon this valley," he said.

So there it was.

Disappointment tasted like blood, like iron, like biting through her tongue. Her mother's warnings come to pass, her orchard's frailty, the predictability of men, they all tasted the same. The whispers that had been gathering all through this liars' spring now blossomed into accusation, rooted in fear more fertile than the still-frosted earth. She looked at each of her neighbors in turn, but not one looked back. They were looking to him, to Enoch Abrams and the Bible he held.

"I have set no curse upon the land," Silence said, but words were nothing but breath when spoken by a woman, and her denial only fueled their suspicion. The Twisdon child raised his hatchet and shook it menacingly, looking so much like her own boys when they played at soldiers that her heart ached with the absurdity of it.

"You are not a God-fearing woman," Enoch Abrams said. "Your mother was not a God-fearing woman. Your grandmother—"

"Was not a woman at all," said Zadock Abrams, to a snicker of laughter.

Enoch continued undeterred: "For as long as your unnatural line has claimed this land, there has been evil upon it. This witch weather is proof of the corruption within. My family and I, we were content to leave it be when it harmed only your own—"

"You have never been content to leave it be," Silence snapped, anger roiling through her in a cold black wave. "Your grandfather did not leave it be when he set his fool's militia upon my grandmother under false pretenses. Your father did not leave it be when he hounded my mother to the grave all for want of a few fertile acres. Do you think me a fool, to believe in your good intent? This spring may be wicked, that I do not deny, but it is not my doing, and my family suffers as much as yours. You have been so blinded by your greed for our—"

"Mum?"

She had not heard the cabin door open. She knew before she turned: it was Prudence, always Prudence, early riser, hard worker, a child who had never caused her parents a minute of fuss. She stood in the doorway, her small pale face etched with worry.

"Go inside, child," Silence said.

But there was John at their daughter's back, his hand on her shoulder to push her aside.

"What is this?" he asked, glaring at their gathered neighbors.

John looked untidy and half-wild, his shirt untucked, his beard untrimmed. Silence knew what they said about her family—her useless husband, her feral children, and her so cold and unnatural a woman—and in knowing, it was hard to hold on to the anger that had straightened her spine. The black wave of fury ebbed, and weakened, and became gray, gray as the wrongful winter day around them, gray as the hesitant morning light, and it seemed to her beyond absurd that she should be here with her water pail, defending a miserable little house and a miserable worthless husband and seven children she could scarcely look at some days, each one of them an ache in her belly that had not faded when they'd ripped themselves free, all because she wasn't a witch and she hadn't set a curse upon the land, and wouldn't even know how, however attractive the idea might be.

Her husband was talking. Enoch Abrams was talking. They might have been speaking in tongues, for all their words meant to her, the empty rumbles of men. They would pretend now the quarrel was about their land, their religion, their rules, their pride, the things men claimed for themselves while women toiled behind them, working until their fingers bled so that husbands and sons could bluster and rage.

She looked back to the house. Prudence still lingered in the doorway, disobedient for the first time in her young life.

Go inside, Silence thought. Go inside, my child, go back to sleep.

"You will leave this land," John was saying. He strode forward, more shambling than imposing.

Enoch Abrams's lips curled in a sneer. "Your wife has brought wickedness to my valley. Our crops cannot take root because of the evil she has set upon us."

"Your valley?" John scoffed. "Do these men gathered behind you know how you covet their farms?"

"Farms made useless by witchcraft," Enoch Abrams countered. "By *her* witchcraft."

He raised a hand and extended a finger. Silence did not let herself step back. She did not quake in fear and she did not flinch when John slapped Enoch Abrams's offending finger down. She did not retreat when Gideon and Zadock charged toward him.

They would say, later, she was a woman of ice and stone, to watch open-eyed and unmoving as Gideon's musket jerked and fired, to remain still as John yelped in pain, scorched by the muzzle flash if not the bullet, as he swung blindly in retaliation, as the Bible knocked from Enoch's hands fell to the ground and the pitchfork brandished by Zadock, a barely formed man of greed and ire, swung and jabbed and found home in a hunger-tight gut.

They would say she was an unnatural woman to watch with such clear eyes as her husband, her own husband, stumbled with his hands clutched to his middle. The red seeping between his fingers was the only color on a gray, gray morning. Her neighbors faded into the wood, silent and cowardly, leaving a woman alone with seven children and a dying man, and a winter frost that would not break no matter how purposefully the days marched toward summer. They would say she was as cold as the unthawed ground to lift her eyes to the orchard as her husband passed, that the trees concerned her more than the man, but John Derry had not been born on this land. The orchard would shudder briefly for him when he passed, not weep as it had for her mother and grandmother. The lasting wounds would be hidden beneath the skin of the wife and children he left behind.

"Silence," John said.

Prudence was crying, the other children waking, the morning full of sound and fear, but their screams might have come from another valley, or another world, so muffled were they to their mother's ears. Silence's hands were hot with her husband's blood.

She did not remember falling to her knees beside him. She did not remember pressing her palms to the wound in his gut.

"Silence," he said, and he died.

She did not remember touching his face, but there was a smear of blood there, where his weathered skin met his graying whiskers, just below his eye.

17

ON SATURDAY AFTERNOON Abrams Valley was crowded with tourists and day-trippers, families and couples and the occasional lone hiker wandering around. It was nothing compared to the crowds that filled Miami beaches on a typical weekend, but after only a week in Vermont, and most of that spent quietly in the orchard, the presence of so many people gave Sorrow a self-conscious itch between her shoulders.

She stopped outside a café called Cozy Coffee. There was a busy ice cream shop to her right, a store offering canoe rentals and fishing lessons to her left, and nobody was paying any attention to her except a golden retriever watching from a shady spot beneath a bench. There had probably been hip coffee shops and trendy food stores in town when she was a child, but she had certainly never gone into them. If she had, she would have been shooed out as soon as the shopkeepers saw her handmade clothes and muddy shoes. She could still hear the whispers: *It's the Lovegood girl, poor little thing. Why doesn't her mother watch her properly?*

She wasn't wearing a patched skirt and ill-fitting hand-me-down boots now. She had as much right to be here as anybody. When she had asked for the car keys and made up an excuse about wanting a Wi-Fi connection, Verity had only laughed and said, "I'm surprised it's taken you this long. This has to be a different pace of life than what you're used to." She had handed over the keys without question, and all the way into town, guilt had gnawed at Sorrow's insides. She hadn't *lied*. But she hadn't been entirely honest either.

She pulled open the café door and stepped inside. It was a small place, decorated with bright patches of blue and yellow, and only about half of the dozen mismatched tables were occupied. There were a few people working on laptops, two women chatting while babies slumbered in strollers, an old man paging through a newspaper, and Julie Abrams.

Julie sat alone at a small table by the window. The pink streaks were gone from her hair, and her face was more angular than Sorrow remembered, making her look years older than twenty-four. Her hands were resting on the keyboard of her laptop, but she was staring out the window rather than looking at the screen. What struck Sorrow most of all was how thin she was: arms like sticks, collarbone jutting like blades, the kind of thin that would have

Sonia remarking how unhealthy she looked and Andi scolding her for being judgmental of somebody else's body.

Sorrow stepped up to the counter to order some iced tea. While it was being made, she kept glancing over her shoulder, afraid Julie would see her and slip away. Sorrow had found out—by asking Kavita, who had asked Mahesh, who had asked his girlfriend, who worked at the café—that most afternoons Julie could be found here with her computer. Filling out job applications, apparently, which seemed to Sorrow the kind of thing that shouldn't have been anybody's business, but this was Abrams Valley, and Julie was an Abrams. People had noticed that she wasn't working. They definitely noticed when she fled her parents' house every day.

Tea in hand, Sorrow approached Julie's corner table.

"Julie?" she said.

Julie started and looked up. Her eyes widened, and she slid her headphones off.

"Um, hi," Sorrow said. "I'm—"

"You're Sorrow."

"Yeah." She had considered and practiced a dozen smooth introductions on her drive into town, but none of them felt right now that she was standing here. There was only one way to start. "Can I ask you something?"

"I guess," Julie said warily.

"You were her friend, weren't you?" Sorrow said. She put a hand on the back of the chair opposite Julie, gripped it nervously to steady herself. "You and Patience were friends."

Julie studied her, and as the silence stretched Sorrow grew

certain she was going to deny it. She was going to scowl, say she had no idea what Sorrow was talking about, say she would never be friends with a Lovegood girl, demand that Sorrow leave her alone, and she would say it loudly enough that heads would turn throughout the little café, and Sorrow would slink away in embarrassment, and her memory of that gray day in the orchard would be only that, a memory, not a key, not a door, not an answer.

Then Julie said, "Yeah. We were. For a little while."

It wasn't an invitation, but Sorrow pulled out the chair and sat down. She jostled the table with her knee, grabbed the edge to keep it from rocking. "But you kept it secret, right? I didn't know until that day. When we saw you in the orchard."

Julie didn't ask what day she meant. "We didn't hang out for very long. Just those few months when I wasn't at school. Why?"

"I was just wondering—"

Sorrow's voice cracked; she took a sip of tea. Her face was growing warm, and the longer Julie looked at her with those suspicious blue eyes, the worse she felt. She had been hoping that when she mentioned Patience, Julie would smile, she would open up to her, she would offer to talk, to remember. But Julie was leaning away from her and she was twisting the cord of her headphones in her fingers, and maybe Sorrow had gotten it all wrong. She had only that one memory, a cold day in the orchard, a single fraught conversation clipped from the end of a friendship she hadn't even known existed before that moment.

She set her cup down, caught a drop of condensation with her fingertip.

"I just want to talk to somebody who remembers what happened."

There was a pause. Then Julie said, quietly, "Everybody remembers what happened to her."

"I mean, not—that's not what I mean," Sorrow said, but when she looked up, Julie's expression was softer, more considering than suspicious. "I mean somebody who knew her. Who liked her. She didn't have many friends."

Julie took a breath, let it out. "Yeah, she mostly kept to herself, didn't she?"

Not by choice, Sorrow thought, but she didn't want to interrupt.

"And it didn't help that she was kinda weird—sorry." A smile quirked Julie's lips. "But you know she was."

"I know." Sorrow's heart was thudding. "It runs in the family."

"I liked that. I did like her. She was different. She was fun." Julie picked up her cup, set it down again when she saw it was empty. "But yeah, we kept it secret. I was petrified my parents would find out."

Tell me about the night she died. The words were right there, hammering at the front of Sorrow's thoughts. Tell me why your sister thinks Patience started the fire. She held them back. Ethan had denied it, had made a good case for why it wasn't true, but Sorrow couldn't get past the echo of Cassie's words going around and around in her mind, compounded with every turn by the force of Cassie's bitterness, the venom in her voice when she'd realized who Sorrow was. Nobody said something like that without a reason, and being a jerk out of the blue to somebody you didn't even know wasn't a reason.

"Can I ask—how did you even become friends?" Sorrow asked. "With our families so . . . you know."

Julie didn't answer right away, but her expression was thoughtful now, not guarded. "I guess the first time I actually talked to her, it was just random chance. I was home that winter—the school counselors decided I needed a break—but I hated being cooped up in the house all the time, so I spent a lot of time outside. Just walking around and stuff." Julie turned toward the window, and the look in her eyes was unfocused, distant. "I was on the trail up to Lily Lake when I realized there was somebody behind me. It was the middle of winter, so there weren't many hikers. . . . Do you mind hearing this? It doesn't bother you?"

"No, it's fine," Sorrow said quickly. "Really. I want to know."

Another shrug of those razor-thin shoulders. "She told me I looked sad," Julie said.

You do, Sorrow thought. She dropped her gaze to the table, where Julie was fidgeting with her headphones cable. Her fingers were childlike and small, her wrists bony, and Sorrow had the sudden urge to reach out and still her nervous motions.

"About the last thing I wanted to do was talk to the creepy Lovegood girl who was following me in the woods, but . . ." Julie lifted a hand to tuck a strand of pale hair behind her ear. Sorrow watched the motion without thinking, looked away quickly when she met Julie's eyes. "She just sort of walked beside me for a while, telling me about how she always came out to the woods when she was feeling sad, because she liked to think that the . . . she felt like the trees and the mountains and, I don't know, the rocks or whatever, they would listen to everything she said even if she didn't say it out loud."

Listen, Patience had said, pressing her hands to the granite in the caves by Peddler's Creek. *Listen,* and Sorrow had tried, oh, how she had tried, but all she'd heard was the moan of wind through the trees.

"I knew it was just, you know." Julie smiled. "Lovegood weirdness. But it made me feel better. I guess we became friends after that. But it was, I don't know. We didn't have much in common except wanting to get out of Abrams Valley."

Sorrow felt something pull inside her chest, a dense knot that was part jealousy, part yearning.

Julie wasn't looking at her. "All we ever talked about was how much fun it would be to, like, take a road trip across the country, to see the ocean, travel. Go to California or England or Japan or whatever. You know, the stupid things people dream about when they're stuck in a town like this."

Sorrow had never known Patience wanted to travel. She had never known what Patience wanted at all beyond the small things that had defined their lives: warm weather and rich harvests, good days for their mother and smiles from their grandmother, the chance to go to town, the possibility of going to school. The girl Julie was describing might have been a stranger, and a stranger she would always remain. Even if every memory came back, Sorrow wouldn't ever remember this Patience, sharing troubles and planning an escape and looking to the future. Sorrow had been eight years old, a tagalong little sister, and Patience had kept her dreams secret.

"I'm glad she had a friend," Sorrow said weakly. She didn't know what else to say.

"It's not like we ever could have done any of it," Julie said, but her voice was different now. Gone was the quiet warmth, the gentle sadness. She sounded, if anything, angry, and the change sent a chill through Sorrow. "Can you even imagine? Our moms would have flipped the fuck out. I don't know what the hell happened between them way back when, but even when I was fifteen I wasn't dumb enough to risk dredging that all up again."

Sorrow's stomach dropped. "What do you mean, what happened between them?"

"That's what I don't know," Julie said. "Whatever it was, it was before I was born."

"No, I mean—" Sorrow shook her head, trying to settle her buzzing thoughts. "Are you talking about something besides the usual family stuff?"

Julie tilted her head. "You know they used to be friends. Your mom and mine."

"*What?*" A man working at the nearest table looked up with a scowl. Sorrow lowered her voice. "No, they didn't. That's not—"

Verity used to say, when she warned them away from the neighbors: friendship with the Abramses would only lead to heartache. More than trouble. More than police at the door, social workers in the kitchen, whispers around town. *Heartache.* It hadn't meant anything to Sorrow as a child, that painfully intimate characterization of consequences. Their lives were a spiderweb of rules, guidelines they had cobbled together to avoid upsetting their mother, and Sorrow had never tried to tease out the reasons behind any particular tender spot. Don't talk to the Abramses. Don't make friends with the Abrams girls. Heartache.

"Are you sure?" Sorrow asked. "I mean, I'm not saying you're . . . I have never heard that before in my life."

"I don't think most people know. I only found out because I found a picture of them together," Julie said.

Sorrow stared. "No way."

"Yeah. When I was a kid," Julie said. "I was playing dress-up with my mom's old things in the attic, and there were all these old boxes of pictures from my dad's uncle. And there was your mom and mine. Like, forever ago. Back in the eighties or nineties."

Sorrow's head was spinning. Julie wasn't lying; she didn't have any reason to lie. Sorrow took a sip of tea, took a breath, but she couldn't seem to get enough air. Her voice was high and strained. "Did you ask her about it?"

Julie rolled her eyes. "Well, yeah, but she yelled at me and told me it was none of my business. So I asked Aunt Jody—Ethan's mom—since she's kind of an outsider and not stuck in the middle of the whole family thing, but I guess it was before she met Uncle Dean. She didn't know anything about it."

"Did you—did Patience know?" Sorrow asked.

"I don't think so," Julie said. She snapped her laptop closed and wound the cable around her headphones. "It was ancient history even then. We only ever talked about getting away from our families. Look, I've got to get going."

It stung, to hear again how much Patience had been looking outward, and how little Sorrow had noticed, but she couldn't think about that now, and she couldn't be distracted by Verity and Hannah. Julie was packing up her stuff to leave, and Sorrow hadn't asked her what she had come to ask.

"Can I ask you something else?" she said.

Julie hauled her bag onto her lap to slide the computer in. "What is it?"

"I, uh, talked to Cassie the other day."

Julie looked up. "You did? Why? What did she say?"

It was much more of a reaction than Sorrow had been expecting: Julie spat the words so sharp and fast Sorrow leaned back, startled by her vehemence.

"She, uh, she said . . ." Sorrow couldn't remember how she had decided to ask. Everything she had practiced had vanished into a blank space in her mind. "She said it was Patience."

"What was?"

"The fires," Sorrow said. "She said Patience started the fires."

Julie stared, unblinking, for a long moment. "She didn't say that."

"Yes, she—"

"She wouldn't say that." Julie was a flurry of noise and motion, shoving her headphones into her bag, winding up her computer's power cable. "You must have misunderstood her."

"I didn't misunderstand. I didn't—"

"Why were you even talking to her about that? Why would you even ask?"

"I didn't ask!" Sorrow said, her voice rising with frustration. "I didn't bring it up! She did. She said—"

"Is that the whole reason you came to find me?" Julie asked. She stood up so quickly she jarred the table, and Sorrow's iced tea sloshed from her cup. "Pretending to bond just so you could ask that?"

Sorrow's face burned with shame. She couldn't meet Julie's eyes, but she had to ask. She had to say the words before Julie stormed away.

"Is it true?" she asked. "Is that what people think?"

"No," Julie said. "Nobody thinks that. Cassie doesn't know what she's talking about."

"Then why would she say it?"

The café door opened and a group of men in cycling clothes came in, and the small space was filled with the sound of their voices, laughter, their bike shoes clicking noisily over the floor. Sorrow turned to watch them, then looked up at Julie.

"What happened to Patience . . ." Julie sighed, and it was as though all the anger drained out of her. "It was an accident. A sad, awful accident. Why do you want to bring it all up now? It's only going to hurt people."

Tears of embarrassment stung Sorrow's eyes.

"You should focus on remembering her when she was alive. Remember the good things."

There was a protest lodged in Sorrow's throat, but she couldn't find the courage to say *I'm trying. That's why I'm asking. I'm trying to remember.* It didn't do any good. Everything she remembered, everything she asked, only led to more questions, and it was getting harder and harder to know what the good things were, when so much of her childhood had been a minefield of words they did not say, questions they did not voice, secrets they did not share.

"The rest of it doesn't matter," Julie said. "I have to go."

She left without looking back.

18

THE DAY OF the 253rd anniversary of the Battle of Ebenezer Smith's Stockade was hot and bright and clear. The air smelled of sunscreen and fried food, apple cider and cut grass, and the occasional whiff of a thru-hiker who had been too long without a shower. Along Main and Champlain Streets tourists and locals alike wandered among the farm stands and food tents, and everywhere there were kegs and bottles of Abrams Valley cider.

"Okay," Kavita said. "You're going to have to explain the significance of this day in a way that makes sense to somebody who didn't grow up in this weird little town."

Sorrow was standing near the edge of the park with Kavita,

Mahesh, and Ethan. She hadn't planned on coming into town for the festival, but when Kavita and Mahesh had shown up that morning to invite her, she hadn't been able to think of a good reason to say no.

"It's not that weird," Ethan said.

"I hate to break it to you," Kavita said, "but it is. This entire town is obsessed with the history of two families, to the point where I swear people are on the verge of asking me what side I'm on. It's weird and creepy and kinda backward."

"For what it's worth, I think it's weird too," Sorrow offered. "And if you're expecting real historical significance, you're going to be disappointed."

Eager parents were setting up folding chairs and spreading picnic blankets around the plywood stage while a couple of frazzled-looking women tried to wrangle excitable five-year-olds into formation. Sorrow kept looking around, casting uneasy glances over faces near and far, but she didn't see Julie or Cassie Abrams anywhere. She didn't even know what she would do if she did. Pretend she hadn't? Look the other way? She didn't particularly want to see Cassie again, but she didn't like the way her conversation with Julie had ended the day before. She couldn't stop thinking about what she could have said, how she could have been more honest, more open about wanting to know about the fire, yes, but also how desperately she just wanted to talk about Patience. To say her name and not flinch from it. To sit with somebody who had liked her. She could have said that. She thought Julie might have understood, if only Sorrow had tried.

But she hadn't, and a day later she was left looking around the park, half hopeful and half anxious, eyes following every blond woman glimpsed from a distance.

"So what's the deal?" Kavita asked.

"The deal," Ethan said, "is that in 1763, after the end of the French and Indian War, there were some people around here who wanted to get rid of some unwanted neighbors, so they came up with this plan to stage a raid on an English farm and blame it on people they claimed were French sympathizers."

"When he says 'some people' he means his ancestors," Sorrow said, "and the unwanted neighbor was my ancestor Rejoice Lovegood—who was married to a French man, but he wasn't even around when all this went down. He was off in the mountains somewhere."

"You know that normal people don't know the names of their ancestors back like ten generations, right?" Kavita said.

"Twelve," Sorrow said.

When Kavita looked at her, she only shrugged. She had known it wasn't normal ever since the day her third grade teacher in Florida had sat the class down with safety scissors and stacks of construction paper and asked them to make family trees. The teacher had been prepared for grandparents and stepparents, adoptions and mixed families, but she hadn't known what to do with the quiet little girl who kept writing name after oddball name on branches of an ever-growing tree long after the rest of the class had lost interest.

"Sure, twelve, whatever," Kavita said. "So his family wanted your family's land, and they decided to start a fight and blame it on the French, which was somehow going to drive your ancestor away, even though the war was technically over?"

"That's about it," Ethan said.

"I'm not remotely surprised this whole thing comes down to white people fighting over land that wasn't even theirs in the first place," Kavita said. "I'm guessing it didn't work."

"Still here," Sorrow said, giving a little wave.

"So what happened?" Mahesh asked.

"You have to watch to find out," Ethan said. "Stop trying to spoil it."

"It's history, dude, not *Game of Thrones*. You can tell me the ending."

"Those kids have worked really hard."

"It is insane that you make children act it out every year," Kavita said.

"It's not always children," Ethan said. "Last year it was the over-fifty community theater group."

Kavita looked at him.

"And the year before that it was the kennel club. My ancestor was Mr. Timmons's corgi and Sorrow's was the Greens's golden-doodle. That one." He pointed across the park toward a large dog sniffing aggressively at an alarmed woman in a sun hat. "And a few years ago it was members of the organic farm co-op. But," Ethan added thoughtfully, "the dogs were better actors. Looks like they're about to start."

On the plywood stage at the center of the park, the kinder-garten teacher bounced on her toes and waved her arms to get the attention of her actors and their audience.

"You like this," Sorrow said to Ethan. "All this celebration stuff."

He shrugged unselfconsciously. "Yeah, I guess. It's pretty ridiculous, but it's ridiculous in a different way every year. People do it on purpose—try to top last year's chaos. You never came when you were a kid?"

"No. Not that I remember."

But she did remember, with perfect clarity, Patience asking their mother if they could go into town for the festival, just to see, and Verity refusing. They would not help celebrate the day the town turned against their family, Verity had said. They did not owe anybody that. Patience hadn't argued, and at the time Sorrow had been relieved, but she wondered now what would have happened if Patience had pushed back. If she had convinced Verity to let them venture beyond the boundaries of their orchard without suspicion, without fear, if only for a single summer afternoon. If one small concession would have led to more, and Patience wouldn't have had to be so secretive with her dreams of school, college, travel. If she would have ever been able to admit out loud how much she wanted a bigger life than the one their mother and grandmother had chosen.

A shout called the crowd's attention to the stage. The teachers had divided the children into groups, all looking equally confused about what they were supposed to be doing. After a couple of squealing, unsuccessful attempts to use a microphone, one woman gave up and started speaking without it.

"Who are we supposed to be rooting for?" Mahesh asked.

"The kid in the black hat"—Ethan pointed to the little boy wearing an oversized Pilgrim hat made of cardboard and construction paper—"he's Clement Abrams."

"Definitely don't cheer for him," Sorrow said. "He was a creepy, misogynistic, fire-and-brimstone preacher. Like a hundred years late to be a proper Puritan, but totally a Puritan at heart."

"True," Ethan said. "Don't root for him. And the kids over there, that's Ebenezer and Eliza Smith. They're the ones who are going to be attacked."

A red-haired girl with a paper bonnet over her braids and a too-big apron had a baby doll dangling from one hand and a glower on her face. The boy playing her husband, Ebenezer, was sitting cross-legged at the edge of the stage, plucking dandelions from the grass and eating them.

"Mama Smith looks like she's not taking any shit. I'll cheer for her," Kavita decided. "Unless she murders anybody's ancestors. Does she?"

"No, she's good," Sorrow said.

"Where's your ancestor? Isn't she in this too?"

"I'm guessing she's the one in the corner there with the black dress and the pointy witch hat." Both of which, Sorrow noted, were trimmed with distinctly anachronistic glitter that sparkled in the sunlight.

"Oh, I see her. This isn't going to go all Salem witch trials in the twist ending, is it?"

"Not unless they're taking a lot of creative license," Ethan said.

"What's with the kid with the historically accurate Super Soaker?" Mahesh asked.

"That's the weather," Ethan said.

What happened on that night in June of 1763 was that it started raining as Clement Abrams and his eager but not particularly skilled militiamen were disguising themselves as French soldiers and Abenaki warriors, taking up their long muskets and farm tools, and sneaking through the downpour to surround the Smith homestead.

What happened in the play was that at the first squirt from the Super Soaker, little Clement Abrams in his paper hat promptly burst into tears.

"Please tell me that's also historically accurate," Kavita said.

The crowd tittered with laughter, which only made the boy cry harder. The teacher waved frantically, trying to stop the rainstorm, but the girl armed with the Super Soaker ignored her. The rest of the raiding party—now leaderless—belatedly remembered to encircle the Smiths and shake their plastic Halloween tridents in an enthusiastic, if confused, display of menace.

Eliza Smith, exactly on cue, kicked her dandelion-munching husband to his feet and pointed imperiously across the stage. Rejoice Lovegood, grinning beneath her sparkling witch hat, waved happily back at her.

The real Eliza Smith, upon waking to discover her house under siege by unseen assailants shouting in bad French, had sent her husband to the nearest neighbor for help. That neighbor was Rejoice

Lovegood, who was clever enough to realize that Ebenezer Smith's tale of being attacked by wild natives and mad Frenchmen was perhaps not the most accurate representation of the events currently unfolding at his farm. She sent him back to his wife and took it upon herself to visit the other farms in the valley to find out what was going on.

"She went from house to house all night," Sorrow explained. "None of the men in the raiding party had bothered to tell their wives what they were doing, but it didn't take long for them to figure it out. They marched up to the Smith house to confront their husbands."

The girl playing Rejoice Lovegood raced gleefully around the stage with her arms spread wide. She knocked into her classmates as she ran, and one by one little girls in paper bonnets joined her.

"I'm guessing this doesn't end with everybody going home and having a laugh over the big misunderstanding," Kavita said.

"Not quite," Ethan said. "When the raiding party heard somebody else coming through the forest, they thought that a real raiding party had found them, so they ran out of hiding and—well. That."

Onstage, Eliza Smith hurled her baby doll at the raiding party, striking the still-teary Clement Abrams in the face.

"She threw her baby at him?" Kavita said.

"No, she shot him," Ethan said. "The teachers probably thought toy guns were too violent."

Clement Abrams screwed up his face to howl even louder.

"She killed him?" Mahesh asked.

"If only," Sorrow replied.

"Hey," Ethan said mildly. "I wouldn't be here if she had."

"He survived," Sorrow said. "He claimed it was God's will, which, whatever, it would have been fine, but he *also* said—"

There it was: Clement Abrams pointing a wobbly finger at Rejoice Lovegood and her grinning posse of little girls.

"He also said that Rejoice—my ancestor—had bewitched Eliza Smith, and the only reason his men were in the woods that night was because they had gone to save her. And that Rejoice had tried to stop them by flying house to house—"

"Hence the witch hat."

"Right. He said she had bewitched all of their wives and made them abandon their children to attack their husbands."

"And people believed that?" Kavita said.

"It didn't matter if they believed it or not," Sorrow said. "Nobody was going to believe his stupid story about the French anymore, so blaming a witch was the next best thing. I guess people liked that better than they liked thinking their neighbors would attack a family while they slept and risk restarting a war they were all only just getting used to being over."

The scene onstage had devolved into chaos. The teacher was still trying to get the kids to remember the final act of their play, but the actors were drifting away toward their parents, and confused applause from the audience drowned out the rest of what she was saying.

Sorrow watched the kids scatter, and as she was following little Rejoice Lovegood's sparkly hat through the crowd, a glimmer of long blond hair caught her eyes. Her heart skipped, but the woman disappeared behind a group of senior citizens in sun hats, and she couldn't tell if it was Julie.

"The kids did better than the co-op," Ethan said, "but it still wasn't as entertaining as the dogs. The dogs actually made it all the way through to the end."

"That's not the end?" Kavita asked. "What's missing?"

Sorrow said, "Well, after they accused Rejoice of witchcraft, they had to arrest her, but . . ."

A dark room, a barred door, and winter air so cold her skin burned. She looked down at her hands, pale and dirty from scrabbling in dark corners—

Sorrow blinked. Again, and looked up, and the park quivered around her.

It had been summer when Rejoice Lovegood was arrested. Not winter, not cold.

"But what?" Kavita said.

She was confusing the story with the memory of hearing it told. She had listened to her mother's stories on so many winter nights, the whistle of wind in the chimney a constant accompaniment to Verity's voice. That was the reason for the blending in her mind, the overlap of history and memory.

"Uh," Kavita said. She nudged Sorrow's shoulder. "Earth to Sorrow?"

"And, um, she escaped," Sorrow said. The sensation of cold vanished, replaced by the weight of the afternoon sun. She rubbed a hand over her face, pushed back her Phillies hat, and cringed when she felt the sweat beneath it. "She broke out of the room they stuck her in, and when she figured out the Abramses were already trying to move onto her land, she drove them away."

"Why don't you tell them how she did that?"

Sorrow turned. Cassie Abrams was standing behind her.

"What?" Sorrow said.

Cassie's smile was full of teeth and gone in an instant. "You left out the best part. Don't you know how she drove them away? It wasn't like she just showed up and said boo and they ran screaming."

The sun was on Sorrow's back but she felt it all around her, pressing in from every side, and it shouldn't have been that hot. It hadn't been that hot only moments before. Her throat was parched, her mouth sticky and dry.

"She set them on *fire*," Cassie said. Her words shimmered through the air between them. She could have been crowing, she could have been shouting, but she was speaking so quietly that people all around were turning their ears to listen. "Sound familiar?"

"It wasn't—" Sorrow's voice cracked; she cleared her throat. The heat of the sun softened, the space between them settled, as the word *fire* sank into the grass. She knew this story. This was *her* family's story, and she wasn't going to let Cassie distort it just to embarrass her. "Don't be stupid. She set a woodpile on fire because they were collecting logs to build a cabin. Not exactly the same thing."

Cassie dismissed this with a roll of her eyes. "Whatever. She was the one with the granddaughter who went so fucking psycho she murdered six little kids, so I guess that level of crazy is genetic."

"Jesus, Cass," Ethan said. "What are you—"

"I'm not talking to you," Cassie said. She didn't even look at him. She stared only at Sorrow, her blue eyes narrow and angry. "It's never really gone away, has it?"

Sorrow knew her face was bright red, and she put on what she hoped was an unimpressed expression. "You're talking about ancient history like anybody still cares."

Cassie said, "What the fuck were you doing yesterday?"

"What? Yesterday? I didn't even see you—"

"Oh my god, give me a break. Are you stupid? My *sister*. Why the hell have you been harassing my sister?"

There was a drumbeat of dread beneath Sorrow's ribs. "What? I was just talking to her."

"What do you want from her? Why the fuck are you bothering her?"

"Okay, seriously, come on." Ethan reached for Cassie's arm. "What are you talking about?"

Cassie jerked out of Ethan's reach. "You stay the fuck away from me. You don't get to say anything. You've made it clear which family you want to be part of. You're a fucking *traitor*."

"Wow," Kavita said. "Overreaction much?"

Ethan stepped back, hands raised in surrender. "You're not exactly making me want to change my mind."

"This isn't about you!" Cassie shouted, and with a frustrated cry she threw her cup of cider at him. It hit him square in the chest, splashing all down the front of his shirt.

There was a nervous ripple of laughter from the crowd around them.

Ethan wiped apple cider from his face. "Go home, Cassie. Stop being an idiot."

Cassie had already whirled back to face Sorrow. "You made her *cry*."

"Who? Julie?" Sorrow said, incredulous. "She was fine when she—"

"She's not fine! Why can't you just fucking leave her alone?" Cassie spun around and shouted at the crowd. "All of you! Just leave us the fuck alone!"

She stormed away, shoving at tourists and kids who got in her way. A mother slapped down a child's pointing hand. Nearby a boy laughed, a snorting derisive sound. Murmurs of conversation resumed, and the park unfroze as one by one people realized they were staring.

"Right," Kavita said. "So I'm guessing that's not normally how the play ends?"

Mahesh snickered, but he stopped abruptly when Ethan glared at him.

19

WHEN THE SUN began to set and the town was emptying for the night, Kavita and Mahesh gave Sorrow a ride home.

"Don't let Cassie get to you," Kavita said, twisting around in the front seat. "She's not worth the angst."

Sorrow looked through the window at the darkening mountains and fields. They were passing the old Roche farm, which had once been the Smith homestead. "Has she always been like this? I mean, since you've known her?"

"You mean, starting random fights in public for no apparent reason?" Kavita said. "Not really. I've never seen her flip out like that before."

"Maybe because nobody has ever stalked her sister before," Mahesh said.

"I didn't—"

Kavita rolled her eyes. "He's joking. Honestly, she should be happy anybody is even talking to Julie."

"What do you mean?" Sorrow asked.

"Nothing. Just that Julie's got that whole sad broken-girl thing going on, and it's not like Cassie going around yelling at people is helping."

Sorrow wanted to be reassured by Kavita's words, but she still felt the same hot crush of shame she had felt when all the town's eyes were on her and Cassie, and with it a sting of guilt telling her: Cassie said she had made Julie cry.

That didn't feel like the kind of thing Cassie would make up for no reason. It hadn't been calculated, not like the other things she had said, accusing and needling to get under Sorrow's skin. It had felt honest, raw and angry and true, and that possibility made Sorrow sick to her stomach. She hadn't wanted to upset Julie. She hadn't meant to hurt her.

The open fields of the Abrams land gave way to the Lovegood orchard. Mahesh nosed the car into the driveway.

"You can drop me here," Sorrow said. "Thanks for the ride."

"See you Monday," Kavita said. "It'll probably be crazy busy with Fourth of July campers."

A wave from Mahesh, a good-night from Kavita, and Sorrow slammed the door shut. Mahesh turned the car around and they headed down the road a few hundred yards. The taillights glowed red in the twilight, chased them up to their house, blinked out.

Sorrow walked up the driveway, reluctance dragging every step.

Verity would ask her about the festival, and Sorrow would have to decide how to answer. She didn't want to lie. She didn't want to tell the truth. She hated the feeling that every possible thing she could say to her mother was a potential land mine, and she was navigating a path so narrow she could barely keep her balance.

It wasn't normal, to approach every conversation like that. That wasn't how families were supposed to talk to each other. It was another thing Sorrow hadn't understood until she moved away, until her father put her into therapy, until she met and spent time with Sonia's family, who shouted out their concerns rather than burying them, who talked over everybody's problems and faults and decisions ad nauseam. It had terrified her at first, the way Sonia would march over to her sister Lu's house after Lu lost a job or had a bad breakup, demand she get up and get dressed and go out, growing louder and louder and refusing to back down, throwing open the curtains rather than drawing them, forcing out laughter rather than smothering Lu in whispers.

Sorrow knew it wasn't at all the same thing; a bad day wasn't comparable to a chronic illness. But as a scared, grieving child in a strange place, all she had understood were raised voices where there should have been quiet, recklessness where there should have been caution, a noisy, stubborn defiance of every rule she had lived by in her mother's house.

The careful way she and Verity stepped around each other wasn't how mothers and daughters were supposed to communicate.

It certainly wasn't how Andi spoke to Sonia; Andi always felt free to say whatever she wanted, even if she knew it would make Sonia angry or it wasn't anything Sonia wanted to hear. There had been times when Sorrow had been frozen with anxiety about telling their parents about something—a bad grade on a test, a fight with friends, even a desire to stay home rather than go to the beach—and Andi would laugh at her, and then her laughter would pass and she would turn thoughtful, and finally she would help Sorrow figure out what to say.

But Andi wasn't here, and Sorrow wasn't even sure she would help. She didn't know how they were with each other now, after their phone call the other day. She didn't know if she had ever told Andi enough about Verity for her to understand.

She reached the corner of the house, but before walking around to the back she stopped, and she leaned against the wall beside the spigot and coiled-up hose, and for a moment she let the homesickness wash over her. She imagined turning around. Walking back to the end of the driveway. Calling Andi or Dad or Sonia and blubbering out that it had all been a mistake, that she shouldn't have come back to Vermont, where nothing was like she had expected, where everybody knew her family but didn't know a thing about her except her crazy mom and dead sister. Admitting that the only reason she had come back was because there was something wrong with her mind. Revealing the black spots in her memories where the past had rotted away. Telling them, through her tears, how desperately she had hoped that patching old wounds with stories and rumors would settle the jittery fear she had been carrying in her chest since that day in the Everglades, when she had realized she'd grown into the kind of person who couldn't even remember important things about her own sister.

Sorrow sighed and pushed away from the wall. She wasn't going to leave, and she didn't need to add her own blows to the embarrassment Cassie had already heaped on her today.

She walked around to the back of the house. The light in the kitchen was on, casting squares of warm yellow through the window and screen door. Verity sat in one of the rocking chairs with a bundle of knitting on her lap.

"There you are," she said.

Sorrow's steps faltered. She had been hoping to offer a quick *hello, did you have a nice day?* and *good night* before escaping up to her room, but Verity sounded as though she had been waiting for Sorrow, and worrying, even though it wasn't yet eight o'clock. She hadn't asked Sorrow to be home by any particular time. She hadn't asked her to call. Sorrow hadn't done anything wrong.

"Yeah," she said. "Here I am."

"Are you hungry?"

"No, I had some stuff," Sorrow said.

"How was the festival?" Verity asked.

Sorrow paused with her foot on the porch step. In the light from the house Verity's face was half illuminated, half shadowed. Sorrow couldn't tell if she was upset. She didn't know how she was supposed to answer.

"It was fine," she said. "Kind of ridiculous, but also kind of funny. I guess it's always like that."

"So I've heard," Verity said.

Sorrow crossed the porch, reached for the door, changed her mind. She settled into the other rocker instead. It was a warm, clear night with crickets singing all around and stars emerging from a velvet sky.

She asked, "Grandma already go to bed?"

"I think she's reading." Verity passed the bottle of hard cider to Sorrow.

"You know I'm only sixteen, right? Which means I'm technically not supposed to be drinking this."

"I won't tell if you won't," Verity said. Then, after a pause, "It was hot today. It wears her out more than she likes to admit."

"Yeah," Sorrow said.

But immediately she wondered if she ought to have denied it, claimed she hadn't noticed any signs of Grandma's advanced age. She had been seeing, but not thinking much about, the way Grandma was slower to rise when she knelt in the garden, her longer breaks and earlier bedtimes, the way she sometimes ate so little at dinner it might have been a child's portion. She was still steady on her feet, clear-eyed and active, but Sorrow, when she paid attention, could see the years bearing down on her, an invisible burden carried softly, quietly, her silence hiding any complaints or fears she might have. Sorrow didn't know if Grandma would voice them even if she could. Grandma used her pen and notebook to answer questions, make suggestions, make lists, and give instructions, but not once since she'd been back had Sorrow seen her put a single line into one of her private journals. If she had any place to share her worries, her mind and her heart, Sorrow didn't know about it.

"Why did we never—" she began, but she paused, her courage faltering. She took a breath and tried again. "Why did we never go to the festival when we were kids?"

"There never seemed to be much point," Verity said. "I don't care to hear what they think of our family history."

"They didn't make our ancestor the bad guy," Sorrow pointed out. "Pretty much the opposite, really."

"It may have seemed that way to you," Verity said.

Sorrow frowned at the dismissive note in Verity's voice. She didn't even want to talk about the festival. It was just such a stupid thing, so pointless, to have been built up so huge in Verity's mind as an attack on their family, when it was clear nobody else took it seriously anymore.

She took a swig of cider, slouched down in the chair, pressed her toes to the porch to set it rocking. The night was still hot, the heat of the day slow to fade. Sorrow's mind rattled with things she could say—wanted to say, didn't want to say—and there was a low nervous itch building in her chest as the light failed and the darkness deepened. She shifted in her chair, jeans sliding over a seat polished smooth by decades of use.

She was so tired of swallowing the things she wanted to say because Verity didn't want to hear them. She was so tired of feeling like her only option was to sew her mouth shut and slink away. She had come back to the orchard because she wanted answers, but all she had found were more questions, and if she kept waiting for the right moment to ask them she would never say anything at all.

"Did you used to be friends with Mrs. Abrams?"

Verity stopped knitting; her eyes remained fixed on the needles. "Where did you hear that?"

Her voice was flat, and her hands were still in her lap, knitting needles crossed and unmoving. Sorrow's skin prickled with discomfort. It wasn't the firecracker response she'd expected, but still her instinct was to change the subject. Retreat, backtrack. Apologize for asking. She was only asking. She wasn't doing anything wrong. But she knew that flat tone, the one that felt more like emptiness than sound. A chill traced down her spine.

"Julie told me," she said. Her mouth was dry, the words taking up too much space. "She said there's a picture of you two together."

"What were you doing talking to Julie?" Verity asked.

"I was just talking to her. That's not the point. Did you used to—"

"You know you're not supposed to spend time with those girls."

"It's not *those girls*, it's only Julie, and come on. I'm not a little kid anymore." Sorrow tried to make it sound like no big deal, but her voice was unsteady, her hands shaking. She had known how Verity would react, and now it was too late to take it back. She didn't *want* to take it back. She wanted an answer. "I can talk to whoever I want and—"

"Not the Abrams girls," Verity said tightly.

"Why not? What does it even matter?"

"You know why," Verity said. "Their family has only ever tried to hurt ours."

"I'm not talking about history. I'm talking about now," Sorrow said, frustrated. "I'm talking about you and Mrs. Abrams. Is it true?"

"We aren't friends with the Abramses," Verity said.

"Patience was."

If Verity had been still before, she was now carved from stone.

"She was friends with Julie," Sorrow went on, and now that the words were escaping she couldn't stop them. "They kept it secret because they knew you and Julie's parents would freak out. That's why I wanted to talk to her. I wanted to—she knew Patience, and you won't talk about her, and I just wanted to, I want to—" There was a hot sting in Sorrow's eyes, a catch in her throat, and she was breathless, her heart racing. "I just wanted to talk to somebody who remembered her. Who wanted to remember her."

For a long, long moment Verity said nothing. She sat unmoving with her knitting bundled on her lap, half of her face in shadow. Sorrow watched her, growing more and more tense as the silence stretched. She turned her gaze away. Looked back. Verity wasn't looking at her. A moth tapped frantically against the window above her head, trying to reach the light inside.

When Verity finally moved, it was such a surprise Sorrow flinched. She snapped the knitting needles together—a soft metal clink—and wrapped the loose yarn around them. She stood so quickly the rocking chair tapped against the wall.

"She was my daughter," Verity said. Her voice was low, but in that moment it was the loudest sound in the world, drowning out the insects and the wind and the whole of the night. "I remember."

"I didn't mean—"

"You've never wanted to talk about her before," Verity went on.

She reached for the screen door and pulled it open. She didn't look at Sorrow. "There were times when I wasn't even sure you remembered her, the way you were on the phone. It was like you became a completely different girl when you moved away, and that one didn't remember the things I remembered, didn't want to—you never wanted to—it was like you didn't even know what I was talking about, like you—"

Verity's voice caught. Her lips worked a moment, words unspoken. Sorrow watched, frozen, unable to speak, her gut churning with guilt and anxiety and a white-hot flush of shame.

"I remember everything about her," Verity said. "I could never forget."

She stepped inside and let the door fall shut behind her.

Sorrow jumped to her feet to follow. "I was eight years old," she said, wrenching the door open. "I had no idea what was going on because you never told me anything. If I never talked about her it was because I didn't know I was allowed to!"

"I have never forbidden you from talking about your sister," Verity said.

"You didn't have to," Sorrow spat back. "By the time Patience was gone I was already so well trained you didn't have to say a word, did you? Our whole fucking lives were about making sure we never said the wrong thing because it would upset you, and that meant we couldn't say anything because *everything* upset you."

"You are not being fair," Verity said. "You don't understand what you're saying."

"What the fuck is there to understand?" Sorrow was shouting now, her voice made louder by the close walls of the house. "It was my childhood! She was my sister! Did you even *know* she was friends with Julie? You didn't know until this fucking second, did you?"

Verity's eyes narrowed. "Don't use language like that when you're speaking to me."

"I *really* don't fucking care what you think of my language right now. You won't even answer my questions and you never knew the first thing about Patience because you never wanted to hear about how much she wanted to go to school or, or travel, or visit Dad, or have friends. She never wanted to do anything awful or unusual! She just wanted to be normal! What kind of crazy fucked-up heartless mother doesn't even let her daughters have *friends*?"

The words fell between them like stones, and in the thunderous silence that followed, Verity was pale and sharp and unbending, older than Sorrow had ever seen. She wanted to take it back. She wanted to shout it again, even louder, loud enough to echo through the orchard and make every branch on every tree tremble with the same ache she felt inside.

"I am not going to listen to you speak to me like this," Verity said. She turned her back to Sorrow, and there was a moment's hesitation, a glance toward the stairs, toward the back door.

"So you're just going to run away again, like you always do."

The words were out before Sorrow could stop herself. Verity ran up the stairs—how familiar that sound was, the flight-quick drumbeat of her shoes—and when she slammed her bedroom door

Sorrow felt it vibrating through her skin, through her bones, felt it a hundredfold, the relentless echo of every single time she'd heard it before.

There was a soft creak of floorboards; Grandma was standing in the kitchen doorway in her faded flower-print robe.

"What?" Sorrow said. Her face was burning and she felt sick, but she still wanted to shout. "I didn't say anything that wasn't true."

Grandma didn't shake her head. She didn't frown. She didn't lift an eyebrow or tilt her head in disapproval. She didn't do anything at all except look at Sorrow, and look, and look, the weight of her gaze so heavy and so silent, as though she was trying to see the stranger beneath her granddaughter's skin.

20

AFTER A STIFF, nearly silent breakfast, Verity announced that she had errands to run and would be out for most of the day. She didn't invite Sorrow to go with her.

"Have fun," Sorrow muttered.

Verity set her mug and bowl in the sink, fetched her purse and keys, and she was gone with the snap of the screen door. The sound of the car engine thrummed briefly, then faded as tires crunched down the driveway.

Their fight had sat between them like a tree toppled over a path, and they on opposite sides, neither wanting to find a way around. Grandma, silent as ever, had looked from one to the other, her eyes unreadable, her pen still and paper empty.

Sorrow sighed and scraped her spoon over her bowl. "I guess it's better than her locking herself in her room all day."

Grandma only raised her eyebrows.

"It's not like I was *trying* to pick a fight. I just had a question. Am I not even allowed to ask questions now?" Sorrow didn't know how much Grandma had heard. She cringed to realize that her shouting had probably woken her, but she wasn't going to apologize. Not to either of them. This time, at least, she was not going to be the one to smooth over the rough patch with careful words and platitudes.

Still Grandma didn't reach for her pen, but the tilt of her head was eloquently inquiring.

Sorrow squirmed in her seat. "I heard that she and Mrs. Abrams used to be friends. I asked her about it."

When she glanced up again, her grandmother's eyes were wide.

"What?" Sorrow said. "You do know that in a normal town with normal families, just asking something like that wouldn't be a big deal. I don't even know why it *is* a big deal. And you can't expect me to believe it's because some great-great-great-second-cousin of theirs did something to some great-great-great-aunt of ours. The tourists at the festival might believe that sh—stuff, but come on. I know when it's more personal than that."

Grandma shook her head, but Sorrow couldn't tell if it was disagreement or dismissal.

"Do you mean they weren't friends? Or that I shouldn't have asked? I don't know what you mean."

Grandma reached for her notebook and pen. She wrote a few

words and turned the page for Sorrow to see.

It's not easy for her to talk about.

"Yeah, I figured that out," Sorrow said. "Still doesn't answer my question. Were they friends?"

Grandma held the pen unmoving above the paper for a moment, considered, before she wrote an answer.

They were close, once.

Sorrow hadn't really believed Julie was lying, but the confirmation made the hair on her arms stand up. "What happened?"

I'll talk to her about it.

"Okay," Sorrow said slowly. "Wait, about what? You don't know? Or you don't know if you can tell me?"

There are some things you should know, with her permission. Give her time.

Another sting of annoyance—how *much* time was she supposed to offer, after eight years apart and only a few weeks before she went home?—but it was quickly replaced by a quiver of worry. "What kind of things? What do you mean?"

Grandma shook her head, gave a small sort of half shrug with one shoulder.

"Does it have anything to do with Patience?"

That time Sorrow had no trouble reading Grandma's expression: she had not expected that question. Grandma shook her head emphatically.

Why would you think that?

"I don't, really. I was just wondering."

It's not about that at all.

"Okay."

Grandma tapped the page with her pen, leaving tiny dots of ink beside *I'll talk to her about it.* Then she wrote, *What are you doing today?*

Sorrow carried her bowl to the sink. "I was thinking . . . I was thinking about cleaning up the cemetery a little bit," she said. "Just the trash and stuff. Trimming some things. I don't like that it's . . . I want to clean it up a little. If that's—"

Sorrow stopped. She wasn't going to ask if it was okay. This might not be her home anymore, but it was still her family buried in the cemetery grove. She didn't need permission to care for their graves. She only wanted to do what her mother should have been doing anyway.

Grandma looked at her for a moment, then wrote: *It's a good idea. There are leather gloves and trimming shears in the barn.*

"Right," Sorrow said. "Yeah. I'll need those."

She loaded the old metal wheelbarrow with supplies: spade and hoe, hedge trimmers and gloves, a black plastic bag for garbage. On a workbench she found a hammer and a Christmas cookie tin full of mismatched nails. It wouldn't hurt to see if she could mend the fence, even though she didn't have the slightest idea how to do that. The tools rattled and clanked as she pushed the load down to the orchard. The wheelbarrow's wooden handles were rough, the tire going flat, and she was sweating before she was halfway through the orchard.

The Lovegood cemetery in its hollow was a patchwork of cool shadows and misty morning sunlight, brown-barked trees and green leaves, white headstones and yellow ribbons and purple traps. Sorrow steered the wheelbarrow through a broken gap in the fence and set it down, rolled her shoulders, flexed her hands. A beetle rattled through the air and she started, turned, stared after it. She had looked up the emerald ash borer online, read a handful of articles about its infestation in New England, studied the pictures and lists of what to look for. Its larvae were responsible for the damage, carving snakelike mazes beneath the bark, cutting off the flow of nutrients, starving the tree from within.

In the pictures the beetle was vibrantly green and shaped like the head of a spear, big-eyed and shimmering and so very tiny. It seemed impossible that such a small thing, and so beautiful, could cause so much damage.

The Lovegood ashes were still healthy. Longer-lived than they had any right to be, sturdy and tall, and thriving. Sorrow pressed an open palm to the nearest, the one Rejoice Lovegood's husband had planted for her, at her request, after her death.

Sorrow and her family used to come out to the graveyard for night picnics sometimes, all four of them. They would spread blankets on the ground and gaze up at the stars, talking about this or that or nothing in particular. One such night in early fall, when the evenings were cool enough for sweaters and the mountains were washed in red and gold, Verity told them about a friendly argument the cider brewers had been having that day in town. One of them claimed it was the land, like the Abrams family had always believed, that made the Lovegood's crop of Abrams Valley apples so perfectly bitter for brewing cider. The other had insisted it was the trees and their great age that made the flavor so strong. Verity had laughed as she told this story, a dry-leaf-rustle laugh, and said that it didn't seem to have occurred to either of them that it was both the land and the trees together, sturdy roots sunk deep in soil, anchored to the earth and reaching for the sky, forever entwined. Grandma had moved her hand, a fluttering silhouette to encompass them, three generations lounging on a picnic blanket, and Verity had laughed again, more quietly, and she'd said, *Yes, the family, we're anchored here too.*

Sorrow had imagined them all as trees, their feet firmly planted and their arms spread wide, and she had kicked off her shoes to press her toes into the ground, giggling when the grass tickled her feet.

She had not noticed if there was an edge of unease in Verity's laugh, and she didn't remember how Patience had reacted at all. It wouldn't have meant anything to her, when she was a child, if there had ever been hints that her mother and sister chafed against the confines of their orchard and its history.

Alone in the cemetery, Sorrow pulled weeds and collected trash, chopped at the plants crowding the headstones, kicked and tugged the fence posts upright. She started in the oldest corner of the grove and worked her way along the graves, creeping forward in time with her trimmers and her garbage bag. Her world shrank down to the closed rectangle of the cemetery. Grasshoppers leapt around her and mosquitoes settled on her skin, took flight when she brushed them away.

The knot of anxiety high in her chest was still there, a living thing in her rib cage. She tried to focus on the dirt beneath her knees, the ragged tear of grass, the prickle of thorny leaves on her bare arms, but in her mind she kept replaying the fight with Verity. She imagined a hundred times what she could have said that would have been smarter, less cruel, more convincing, exactly the right thing she had needed to get Verity to *talk* to her, to have a conversation, share a piece of her past, open up rather than shut down. But no matter what she came up with, the replayed fight in her mind ended the same way.

Her, saying things she wasn't sure she meant.

And Verity, fleeing to her room, closing the door.

She was chopping clumps of grass from around Anne Lovegood's headstone when something small and blue caught her eye. Sorrow tugged off her leather glove and parted the grass with her fingers. It was a glass bead on a leather string.

Sorrow pulled it free of the grass, brushed away specks of dirt. Her heart was in her throat.

She'd had one just like this when she was little, only that bead had been red, not blue. She had found it in Grandma's garden one spring day. She must have been about five—young enough that she had been more use playing in the dirt than gardening. She remembered how excited she had been when the dark earth revealed the shiny red bead, the first favor of the year, and how she had whooped and run to show her grandmother. Sorrow had worn the red bead on its leather thong around her wrist the whole day. It barely fit, it was made for somebody even smaller than she was, so when it was time for bed she had taken it off and added it to her collection.

She turned the blue bead over in her hands, watching the sun catch and sparkle in the glass. It wasn't one of the favors she had lost, but it was a favor, and holding it made something jitter hopefully inside of her, an expectant feeling she had almost forgotten.

She hadn't imagined them. They were real. Lost, perhaps, the things she had cherished as a child, but real. She wanted to run to Grandma like she had before. She wanted to drop it into the grass and pretend she had never seen it—but as soon as she thought that, she felt guilty, absurdly, as though she would be betraying the orchard.

Sorrow tucked the blue bead into her pocket. From Anne's gravestone she moved to the next grave, the one belonging to a woman named Mary Covington. As a child Sorrow hadn't questioned her mother's explanation that Mary was Anne's dearest friend. She knew better now, and she felt an amused sort of embarrassment at her childish naïveté—and a twinge of annoyance too, that Verity hadn't tried to explain that Mary had been Anne's partner. Sorrow would have understood, even as a child. Only family was buried in the Lovegood cemetery. After a lifetime together, Mary had outlived Anne by only a few months.

Their daughters were next in the row: Righteous had died as a young woman, only twenty-three, but her twin, Justice, had outlived her by sixty years. Sorrow traced Justice's name on the moss-greened stone. They had grown up to be young women together, but no farther. A child never looks into the future and sees the seasons rolling past with a part of herself missing, a hole where a sister ought to be, a space so vast and so deep it is as though a piece of the landscape has been scooped away.

When she looked up she found the second favor.

Perched in the roots of Justice's ash tree was a small wooden tiger.

It was her tiger. *Her* tiger, the same one she had found as a child. She knew before she crawled a few feet on her knees to reach for it. She knew before she held its familiar shape in her hand, before she pressed her thumb to the space between its little ears, the way she always used to do when she was lonely and wanted comfort. It was exactly as she remembered, a terrific stalking beast made small and still, the ridges on its side an echo of the knife that had carved it. She must have looked past it a dozen times as she was hacking away at the weeds.

She scrambled to her feet, tiger gripped tight in her hand, and she began to search in earnest for more favors. She kicked through the grass where it was high, circled every tree to examine the nooks and crannies of their roots, pulled herself up on her toes to look into low branches. Her excitement quickly gave way to disappointment, however, and the only other favor she found was a single silver button, pressed into the earth by her own footprint near the wheelbarrow.

She dug the button out of the soil and cupped it in her palm with the bead. She shook them together, made a face at the paltry little rattle, and rolled them into the wheelbarrow beside the tiger. Her enthusiasm was gone. She was hot and thirsty, and every time she stepped from shadow to sunlight she could feel the heat on her shoulders, her arms, the back of her neck. She took off her Phillies hat, pulled her hair out of its ponytail and put it up again. She fanned herself with her hat for a moment, looking over the cemetery.

And she stilled. Stopped fanning herself. Lowered the hat. The skin on her neck itched. Her shoulders tensed. Nothing had changed. The birds were still chattering, the insects still humming. No cloud had passed over the sun.

But she felt around her a change like an indrawn breath. She turned slowly.

There was somebody standing at the corner of the orchard.

Her breath caught, the start of a word, but it wasn't Verity. It was Julie Abrams.

Sorrow exhaled shakily, feeling foolish for her nerves. Julie stepped over the fence, but she took only a few steps into the cemetery before stopping again. She was wearing a red shirt so bright it stood out like a vibrant flower blossom against the orchard's layers of green. Sorrow walked over to meet her.

"Hey," she said. She twisted her hat, pulled it over her hair. She had thought, after Cassie's outburst at the festival, Julie would be avoiding her for sure. She didn't know how to feel about being proved wrong.

Julie took off her sunglasses and fiddled with them. "Hi. Miss P said you would be out here."

"You were looking for me?" Sorrow said, then immediately felt stupid. "I mean, yeah. You, uh, you found me."

A flicker of a smile passed over Julie's face, gone so quickly Sorrow couldn't be sure she hadn't imagined it.

"I wanted to give you this," Julie said. She reached into the back pocket of her jeans; Sorrow watched the way her thin arm bent, how her collarbone jutted under her skin. "I went looking for it after we talked the other day. It took me a while to find it."

It was a photograph. Four-by-six on glossy paper, a bright scene overexposed by too much light, the colors washed out by the glare. Two women were sitting on a low brick wall. They were both wearing sunglasses, but Sorrow recognized them immediately. It was Verity and Hannah Abrams.

"Oh," she said. "Oh, wow."

"I told you," Julie said. When Sorrow looked up she expected a smile, but Julie's expression was solemn. "Photographic proof."

Verity and Hannah were sitting so close their shoulders were pressed together, their knees touching, and they were smiling widely. The photographer had caught them laughing. Verity was wearing a dress with a flowing skirt and loose sleeves, and her long hair was braided, altogether looking like she had accidentally wandered into the frame from a Woodstock retrospective, but Hannah was pure early nineties preppy: pleated skirt, square-shouldered blazer, blond hair teased and feathered around her face.

"Holy fashion crimes," Sorrow said. "How old are they? They look really young."

"Mom didn't tell me," Julie admitted. "But she didn't move here until after she was already engaged to Dad, so she was at least twenty-one or twenty-two. I think your mom's a few years younger, isn't she?"

Sorrow didn't know the difference in their ages, but it was true that in the photograph Verity looked younger. She looked like a teenager—fresh-faced, long-limbed, slouching. Even captured in a frozen frame there was an easy way about her that Sorrow had never seen before. At first glance Sorrow might have thought Verity looked like Patience, but nowhere in Sorrow's memories did Patience have that relaxed posture, that careless laugh, bright and summery as though she hadn't a care in the world, leaning into another girl in a way that was cozy, almost intimate.

"Where are they?" she asked.

Sorrow turned the picture over, but there was nothing written on the back. Turned it again and frowned as she studied the space around the two laughing girls. She didn't recognize the brick wall on which they were sitting, nor the neat bed of flowers behind them, the trees arched at the edge of the frame. On the right side of the photo there were the vertical lines of a wrought-iron fence and a brick pillar with a sign on it, but Sorrow couldn't read the words, and she couldn't see anything beyond it. It didn't look like any place in Abrams Valley.

"No idea," Julie said. "Maybe somewhere in Boston. That's where my mom's family lives."

"You didn't ask?"

"When I found it, I got yelled at for going through things that didn't belong to me," Julie said. There was a tired resignation in her voice, as though she was disappointed she even had to explain. "I found it in my uncle Henry's stuff—he was actually our great-uncle. Grandpa Eli's brother. He was the photographer in the family. We still have boxes and boxes of his pictures."

The name Henry nudged something in Sorrow's mind. "He's

the one who died in a car accident?"

"I guess. It was a long time ago."

Verity must have known him, to have been so at ease before his camera, but the other night in the barn, when she'd been talking about Devotion's fight with George Abrams, she had only mentioned Eli, said nothing about Henry.

"This is so weird to see." Sorrow held the photograph out to Julie.

"You can keep it."

"Really?"

"Maybe you can get your mom to tell you something about it."

Sorrow laughed a little and shook her head. "I really doubt that. Not after, what, twenty-some years of pretending it never happened."

"She might change her mind," Julie said. "People get so used to avoiding some things they don't realize it would be better if they just . . . stopped. That what they're hiding from isn't as bad as what they're doing to themselves by hiding."

"Somehow I doubt she'll find that convincing," Sorrow said. "But thanks anyway."

"I wanted to make sure it didn't get lost," Julie said.

Then she was turning, walking toward the fence again, and Sorrow scrambled for something to say, something to keep her from leaving. She hadn't noticed how the quiet of the orchard was weighing on her until Julie had broken it, but now that she did she didn't want to be left alone with the trees and the rows of dead ancestors. She didn't want Julie to walk away and take with her any chance she had of bringing up Patience again, of tugging at that one thread between them. Julie hadn't even said Patience's name, but Sorrow could still feel it echoing around them.

"Hey, Julie?" she called. "Do you think we could . . . I'd like to talk about Patience, sometime, again? If we could?"

But instead of answering with a yes, a no, a maybe, Julie looked at Sorrow for a long time, so long Sorrow grew uncomfortable under her gaze.

Julie said, "I heard about what Cassie said yesterday."

Sorrow's stomach twisted. "I never—"

"It's okay. I just wanted you to know—I didn't think you were bothering me. Not like that. Cassie's just . . . confused, and angry about a lot of things. But I didn't mind. I don't want you to think you upset me."

"Oh." Sorrow nodded uncertainly. "Okay. I mean, that's good, that I wasn't . . . yeah."

"I just wanted you to know that," Julie said, and she was walking away again, her blond hair gleaming in the sun.

Sorrow watched her until she disappeared into the trees. She looked down at the photograph in her hand, two faces familiar but so unlike the women she knew them to be, and tucked it carefully into her back pocket.

21

VERITY RETURNED IN time to make dinner, and Sorrow made an effort to act normal at the table, but a day apart had not lessened the tension between them. Grandma kept looking at each of them with a pinched frown. It was a relief when the dishes were washed and Sorrow could escape to her room.

When Verity came up for bed a little while later, she tapped on Sorrow's closed door and said, "Good night, sweetheart," but by the time Sorrow decided to answer she was already gone.

The night was hot and Sorrow's bedroom was stuffy. She kicked her quilt down to the foot of the bed, tugged the sheet up. Her window was open, but the air was humid and heavy, without the slightest hint of a breeze. There was a moth on the dormer ceiling above her, unmoving, a flat black triangle against the white paint. Somewhere outside, a bird chattered angrily, then faded, and the night was quiet.

After arguing with herself for a couple of minutes, Sorrow rolled out of bed and snapped on the light. The favors she'd found in the graveyard were sitting atop her dresser, right where her collection used to be. She touched her fingertip to the smooth spot between the tiger's ears. She remembered clearly where she had found it the first time: in the branches of the black oak on the hill, ten or twelve feet above Silence Lovegood's grave. Patience had been teaching her to climb the tree and trying to get her to guess which of the branches had held the rope where Silence was hanged. Sorrow had grown annoyed with her sister—the tree wasn't *telling* her anything, it was only a *tree*—but her annoyance had changed to smugness when she'd found the tiger, and Patience had admired it with just a hint of jealousy in her expression, and she'd said, "Maybe it's telling you something different."

Sorrow dug Julie's photograph out of the top drawer. She had stashed it there earlier, in the same spot where, with the laughable solemnity of a child, she had always hidden her most secret favors. She couldn't remember now, what those secret favors had been. When she walked through her old collection in her mind— the tiger, the watch, the beads and coins and lady's fan—she felt as though she was still grasping into dark places, reaching gingerly into corners and cracks, not even knowing what she was looking for. She felt a space where something ought to be—small and solid, tucked in her pocket—but like every other gap in her memories, every time she focused on it, it was as though a thicket of branches closed over the past.

It wasn't growing any less frustrating, the longer she was in Vermont, to have her own mind be so unyielding, even when she was only trying to remember things that mattered as little as trinkets she had found in the orchard.

She dropped onto the bed and examined the picture in the lamplight. How strange it was, to be looking into a corner of her mother's past she hadn't even known existed before. There were no lost memories here, no murky mental traps to find her way around, no flaw like the fog-filled canyon running through the center of her own mind. There were only secrets of the mundane variety. Two women who were once close enough to sit with their shoulders and knees touching, their heads thrown back in laughter, their hands drifting toward each other, no longer.

Sorrow set the photograph aside and turned off the light.

When she woke later she was shivering violently. It took a moment for her to register the cold, and in those few sleep-muddled seconds she saw blue lights flashing on the white dormer ceiling.

Her heart thumped in fear and she blinked rapidly, shook her head so fast her hair rasped against the pillow, and the glow was gone—a stray wisp of a memory. There was no light through the window but moonlight. Sorrow fumbled for the quilt at the foot of the bed, pulled it up to her chin and kicked her legs to generate heat. Only after a minute or two of groggy confusion did she realize she ought to close the window. She rolled up onto her knees to reach for it. Her breath was an opaque puff, and the orchard gleamed silver. The moon was sitting low over the trees, casting long, sharp shadows.

Sorrow's hand stilled on the window frame.

She had left the window open every night since she'd arrived, because the upstairs of the house grew unbearably stuffy during the day. The nights were cool in the mountains, but never like this. It wasn't supposed to be this cold. It was the end of June.

Sorrow slid the casement down and it dropped with a snap. She checked the time on her phone: half past midnight. The house was quiet. Completely, totally quiet. She sat in the center of her bed with her quilt wrapped around her, looking from the window to the door. She didn't know what to do.

It wasn't supposed to be this cold, and the bite on her skin, the ache in her ears, they sparked something in her memory. Blue lights through the window. She had forgotten before, what that looked like, how it felt to wake and see her bedroom cast in shifting colors all wrong, but she was remembering now, the cold and the light, those sensations long buried. There had been voices in the kitchen.

She pushed herself out of bed and winced over the cold floor. She opened her bedroom door, paused to listen. There were no voices. No visitors. She shook her head. She was not going to confuse past and present.

Down the hall Verity's bedroom door was closed. Sorrow slid her feet along the floorboards and stopped in front of it. She remembered this too: standing here. Smaller, younger. Her nose cold and running from being outside. She was going to ask Mom for a story.

She had opened the door. Something small and white had crunched under her foot.

Sorrow reached for the doorknob, and the door wavered before her, like a pond in moonlight, disturbed. She stopped, fingers resting on the cool metal. Her chest hurt. She hadn't noticed the panic rising, but there was a racing fear squeezing her lungs with every breath. She didn't want to open the door. She had to. She didn't want to. She turned the knob.

She squeezed her eyes shut. The cold didn't mean anything. It didn't mean anything.

Witch weather.

It didn't mean anything.

But the words were whispering through her mind, whispering and slithering, echoes of women overheard in town, men at Patience's graveside, taunts and rumors, gossip milled for years and years. An early frost: witch weather. A late spring blizzard: witch weather. Years of hardship remembered generations later. Failed crops. Harvests eaten through with disease and rot. Unseasonal, unnatural, suspicious, wrong. That's what happens when you anger the Lovegoods, and, boy, those women are easy to anger. That was what they said in town, half a joke.

But that had never been what the Lovegoods said among themselves. The orchard did not shudder in response to every sling or slight. The witch weather wasn't revenge.

It was the orchard's way of mourning.

Sorrow pushed the door open.

Verity's room was lit by moonlight. Sorrow could just make out her shape on the bed. Curled on her side, only taking up half even though she slept alone. Her back was to Sorrow.

Sorrow took a step forward, then another. Her third landed on a board that creaked loudly and she froze, her heart thundering. Verity didn't stir. Sorrow couldn't tell if she was asleep. She wasn't moving. She wasn't making any noise. She couldn't tell, she couldn't hear, she had to know—

Verity snorted softly and let out a low whuffling breath.

Relief hit Sorrow so hard she stepped back, right onto the creaking board again. She waited until she heard another breath, and another. The gentle inhale, the soft exhale. Verity was fine. She was only asleep.

Sorrow backed out of the room and shut the door quietly. Adrenaline and cold racked her entire body, made her hands shake and her teeth chatter. She picked her way down the stairs and into the kitchen. She filled the kettle and set it to boil on the stove. As it warmed she paced anxiously around the kitchen, tried to decide if she wanted to start a fire or not. She didn't think she would be getting back to sleep anytime soon, even if she could find a way to get warm. By the time the water was boiling and her tea was steeping, Sorrow was so annoyed at her own indecision she stalked over to the woodstove just to have something to do besides fret.

She started piling kindling and balled-up newspapers into the woodstove, but when she reached for the long lighter she stopped. She might be doing it wrong. It was all too easy to imagine smoke billowing out of the stove as the paper crumpled to ash. So easy, in fact, that as soon as the idea came into her mind she couldn't shake it. She would do it wrong, she would make a mistake, the fire would rage out of control, it would engulf the kitchen, chew away everything bright and new. It had never been her chore anyway, starting the fires, that had always been Grandma's—

Grandma. Sorrow jerked away from the stove so quickly she slammed her knee into the iron door. *"Fuck,"* she whispered. She rubbed at the sore spot as she scrambled to her feet and limped down the hall to Grandma's room. She paused only a second before opening the door.

The curtains were drawn tight, blocking out the moonlight, and Sorrow had to blink for a few moments to let her eyes adjust. The room smelled of flowers and earth and laundry detergent. It was quiet. Grandma was a featureless shape on the bed. It was so incredibly quiet. Sorrow's heart, already racing, stuttered with anxiety. She needed to see. She needed to be sure. She reached for the light, stopped with her fingers on the switch.

A loud snore rumbled from beneath the blankets.

Heart still thumping wildly, Sorrow shut Grandma's door and returned to the kitchen. She picked up her tea, but the first sip was too bitter, almost metallic, and she set the mug down. She started toward the woodstove, changed her mind, turned on her heel. Verity was fine. Grandma was fine. She was fine. All three of them were alive and well. She didn't know where this discomfort and restlessness was coming from. She felt as though she had woken in ill-fitting skin, and with every minute the sense of *wrongness* grew stronger. Verity was fine. Grandma was fine. She was fine. It was so cold.

Sorrow pulled the back door open. Everything was silver in the moonlight. She couldn't tell if there was frost on the garden. Grandma would be crushed if her garden was wrecked by frost in the middle of summer. Sorrow grabbed a sweater Verity had left draped over a kitchen chair, jammed her feet into her sneakers, and darted outside.

Her breath was a bright puff of mist. Everything was the wrong color, silver and gray and black. Grandma's garden looked like it had been carved from marble.

She stepped down from the porch and crossed the lawn. Her shadow was long and wavering, and the grass was damp with cold dew—not crackling with frost. She touched the top leaves of one beanstalk, holding the baggy sweater against her chest as she leaned forward. She half expected the leaf to snap when she brushed her finger against it, but it gave, still perfectly supple. She touched others with the same trembling fear. None of them were frozen and stiff. It wasn't cold enough to frost. Not yet.

Sorrow straightened and looked around, casting her gaze over the barn and the chicken coop and the dark edge of the orchard tipped with silver. She ought to check the apple trees too.

She twitched her knees, but she couldn't bring herself to take a step. Blades of grass tickled her ankles. The orchard at night had never frightened her when she was a child; she wasn't going to let it frighten her now. But it was cold, and she would rather be back inside, drinking her tea, calming down, going back to bed.

A soft breeze rose. The air was bitingly cold; it laced through the knit of her sweater and sent a shiver through her entire body.

Leaves turned in the garden, rustling quietly, and more distant, more softly, the trees in the orchard did the same.

The wind stilled, and it was quiet.

There were no crickets. She didn't hear any night birds or owls. No crackle of small nocturnal creatures scurrying along the ground. She couldn't hear the peep of the frogs that sang in the soggy field below the house.

The orchard was absolutely, achingly silent.

The stillness lasted seconds, minutes. The only way Sorrow could measure the passage of time was in the racing of her own pulse.

Witch weather. She moved her lips as the wind rose again. She heard it before she felt it, chasing through the leaves in the orchard like an approaching rainstorm. The touch of cold on her skin, on her bare legs, through the sweater, that came after. It stung her ears and made her eyes water and carried with it, faintly, the scent of smoke.

Sorrow spun around, poised to run, fear stinging like ice all over her skin. There was a fire nearby.

The rational corner of her mind was thinking: It was a cold night. It was a fireplace or woodstove. She was in the mountains, surrounded by farms. It didn't mean anything. It could be anywhere, drifting on that unsteady wind. Next door or a mile away.

She tilted her head and breathed in.

The wind was from the north.

To the north lay the cider house.

Sorrow was striding across the lawn before she made a decision.

There was something wrong in the orchard. She could feel it in her chest with every painful heartbeat, in her lungs with every shallow breath, in her skin and in her bones, the echo of a deep old ache rising from the soil and the roots and the ancient mountains. She had known from the moment she woke up.

When she reached the old dirt road around the field, she broke into a run, hit the edge of the orchard, and flashed from moonlight to shadows. She ran north, tracking the smoke and the wind, and slowed to a walk only when she rounded the hill and the road tilted down toward the meadow between the Lovegood and Abrams farms.

The wind was soft and teasing, tugging at her hair, chilling her sweat-damp skin. The scent of smoke was stronger now. She couldn't see if there was a tendril rising from the chimney of the Abrams house across the valley. All she could see was the front porch light, a glint on the other side of the moonlit field, so bright that even at this distance it stung her eyes, and in the space between wincing and looking away she had a disorienting memory of looking across this same valley, seeing light shining from several windows of the Abrams house, smelling smoke in the air.

She pressed her fingers into the stitch in her side and sucked in ragged, gasping breaths that tasted of iron, and she started down the hill.

When the cider house came into view, she stopped.

In an orchard awash in silver moonlight, the cider house was a black hole, a gap in the night, but there was a weak, wavering light inside. There was a fire in the cider house.

Sorrow charged down the hill, heedless of the uneven ground. Branches snagged her sweater and grass whipped her bare legs, and her feet pounded so hard she felt every step in her teeth. She stumbled twice, fell the second time, but she was scrambling to her feet before the sting of pain on her palms and knees registered.

She stopped at the edge of the meadow. Warm yellow light danced nimbly over the interior of the ruin, casting the charred black boards with a golden sheen. Smoke rose through the shattered roof—the thick, fragrant kind that came from burning damp wood. Sorrow took a few faltering steps forward. She didn't know who was in there. She didn't know how bad it was. She didn't have any water; she couldn't put it out herself.

She should go back to the house and call 911. She needed a closer look. She needed to see if somebody was inside. The sweat on her skin grew clammy in the cold. She began to shiver. She had to do something.

She crept through the meadow, and as she drew nearer she saw the light was coming from the hole in the floor. The fire was in the cellar.

Sorrow stepped over the bottom of the broken wall and tested the floorboards. They didn't bend, didn't give, so she stepped gingerly inside and slid toward the hole. A board creaked beneath her, loud as a shot, and she stopped. The cellar was about ten feet deep, and there was no ladder. She had no way to get down.

She took several breaths before dropping to her knees. She covered the last few feet to the hole at a crawl.

"Hey." She stretched her neck out to look in the cellar. She heard the fire crackling softly. Gentle heat caressed her face. "Hello? Is somebody down there?"

The rising smoke stung her eyes; she wiped the tears away and leaned out farther. The fire was small and contained within a ring of charred debris.

"Hey!" Sorrow said, louder. She dipped her head, trying to see all corners of the cellar. "Hey, if you're down—"

There was somebody right below her. She jerked back in alarm.

Blue jeans, red shirt.

Shoes that didn't touch the ground.

"Hey, are you—"

She had to be wrong. She needed to be wrong.

She looked over the edge again.

Shoes that didn't touch the ground, blue jeans, red shirt. A curtain of blond hair obscuring half of a mottled but familiar face.

It was Julie Abrams. There was a rope around her neck, the other end knotted to a beam, and a toppled stack of apple bushels beneath her. The flickering firelight cast a warm flush over her skin, but she wasn't moving. She wasn't swinging or twisting. She wasn't struggling or choking or gasping. She was dead.

22

EIGHT YEARS AGO

THE RAIN BEGAN in the afternoon and continued into the evening, and the lights flickered off after supper. Patience lit lavender
candles and set one in every room, filling the house with small cir-
cles of light. Sorrow usually liked the house in candlelight, the shy
dancing shadows on the walls, but that night she tensed with every
lash of rain and gust of wind.

The third or fourth time she jumped and looked out the window in alarm, Patience noticed and laughed. "What's got you so
jittery?"

"Nothing," Sorrow mumbled. She didn't dare admit she was
afraid the candles would topple and set the whole house on fire,

that she couldn't stop thinking about that burned corner of the Abrams barn and how wrong it had looked, that big chunk of building gone, as though a massive beast had taken a bite and left a black wound behind.

Mom had gone up to bed shortly after dinner, and a little while ago Grandma had set her pen aside and closed her leather journal before going to her own room. It was only Patience and Sorrow now. Patience had been forcefully cheerful all afternoon, ever since they had returned from the orchard, acting like nothing had happened. She hadn't even glared or pinched Sorrow to remind her not to say anything. Sorrow, true to her word, hadn't mentioned Julie when Mom asked if they'd had a nice walk.

"It's only a storm," Patience said.

"I know," Sorrow said, but another gust of wind rocked the house and she tensed, every inch of her body aching with worry. She shoved her chair back and stood. "I'm going to bed."

Patience turned a page in her book. "Take a candle up with you, but make sure you blow it out before you fall asleep."

"I *know*," Sorrow said. "I'm not a baby."

"Good night, baby," Patience said.

Sorrow stuck her tongue out and stomped up the stairs. She dutifully brushed her teeth and used the toilet and changed into her pajamas, and when she was alone in her room, with the door closed and the window rattling ominously, she blew out her candle. She had placed the eyeglasses from the cemetery on her dresser with the rest of her collection, propped up on the back of the small wooden tiger. She could see them even now, in the dark, as a pale circle where the one cracked lens reflected the weak light from outside.

A little while later, through the angry splutter of the storm, she heard footsteps on the stairs: that was Patience coming up for bed. Even later she thought she heard a door open, and footsteps in the hall again, but quieter, but she only had time to wonder if it was Mom or Patience before she fell asleep.

It was still dark when Sorrow woke, but her room was bright with light dancing over the ceiling. She frowned up at the shifting pattern of blue and white. She didn't want to get out of bed. She had thought the weather was turning and spring was on its way, but outside the cocoon of her blankets her bedroom was cold, so cold her nose was running and her ears ached. She could see the bright lights even when she squeezed her eyes shut, so she pushed herself up onto her knees to look outside. There was a layer of frost over the inside of the window. She swiped a small circle clear.

There was a police car parked in front of the house. The rain had turned to snow while she slept, and fat flakes drifted in lazy whirls. A man was standing beside the car, speaking into a radio. There was a fine dusting of snow on his broad-rimmed hat.

Sorrow scrambled out of bed and ran down the stairs. Mom and Grandma were in the kitchen with Sheriff Moskowitz.

"Hello, Sorrow," the sheriff said. He offered a quick smile, but his blue eyes were solemn. "Did we wake you with all our stomping around?"

Mom was standing by the back door, dressed in her coat and boots; she was holding her hat and gloves. "Go back to bed," she said, her voice sharp with impatience.

"What's wrong?" Sorrow asked. "Where are you going?"

"There's another fire," Mom said. "It's the cider house."

Sorrow gaped at her. "Our cider house?"

"One of the Abrams girls saw it from her window," the sheriff explained. "The firemen are down there now. They'll get it under control."

"I need to go out there," Mom said.

"I'll take you out once we're sure it's safe. One fire in the area could be an accident, but two makes me think somebody might be doing it on purpose." Sheriff Moskowitz looked first at Mom, then at Grandma. "Are you sure you haven't seen any strangers around lately? Kids from town looking to make some mischief?"

"No," Mom said. "We haven't seen anyone, and that's not going to change no matter how many times you ask. I'm not going to wait—"

"Miss P?" the sheriff said to Grandma. "Seen anybody around?"

Grandma shook her head, and Sorrow braced herself, tense from head to toe. She wanted to run away to her room but it was too late. The sheriff was already turning to her. She shrank under his gaze.

"And you?" he said. "Did you see any strangers in the orchard today?"

She hesitated before shaking her head exactly like Grandma. Julie wasn't a stranger. She was Patience's friend, but that was a secret, and Sorrow wouldn't reveal her sister's secrets.

"All right. Is Patience here? She might have seen something."

Mom reached out and pulled the back door open; cold air flowed into the kitchen. "It's the middle of the night. She's asleep, like Sorrow should be, and I'm not going to wait here for you to decide when I get to see what's happening on my own land."

"I'd like to have a word with Patience first," the sheriff said.

Mom started to say something, but Grandma moved her hand, a quick tap of fingers on the tabletop. Mom sighed and shut the door. "Sorrow, go wake Patience and ask her to come down."

Sorrow was only two treads up the steps when the front door opened and another police officer came in. He stomped his boots on the doormat and took off his hat. He was a younger deputy; his cheeks were pink with cold and there were snowflakes melting on his shoulders. He glanced at Sorrow as he passed. He held a radio in his hand.

"Geoff," he began.

The sheriff held up his hand. "Go ahead, Sorrow. Get your sister for us."

Sorrow ran up the stairs, but she stopped on the top step to listen.

"They think there was somebody trapped inside," the deputy said.

An awful silence fell over the kitchen.

"What?" Mom said, as sharp as the sound of wood cracking.

At the same moment the sheriff said, "Are they sure?"

"In the cellar. They couldn't tell until—"

"That's impossible." Mom's voice. "Who would be in our cider house? Nobody goes in there."

"M-ma'am," the deputy stammered. "The firemen said—"

"We're not going to jump to conclusions," said the sheriff. "We'll need some more help, so start waking people up. But keep your mouth shut until we know more, do you understand?"

A faint "Yes, sir" from the deputy. The narrow dark hallway felt like a box around Sorrow, pressing from all sides, and her lungs hurt so much it was hard to breathe.

"There's got to be a mistake," Mom said. "Nobody would be— this isn't—it has to be a mistake."

"Let's not panic until we have all the information," Sheriff Moskowitz said.

Sorrow raced down the hall to knock on Patience's door. Softly at first, then more insistent.

"Patience?"

There was no answer.

"Patience? You have to wake up. The police are here."

Still no answer. She pushed the door open.

"Patience, Mom said you have to . . ."

She felt the yawning hollowness of the room as she fumbled for the light switch.

The covers were mussed up, the pillow dented, but Patience's bed was empty. Sorrow leaned into the room, looked in each corner. The room was small, like Sorrow's, with no closet. There wasn't anywhere to hide.

"Patience?"

She checked the bathroom, Mom's room, even her own room, still filled with eerie blue light. She looked in Patience's room again,

even peeked under the bed. There was no sign of Patience anywhere. A nervous flutter beat like butterfly wings at the back of
Sorrow's throat.

She ran down the steps. "She's not here!"

There was a long silence. The deputy's mouth was hanging
open.

"That's not—" Mom began, but she stopped. "She hasn't gone
anywhere. I would have heard. I would have . . ." Mom pushed by
Sorrow to get to the stairs, ran up with heavy, echoing footsteps.
"Patience! Patience, come down here!" She sounded both too loud
and too far away. Sorrow flinched when Mom's boots hit the steps
again and she returned to the kitchen. "I don't know where she
went. She must be—"

"Ma'am," said the deputy. His radio crackled with incompre-
hensible noise.

"No," said Mom. She shook her head. "No. I'll look in the barn.
She's probably—she keeps books there. She's, she's . . . she's gone
out."

"Mom?" Sorrow's voice wobbled. "Mom, where's Patience?"

"Verity," the sheriff said.

Mom only shook her head and whispered no again.

"Verity." The sheriff's voice was low. "We don't know—"

Mom lunged for the back door and yanked it open. In a flash
she was outside. The sheriff ran after her.

The deputy gave Grandma an apologetic look. "I'm sorry," he
said. "We'll be—we have to—"

Then he was gone too.

Sorrow wanted to follow, but Grandma caught her around the shoulders before she took one step.

"Let me go!" Sorrow said, twisting and tugging. "I want to go!"

Grandma's hold was too strong. She shut the door firmly, pulled Sorrow into her lap, and held her tight. Sorrow was too big to sit in her grandmother's lap, too big to be coddled and cuddled like a baby. But she gave up struggling and snuggled her face into Grandma's shoulder.

"Grandma? Where's Patience? Where's Mom going?"

They sat there together, Grandma silent and Sorrow sniffling, in the anxious quiet of the farmhouse, until the sheriff's deputy returned with the news.

The firemen had found a body in the cider house. It was Patience.

23

JUSTICE LOVEGOOD

1856–1939

WHEN JUSTICE WOKE before dawn and felt the cold in the air, deeper and crueler than it had been the day before, she considered not getting out of bed. The old house, the old blankets, her tired old bones, they were no protection against a cold so deep, and the long years of her life stretching behind her no shield against what it meant.

It was too cold, too early. The fruit had only just ripened on the trees, and already it was frozen. There would be no harvest this year. It was only the first of September, but winter was here to stay.

The year was 1919, and in the span of half a decade Justice's family had shrunk from a noisy, boisterous crowd of daughters and sons and husbands and wives to a small, quiet knot, barely enough to fill the house anymore. The most recent to pass had been her niece Charity, gone in her sleep a few days ago, now buried beneath the first early frost.

With Charity gone they were three: Justice, her daughter, her granddaughter.

Today the morning was even colder.

Justice dressed in the half-light of a gray dawn, pulled on an overcoat patched at the elbows, and stepped outside. There was a line of footsteps already scraped through the frost, and when she saw it despair washed over her again, thicker and blacker now, a fog as heavy and dark as a midwinter storm. She had not heard her daughter Faith rise from her bed in the night. She had not heard her walk down the creaking stairs and through the door that squeaked on its hinges. If she hadn't been so tired, her back so sore from wielding a shovel the day before, she might have heard. They had buried Charity yesterday, although she had been slipping away for much longer, ever since three telegrams had arrived, one cruel blow after another. All three of her sons, barely old enough to be called men but old enough to go to war, were gone.

Justice was an old woman, and she felt old in every limb, every joint, but until that summer she had not thought herself old enough to see her grandsons die. They were only boys. Boys with uniforms and guns, but still children in her heart. Neither had she thought herself old enough to hold Charity while she wept, to watch her grow pale and silent as summer turned toward fall, to see the moment her spirit failed, to count the days until her last breath.

It seemed so very unfair that the longer she lived, the more grief clung to her like long evening shadows, a weight no new dawn could chase away.

She followed Faith's path, although she knew where it led and what she would find at the end. She plucked apples as she walked and found every fruit on every tree, and all those fallen to the ground, frozen solid, bitter pale flesh turned hard as stone. She flung the first few into the orchard with furious force, but dropped the last one, tired, feeling foolish for her outburst, impotent in her anger.

They had gathered only three bushels before Charity died and the first frost came.

Three bushels. Justice walked through the orchard in old shoes worn thin at the soles, and in her mind she counted: jars in the root cellar, strips of meat drying in the shed, goats in the pen, firewood stacked beside the barn, what she could ask of neighbors and what would be offered, coins in the metal tin on the shelf, and three bitter bushels. It did not add up to much.

The ground dipped into the hollow, the cold deepened, and the cemetery grove was just ahead.

Justice and her twin, Righteous, had given birth within days of each other, and they had mixed up their babies long ago, laying them side by side in the same crib one night. It was said a mother ought to know if the child suckling at her breast was her own and not her sister's, but they hadn't, and they had laughed about it. Their grandfather, old and forgetful by then but still doting on his great-granddaughters with a white-whiskered smile, had fashioned tiny bracelets for each girl, a single glass bead on a leather tie. Red for Charity, blue for Faith, and a laughing hope the right baby had got the right bead. The girls had grown up as though they were a second set of twins, sisters rather than cousins, and they had married a pair of brothers and raised their own children as siblings—Charity's three boys, all killed near the German border before Armistice, and Faith's daughter Joyful, the one who remained, once spoiled as a beloved little sister, now an only child, prone to singing and talking too loud to fill the silence her brothers had left behind.

When Righteous had died, Justice had thought she could not survive without her twin, her other half. She had been killed in what all claimed was a hunting accident, never mind that it had happened in broad daylight, on a clear day, not half a mile from the border of the Abrams farm.

But somehow, achingly, tiredly, as though her bones were hollowing out with every passing year, Justice had endured. She had lived when her sister could not. She had their daughters to care for, and an orchard to protect.

Faith had not been able to do the same. She lay now on her sister's grave, atop the mound of soil not yet settled. She was wearing only her nightdress, and her feet were bare. Her hair was as dark as polished wood, her skin the same pale blue as the ice-cracked dawn sky.

Justice stood beside the grave for a long, long moment, looking down at both of her girls. One curled like a child on the ground above the grave, the other buried below, and she thought: If a single bird dares loose a song, I will shatter. If a single breath of wind disturbs the crackling dry leaves, I will begin to scream and I shall never stop. The silence was her armor, its reaching tendrils snaking through her ribs to turn her tired old heart from muscle to stone. If it broke, she would too, and the pieces would be too scattered to ever come together again.

She knelt beside her girls, knees cracking, and brushed the frost from Faith's skin. The flesh was still soft, still pliable. Faith's eyes were open, her face angled upward, as though she were gazing at the ash tree she had, only yesterday, planted for her sister. She looked older in death, waxy and hollow.

Justice's knees ached and the sting of frost crept through her old dress and overcoat. She could stay, if her body did not find the strength to rise. The blood could grow sluggish in her veins. Her breath could crystallize. The ground was frozen. They would not be able to bury Faith until spring, and the orchard would mourn. The winter would be long and bitter. How many deaths, how much grief would it take to bring about a winter to last forever? How cold could the orchard become before tears turned to ice, carving tracks down cheeks?

She could stay with her girls.

But in the house her granddaughter, Joyful, would be rising to set a fire in the stove and heat yesterday's porridge, and she would be singing, singing like the first brave robin to emerge after a snowstorm, singing though her heart was broken, and

Justice could not make her eat breakfast alone.

Justice wiped the tears from her cheeks—almost scalding on her fingers—and rose.

Three bushels of apples would last longer with only two mouths to feed.

24

SORROW WOKE GROGGY and disoriented. Her muscles were sore, and when she bent her legs the sheet rubbed over the raw skin on her knees. She felt the same sting on her palms when she touched the scrapes. Her head was pounding, but she remembered running, and falling, and night and cold and—

Her chest squeezed so tightly she couldn't breathe. She kicked free of her blankets and sat up, dropped her feet to the floor and bent over her knees. The room pitched and swam. She shut her eyes until the dizziness passed.

Julie. She had forgotten.

The cold. The eerie quiet. The smoke in the air, the fire in the cider house.

And Julie, hanging in the cellar, dead.

The last of Sorrow's sleep-muddled confusion fled, and she remembered everything. She had spent too many minutes frozen in panic and indecision. Shouting Julie's name. Trying to reach her from above, trying to find a way down into the cellar. There was no ladder, nothing to climb, no way except jumping, and if she did that, she couldn't get back out. Finally Sorrow had run back to the house as fast as she could, tears streaming down her face and sobs shuddering through her. She had been dialing 911 when Grandma came out of her bedroom—Sorrow had made enough noise to wake her—and it was Grandma who fetched Verity while Sorrow shakily, haltingly, told the dispatcher what she had found.

Julie, who had been alive and smiling only hours before, her hand warm as she passed the photograph to Sorrow, her eyes the color of the sky.

You made her cry, Cassie had said, but Sorrow hadn't seen it. Not in the café, not in the cemetery. Not once in the brief time they spent together had she looked at Julie and seen misery. She should have seen. She should have known.

Sorrow shoved the window casement open and breathed in the crisp morning air until the sudden surge of nausea subsided. It wasn't as cold as it had been the night before, but a chill lingered in the air, and during the night, clouds had gathered over the valley. They must have rolled in after she returned to the house. She remembered glinting stars above the dark orchard, clean and bright in the cold. She sucked in another breath—it was just cold enough to sting her throat and send a shiver over her skin—and shut the window again.

Feeling shivery and off balance, as though the earth had tilted while she slept, Sorrow rose and dressed. She had the absurd, embarrassing thought that she was putting on the wrong clothes and she ought to choose more carefully. What were you supposed to wear the day after you found somebody dead? The sheriff had come to the house last night, after Sorrow made the call, but she was likely to return today. Sorrow would have to talk to her again. She would have to talk to Verity. She wanted to go back to bed, pull the curtain over the window and a blanket over her head, keep her door closed and the unseasonal cold shut firmly outside.

Sorrow rubbed her eyes again, took a deep breath, and went downstairs. The kitchen was empty; there was a used bowl and mug in the sink. Through the screen door she saw her grandmother walking the perimeter of the garden. Grandma stopped every few steps to examine the plants, bean stalks, tomatoes, pumpkins, squash. It didn't look like there was any frost over the garden and lawn, but there was a damp sheen to everything the sun had touched.

Cold at the end of June. Witch weather. Sorrow's heart ached.

Sorrow should go out to join her. Offer to help, ask if there was anything she could do. But she couldn't figure out what her first words should be—what were you supposed to say on a morning like this? She couldn't even decide if she wanted to eat breakfast. Make tea. Do her chores. Call her parents in Florida. Call Dr. Silva. Walk out to the orchard to see if the police were still there. Walk down the driveway and down the road until the air warmed and the clouds cleared. Keep walking and never come back. Do something. *Do something.*

Anything was better than standing in the kitchen, arguing with herself. She set the kettle to boil, then collected the clothes she'd been wearing last night into a pile with the rest of her laundry. After she had shoved it into the machine and set the cycle running, she returned to the kitchen to find Grandma had come inside.

"I really wish you guys drank coffee," Sorrow said. "I don't think tea is going to be enough this morning."

Grandma's smile was small, and Sorrow cringed.

"Sorry," she said. "I'm not trying to be—you know—flippant."

Grandma opened her arms, and Sorrow stepped gratefully into the hug. Grandma smelled earthy and green, and her shoulder where Sorrow rested her cheek was cool with clinging morning mist.

"Is the garden okay?" she asked.

Grandma released Sorrow from the embrace and, after a moment's thought, nodded.

"I was worried, with how cold it was last night. It was really cold. Did it frost? I thought for sure it was frost, I mean, it felt like it, but I'm not used to the cold anymore, so I was probably overreacting. I'm glad it didn't." She was babbling to fill the silence and didn't know how to stop. She was relieved when the kettle began to hiss—it never really managed a full whistle—and she could occupy herself making oatmeal and tea. "Where's Verity?"

Grandma pointed outside.

"I guess it's kind of late. Is she getting started in the barn? I know she wanted to start cleaning it out."

Grandma was shaking her head.

"Then where is she?"

Grandma pointed again, this time to the north.

A knot tightened in Sorrow's stomach. "She went out there? Why?"

Grandma's only answer was a shake of her head.

"I don't think she should—" Be out there. Be alone. Invite the memories in. Sorrow's breath was short, her chest tight. "I'm going to get her."

She left her tea steeping on the counter and marched into the orchard. It still *looked* like an ordinary overcast summer day, all the grass thick and full, all the trees heavy with green leaves, but the cold deepened when she stepped into the shade of the orchard, the more she found that was wrong. There were no leaping grasshoppers or lazy bobbing bees, no chasing squirrels or chattering birds. There was a hush over the orchard as oppressive as the gray clouds, and every flower she spotted in the grass beneath the trees was wilted.

She was wearing a flannel shirt, but the fabric felt too thin in the deepest orchard shadows, and she found herself shivering every time she stepped from sunlight to shade. One night. It had taken only one night of cold to brown and shrivel the blossoms, to silence the birds, to chase away the bees. The only sound was the gentle, sporadic patter of drops falling from the leaves. After so many days of persistent shimmering heat, it felt as though the volume had been turned down on the morning.

Sorrow slowed as she reached the point where the dirt road dropped down to the property boundary. She had expected to see a police car outside the Abrams house, or people milling around the cider house, but there was neither. Both places looked deserted.

She found Verity about halfway down the hill. She was sitting at the base of an apple tree with her knees crooked up, and in profile, from several feet away, she looked so much like Patience that Sorrow's breath caught. The illusion faded quickly. Patience had never worn jeans, never cut her hair short, never worn an expression of such careful blankness she might have been carved from stone.

Sorrow picked her way along the hillside and sat beside her.

She thought about asking, What are you doing out here?

She thought, What are you thinking about?

And, Did you go down there?

And, I know you're thinking about Patience.

The police had come to the house last night. The sheriff was a woman named Reyes, and she had told them Julie's death did appear to be suicide, but there would be an investigation to determine the cause of death. She wanted to know why Sorrow had been out in the orchard in the middle of the night. Sorrow had told her about the cold, going outside to check for frost, smelling smoke.

She told the sheriff, too, about both times she had spoken to Julie.

"She didn't seem depressed," Sorrow had said, painfully aware of Verity sitting beside her at the table. She could not meet her mother's eyes, so she had looked at her hands, at the sheriff's pen and notebook, at the mist on the window, at the clock on the stove ticking through the early hours of the morning. "It didn't seem like there was anything wrong."

Sheriff Reyes had taken her leave sometime around 2:00 a.m., with a promise to provide more information when she had it.

Sitting beside her mother on the hillside, Sorrow drew her legs up, mimicking Verity's posture, and she said, "Doesn't look like anybody's over there."

"They left a little while ago," Verity said.

There was a sour taste at the back of Sorrow's throat, a sting in her eyes, and she was suddenly, overwhelmingly tired. She shouldn't have come out here. She didn't want to hear that flat tone in Verity's voice. She didn't want to talk about the Abramses and the daughter they had lost. She didn't want to feel the damp earth beneath her, the dripping dew pattering on her arms like rain, the cold breathing from the shadows. She didn't want to feel the well of Verity's silence beside her.

And she didn't want to have to talk about Julie. She didn't even want to think about Julie, and how she had been alive and warm in the ash grove, silent and hanging in the cider house, one and the other, both at the same time, a cycle and a blur, and it was no use. There was nothing she could do to turn her thoughts away from the awful certainty she had felt leaning into that firelit cellar. She felt the shock of seeing Julie's face over and over, every time she tried to think about the weather or the orchard or her mother's waiting silence, like a wound that would never stop tearing open.

She blinked rapidly and turned away, rubbed at her nose to quiet a sniffle.

"Are you coming back to the house?" she asked. "Grandma's in the garden."

"Does she want to scold me for not doing my chores?" Verity said.

There was a spark of annoyance in her voice, a ripple in the awful flatness, but it didn't make Sorrow feel any better. She didn't know what she could say that would draw Verity to her feet, turn her away from staring at the cider house, and bring her back to the house—and even if she found the right words, she didn't know if it would matter. The cider house would still be marring the orchard in a tumble of charred wood. Julie would still be dead. Patience would still be eight years gone and everywhere all at once, filling every space between them with thistle barbs and thorns.

Verity said, "They keep telling me I should tear it down."

Sorrow didn't need to ask, but she couldn't leave those words dangling and unanswered. "Yeah?"

"Some kids got into it a few years ago," Verity went on. "They were using it as a sort of hangout. Smoking pot and drinking and—well, you would know better than I do what teenagers do these days. They were coming over for weeks before anybody noticed. I don't know what they"—a flick of her wrist toward the Abrams house—"were doing that they didn't notice a party practically in their yard—no, that's right. They were in Europe that summer."

The pause that followed was where any other morning Verity would make a wry comment about how tough it must be to spend the summer in Europe, how wrong it was that the Abrams family cared so little for their land they could abandon it for months at the height of summer. Any other morning she would have laughed, not in envy but in mockery, before going on.

Verity cleared her throat. "One of the kids fell and broke his wrist. His parents threatened to sue—with Paul egging them on, obviously. He was the only reason they were talking about it."

"Did they go through with it?" Sorrow asked.

"They realized pretty quickly that a lawsuit would mean having a public record of their son's illegal activities, and college admissions might not like that. They dropped it."

"You never told me any of that."

"You were twelve," Verity replied. "It didn't amount to anything."

"You didn't tear it down," Sorrow said.

She could guess why: if the entire town had been telling Verity and Grandma to tear down the cider house, they would have dug in their heels and done the exact opposite. Lovegoods did not allow the people of Abrams Valley to push them around—not even if it was only common sense, that a dangerous old ruin and eyesore should be removed. It was such an ugly thing, a black blight on the green land.

"It's not the first cider house to stand where it is now," Verity said.

"Yeah, I know."

"The first one wasn't torn down, not really. It was—"

"A terrible winter." Sorrow rubbed her hands together; she couldn't tell if the morning was getting warmer. She wished Verity hadn't chosen a spot in the shade. "I know."

When the winter of 1919 had come too soon and lasted too long for Abrams Valley—witch weather, Sorrow thought, the words minnowing through her mind—Justice and her granddaughter, Joyful, had taken the cider house apart piece by piece, board by board, preferring to strip the entire building to the ground for firewood than sacrifice a single apple tree. Making a game of that winter had been one of Sorrow's favorite snowy day activities as a child: melting snow in a pot on the woodstove, piling blankets into a corner to nest, bringing log after log in from the woodpile, turning misery from another century into an afternoon of make-believe.

"What does that have to do with anything?" she asked. "You should have torn it down."

Verity wasn't looking at Sorrow. She wasn't looking at the cider house. Her gaze was turned higher, lost in the sky. "They had nobody to help them that winter. They'd lost so much and they were alone—"

Sorrow stood, and Verity stopped.

She couldn't do this. She couldn't listen to Verity tell an old family story as though it were any other morning. She couldn't sit here on the hillside looking down on the cider house and see anything other than the same reminder Julie had seen every day of her life, every time she looked out her bedroom window, all because

Verity clung so desperately, so stubbornly to a past that was likely half-fictional anyway. Every time Sorrow closed her eyes she saw the orchard cast into stark moonlight shades of silver and black. She felt the sting of smoke, the rising heat. She saw the smooth fall of Julie's golden hair and the unnatural angle of her neck. She couldn't have all of that crowding her thoughts and Verity's meandering storytelling too. She needed somebody who would sit beside her when Sheriff Reyes returned, who would reassure her it wasn't her fault she hadn't found Julie sooner, who would lie to her and tell her everything would be okay. She needed a mother to comfort her in the present, not a wraith lost in the past.

"I don't care," Sorrow said. "I don't want—*god*. Why are you even talking about this now? Julie is dead, and it has nothing to do with—with anything that happened a hundred years ago. She's *dead*. And all you give a fuck about is where our stupid ancestors got their firewood."

Sorrow walked away without looking back. She hadn't come out here to start another argument with Verity. She had planned to be calm, reassuring, to make sure her mother was okay and bring her back to the house, where they could all go through the pitiful motions of pretending it was a normal day. That was what she had intended.

But all of the mechanisms she had for being the calm one, for being the person who absorbed other people's emotional ups and downs without wavering, without reacting, always cowering in the quiet center no matter what storm raged around her, none of it was working now. All of the things she normally thought and kept to herself, they were flying from her tongue every time she was near Verity, and she didn't know how to stop.

And every time she blinked she saw Julie's face, warm with firelight.

Verity still hadn't come back from the orchard an hour later, when Sheriff Reyes returned.

"Is Ms. Lovegood here?" the sheriff asked. She was a tall woman with brown skin and short-cropped black hair, and she spoke with a big Boston accent that filled the small kitchen. "I have some information."

"She's out in the orchard," Sorrow said. She thought about adding *she's working*, decided against it. She wasn't interested in lying for Verity today.

There was a pause while Sheriff Reyes waited for an explanation; then she asked, "Will she be back?"

"No idea," Sorrow said. "She didn't tell me anything. Why? Do you need her for something?"

"No, nothing like that," the sheriff said. "I only want to fill her in."

"You can tell me."

"I would prefer to have this conversation with your mother present."

"She's not even my legal guardian or anything," Sorrow said. Through the kitchen window she could see Grandma in the garden, but Sheriff Reyes didn't mention her. Sorrow wondered if she was one of those people who dismissed Grandma out of hand, assuming that because she didn't talk she couldn't hear either and wouldn't be any use in a conversation. "Can't you just tell me? I want to know if . . . I want to know."

Sorrow didn't like the assessing look in her brown eyes, but Sheriff Reyes nodded slightly and said, "The coroner is going to designate Julie's death a suicide. That's what all the evidence indicates."

At once Sorrow regretted asking. She didn't want to know about the evidence. She didn't want details. They were too many in her mind already. The warmth of the fire on her skin, and the lingering scent of smoke. The thinness of Julie's hands, and how they had played with her headphones in the café. The way the sun had shone on her hair in the ash grove.

She only wanted to know how they were sure. "Did she leave a note?"

"Not that we've found. But that's not unusual. Most people don't." A grimace passed over the sheriff's face, like a cloud crossing the sun. "This has already gotten out, thanks to a blabbermouth in the office, so I suppose it won't hurt to tell you. There were recent searches on her phone."

Sorrow's stomach clenched. "What kind of searches?"

"Information on how to make a noose."

"Oh." She shouldn't have asked. She didn't want to know that.

"There is one thing I want to ask you about," the sheriff said.

Sorrow looked up to meet her eyes, looked down at the table again. The sheriff must have heard about what Cassie had said at the festival. "What is it?"

"I'm wondering if you know why she chose that old building," the sheriff said. "Most people seem to think she picked it to spite your family, but nothing else I've heard about Julie makes her sound spiteful. Her parents insist—pretty strongly, I might add—it was more about convenience than making a statement. That it has nothing to do with your family. I'm inclined to agree with them." Sheriff Reyes paused, and when Sorrow didn't answer she went on, "But, as everybody keeps reminding me, I'm a newcomer around here. I've only lived here for five years, which might as well be five days in this town. What do you think?"

Sorrow traced her fingertips along the woodgrain of the table. That didn't sound like Mr. and Mrs. Abrams, vehemently absolving the Lovegoods of having any part in their personal tragedy. Ethan had been right when he'd said that if they had any way to blame the Lovegoods for something, they would do so loudly and repeatedly.

But they didn't know what Sorrow knew about Julie and Patience and their brief winter friendship. That secret had felt so huge and terrible when she was a child, but now it seemed no more than a small hot ember, pressing on the inside of her chest.

"You know that's where my sister died," Sorrow said. She looked up at the sheriff to be sure she was listening.

"I do know about that," Sheriff Reyes said.

"They were friends. Not for very long, I don't think. Just a few months. They weren't supposed to be. Our families . . ." Sorrow shrugged. "It was a secret. I mean, they kept it a secret from our parents, because they would get in trouble."

"That's why you sought out Julie when you came back to town?"

"I just wanted to talk to her. I didn't think—I didn't mean to upset her. I wasn't trying to do that. I just wanted to see if she remembered Patience. I didn't—oh, god." Sorrow put her hand over her mouth and choked back a sob. "I didn't know. I didn't know it would hurt her just to ask."

"Sorrow." Sheriff Reyes moved her hand like she was going to reach out, changed her mind and rested it on the table. "I didn't know Julie, but I do know that something like this doesn't happen because of just one conversation. Her family and friends tell me she's been troubled for years."

Sorrow nodded, but she couldn't bring herself to say anything. She didn't know Julie either. She never had. They'd spoken twice, and all of the enthusiasm for those conversations, every feeling of connection shared between them, every possible future meeting where they might talk again, those had all been in Sorrow's head.

After the sheriff left, the day passed quietly. Verity returned to the house after Sorrow and Grandma had finished lunch, and she stayed only long enough to claim she wasn't hungry before vanishing into the barn. Grandma did what she could for the cold-nipped garden, then came in to sew in the living room, and Sorrow sat in the kitchen with her summer reading books. She tried to let the steady chug of the sewing machine soothe her, but every glimpse of motion outside the kitchen window, every change in the light, made her look up, half hoping and half dreading it would be Verity on her way inside. The clouds showed no signs of breaking.

Sorrow went to bed early, still exhausted from the night before. She lay on her bed, curled onto her side beneath an extra blanket, and squeezed her eyes shut. She kept thinking about Julie in the cemetery grove, the sunlight shining on her hair, secrets and questions stretched between them delicate as spider silk, and her smile, always her smile, soft and sad and so very alive.

And thinking about that led, every time, to Julie in the cider house.

Sobs pressed at the back of Sorrow's throat and hot tears streaked her face. Her heart was racing for no reason she could identify. She pressed her fingers to her wrist to feel her pulse and tried to count the beats, tried to draw in slow, even breaths, but nothing helped.

She was still lying there, choking on sobs she couldn't stop and rubbing tears from her cheeks, when Verity came upstairs.

Please come in, she thought, staring at the closed door. Please come in.

She wanted Verity to knock softly and open the door when Sorrow answered. She wanted Verity to ask if she was all right. Sit on the edge of the bed. Put a reassuring hand on her shoulder. She wanted to not be alone.

But Verity didn't tap on the door. She walked down the hallway to the end, paused, returned, and did it again. She paced back and forth, back and forth, her soft steady footsteps lulling Sorrow halfway to sleep.

The sound of her steps changed: she was going downstairs.

Sorrow held her breath. Waited, waited—and there it was. The back door opening, the screen snapping shut.

She exhaled and rolled onto her back. She fell asleep still waiting for Verity to return.

25

THE NEXT DAY dawned cool and gray, with a layer of clouds hanging stubbornly over the valley. Grandma was making bread when Sorrow went downstairs. She looked up from her kneading to offer a quick smile, which Sorrow couldn't quite manage to return. She sat at the table and watched for a minute or two. Grandma's arms were dusted with flour up to her elbows, and there was a stray speck on her nose. The door was open, and beyond the screen the orchard was muted under the cloudy sky, all the uncountable shades of green murky and dark where before they had practically glowed in the sunlight.

Sorrow had barely slept. She had tossed and turned restlessly for hours until finally drifting off to dream about racing through the orchard on a cold winter night, surrounded by smoky shadows and chased by raging fire, and every time she looked back to see how close the flames were, the trees rustled and shuffled and bent to block her view. She had awoken disoriented and nauseated, and even after shoving her window open and gulping in the chilly night air, she hadn't been able to settle her stomach or her nerves.

And as soon as the shifting dream images faded, she was thinking about Julie again, and the way the firelight had glowed on her skin, how it had made her look warm and alive. Sorrow had showered twice since the cider house but still every breath smelled of smoke, and even when she was nested in her bed beneath two quilts she felt chilled all over.

"I don't know what to do," Sorrow said.

Grandma's hands stilled. She turned to Sorrow.

Sorrow hadn't meant to say anything. She looked down at the table, tears filling her eyes, and she swallowed. "I keep thinking about her," she said, her voice small. "I can't stop seeing her."

A hysterical burble of laughter rose in her throat, and she pushed it down, covered her mouth with her hand to keep any sound from escaping. It wasn't funny. There was not a single thing funny about it, but all she had been doing since she arrived was trying to remember something terrible, thinking about Patience and how she had died, and now all she wanted was for her mind to *stop*. She didn't want any of it in her thoughts now. She didn't want to think about anything.

Grandma pulled out a chair beside Sorrow and reached for her hand. Sorrow let her take it, squeezed her fingers, and held on.

"I remember a lot of casseroles," she said.

Grandma tilted her head in question.

Sorrow sighed and rubbed her free hand over her face. "I keep thinking I don't know what to do, and trying to remember what other people did, and that's what I remember after Patience died. A lot of casseroles."

She couldn't imagine how Hannah Abrams would react to a counter full of foil-wrapped baking dishes. She remembered Hannah that afternoon in the grocery store parking lot, so perfectly put together, so aloof, and how that aloofness had turned cold when Verity came out of the store. It was impossible to picture her breaking down in grief, or comforting Cassie, or standing beside her husband while the funeral director told them about different styles of coffins.

"I wonder how Cassie's doing," she said. "I mean—that was a stupid thing to say. This must be awful for her. Maybe—oh, god, I wonder how Ethan's doing. We should have called him yesterday. I should have called, right? Is that the right thing to do?"

Grandma let go of Sorrow's hand to pick up her notebook. *We can ask Jody if the family needs anything.*

"Right. Yeah." Sorrow had never spoken to Ethan's mother, but Grandma was right. This was the kind of thing mothers were supposed to deal with. "Okay, so that's—oh, shoot. I think I'm scheduled to work today."

For a moment the prospect was an appealing one, however shaky she was feeling. To escape a repeat of yesterday's long, heavy silence, to break through the imaginary wall around the orchard and remind herself she wasn't eight years old and stuck here dreading the sound of a police car on the driveway. The store could be a refuge, if only for an afternoon, with Kavita's endless chatter and tourists wandering in to ask questions about tents and bears and blisters.

But it wouldn't only be Kavita, and it wouldn't only be tourists. At some point the bell over the door would jangle, and it would be Mrs. Roche or somebody like her, locals Sorrow knew by sight if not by name, and even if she weathered the unsubtle staring she would hear the whispers: Isn't that the girl who found . . . ? Oh, yes, she's the one. She's the Lovegood girl. Everybody in town would be talking about Julie, and that it had been Sorrow who found her. An Abrams tragedy on Lovegood land. That was too juicy too resist.

"I guess I can call them and see what they say," Sorrow said.

Grandma didn't offer an opinion either way. She patted Sorrow's hand one more time and stood to go back to her dough. Sorrow stared at her shoulders, willing her to shrug, to nod, to do *something* to indicate whether Sorrow was doing the right thing. For the first time since she had come back to Vermont—perhaps the first time in her life—she felt a spike of genuine anger at her grandmother's silence.

But Grandma only kept kneading.

Sorrow sighed. "I'll call them," she said.

It was Helen Ghosh who answered, and she told Sorrow at once she didn't need to come in.

"I can if you really need me to," Sorrow offered. She couldn't decide if she was relieved or dismayed. "And tomorrow is fine."

"Don't worry about it," Helen said. "We'll be fine. We'll just make Kavita work extra." There was a muffled "Hey!" in the background, and Helen said, "Speak of the devil; she wants to talk to you. Take care of yourself, Sorrow. Let us know if you need anything."

A rustle as the phone changed hands, and Kavita said, "You should consider yourself forewarned that if you take Mom up on her offer, it will be food, and food will probably be a pot of masoor dal big enough to drown in."

"That doesn't sound like a bad thing," Sorrow said, "but we're *fine*. Nothing happened to us. It's just, you know."

"It's fucked up, is what it is," Kavita said. "I can't believe she did that. I mean, everybody knew she had problems, and it didn't take a rocket scientist to see she had an eating disorder of some kind, but . . . I thought her family was the kind that would get her into therapy if she needed it."

Sorrow thought about what Sheriff Reyes had said about Julie being troubled for a very long time. There was an ache in her throat, a knot of choked-back tears; she rubbed at her chest right below the hollow of her neck. "Maybe they did. Maybe it wasn't enough."

"Yeah. Have you talked to Ethan?"

"No. Not yet."

"Me neither. He's been doing the one-word text answer thing. Mahesh is going over there later." A brief pause, then Kavita said, her voice serious, "But, really, are you okay? That has to be—I mean. It is so fucked up."

"Yeah, I'm fine," Sorrow said.

A lie, such a lie, but she couldn't give voice to the quivery feeling in her chest, the way her mind turned in every unwary moment
to her walk through the silvery cold moonlight, the glow of firelight below, and Julie's hair falling over her face in a sleek curtain.
She squeezed her eyes shut and she held her breath, terrified for a
moment that Kavita was going to ask her, what was it like, what did
you see—all the things Sorrow couldn't bear to talk about again.

But Kavita didn't ask, only told Sorrow she'd see her later and
said good-bye.

Sorrow turned to Grandma. "Is Verity already outside? What's
she working on?"

Grandma wrinkled her brow.

"You don't know?"

A shake of her head, and Grandma glanced upward.

"Or you mean—she hasn't come down yet? But it's—"

Sorrow looked at the clock on the range. Almost ten. Hours
past the time Verity normally woke. "What do you mean? Did she
come down or not?"

Grandma only shook her head again, and her expression was
uncertain. Sorrow stood up—her chair scraped loudly on the
floor—and she ran for the stairs.

Verity's door was closed. Sorrow should have noticed. Verity's door was always open when Sorrow emerged in the morning
because Verity was always awake first, but today it was closed. She
had walked right by. She hadn't seen. She reached for the knob. Her
heart was pounding and her breath was short and she felt the same
wild, irrational fear she had felt the other night, when she'd woken

in the cold and known something was wrong. She didn't even know where it was coming from, this anxious fear of what lay beyond that door. She was probably overreacting. Verity had been up late last night. She could have slept in. She was allowed to do that.

Sorrow let go of the knob and knocked softly. "Verity? Are you awake?"

The stairs creaked behind her: Grandma was following.

"We just want to see if you're up," Sorrow said.

Still no answer. Sorrow looked at her grandmother for help, but Grandma looked as lost as she felt.

She turned the knob. It would be dark beyond the door. A darkness deep and growing, shadows reaching from every corner of the room, and the air would be stuffy, close, sickly. She didn't want to open the door. She didn't want to see what was on the other side. A shape in the bed, unmoving.

She pushed the door open. "Hey, we're wondering where you—"

The window and curtain were open, filling the room with soft light and fresh air. Verity was sitting on the edge of her bed. Her hair hung in messy strands around her face. She was wearing her cotton sleep shirt over a pair of jeans, as though she had started to get dressed but had run out of energy before she could finish.

"Hey," Sorrow said, and she stopped.

She looked around the room, gaze darting into every corner. There was a glass of water on the table, mostly full. A book beside it. A lamp, off. A pair of shoes on the floor. A knitted afghan draped over a chair. She didn't know what she was looking for. The curtains drifted in the breeze, billowing gently. It looked normal. Everything was as it should be except Verity, half dressed at ten in the morning, staring at Sorrow in confusion.

"Sorrow? What do you need?"

"We were only . . ."

Sorrow glanced at Grandma in the doorway. She didn't know what she was supposed to do. She didn't know what to say. She needed somebody to tell her how to deal with this.

"We were only wondering," Sorrow said, "if you were feeling okay."

"You barged in here to ask me that? Why wouldn't I be?"

"But you—you never sleep this late."

Verity rolled her eyes—actually rolled her eyes, like she was the teenager and Sorrow the mother—and said, "I'm not sleeping. I'm wide awake."

"Yeah, okay, but . . ."

"I'll be right down." Verity swept her hair back from her face and stood. "Are you going to stand there and watch me get dressed?"

Verity wasn't crying. She hadn't locked the door. She wasn't curled insensible beneath her blankets. She was awake. Standing. Getting dressed. She was talking to Sorrow, even annoyed with her. She had never been annoyed on her bad days. On those days, the very worst, no matter how many times Patience and Sorrow had tried to plead and pester her out of bed, she would only roll over and say she was too tired. This wasn't like that. This wasn't *like* that.

But Sorrow couldn't move. She couldn't turn around and walk out of the room. She couldn't let Verity close the door again. Every one of her oldest instincts was telling her to take Verity's hand and tug her outside, pull her stumbling and blinking into the sun. *She just needs a bit of fresh air*—Sorrow couldn't remember who used to say that to her. It was a lie then and a lie now, but still the words fluttered moth-frantic in her mind: she needed sun, she needed air, she needed Sorrow to do the right thing, say the right thing, and when she did what her mother needed, that sinking lethargy would snap away, and with it the fear clawing at Sorrow's insides like brambles. She couldn't move. If she left, anything that happened would be her fault.

"Sorrow." Verity walked to her wardrobe, opened the door, began searching through the clothes inside. "I'll be right down. Five minutes. Not even five. Two."

Grandma touched Sorrow's elbow. Sorrow looked at her, and Grandma gestured toward the door. Still Sorrow hesitated.

"Sorrow," Verity said. "Earth to Sorrow. I'll be right down."

Her gaze slid to the side, and she fussed with the clothes in the wardrobe, straightening shirts on hangers, and that was when Sorrow saw the pink in her cheeks, on the tips of her ears, saw the wry twist to her mouth, and she understood: Verity was embarrassed. She was embarrassed to have been caught half dressed and momentarily overwhelmed. She was embarrassed that Sorrow had charged up here to find her.

Sorrow turned, her face growing warm, and pretended not to see Grandma's approving nod. "Okay. I'll just—there's breakfast. When you're ready."

She hurried downstairs, followed by Grandma. She sat at the table for an interminable few minutes until she heard Verity's footsteps on the stairs. She jumped to her feet and grabbed the kettle.

"I can make tea," she said.

"No point," Verity said. Her voice was bright, unusually high. She breezed past Sorrow to the back door. "Half the morning's gone. I've got work to do."

"I can help," Sorrow said quickly. "What've you got planned?"

Verity was already stepping onto the porch. "Nothing interesting. I'll just be clearing up some of the winter deadfall around the fence on the south side. You help Grandma."

The screen door clacked shut. Sorrow watched through the window as she crossed the lawn and disappeared into the barn, and when she looked away she saw that Grandma was watching too, a worried wrinkle creasing her brow.

Verity didn't return to the house until it was nearly dinnertime, and then all she did was pick at a few bites before shoving her chair back and declaring, "I'm disgusting. I need to shower." And her voice was so airy, so dismissive, so unlike how she normally sounded that it put Sorrow immediately on edge. "Go ahead and put this away. I'll heat up something later."

She vanished upstairs and didn't return for the rest of the night.

After the kitchen was cleaned up, after Grandma had gone to bed, when Sorrow was alone in her own room, she turned off her light and lay down. As soon as her head hit the pillow her heart was racing again with the same panic she had felt the night before. She sat up and crossed her legs, hugged her pillow to her chest, and sucked in painful, gasping breaths. It didn't help. Tears sprang into her eyes and she scrubbed them away, and her heart was pounding so hard she could feel it in her neck and in her fingertips. The room was too small. She had to get out. She scrambled off the bed and to the door.

And she stopped again, hand on the knob. Leaned her forehead against the solid wood and closed her eyes. What was she going to do? Bust into Verity's room when she was trying to sleep? Verity had been up today. She had been outside working. Outside in the sun, in the fresh air, and that was what everybody said she was supposed to do. That was good. That was fine. It was *fine*. Sorrow was freaking out for no reason. She didn't know what was wrong. She kept picturing herself opening the door to Verity's room over and over again, and finding not bright morning light, but darkness at midday, the air stuffy and stale, a too-still body in the bed, the soft crunch of something under her shoe, and she didn't know *why* that was all she could see. She couldn't remember. She tried and tried and tried, but every time she stepped into that room in her mind, every time that small person she used to be walked toward the bed, toward the shadowed shape she knew to be her mother, her mind shuddered and twisted and shied away, and there was a hedge of brambles around her, high enough to reach the sky, thick enough to block the light, and she still couldn't remember. She could creep and peer and sneak through the labyrinth of her own memories, pressing like a bruise around the edges of what she couldn't remember, but those bending, rustling branches were always there, blocking her path, turning her away.

She slid to the floor and pulled her knees up to her chest.

No matter what she remembered or didn't, no matter what she found or left buried, no matter what was going on with Verity, Julie was still dead. Sorrow could still see her. The shine of her hair, the tilt of her neck. She could still smell the smoke.

Sometime later, Sorrow heard her mother's door open. Verity began pacing up and down the hall, from the top of the stairs to Patience's bedroom at the other end, a constant slow rhythm, socked feet on floorboards the only sound in the tired old house.

26

FOR THE THIRD day in a row, the dawn was overcast and gray and chillier than midsummer ought to be. Sorrow wrapped herself in a sweater and took her tea out to the back porch. She was the first one up. She had awoken slumped on her bedroom floor, stiff all over from sleeping curled up by the door. If she had dreamed, she didn't remember it, and every time her mind turned toward what memories might still be hiding in the maze of her muddled brain, she felt so tired she wanted to give up thinking about it at all.

She had told herself, when she first began to remember, that it would be like piecing together a puzzle. Once she found enough pieces, once she fit together the corners and edges, the rest would fall into place, and for the first time she would have a complete picture of everything she had been missing.

She remembered the day before Patience had died. She remembered the night of the fire. She remembered how cold it had been. She remembered watching through her bedroom window as snowflakes whirled down in the blue and white lights of the sheriff's car.

She remembered burying Patience in the ash grove.

Verity at the graveside with a doctor behind her.

Leaving with her father and not knowing if she would ever return.

She didn't remember what had happened in between.

Your mother is sick. Your mother isn't well. Your mother is going away for a while. That was what Sorrow remembered, but none of it came from her own memories, only from the explanations and excuses others had offered over the years. Verity had always been depressed, off and on, for as long as Sorrow could remember, and she was fairly certain there had never been any kind of treatment before Patience died. That had been the breaking point. During those few weeks between Patience's death and Sorrow leaving for Florida, something had happened that had pushed Verity and Grandma and Dad to all agree that Sorrow could no longer live in the only home she had ever known.

She had asked, once, a few years ago. Dad had only said: *Your mother had a breakdown.*

What a useless word, *breakdown*, so big and so small all at once, meaning nothing and everything, no more than a way to avoid the truth. But at the time she had accepted it. It had all seemed so very far away, not her own life and her own memories anymore, but somebody else's, the history of some poor little girl and her sad family tragedies.

She heard Grandma moving around in the kitchen. The light was changing, the orchard's shades of gray sliding into dreary green, and the trees were emerging from the misty darkness as distinct shapes. Somewhere behind the clouds the sun was rising. Sorrow didn't want the day to start yet. She wasn't ready for more hours of worrying about whether Verity was coming downstairs, whether she should go fetch her, whether Grandma was paying enough attention, if it was even fair to expect Grandma to do more, if this was normal, if this was wrong, and why she didn't know any of those things. How she could be sixteen years old and not have the slightest idea how to ask if her mother was okay.

Her tea had grown lukewarm when she heard a car coming up the driveway. She tensed, then relaxed. It was too early for the police, and she recognized the grumble of Ethan's Jeep. He came around the corner of the house a minute or so later. He was dressed in his grass-stained work clothes, and his Red Sox hat was jammed into the back pocket of his jeans. He looked younger without it, his hair uncombed, his expression uncertain.

Sorrow slid a few inches to the left to make room on the step. "Hi," she said.

"Hey." Ethan sat down beside her.

She took a sip of her tea. "We meant to call you yesterday."

Sorrow said *we*, but in truth she had considered it, then forgotten, and Verity had never mentioned it at all. It should have been Verity to suggest it in the first place. She was the one who liked Ethan so much she wished he were a Lovegood rather than an Abrams. Sorrow barely knew him; she wasn't even sure if they were friends.

But his cousin had died, and she should have called.

"It's fine," Ethan said. "Things have been . . . I don't even know. So messed up."

"How are you doing?" she asked.

"I don't know," Ethan said. "I know I'm here early, but I had to get out of the house. Mom is all over the place because she can't decide if she's supposed to be helping or not, because she can't stand talking to Aunt Hannah and Uncle Paul anymore, but this is *Julie*, and Julie was never the problem, and . . . Two days of listening to her go around and around and I, uh, I told her you guys needed help today."

"That's okay," Sorrow said. "You can use us as an excuse anytime."

"I just can't . . . Part of me keeps thinking, I can't believe she did this, but part of me isn't surprised at all. That's an awful thing to think, isn't it?"

"I don't know," Sorrow said.

"She tried before," Ethan said. "When she was in high school. At least once that I know of. She was away at boarding school, and she—I think she got drunk and climbed up on a school building or something. I was just a kid, nobody told me anything. But I remember how she came home in the middle of the school year and nobody would talk about why."

The school counselors decided I needed a break. That was how Julie had described it that day in the café.

"But I thought they got her help," Ethan said. "I thought, after that . . . I thought they got her help."

"I don't think it always works that way."

"I don't even know if there were other times after that."

Other times, he said, like they could have been talking about anything. Julie had tried to commit suicide as a teenager, had succeeded eight years later, and the space between was filled with unknowns and euphemisms, careful avoidances and awkward silences, all the ways people had of talking around a thing they were too afraid to face.

"She mentioned that when I talked to her," Sorrow said.

"She did?"

"Well, not really. She just said she was sent home from school. She didn't say why. She and Patience became friends for a little while after that." Sorrow turned her tea mug in her hands. "The sheriff asked me if I knew why Julie picked—why she went to the cider house."

"I didn't know they were friends," Ethan said.

"I'd kinda forgotten about it, until recently. I don't think anybody was supposed to know," Sorrow said. "It was a secret. They weren't even allowed to talk to each other. But you know it was . . ." Her voice caught, and she breathed for a moment to steady herself. "You know she was the one who saw the fire that night? From her window."

"Yeah," Ethan said softly. "I know."

"And she had to look out there every day and see where her friend died and it was just a—a reminder, every day, and she couldn't even tell anybody and . . ."

And Sorrow had tracked her down in a café and asked her about it without warning. It was never only one conversation. That was what Sheriff Reyes had said, and Sorrow knew if she asked, Dr. Silva would say the same. But it must have been painful for Julie, and that was an awful feeling, knowing in retrospect that she might have helped rather than hurt, if only she had known.

"Our families are so fucking stupid," Ethan said.

"Yeah."

In the kitchen the water was running, and there was a soft clatter as Grandma searched through utensils in a drawer.

"I remember talking to her," Ethan said.

"Julie?"

"Patience."

Sorrow looked at him. "You do?"

"A little. There was this one Christmas. I was like six or seven. Young enough that my parents were still trying to make the whole happy-family holidays thing happen. We were over at my aunt and uncle's for presents and food and everything, and of course everybody started fighting about . . ." Ethan let out a long sigh. "Something. I don't know what. They always did. Cass was crying. I decided I'd rather go outside and just . . . get out. Away from all the shouting. It was getting dark and it was snowing, but I went anyway. I knew I wasn't supposed to go over to your place. That was like the number one rule, right? But if you tell a dumb kid to stay away from the scary ladies in the haunted orchard next door, what's the first thing he's going to do when he gets a chance?"

Sorrow imagined a tiny towheaded Ethan tramping away from the noise of a family argument under a dark gray December sky, and the forbidden orchard next door his only escape.

"I'm guessing you didn't get caught," she said.

"Not by anybody in my family," Ethan said. "Your sister caught me, though. Or, not caught me, she just found me and asked me if I was lost."

Patience would have smiled through the falling snow, soft and kind and just a little bit teasing, her cheeks pink beneath her green wool hat, her hazel eyes warm.

"I said I wasn't. I don't think she believed me. She asked me if I wanted her to show me the way home and I said no, so she asked me if I wanted to climb a tree instead," Ethan said. "That sounded way better than going home, so we went up to that huge oak on the hill, and she helped me up onto one of the low branches—not that high or anything—and climbed up there too. She asked me if I ever stopped and listened to the snow falling."

Patience had asked Sorrow the exact same thing once, and Sorrow had laughed, told her she was being stupid, told her there was nothing to hear. Patience had laughed right back at her and said she didn't know how to listen. She was always so sure she knew better. Sorrow didn't know where that certainty had come from. She couldn't imagine ever being that sure about anything.

"She said if I listened hard enough," Ethan went on, "I could hear the orchard whispering. Not like it was creepy or anything.

She said it like it was . . . just the way it was." He was quiet for a moment. "When it got dark she walked me back to the fence, and she told me I could come back anytime I wanted to get away."

Sorrow took a sip of her tea. The clouds didn't seem to be lifting as the morning crept along. If anything they were hunkering down, sinking over the mountain peaks, threading a mist as fine as cobwebs between the trees. It wasn't chilly enough to be uncomfortable, but still she could feel the cool air on her arms and legs, a light touch on her skin.

"Is it cloudy like this in town?" Sorrow asked.

If the question surprised him, he didn't show it. "Yeah. It might rain later."

"That would be good."

Sorrow scraped the heel of her shoe over the packed dirt at the base of the porch steps. She wondered if locals were looking at the sky with suspicious eyes, whispering about witch weather, wondering when it would break. It hadn't stayed cold, not like in the old stories where the unnatural weather lasted weeks or months, but the sun remained stubbornly hidden.

A minute or so of quiet, then Ethan exhaled tiredly, slumped against the porch post, and rubbed his eyes. "I can't even imagine what this must be like for Cassie."

Sorrow felt a pang in her chest. "Have you talked to her?"

"No. I tried to go over there, but my aunt told me . . ." His lips twisted, nothing like a smile. "Well, she said to come back later, and shut the door in my face. Cassie hasn't answered my texts. I think they took her phone away."

"Why would they do that?"

"I don't know. I have no idea what they're doing. It's not like she would even want to talk to me, but . . ." A shrug, and Ethan put his hands down to push himself off the step. "We should probably help Miss P with breakfast."

There wasn't much to help with. Grandma had made muffins, and Sorrow fixed more tea while Ethan set out plates. They sat at the table together, but nobody launched into the usual morning conversation about what projects they would work on around the farm that day.

After a couple of minutes of silence, Ethan asked, "Where's Verity?"

Grandma and Sorrow looked up at the same time, casting their eyes toward the ceiling. When Sorrow dropped her gaze again, she saw that Ethan had noticed.

"She'll be down," she said.

He said, "Okay," and didn't ask for an explanation, but after a minute he was doing it too: looking up at the ceiling, listening, waiting.

They had finished eating and were cleaning up the dishes before there were footsteps overhead. Sorrow was tense from her neck all the way down her back. She only wanted Verity to come downstairs. Just come downstairs and stop making them worry.

Verity's bedroom door opened. Footsteps in the hallway. The bathroom door closed. Sorrow told herself to relax. The bathroom door opened again—strange how she had learned so long ago to recognize every sound in the house without even thinking about it, the squeak of every board and hinge loud in her memory even when everything else had faded. Verity was walking, but it shouldn't be taking her that long to reach the stairs. It was only ten or twelve steps.

Sorrow draped a dish towel over the edge of the sink. She was stepping toward the doorway when she heard the top stair creak, then a pause, and what sounded like the slap of a hand on the wall, a startled curse—*"shit"*—followed by a series of loud thumps.

Sorrow ran out of the kitchen to find Verity sprawled at the bottom of the stairs. Her limbs were splayed awkwardly, her hair over her face.

"Oh my god." Sorrow dropped to her knees and touched Verity's shoulder, reached for her face. "Are you okay? Holy shit, did you fall? Are you okay?"

Verity moved her head, let out a groan.

"Are you okay? Are you hurt?"

Verity brushed Sorrow's hand away. "Stop poking. I'm fine."

"Are you sure? Can you move? Can you sit up?"

Verity lifted her head and gave Sorrow a baleful glare. "I'm *fine*. I just lost my balance."

"How did you lose your balance? It's only the stairs! Did you hit your head?"

Sorrow reached out to grab Verity's chin, lifted her face to look her in the eye. She didn't even know what to look for. Verity's eyes seemed normal. She was avoiding Sorrow's gaze, but her pupils weren't pinpoint small or blown wide. A touch on Sorrow's shoulder—Grandma, leaning down to look too.

Verity pushed Sorrow's hand away a second time and shifted around so she was sitting on the step. "Stop crowding me. I'm fine."

"Should I call 911?" Ethan was standing in the kitchen doorway; he already had the phone in hand.

Verity's gaze snapped up to him. "What are you doing here?"

Ethan blinked, taken aback. "I, uh, came over to—should I?" He was asking Grandma, not Verity.

"You're not supposed to be here today," Verity said. She looked away from him quickly, her cheeks burning pink. "We didn't ask you to come over."

"But I—"

"Put the phone down."

"What the fuck," Sorrow said. "He's only trying to help. You *fell*. You could be seriously hurt."

"I'm not hurt at all. I'm fine," Verity said. "I'd be a lot more fine if you weren't all crowding around me like I'm some kind of zoo animal."

Sorrow gave Ethan an apologetic look. "Just wait outside?"

He nodded and hung up the phone; the screen door clapped as he went out to the porch.

"Do you need a doctor?" Sorrow said. Her voice was shaking; she swallowed, hard, and her throat ached. "Did you hit your head?"

"Nothing happened," Verity said. She put her hands down to lever herself up, but she changed her mind and sat on the step again. "I just got a little dizzy. I missed the top step."

"Okay, but, how did—" Sorrow looked up at Grandma, down at Verity again, her mind buzzing with an awful possibility. "When did you last have anything to eat?"

"What? I had dinner with you last night. Don't be stupid."

Some part of Sorrow's mind was mildly shocked at Verity's words—she had never called Sorrow *stupid* before, she didn't say things like that—but she brushed it aside, because Verity was avoiding her eyes, turning her head this way and that to keep from looking at Sorrow and Grandma.

"You barely ate two bites last night." Sorrow's voice was so unsteady she nearly choked on the words. "You didn't have any lunch or breakfast. You were working outside for hours and—did you even have any water? You were out there for hours. Did you eat the day before that?" The question rose to a frightened pitch. She couldn't remember. She hadn't been paying attention. How could she not have been paying attention? She looked up at Grandma. "Has she eaten anything? When did she last eat anything?"

Grandma shook her head.

"What the fuck!" Sorrow shouted. "That's not an answer! How can you not know? It's been three days? Is that how long? How can—"

"Stop shouting, Sorrow," Verity snapped. "You're overreacting."

"Don't tell me to stop shouting when *you're not eating*! What the fuck are you even—"

Grandma touched Sorrow's shoulder, and Sorrow closed her mouth with a click. Grandma nudged her aside, and Sorrow stepped back, crossed her arms over her chest, uncrossed them, wrapped them again around her middle.

Grandma eased herself, knees cracking, to squeeze in beside

Verity on the stairs. She unclipped her pen from the string around her neck and wrote something in her notebook.

"No," Verity said. "I don't think that's—"

"What?" Sorrow said.

Grandma was still writing.

"Do you need a doctor?" Sorrow asked. "Does she need a doctor?"

Grandma's hand stilled, and for a moment neither of them moved. There was worry in the lines around Grandma's eyes, and in the shadows on Verity's face there was doubt and stubbornness and something almost like shame.

Verity let out a breath. "Fine," she said. "I'll call her."

Grandma nodded shortly. She held out a hand, and Sorrow helped her to her feet. Verity refused the same help, but she kept one hand on the wall as she stood and made her way into the kitchen. Grandma nudged Sorrow's elbow and pointed to the back door.

"But," Sorrow began, and Grandma pointed again.

Sorrow let herself be steered outside, across the porch and down the steps, Grandma following right behind her. Ethan hadn't left; he was waiting on the lawn.

"Is she okay?" he asked.

"I don't know," Sorrow said. "I don't think she's badly hurt. Who is she calling?"

Grandma held out her notebook.

On the first line: *You have to call Dr. Parker.*

The name was familiar. Verity's psychiatrist, the woman who had been treating her since her first hospitalization eight years ago.

She had come up during their phone conversations over the years.

And on the second: *You are scaring your daughter.*

A storm of questions crowded into Sorrow's mind. This was terrain she didn't know how to navigate. She hadn't even noticed that Verity wasn't eating—but that wasn't entirely true. She had noticed, but she hadn't known she was supposed to pay attention. Long hours of quiet, days spent in bed, a quiet retreat from the world, these were the things she had been worrying about, the anxious thoughts gnawing at her mind like bugs hollowing out a fallen log, but she hadn't known to look for this one.

She and Grandma and Ethan stood side by side at the base of the steps, staring toward the house, waiting. They could hear only the murmur of Verity's voice, see only her silhouette through the screen door. Sorrow rubbed at her arms. The air was damp and misty, teasing her skin with the faintest promise of rain. She hadn't known. She should have known.

27

DR. PARKER WAS an older woman with buzzed gray hair and horn-rimmed glasses. She wore a brown cardigan, a flowing long skirt, and hiking shoes. She didn't look like a psychiatrist; she looked like any woman who might be browsing the weekend farmers' market, arguing over the price of ramps and fiddleheads.

"Sorrow," she said, and she smiled. "You are Sorrow, aren't you?"

Sorrow nodded stiffly.

"My name is Miranda Parker. I'm your mother's doctor."

"Are you going to—can you check her out? She fell—"

"She told me about that. How are you feeling?" Dr. Parker blinked at Sorrow expectantly.

Sorrow stared right back at her. "I'm not the one who fell down the stairs." And I have my own therapist, thanks, but she kept that thought to herself.

"You did have a very traumatic experience the other day," Dr. Parker said. "It's okay if you're not fine. Is your grandmother here?" Dr. Parker leaned to look around Sorrow. "Good morning, Miss P."

Grandma stood in the doorway to the kitchen with her arms crossed. She didn't even nod a greeting.

"Where is Verity?" Dr. Parker asked.

"Upstairs," Sorrow said. "She went to get dressed."

"Well." Dr. Parker was still smiling. "Let's go talk to her. May I come in?"

Sorrow stood aside to let her through the door. The doctor had said *let's* but she brushed by Sorrow to climb the stairs; she didn't have to ask where to go. Sorrow considered following, then considered eavesdropping, but in the end she shuffled into the kitchen to sit with Grandma. She wanted to feel better that an adult, a professional, was here to take over. She wanted to be relieved there was somebody who could help. Instead she only felt tired and anxious and sick to her stomach.

And angry. She was angry too. Verity was a grown woman. She shouldn't need somebody holding her hand just to remind her to eat. She shouldn't need somebody watching her just to be sure she didn't get so dizzy she fell down the stairs. She could have been seriously hurt. The wrong angle, a different tumble, and she could have snapped a bone or given herself a concussion or broken her neck and it was so *stupid*, so incredibly stupid, and the longer she stewed on it the angrier Sorrow became.

"Dr. Parker has been here before?" she asked.

Grandma nodded.

Sorrow looked at her, eyes narrow. "Has this happened before? The not eating?"

A pause, then another nod.

"Well, I didn't know that. I had no fucking idea."

Grandma raised an eyebrow, and Sorrow fidgeted in her chair.

"Sorry. But I think I'm entitled to a little bit of bad language. What are they talking about? What's Dr. Parker like?"

Grandma toyed with her pen a moment before answering: *She has very firm ideas about what's best.*

Sorrow sighed. "Yeah. I don't like her either."

That earned her a small smile, and Grandma reached out to squeeze her hand. Sorrow only let go when Dr. Parker and Verity came down the stairs.

"I'm going with Dr. Parker for a while," Verity said.

Sorrow shoved to her feet. "Going where? Do you need X-rays or something?"

Verity paused at the front door. When she looked back at Sorrow, her expression was tired, but her eyes were clear. "I already told you I'm not hurt. If it rains later, you'll need to make sure the French drain on the side—where's Ethan?"

"Uh, he left," Sorrow said. "You know, after you yelled at him for trying to help?"

Verity looked momentarily chagrined. "He didn't have to leave."

"Well, I'm sorry that your favorite kid who you like better than your real kid took off, but will you—what's that?"

Sorrow pointed. Verity was holding an overnight bag in one hand.

Verity shifted away from her, turning toward the door. She had her purse over her shoulder, a jacket on. She hadn't just gotten dressed. She had packed to leave.

"Where are you going?" Sorrow said. "Are you *leaving*?"

Dr. Parker stepped between them. She was still smiling, her expression as mild and pleasant as could be, but her voice was firm when she said, "Go on outside, Verity. I'll talk to Sorrow for a little bit."

"Wait, no, don't—"

But Verity was already going outside, her head ducked and shoulders hunched like she was glad to have Dr. Parker telling her what to do. When the front door snapped shut, Dr. Parker turned to Sorrow and said, "We're going to my office to talk for a little while, then decide what happens next."

"What does that mean? Decide what?"

Dr. Parker's expression was patient and sympathetic. "This is the first time you've visited your mother since you were a child, isn't it?"

There was no censure in her voice, but still Sorrow heard an accusation. "Yeah. But we talk."

"I know that, and I've always thought that was healthy for both of you. But it's important for you to realize that there's a lot you don't know about how your mother manages her illness. Not," Dr. Parker added pointedly, when Sorrow opened her mouth to respond, "because you don't care, or because you aren't old enough to understand, but because it's very personal and very difficult for her. I know it doesn't seem like it right now, not after the terrible few days you've had, but the fact that Verity called me this morning is a good sign. She's asking for help, and that's a good thing."

Sorrow didn't like the way Dr. Parker was looking at her, knowingly and maybe a little bit condescendingly, like she was waiting for Sorrow to catch up to something everybody else had already figured out. It didn't feel like a good thing. It felt like Verity had stopped eating for three days, risked injuring herself seriously with a fall, and then decided to run away, leaving Sorrow and Grandma behind.

"You didn't answer my question," Sorrow said. "Where are you going?"

"If she doesn't feel up to coming home today, we'll do as we've done before and admit her for an observation period," Dr. Parker explained.

"You mean admit her to a hospital. That's what you mean, right?"

"It's a possibility. We're going to talk about it."

"But she's—but before this week, before our neighbor—"

"I know about the Abrams girl."

"Julie," Sorrow said, her voice hoarse. "Her name was Julie."

Dr. Parker nodded slightly. "I know about Julie. And I agree that her death is a large part of why your mother is struggling. But it's not the only major change in her life recently, is it?"

"No, but—"

She meant Sorrow.

Here, now. Visiting for the first time in eight years. That was what Dr. Parker was talking about. Verity had never invited her. Sorrow had done that all herself. She had insisted. All she had cared about were her own reasons for coming back, and she had never once thought that she might be steamrolling decisions Verity had made to protect herself.

"Sorrow," Dr. Parker said.

Sorrow hated that she said her name with such familiarity, like they knew each other.

"This isn't a bad thing. The fact that she recognizes that she has to take care of herself following these difficult days is a good thing."

"She wasn't even going to call you until Grandma told her to," Sorrow pointed out.

Dr. Parker was unfazed. "And it's good that your grandmother is looking out for her too. Trust me, Sorrow, what Verity is doing right now is exactly what she should be doing to take care of herself. This is her life, and she is handling it the best she can."

"When will she be back?" Sorrow asked.

"Nothing is decided yet. We'll be in touch later, okay?" Dr. Parker smiled. "Try not to worry."

Sorrow watched them drive away, and she stood there in the open door for a long time, staring at the driveway and the maple trees. The wind rose, rustling the leaves and pushing damp, cool air into the house. She felt a spattering of droplets on her arms. She wiped them away, leaned out to look at the sky. The clouds were so low they obscured the tops of the hills, shrouded the trees with gauzy gray. It would be raining soon. She didn't even know what a French drain was, much less why Verity was worried about it. She wondered how that would go over if she called Ethan: She didn't say she was sorry for snapping at you, but she does want you to fix the drainage.

Sorrow shut the door and went inside. She joined her grandmother at the kitchen table again, took a breath, and said, "I have a lot of questions."

She thought her voice was admirably steady, all things considered, but her lips were dry, her hands trembling. She curled her fingers into a fist and tucked them in her lap. Grandma politely pretended not to notice. She opened her notebook and picked up her pen.

"Were you avoiding Dr. Parker on purpose?" Sorrow asked. "You didn't even come to the door."

A crook of one eyebrow answered her question even before Grandma started writing. *We've had disagreements in the past.*

"So you left me to deal with her. Thanks for that. What did you disagree about?"

About what's best for my daughter.

"What do you mean?"

Instead of answering, Grandma tapped the pen thoughtfully on the page.

"Do you know how long she'll be gone?"

It depends. Could be only a few days. Could be longer.

"How many times has she been to the hospital before? Since the first?"

Three since then.

"Three?" Sorrow thought back, counting through the years.

She didn't want you to know.

And Sorrow had never asked.

When they talked on the phone, she asked about the farm, about the town, about the mountains and the weather, but no matter what she heard in Verity's voice, no matter what silences fell between them when they ran out of things to say, she didn't ask. Even without the specter of Patience in her mind, shaking her that last day in the orchard and saying, *Don't you dare*, she had never asked.

"I don't even know where she goes," she said helplessly. "Where is the hospital?"

The inpatient facility is in Burlington, ever since Dr. Parker transferred.

Sorrow considered that for a moment. There were so many things she had failed to do, and every one felt like a deep furrow inside her, wounds old and new being ripped open and exposed.

But that wasn't all that was going on. There was something else missing.

"I get the feeling everybody thinks I know something that I'm not sure I know," she said carefully. She watched her grandmother's face as she spoke. "But I'm not an idiot. I know that nobody checks into a psychiatric hospital just because she's feeling bad. I know there's more to it than that. But I don't remember. There's just this . . . space. Dad's only ever told me that Verity had a breakdown. He's never told me anything else. Maybe I should have asked, even if I didn't want to know. But I want to know now."

Grandma waited, pen hovering above the page. She was looking at Sorrow like she couldn't quite figure out what Sorrow was asking. Like she was waiting for Sorrow to come around to the answer herself.

"Even you're looking at me like that. What is it? What is it that everybody thinks I remember?"

A slow nod, and Grandma began writing.

Rain struck the window in a sudden burst. The storm was rolling across the western orchard in broad gray sheets. They would have to close the windows. They had to check the drainage. There was still work to be done.

When she turned away from the window, Grandma had finished writing.

You were the one who found her.

28

EIGHT YEARS AGO

AFTER PATIENCE DIED, spring came to Abrams Valley, but not to the Lovegood farm.

The rain cleared, the days warmed, and blue skies reigned. A soft green blush crept over the land as tender grass sprouted and trees unfurled their first leaves. The last lingering patches of snow sank into the soil, and the air was rich with the scent of damp earth. Bees emerged from wherever they hid during the winter, and with them mosquitoes and flies, ticks and crickets, the incessant insect hum punctuated by the cheerful chatter of birds and the chiming chorus of spring peepers.

The mountains and valleys were returning to life after a long winter, but the Lovegood orchard wasn't waking with them.

Sorrow stood at the window in Mom's room, her elbows folded on the wooden sill.

"Grandma's planting beans today," she said. "Beans and carrots and peas. She says it's warm enough."

In the garden below, Grandma's pale blue dress and yellow straw hat were the only spots of color. The garden and yard were still brown, and every morning there was a crackle of frost that took far too long to burn off. None of the early flowers had sprouted from their bulbs, and even if they had, the biting chill would have shriveled the petals as soon as they blossomed.

"I hope it's finally warm enough," Sorrow said, a little quieter.

She crossed the room to her mother's bedside. Mom's eyes were damp and there were dried tear tracks on her cheeks. Sorrow brushed a strand of dark hair back from her face; her skin was warm to the touch.

"Sorrow," Mom said, her voice as hoarse as sandpaper.

"Mom?" A bright burst of hope flared in Sorrow's chest.

Mom took in a shaky breath, as if to brace herself. "Are they going to let her come home?"

As quickly as it had sparked, Sorrow's hope pinched out. "I don't know," she whispered.

"She's my little girl," Mom said. "I want her to come home."

"I know, Mommy."

"It's so cold. We need her home. The orchard needs her."

"I know."

It had been two weeks since Patience had died, but they

weren't yet allowed to bury her. Sheriff Moskowitz had explained to Grandma that the police investigation wouldn't be finished until they were certain the fire had been an accident. Only when that was settled could Patience have a funeral.

Sorrow kissed her mother's cheek. "We're going to make chicken and biscuits tonight. It'll be really good. I know you like that." She rounded the bed and walked to the door, but before she left she looked back. "It's a lot nicer today. Maybe you can come out and sit in the sun for a little bit?"

Mom didn't answer. Sorrow left her alone.

Sorrow wanted to help, but she didn't know what to do. Mom never wanted to eat, and at night she only slept when she took medicine. She didn't get dressed in the morning and she hadn't left the farm in over a week. The last time, when she had taken Sorrow into town for groceries, she had started crying in the middle of the store, big, fat tears rolling down her cheeks while her shoulders shook and her breath shuddered. Sorrow had pulled her arm and pleaded with her to leave, until finally they'd abandoned their cart and walked out empty-handed. The clerks and other customers had gaped and whispered, but nobody had tried to help.

Sometimes Sorrow woke to hear Mom pacing up and down in the hall, from the top of the stairs to the closed door of Patience's room. She walked back and forth, over and over, the slow rhythm of her steps lulling Sorrow to sleep.

The worst of it was that some days when Sorrow woke, first thing in the morning or in the middle of the night, there was a moment when she forgot. She forgot Patience was dead. Before she opened her eyes, before she felt the sun through the window or heard the rooster crowing to accompany dawn birdsong, there was a moment where her traitorous mind listened for the sound of voices downstairs, the familiar morning chatter of Mom and Patience making breakfast. For Patience's steps quick on the stairs, for the turn of her bedroom doorknob, for a cheerful voice calling *Wake up, sleepyhead, wake up—*

Then she would remember, and everything would crash over her like an avalanche.

Sorrow pulled on her bulky green sweater and heavy boots and went out into the orchard. She searched the apple trees for opening buds, but after she checked ten trees in a row and found none, she had to admit nothing had changed since yesterday. Not a single apple tree was sprouting its leaves. The orchard was as grim and gray as it had been in the middle of winter.

Witch weather. That was what Mrs. Roche had called it when she'd stopped by with a casserole the other day. She had sipped the tea Grandma made for her and nodded knowingly toward the kitchen window and she'd said, "This witch weather will break soon, Perseverance. It will break."

Sorrow stopped looking for spring leaves and began looking for favors instead. In the pocket of her skirt, she was carrying the eyeglasses she had found in the cemetery, as she had carried them every day since Patience had died. Sometimes she took them from her pocket and put them on—carefully, as Patience had shown her—and squinted at a world that was half clear, half fractured, blurred almost beyond recognition.

She didn't like that they were the last favor she would ever find while walking through the orchard with Patience. It gave her a cold, squirmy feeling in her stomach to remember how she had told Patience she didn't like them. She could never take that back now.

There should have been more favors by now. Even if the weather wasn't warming like it should, even if the trees weren't budding, there should have been *something*. If she found a pretty seashell or polished stone, something bright and colorful, she could bring it to Mom and cheer her up. But the orchard didn't offer so much as a single Indian Head penny.

What she found instead, nestled at the base of an apple tree, were the corpses of two little birds.

Sorrow stared down at them for a long time, a curious hollow ache growing inside her.

They were tiny, no more than a few days hatched. Scattered around them were the remains of frail blue eggshells.

She lived on a farm, in the woods; she had seen dead things before. Last winter during a bad snowstorm a buck with broad antlers had been caught on the fence between the orchard and the nature preserve. Mom hadn't found it until it was already dead and the meat spoiling. For weeks every eastward turn of the wind had carried a foul, septic stench. Birds had picked at the corpse until it had shrunk down to a saggy sack of fur and bones.

No predator or accident had killed these chicks, only the cold. They had hatched expecting springtime warmth, found bitter clinging winter instead, and died before they had a chance to live.

A burst of song drew Sorrow's attention upward. There was

a nest huddled in the tree, and hopping along the branch beside it was the mother bluebird. She jumped back and forth, back and forth, her wings fluttering anxiously, chirping out a question to anybody who could hear. Each time she reached her nest she looked into it again, as though she might find it not empty that time.

Sorrow shoved a pile of leaf debris over the chicks and hoped the mother bird wouldn't find them.

She walked north, toward the cider house, an uncomfortable tickle of guilt making her glance over her shoulder every few steps. She wasn't allowed to go near the ruined building, but she didn't want to get too close anyway. She only wanted to see, even though she hated the way it looked, so burned and broken. She stopped halfway down the hill. Slid to the ground with her back to an apple tree and hugged her knees to her chest.

The cider house was a smudge of black through the naked trees, a hole where light and color ought to be. Half the roof was caved in, but the building hadn't collapsed. The meadow was brown and yellow, free of snow but still winter-dormant, and the grass all around had been churned up by fire trucks and police cars. The ambulance had taken Patience away after the firemen put the fire out.

They had known it was her at first by the dress she wore and the barrettes in her hair, later by tests they did in a laboratory.

Sheriff Moskowitz had explained that to Mom and Grandma when Sorrow wasn't supposed to be listening. He asked if Patience had a boyfriend. He asked if they had seen Patience talking to strangers. He asked if she had ever sneaked out or lied about where she was going. He asked if they had any idea what she would have been doing out in the orchard that night. To every question, Grandma shook her head silently and Mom said, "No, nothing, no," repeating herself until the words became meaningless sounds.

Nobody asked Sorrow anything. She expected it every day, for the sheriff to return to the house and demand to speak with her, for him to sit her down and look at her with his sad eyes and say that he knew she was lying, he knew everything, and it was time for her to tell him. And when he did, the secrets Sorrow had been holding inside would crack open like a hornet's nest.

But a week passed, then another, and the sheriff did not ask. He said hello to her when he came to the house, ruffled her hair fondly, but he never looked her in the eye and said he knew she was hiding something.

She watched the Abrams house for a long time. Their car was parked outside, but Sorrow didn't see anybody. Mrs. Roche had said they would soon be leaving to stay with Mrs. Abrams's family in Boston, because Julie was so upset from seeing the fire she had been crying and crying for days. The other Mr. Abrams and his family were going to watch the house while they were gone. A blue tarp fluttered over the burned corner of the barn, lifting and falling with every gust of wind like a creature breathing. The Abrams fields were brown near the fence, but farther away their land was greening as the weather warmed. Bushes along the driveway erupted with small white flowers. A pair of jays chased each other across the meadow, dipping and diving, and swept into the woods.

The sight made Sorrow's insides ache. She didn't want to look at it anymore, but she didn't want to go back to the house either, where everything was cold and quiet and wrong. She wanted to run into the mountains and hide and never come back, the way Grace Lovegood had when her mother had killed her sisters and brothers. Run away to crawl into a fox's burrow, alone and scared until she heard the shouts of townspeople looking for her. Then she must have crawled out of her hiding place and—

Sorrow didn't know where she went next. She had never heard the rest of the story. She didn't know who had taken care of Grace after her mother was hanged, if there had been anybody at all.

She could ask Mom. Sorrow stood slowly and brushed dried leaves from her skirt. When she got back to the house, she could ask Mom to tell her the rest of the story. She hadn't asked for a story since before the fire, but Mom wouldn't refuse, no matter how sad and tired she was. She never refused a story. Sorrow would bring her a cup of tea sweetened with honey and climb into bed next to her, and Mom would sit up with the pillow bunched behind her, her voice growing less hoarse and less distant the more she talked, and when she was finished they would go downstairs together to help Grandma make chicken and biscuits for dinner.

Emboldened by her decision, Sorrow ran back to the house. By the time she reached the fallow field, she was breathless with excitement. She knew how to help Mom now. She skipped along the dirt road and up the hill. The day felt a little warmer than it had before, the sun a bit stronger. She knew this was the right thing to do.

Grandma was sitting on the back porch with her quilting frame. The needle was still stuck in the fabric, untouched.

"I'm going to ask Mom for a story," Sorrow said.

She yanked the screen door open, and Grandma reached out, her knobby fingers beckoning.

"Grandma?"

Grandma gestured her closer. She pulled Sorrow into a hug and pressed a kiss to the side of her head.

Sorrow squirmed away. "I'm going to get her to come down for dinner. You'll see. I promise."

She was halfway up the steps before she remembered she wanted to make tea, so she had to go back down, set the water to boiling, and find Mom's favorite mug, the one she had bought from a potter named Eulalie at the farmers' market. Patience had always called it the Eulalie Mug, but Sorrow didn't know if it was okay to call it that anymore. She didn't know if it would make Mom smile or cry. She decided she wouldn't call it anything, not until Mom did first.

When the tea was finally ready, she carried it upstairs, wincing when a few hot drops sloshed over the side. She opened the bedroom door with her free hand.

"Mom?"

Mom's room was dark and stuffy; she must have closed the window and drawn the curtains after Sorrow left. In the faint light from the hallway she could barely make out Mom's shape in the bed.

"Mom, I brought you tea. With honey."

Sorrow's boot crunched on something on the floor. She looked down.

It was a small pill, now ground into white powder. There was another one a couple of steps ahead. A small orange bottle lay on the floor beside the bed. Sorrow set the tea on Mom's bedside table and picked up the bottle.

"Mom, you dropped your medicine." She shook the bottle; there was only one pill left inside. "Mom?"

Sorrow reached for her shoulder to shake her awake. Mom groaned softly but didn't open her eyes.

"Mom? Come on, Mom, wake up."

Sorrow's heart began to beat quickly. Her hands were shaking. There was a line of spit trailing from Mom's mouth, glistening and wet on her jaw.

"Mom? Please wake up. Mom?"

Sorrow shook her again. Mom didn't even groan this time.

"Grandma!" Sorrow ran into the hallway and shouted from the top of the stairs. "Grandma, Mom won't wake up! Grandma!"

Downstairs the screen door opened, then snapped shut, and Grandma was hurrying up the stairs. She pushed past Sorrow and perched on the edge of Mom's bed. Grandma shook her shoulders, patted her cheeks gently.

"I tried that." Sorrow's eyes were hot with tears and it was hard to breathe. "I *tried* that already!"

Grandma picked up the pill bottle and shook it, just as Sorrow had done.

"It was on the floor," Sorrow said.

Grandma dropped the bottle onto the bed and grabbed the pen and notebook she wore around her neck. She scribbled some words and shoved the page at Sorrow.

Go to Abrams. Tell them to call ambulance.

Sorrow stared at the words on the page. "The Abramses? But—"

Grandma shook the page. When Sorrow still didn't move, she stuffed the note into Sorrow's hand and turned her to the door with a shooing motion: *Go.*

Sorrow ran. Down the steps and out of the house, around the yard to the driveway, and she sprinted through the orchard so fast she felt every jolting step in her bones and her teeth. She knew Mom would hate that she was going to the Abramses, hate that she was inviting them into family business, but she didn't stop, didn't even pause, and in a flash she was stumbling down the hill to the cider house meadow. She cut herself twice ducking through the barbed wire fence, and blood blossomed on her hand and wrist as she sprinted through the field on the other side.

Then she was pounding on their door, and Mr. Abrams was answering. His eyes went wide with surprise and his voice was booming and scary, but Sorrow could barely understand the words. He guided her inside, bewilderment etched all over his face. Sorrow had never been in the Abrams house before. Mr. Abrams seemed tall and alien and terrible, looking down at her, waiting for her to explain herself. Sorrow sucked in several breaths before she remembered Grandma's note. She handed the crumpled paper to Mr. Abrams, and her legs gave way as he read it over. He asked her twice what was going on, but she couldn't answer. He shouted for Mrs. Abrams and ran to the phone. Sorrow thought, as she wheezed through the taste of iron at the back of her throat, that she needed to tell them Mom was sick, needed to tell them that she had never seen Mom so still and so limp. Mom would hate it. She would hate it more than she hated anything, that Sorrow was here asking the Abramses for help, but Sorrow didn't care. She didn't care if Mom hated her forever and ever as long as they helped. She needed to make them understand. She had never seen Grandma so scared.

29

PRIDE LOVEGOOD

1914–1980

WHERE ONCE THERE had been a narrow muddy track, carved up by two hundred years of cart wheels, there was now a ribbon of level, graded dirt wide enough for two vehicles to pass. Every step Pride took stirred up a cloud of dust around her ankles. The day was warm, summer's last glimmering, but autumn had begun to turn the mountains gold and red.

The seven miles between town and the Lovegood orchard had seemed a tiny distance when Pride was a child, when her feet had been so swift there was nobody who could beat her in a footrace, not even boys who were three or four years her senior and propelled by stubborn arrogance. It felt a lot longer now. She ought to have hitched a ride from where the Greyhound dropped her off in town, but nobody recognized her anymore, and every face she'd seen had belonged to a stranger.

It was hard to remember their names now, those sulking boys with dust on their faces. It didn't matter. She was sixty-six years old, and there was cancer in her brain. She had told the doctor, in his grim little office lined with posters of human bodies stripped down to component systems, that she would like to spend her last days in the mountains rather than a sterile hospital room. Her doctor had smiled a sad smile, too ancient for his barely-six-years-out-of-medical-school face, and he had said, "Go home. Go while you still can."

So here she was, walking along a dirt road on a late summer day, and the air tasted green, smelled green, felt green in the sticky-slick sweat that gathered beneath her clothes. The orchard was waiting for her, right where she'd left it.

Fifty years away and her memory was hazy. She remembered Ma and Dad and their musician friends drinking smuggled Canadian whisky on the back porch. There had been laughing, carrying on, drifting smoke. The twins, nine years old and wild as animals, shouting that they were going for a swim in Peddler's Creek. The baby had been crying. She remembered that well enough. Baby Devy crying her little head off like she wouldn't ever stop.

But she must have stopped, at some point, because Pride remembered quiet too. A suffocating silence at dusk. Dad and the men hissing at each other, counting bullets. Fear curdling in her stomach, fear and anger and a desperate swallowed scream. Ma in the doorway with her shotgun, her sharp face illuminated when she struck her lighter, and smoke curling around her head like a veil.

The crack of a shot echoing through the twilight.

Pride had stopped walking. There was a phantom ache in her shoulder: the kick of a shotgun. A pain she hadn't thought she would ever forget. Her finger had twitched before she told it to. A silhouette had crumpled in the darkness.

She rubbed at her shoulder, arthritic fingers massaging a bruise that had faded fifty years ago, and she scuffed one foot forward, then the other, creaking her old limbs into motion again.

She stood now at the turn to the Lovegood farm. The trees were heavy with apples; their sharp, sweet scent filled the air. Another couple of weeks and it would be time for the harvest.

She walked up the drive through the tunnel of sugar maples, and with every step she half expected the twins to come whooping from the house to greet her. Cherish taller and faster, Charles two steps behind.

But the twins were gone. They had been dead for more than fifty years, and she remembered how pale their bodies had been, laid out side by side in their best clothes. After Simon Abrams and his wretched brother had ambushed them in the woods, Charles had died at once, but Cherish had lingered a few days longer, going mad with fever until she finally slipped away to join her twin. Charles's funeral shirt didn't fit right; the bullet had caved in his skinny chest. It had started raining the day he died, rained all through that Bloody July, and it was raining still the day the twins were buried together in the cemetery grove. Pride had stood beside their little graves and felt the roots of the old ash trees reaching up for her from beneath the soil, imagined them wrapping around her ankles, dragging her down, down, never letting go.

The baby was the only one left now. Devotion had a daughter and a granddaughter of her own. They had exchanged letters over the years, but Pride had never returned, and, as far as she knew, Devotion had never traveled more than ten miles from the Lovegood farm.

When she reached the house, Pride bypassed the front door—they had never used it anyway—and walked around to the back. The garden was rich with autumn bounty: cornstalks shoulder-high, gourds and pumpkins tumbling from beneath blankets of leaves. The door to the barn was open, but there was nobody about.

Pride had one foot on the porch step, one hand on the rail, when she saw Ma's lighter.

It was sitting there on the railing, set upright in the center of the board. Her mother's old naphtha lighter, the one Dad had given to her after they'd gotten paid for their first successful whisky shipment. It had cost a pretty penny because it was engraved on the side: *To My Joy, With Love and Music, Rosie.* That was what they had called Dad in the clubs and speakeasies. Rosie for Rosenthal. The newspapers had loved that, when he was arrested: *A Lawman's Rosie Murder!*

The lighter was just sitting there on the porch rail, like Ma had set it down to slip inside for a minute, and any second now she would come back out with a hand-rolled cigarette pinched in her fingers, barking orders, making plans.

"The girl found that."

Pride turned, and for one trembling heartbeat she was looking into a mirror. She was the elder by ten years, but in their decades apart she and Devotion had crept toward a median. They were both old women now, their wood-brown hair gone to gray, skin wrinkled around the eyes. Pride wore her hair short, cropped close to her head ever since her first hospital stay; Devotion had a long braid twisted over her shoulder. Pride was wearing a soft tracksuit in pale yellow, clean except for the clinging road dust. Devotion wore rubber barn boots, trousers patched at the knees, a plaid shirt rolled up at the elbows. Joyful and Rosie's girls, the one who left and the one who stayed.

"The girl?" Pride asked.

Devotion jerked a thumb over her shoulder. "My grandbaby. She was playing down by the pond."

Yesterday, Pride would have been hard-pressed to remember the sound of her mother's voice, so smoky and deep and beloved in the clubs, but she heard echoes of it in Devotion's words. Ma had stopped singing after the police took Dad away.

"What are you doing here?" Devotion asked.

"I'm sick," Pride said. Even now she couldn't bring herself to say *dying*. People told her she was supposed to be brave in the face of cancer, but she was only tired. She was so tired. "I wanted to come back one last time."

Devotion crossed her arms and regarded Pride thoughtfully. She had their father's eyes, blue rather than Lovegood hazel, pale as chips of ice, but without any of the spark or laughter.

Finally she said, "You think you can hold off dying until after the harvest? We need a good one this year, and we'll still have time to get you in the ground before it freezes."

Pride had been away for more than fifty years. It wasn't so much to ask. "I can do that."

"Put your things inside. I've got work to do."

Devotion clomped toward the barn in her heavy rubber boots.

Pride didn't go inside as she had been told. She was still the older sister, after all, no matter what sort of stern old woman Baby Devy had grown up to be. She climbed the steps of the porch, one hand on the rail for balance, and tugged a chair a few inches around so she might have a view of the orchard. She picked up her mother's lighter before she sat down. The naphtha inside should have long since evaporated away, but she gave it a flick, just for the hell of it. A small flame flickered, danced, vanished.

30

SORROW'S EYES WERE gritty with exhaustion when she pulled into the hospital parking lot. It was fifteen minutes before nine o'clock and the start of visiting hours, so she rolled down the window, leaned her head against the seat, and closed her eyes. Morning sounds drifted in: traffic around the hospital campus, the high beep of a locking car, a couple of women talking about their weekend plans in a mix of Spanish and English.

She opened her eyes to watch them pass. They weren't Cuban, but that brief catch of voices sent a wave of homesickness through her.

At five minutes to nine she went inside. She hadn't been in a hospital since Sonia's brother Hector had had a heart attack a few years ago. This one was newer, brighter, less crowded than the one in Miami, but the long corridors and antiseptic smell were the same. She found the elevator and followed the signs to the right nurses' station. The woman behind the desk had her sign in, asked what was in her pockets, confirmed that Dr. Parker had cleared the visit. The room she directed Sorrow to was square and bright, enclosed by windows on two sides: one bank facing the hallway and the nurses' station, the other overlooking the parking lot. Ugly chairs and dull landscape paintings lined the walls. There was a male orderly in white dragging a mop over the floor, an old woman putting together a puzzle on a coffee table, but otherwise the room was empty.

Sorrow walked over to the window. Her shoes squeaked on the linoleum. Everything beyond the glass was the wrong color, gray-tinted and dull. The trees edging the parking lot were too far away. She chose a chair and sat down. Not even a minute passed before a reflection in the window moved. She looked up, and Verity was there.

"Sorrow."

"Hi," Sorrow said.

Verity looked at the chair beside her, looked at the one across from her, chose the latter. She wore a long flowery skirt, a soft sweater—they were the clothes of the old Verity, the one Sorrow had left behind. Barely forty-eight hours had passed since they had last seen each other, but Sorrow was more nervous now than she had been in the airport.

"You didn't have to drive all the way up here," Verity said.

"Dr. Parker said I could visit."

"I'm glad to see you, but it wasn't necessary. I'll probably be home tomorrow."

"Probably?"

"Miranda and I are going to talk about it today," Verity said. "We'll decide then."

Just like that? It's that easy? Sorrow didn't say it. She couldn't ask that. She pressed her lips together and swallowed. There were no bruises she could see. Verity's fall down the stairs hadn't hurt her, at least not in any way that left visible marks.

"Did you . . ." Verity took a breath. "Did you want to talk about something?"

Every single thing Sorrow could think to say was the wrong thing. She could ask how Verity was feeling. If she was eating now. Why she had stopped in the first place. Why she had come here. If she had been thinking about swallowing a handful of sleeping pills again. It was all wrong. There was a drumbeat of fear deep inside her chest, so persistent she couldn't remember what it felt like not to have that anxious terror of making a mistake every time she opened her mouth. She was so tired of feeling like she had to make herself small and quiet to avoid upsetting Verity at all costs. It had never worked anyway.

"We used to have this system," Sorrow said.

Verity's lips were parted; she had been about to say something.

"Me and Patience."

There it was, on hearing Patience's name: a faint crack in

Verity's calm mask. Sorrow stamped down the rise of guilt, held it with her breath until it faded. She was allowed to say her sister's name.

"It was this way of warning each other, I guess. When we were doing or saying something that was going to upset you. If I was being obnoxious Patience would go like this"—Sorrow held out her hand, sliced it side to side: *Cut it out*—"and I would know I had to stop. Calm down. Shut up. Stop whining. Stop bothering you."

"You didn't—"

"And the days when you would shut yourself in your room," Sorrow went on, not raising her voice but not faltering either, "we would sit on the stairs and try to figure out what to do to make it better. We never knew what was going to help and what was going to make it worse. But we tried. We had this whole—" Sorrow's voice caught. She inhaled slowly. "It was this whole system. Patience had figured it all out. I don't know what she would be telling me to do right now."

Sorrow had always believed it came naturally to Patience, a chore as obvious as turning the soil in the spring or harvesting fruit in the fall, caretaking their mother as they did their land. But she had been wrong. Patience had had to figure it out on her own, without help, and it had been guesswork and desperation from the start.

"You don't have to do anything," Verity said.

"You said you remember everything," Sorrow said. "But I don't. There's a lot I don't remember about—"

"You were very young," Verity began.

"There's a lot I don't remember about what happened when

Patience died," Sorrow said firmly. "Before I came back here, I couldn't remember anything. It was just this . . . this black hole. This empty space. Dr. Silva thinks I've blocked it all out because it was traumatic. She didn't think me coming back here would help, but she said it wouldn't hurt to try."

"That's why you wanted to visit?" Verity said, her voice small, hurt.

"And it's why I went looking for Julie, even though I knew it would piss you off that I was talking to her. Did you really not know they were friends?"

"I had no idea." Verity exhaled slowly. "I never even suspected."

"What would you have done if you did know?"

Verity plucked at the fabric of her skirt and did not answer.

"They weren't friends for very long. They didn't have a chance to be, did they?" Sorrow leaned to the side to reach the back pocket of her jeans. "She came looking for me the other day. She gave me this."

She held out the photograph. Verity's hand trembled as she accepted it.

"I thought she was just being, like, friendly," Sorrow said. "She seemed kinda lonely. But she was giving it away. They say people do that before they commit suicide, right? Give things away."

Verity sat back in her chair and studied the photo. Sorrow waited.

"I assumed they would have gotten rid of all of Henry's pictures," Verity said.

A small, sour fear at the back of Sorrow's throat subsided.

That wasn't a denial. It wasn't a refusal to talk. It was, perhaps, an opening.

"Julie said they still have boxes of them in the attic," she said. "I don't even know who he was. I've never heard anything about him."

"You remember Eli Abrams, right?"

"Their grandfather? Ethan and Julie and Cassie's? Yeah. A little. Patience called him Mean Old Eli."

"Henry was Eli's younger brother." Verity traced a fingertip over the photograph, the pressure so light it barely bent the paper. "They weren't anything alike. Henry was this bohemian hippie type. He traveled a lot. He'd gotten arrested protesting Vietnam. That kind of thing. Eli considered him an embarrassment."

Sorrow heard the fondness in her mother's voice. "You liked him."

A small, sad smiled played over Verity's lips. "Your grand-mother liked him. A lot. They were going to be married."

"*What?*" Sorrow's voice rose so loud the orderly across the room gave her a sharp look. "Are you serious?"

"I supposed it does seem hard to imagine," Verity said. "But my father had been dead for more than a decade by the time Henry moved back to town, and my grandmother for a few years. Mom and Henry were both in their forties. They weren't kids. They were doing what they wanted, never mind what anybody else said. Eli hated that they were together, of course, but they didn't care. They were in love."

Verity hadn't once taken her eyes off the photograph.

"That doesn't explain why you were all friendly with Hannah

Abrams," Sorrow pointed out.

"She wasn't Hannah Abrams then," Verity said. "She was still Hannah Lowell when I met her."

"Where was that taken? I don't recognize it."

"Massachusetts. Amherst. We were at college together."

"You went to college?" Sorrow managed not to shout that time, but she felt every bit as sideswiped as she had a moment ago. "You never told me that."

"Hearing all of Henry's stories about traveling around was what made me want to go," Verity said. "He was the reason I even applied. He was always saying, there's a big world out there, why not go see it? And I thought . . . it wouldn't be so bad, to get away from Abrams Valley for a while. To get away from a town where just hearing my name was enough for people to see a whole long history of violence and tragedies they would never understand."

Verity would have heard it too, all through growing up: *You're the Lovegood girl.* There had always been more meaning behind the words than Sorrow knew how to translate.

"I never graduated," Verity said. "I didn't even finish my first year."

"But you met her there? You were friends?"

A brief silence. Sorrow could hear the murmur of the TV from across the room, where the puzzle lady was watching a morning talk show, and the chatter of nurses in the hallway. One laughed, a discordantly bright sound. An elevator dinged. The hospital smelled like disinfectant and filtered air and, faintly, drifting from a break room somewhere, popcorn.

"Yes. We were close. She was a couple of years ahead of me," Verity said. She still hadn't looked up from the photograph. "She was from Boston. She was smart. She was beautiful. I'd certainly never met anybody like her. Certainly not in Abrams Valley—not anybody who would ever talk to the Lovegood girl, anyway."

"And you were friends," Sorrow said. Her voice was shaking and she felt an ache in her head, guilt twisting around and telling her she didn't have to ask, she didn't have any right to demand explanations of Verity just to satisfy her own curiosity. "Were you friends? What do you mean by *close*?"

Verity sighed and set the photograph on the cushion beside her. "It was more than twenty-five years ago. It doesn't matter anymore."

And that, Sorrow thought, wasn't any kind of answer.

"Maybe not," she said. "But why don't you want to tell me?"

"We were different people then."

"Different people who were really close? So close you never told anybody about it? Because you look really close in that picture." Sorrow jabbed her finger at the photograph. "But Julie got yelled at for just asking about it, and now you're refusing to answer."

"Why does it matter, Sorrow?" Verity asked tiredly.

Sorrow sank back into her chair. "I don't know. Maybe it matters because of all those times you told me and Patience how much we would ruin everything if we even talked to the Abramses, like the worst thing we could do was try to make friends like kids are supposed to. And nobody says anything that extreme about random friends from twenty years ago. Not even you. Maybe it matters because you were conveniently leaving out the fact that it wasn't

326 · THE MEMORY TREES

about our family history or the stupid feud or people being assholes a hundred years ago at all. It was all about you."

Verity said nothing, and for a long, crushing moment Sorrow was certain she had gone too far. Verity didn't look angry. She didn't look disappointed. She only looked drained. The slump of her shoulders and lines around her eyes made Sorrow want to shrivel up, to back off and apologize for asking, to plead forgiveness for pushing and swear to never speak of it again.

But she didn't. She was so fucking tired of being led around by that pathetic cringing instinct of hers. She was so tired of how assiduously it lied to her. It had always lied to her: If you are good, if you are calm, if you don't upset your mother, if you don't make her sad, everything will be okay. She had been so careful after Patience died. She had crept through the house like a ghost. She had filled the days with gentle little-girl chatter and cheer. She had made tea. She had done her chores. She had never caused her mother or grandmother a single moment of trouble, for the entire span of those two terrible weeks, and it hadn't mattered. Verity had still swallowed a handful of sleeping pills. Grandma had still sent her away. None of it had mattered. Her family would have fallen apart even if she had been having screaming tantrums rather than trying to vanish.

"Were you friends?" Sorrow asked. "Or were you . . . was she your girlfriend?"

Verity looked down at the photograph again, but she left it lying on the arm of the chair. "We didn't call it that," she said. "We didn't call it anything."

"But that's what it was?"

"I suppose."

Sorrow took that in for a moment, turned it over in her thoughts. It wasn't surprise she felt, she decided. It was the uncomfortable sort of understanding that came with figuring out something she ought to have figured out years ago, if only she had been able to look at her mother and see more than her isolation and eccentricities.

"What happened?" she asked.

Verity looked up. "What happened?"

"You went to college. You got a fancy Boston girlfriend." Verity raised an eyebrow, and Sorrow didn't look away. "The Lovegoods and the Abramses were being all friendly with each other and hell didn't freeze over. How did it get from that to the point where Patience and Julie had to creep around like criminals just to hang out? What happened?"

"Our families were never truly on good terms," Verity began.

Sorrow rolled her eyes. "I know, I'm just—"

"I'm answering your question." Verity's voice was the crack of a whip. Sorrow shut up. "Mom and Henry were going to be married. They were planning an autumn wedding. I was so happy for her. She'd been lonely since my father died, even though she would never admit it. We Lovegood women don't admit that sort of thing, do we?" A sharp little twist of a smile, gone in a flash. "I was only away for a few months, but it was long enough that I started to forget how bad things could be between our families. Isn't it funny how all you have to do is step away for a bit, and things start to look different?"

"I don't think it's funny at all," Sorrow said quietly.

"No. I suppose it isn't." Verity looked at her steadily for a moment before going on. "Mom called me a few weeks before the end of the school year. She was—I'd never heard her like that. She was hysterical, barely making any sense. All I could make out was that something had happened to Henry. It was too late for a bus and I didn't know anybody with a car, so I hitchhiked. By the time I got to Abrams Valley, Henry was dead."

"I heard it was a car accident?" Sorrow said.

Verity nodded. "They'd all been having dinner together, the Abrams family, and Henry brought Mom along. And Eli, well, he hated that. He started in on Mom right away. Asking her if she knew all the ways her mother had cheated his family over the years. Saying he knew she had helped Devotion kill his father and cover it up. Henry blew up at him, and they fought, and Henry stormed out of there." Verity paused for a second; her voice had gone hoarse. "He'd been drinking—they'd all been drinking—and he only made it about two miles down the road before he missed a turn and smashed into a tree."

"Oh no," Sorrow whispered.

"It took him most of the night to die. They wouldn't let Mom see him. Eli had his worthless sons pick her up and carry her out of the hospital, like she was a toddler having a tantrum, not a woman who only wanted to hold the hand of the man she loved before he died. And nobody said a word. Nobody helped her."

Sorrowed cleared her throat, steadied her voice to ask, "Grandma told you about it? Afterward?"

"A little," Verity said softly. "I heard the rest from other people.

She was so distraught. I'd never seen her like that. I've never seen anybody like that. I didn't know what to do. I came home to take care of her. She didn't have anybody else. I thought . . . I thought after a few months it would go back to—not exactly normal, but it would get better. But she only kept fading. That's when she stopped talking. Not all at once—I know that's how people remember it, but it wasn't sudden like that. It wasn't like she woke up one day and decided not to speak. The words just dropped away. Every day she said a little less, and she spent more and more time writing in those books of hers." Verity's voice was quiet with old hurt. "By the end of the summer . . . it was an awful summer. We barely had any harvest at all. The trees were sickly, and the apples rotted on the branches, and we couldn't do anything to stop it. By autumn I knew I couldn't leave her to go back to school. I shouldn't have left in the first place."

Sorrow had wondered what was behind Grandma's decades-long silence, but only in the same way she wondered why the sun rose in the east, why snow fell in winter. She had never known her grandmother any other way, and like all children she had assumed the world she knew was the world that had always been. She had never pictured Perseverance in love, or heartbroken, or humiliated, just as she had never imagined that Verity had once dreamed about life beyond the orchard, had even reached out to take it, only to be pulled back.

"Did Patience know any of that?" Sorrow asked.

"Patience?" Verity said, surprised. "No. I don't think so. Why do you ask?"

She asked because even though the hospital walls around her

were modern and white and bland, even though she was miles and mountains away from the orchard, she was still standing in the ash grove where their family was buried. She was still squirming with alarm to hear her sister, her idol, the person she trusted to lead in every situation, telling her in a voice raw with desperation how much she wanted to escape, how she dreamed of leaving, but even her dreams were shackled by the roots of the orchard. In that moment, that cold morning on the last day of her life, Patience had understood something Sorrow had been too young to grasp: the stories were never just stories, and history was never only in the past. If they echoed loudly enough, those long-dead spites and long-buried hatreds, they weren't a legacy but a cage—and she had wanted out.

If only they had been a family who talked about what they wanted as much as they talked about where they had come from, Patience and Verity might have found that in common.

"I know you think I was unreasonable," Verity said. "And you're probably right. Sometimes I feel like my whole life I've done nothing but make one wrong decision after another. I was only ever trying to protect you. All of you. I didn't want Mom to have to face that kind of pain again. I didn't want you and your sister to ever know what that felt like. There were days when it seemed like all I could do to keep you safe was keep you close. I thought we would be safe in the orchard."

"That's not—" Sorrow stopped, and she didn't say: That's not rational. That doesn't even make sense. That's not how it works.

The protests were there on her tongue, but withered before she spoke them. Verity knew that already. The regret seeped through every word she spoke.

"How did . . ." Sorrow had to stop, take a breath. "How did Hannah end up married to an Abrams? After all that? How did she even end up in Abrams Valley?"

"At the end of that summer she came to try to persuade me to go back to school," Verity said. "I didn't even—I refused to see her. I didn't want her seeing how much Mom and I were struggling. I suppose she and Paul met while she was staying in town. I don't know. I never asked. The next time I saw her they were engaged, and everybody in town was talking about how Paul's fiancée had dropped out of law school to marry him. That bothered me, actually. That she dropped out to get married. She's smart. She could have had quite a career."

"That's what bothered you," Sorrow said slowly. "That she quit law school."

"What do you want me to say, Sorrow? Hannah was always going to marry a man her family approved of. Paul Abrams may have been barely one generation removed from farmers, but at least they could trace their roots back before the Revolution. And I was always going to go home to the orchard. I had already decided to have daughters by then. Our lives were on different paths. I met your father when he was hiking through one summer."

Sorrow knew that part of the story: Dad was an Appalachian Trail hiker who never made it to Maine because he got distracted in southern Vermont. She had always imagined it as a summer fling that led to an unexpected pregnancy. She had assumed Patience was an accident, and her too, eight years later.

"Michael and I were never going to want the same things," Verity said, as though she knew what Sorrow was thinking, "but we both wanted you and your sister. You were supposed to come along a bit earlier, but these things don't always go according to plan. Whatever else you think about the choices I've made, don't ever doubt that. We always wanted you and Patience."

Sorrow's face grew warm and she looked away quickly. She knew Verity wasn't being entirely honest with her—there was heartbreak beneath her dismissal of Hannah's callousness, hurt and embarrassment and regrets, the inevitable act of moving on. There was more to her history with Dad than their daughters and the eight years between them. But Sorrow could let her have these small lies. She didn't have to tear the scar tissue away from every one of her mother's old hurts. She had done enough of that already.

Sorrow leaned forward to take the photo back. Julie hadn't known the story behind that picture; she hadn't known anything about it. To her it was a curiosity, an artifact of a forgotten age hidden away in an attic. Sorrow didn't know why Julie would have taken time out of her last day alive to find it for her. Sorrow wasn't anybody to her except the little sister of her long-dead once-upon-a-time friend. It probably didn't matter. Julie was still dead. The girls in the photograph had grown into women who could barely speak to each other. Their families were still torn apart by rifts that would never mend.

"You know," said Verity, "I really hate this place."

Sorrow looked up. Verity was staring out the window. The view was unremarkable: parking lot half-filled with cars gleaming in the sun, strips of grass and trees locked in concrete curbs, roads pulsing with weekday traffic. Nothing from outside filtered into the room. Not the sounds of the traffic, not the heat of the day, not the scents of gas and asphalt and cut grass.

"I hate this place," Verity said again. "I hate the rooms. I hate the beds. I hate the food. I hate wearing this stupid thing on my wrist." She plucked at the patient ID band. "I hate that the windows don't open. I hate that the plants are plastic. I hate that nobody who's here wants to be here. *I* don't want to be here."

Sorrow opened her mouth, but Verity lifted a hand to stop her.

"Let me finish. I hate this place so much I start thinking about leaving the second I get here. But as much as I hate being here, sometimes I need to be. I need . . ." Verity considered her words. "I need somebody else to make decisions for a while, when I can't trust my own judgment. When I can't trust that the way the world looks to me is the way it actually is. I know you think I'm selfish, but all I could think—I kept thinking about when Patience died. You were so worried all the time."

Sorrow nodded.

"I hated that. I hated how scared you were. It wasn't that I didn't notice. I did. But everything was cold and gray. Everything I ate tasted like ashes. It was all dust. Nothing had any texture to it anymore. And sometimes—sometimes I start thinking like that again. Like nothing has changed. When it starts to feel like the world has gone flat and dull, it's like my mind gets stuck on this wheel going around and around, and there's no room for anything else. I can't feel anything else. I don't even want to. I didn't mean to scare you. But I couldn't . . ."

They sat in silence for a few minutes, both of them looking toward the windows, watching the day move beyond the glass. Sorrow knew what she was supposed to say. Her entire life had been rehearsing for this. She was supposed to reassure Verity she wasn't angry. She wasn't upset. She hadn't been scared. It was okay, it was really okay that in those few days after Julie died, when she had wanted so very badly for somebody to see how shaken she was, she had instead faded away to nothing more than an afterthought at the edge of her mother's awareness. But it was fine. She was fine, Grandma was fine, they would be fine. She was supposed to say all of that, and mean it. That was what she would do if she could be a good daughter and granddaughter, the kind of person who could offer forgiveness as easily as she hoarded hurt. It would only take a few small words. She wouldn't even choke getting them out.

"I better get back," she said. She stood up and didn't wait for Verity to do the same. "I don't want to leave Grandma alone too long."

31

SORROW'S PHONE RANG as the elevator reached the ground floor. She silenced it and glanced at the screen.

Dad.

They hadn't spoken since her first night on the farm. They'd exchanged a few text messages—brief, unimportant—but that was all. She hadn't told him that Julie had died; she'd wanted to think of a way to tell him that wouldn't have him freaking out and demanding she come home instantly. But then he'd texted that he was off to Hong Kong for a business trip, and Sorrow had felt a guilty relief for not having to make the decision.

Her phone beeped as it sent the call to voice mail. Somebody bumped into her from behind. She muttered an apology and shuffled out of the way. She didn't listen to the message until she was back in the car with the key in the ignition and the phone on her lap.

"Hey, sweetie, just checking in to see how you're doing." Dad's voice was cheerful and fast, the way he always sounded first thing in the morning. "I'm back stateside—stuck in LA traffic as we speak. I hope you're having fun. Give me a call when you get a chance."

He sounded so normal, so warm, so very far away. Dad had no idea she'd been having anything other than an ordinary summer vacation. He certainly didn't know she had just walked out of the hospital. Sonia always liked to joke that he had the best-worst timing of anybody she knew.

Sorrow deleted the message. It was early in Los Angeles. He was probably on his way to a meeting. He might not have time to talk. But he would notice if she didn't respond at all.

She took a breath and called him back.

Dad answered right away. "Hey! Guess what. Still stuck in traffic."

"It's only been like two minutes," Sorrow said. She made herself smile, hoped it carried through in her voice. "You're not driving and talking, are you?"

"No. The company sent a car."

"Ooh, corporate big shot."

"I think it's more that they're afraid I would go *Mad Max* on my way to the meeting. There are twelve lanes of traffic and none of them are moving. So how have you been? How's Vermont?"

"Oh, it's . . ."

Tell him, Sorrow thought. Tell him. Say it.

But if she said it, if she started with the night Julie died and let the rest spill out, they would be right back to where they had ended their last conversation, and this time Dad would be right. Nothing was okay. Everything was broken and wrong and terrifying, exactly as he had feared and Sorrow had insisted would never happen. Sorrow knew her father. He would be so worried for her he wouldn't even manage an *I told you so* before he was making arrangements for her to go home. A plane ticket and a plan. That was all he could do. He was too far away to do anything else. He had always been too far away.

"Does that significant silence mean things are really good or really bad?" Dad asked.

"Can I ask you something?" Sorrow said.

"Sure," Dad said. "What is it?"

Sorrow gripped the steering wheel with her free hand, so tight her knuckles were white beneath her summer tan.

"Sorrow? Is something wrong?"

"Why didn't you come to Vermont after Patience died? Before Verity went into the hospital, I mean. Why didn't you come back?"

"Oh," said her father, a breathy exhale of a word.

And there was a long, long silence.

"I didn't know you . . ." Dad trailed off, started again. "You've never asked about that before."

"It was, what, two weeks? What could you have been doing for two weeks that you couldn't even—that you didn't even—" Sorrow's voice caught. She pressed her knuckles to her lips, held her breath for a few seconds.

Two weeks of unnatural cold. Two weeks of crushing quiet. Two weeks of crying herself to sleep, stifling her sobs in her pillow so her mother wouldn't hear, and waking every day wishing for spring to come, wishing her mom would get better, wishing her sister would return.

"I wanted to come back," Dad said. "But Verity told me to wait."

Sorrow let go of the steering wheel. That pinch she felt in the center of her chest, it wasn't surprise. You couldn't be surprised by something you had suspected before you asked.

"She told me it would only make it harder for you. That I shouldn't force you to deal with somebody who was essentially a stranger when you were grieving your sister. She told me to give you time. All of you. And I . . . I didn't argue." Dad made a frustrated sound. "I wanted to see you, but she wasn't entirely wrong. I was a stranger to you. We barely knew each other when Patience died, and we didn't for a long time after, did we?"

They had never spoken of it before, those agonizing first months in Florida, after Sorrow had been plucked from the only life she knew, how long it had taken for the nightmares to fade, the tears to dry up, the knowledge that she wasn't going home again to sink in. By then she had been so tired of rebuilding the walls around her heart she had given up in exhaustion. It had taken the two of them months to begin acting, in fits and starts, neither of them knowing how, like father and daughter rather than a lost child and a bewildered man who had been thrown together by an accident of fate.

"That's not a good enough reason," Sorrow said. Her voice sounded like a stranger's to her own ears, hoarse and wet and faint. "I get what you're saying. I get that—but it's not, it's not good enough."

"I know," Dad said quietly. "Has something happened, Sorrow? What's this about?"

"Do you give Verity and Grandma money?"

That caught him off guard. "I—uh, well, yes. I've helped them out from time to time."

"Does Sonia know?"

A brief pause. "She does now, yes."

"And she doesn't care?"

"Honey, what's going on? Is there something wrong?"

Sorrow scrubbed the tears from her cheeks. "Why does something have to be wrong? Do I need a reason to ask questions about my own family?"

"You can ask whatever you want. But you sound so upset and this isn't—this isn't like you."

"Being upset isn't like me?" Sorrow said, laughing bitterly. "Well, isn't that convenient for everybody else. We've always got to have one person in the family who doesn't get upset so everybody else can lose their fucking minds, right?"

"Sorrow—"

"I have to go," she said.

"Sorrow, wait—"

"Talk to you later. Bye."

Sorrow hung up and threw her phone onto the passenger seat.

She reached for the key in the ignition, changed her mind before she turned it. Her phone rang. She ignored it. The voice mail beep sounded. A text, then another. She ignored those too. The only sound inside the car was her own breathing, rough and fast; she put a hand over her mouth to trap the sobs, swallow them down, bury them away somewhere deep inside. It didn't help. Her shoulders were shaking, her throat raw. Her phone rang again, and still she didn't answer. She closed her eyes and leaned forward to rest her head on the steering wheel.

She had come back to Vermont because she had realized, that day in the Everglades, the day she had imagined Patience walking beside her and understood she was older than her sister would ever be, that she didn't know how to move forward into terrain Patience had not explored first. She had been following Patience's example for so long, for so many years even after Patience was dead and buried, she hadn't known she was still doing it until she tried to look forward and couldn't see anything at all except the shadows and gaps and echoing empty spaces behind her.

But none of it had worked like she'd planned. All she had wanted to do was remember the last days of her sister's life, to have a complete picture of the person Patience had been, to know what she had wanted to be. But now Patience's only friend was dead, Verity was back in the hospital, and Sorrow felt more mired in the past than she ever had before.

It was a long time before she felt steady enough to drive away.

32

AFTER DINNER SORROW and Grandma went together to sit on the porch. The rain had stopped and the clouds had finally cleared. The sharp cold had subsided, leaving the evening pleasantly cool. Soft golden light filtered through the apple trees. Grandma had a ball of yarn and two wooden needles in her lap. Sorrow sat in the other chair, rocking idly from time to time, letting her inward restlessness show only in the occasional tap of her feet against the floorboards, the drum of her fingers on the arm of the chair.

All day she had considered and discarded things to say to her grandmother. She had reported that Verity seemed fine and might be coming home tomorrow, but she hadn't been able to add: She told me about Henry Abrams. She had spent hours helping Grandma in the garden and around the orchard, but not once had she found a way to say: I know why you stopped talking. I know what hurt you so badly silence was the only way you could live through it. I know why you and Verity have wrapped yourselves in a protective cloak of loneliness and quiet here on the farm, surrounded by memories and dead ancestors. *I know.*

All the words Sorrow could not say beat a steady rhythm against her ribs. She couldn't say something just to prove she knew, not when it might hurt Grandma to have the truth drawn unexpectedly into the open after she had locked it away so long ago.

The sun sank, the shadows lengthened, and the only sound between them was the creak of rocking chairs on the porch and the occasional slap of a hand brushing away a twilight mosquito. After a while, Grandma let out a quiet sigh, picked up her needles, and began to knit. The soft tap of wood on wood joined the chorus of crickets and evening songbirds.

The phone rang; the noise was so loud and so unexpected Sorrow jumped in her chair.

"I'll just—get that." Her heart was thudding as she stepped inside to answer. "Hello?"

"Uh, hi, Sorrow? It's me. Ethan."

A wash of relief: she had feared it would be Dr. Parker. "Oh. Hi."

"Look, this is kind of—have you seen Cassie?"

"Cassie?" Sorrow's relief turned to confusion. "Uh, no. I haven't seen her since the festival. Why?"

"Nobody knows where she is."

Sorrow felt an electric spark down her spine. "Since when?"

"Nobody's seen her all afternoon," Ethan said. "Aunt Hannah doesn't know exactly when she went out. They thought she was in her room."

"She's not answering her phone?"

"Her parents have it. They're calling her friends, but nobody's seen her."

"Right. Right, you said . . . yeah." They had taken her phone away after Julie died; Sorrow remembered Ethan mentioning that. "Do you need help looking for her? I wouldn't even know where to start, but I can help."

"I don't know if that's a good idea," Ethan said. "They don't know I'm calling you."

Calling the Lovegoods for help with an Abrams family problem. Sorrow bumped her head softly against the wall and tasted, faintly, iron at the back of her throat, a drifting memory of that day she had run to the Abramses for help, so terrified she was doing the wrong thing.

"Right. Yeah. Have you . . ." Oh, she didn't want to say it. She did not want to ask. "Has somebody looked in the cider house?"

"I did," Ethan said, his voice quiet. "Just now. She's not there. I don't know if it's . . . fuck, I don't even know how freaked out we should be. But Aunt Hannah called me. She called *me*. She would never talk to me willingly unless she was really worried."

"Yeah. Okay. What can I do?"

"I don't know yet. I don't know. If she shows up at your place and she's . . . can you call me?"

"Yeah, definitely."

"Thanks. Yeah. Thanks."

"I hope you find her soon," Sorrow said.

A pause, then Ethan said, "Yeah. Me too."

Sorrow went back outside and dropped into her chair. "That was Ethan. Nobody can find Cassie. They don't know where she is."

Grandma's eyes widened, and she lifted her hand in her usual *go on* gesture.

Sorrow shook her head. "That's all he said. I don't know if they think she's . . . I don't know. They wouldn't even let Ethan talk to her a few days ago. I feel like I should do something."

Grandma tilted her head to the side, and Sorrow made a face.

"I know. I'm the last person they want around. But I still feel like I should—"

The porch faced west. The sun was sinking before them, kissing the tops of the hills, just high enough to cast long bright rays through the apple trees, creating a striped pattern of light and dark over Grandma's garden.

In one of those bars of sunlight, something glinted on the lawn.

It hadn't been there before. She and Grandma had been sitting here for half an hour or more, watching the sun go down. She would have noticed that sparking bright reflection in the grass.

"Like I should do something," she said absently. She stood; the chair rocked gently behind her. "I told Ethan I could help."

She walked to the edge of the porch. Dropped down one step, another, stepped onto the hard-packed soil. Walked across the lawn until she stood above the glinting object.

It was a pair of old-fashioned wire-rimmed eyeglasses.

Sorrow's heart beat quickly.

One of the round lenses was missing, the other broken down the middle in a lightning-shaped crack. She picked them up gingerly. The wire frame was warm to the touch.

She glanced back at the house. Grandma had risen from her chair.

A child could believe impossible things. A child with a home embraced by trees so old and roots so deep they were part of the mountains themselves, filled with small treasures, fading and growing with a cycle that sometimes had nothing to do with the seasons, she could rise every morning with the sun and work chores to tend the land, tame it just enough to make it nurturing, but not so much to make it docile. She could remember the stories her family had always told, passed down mother to daughter, woman to woman, words made breath through generations, and believe it was possible to pluck those stories from the soil with careful little-girl fingers. History never truly loosed its grip on the present. The past was never only memories.

Patience had placed the glasses on Sorrow's face, her fingers warm from being tucked into her mittens. She had laughed at the find, delighted by proof that winter was ending. Sorrow had wanted to laugh. Oh, how she had tried, so achingly aware of the gap between the girl she was supposed to be and the one she was inside. Patience had believed the glasses were Sorrow's first favor of the year, but Sorrow had been keeping a secret from her. In her pocket there had been a weight, so small nobody had noticed, so heavy it had threatened to press her into the earth.

She could feel it even now, a solid square against her ribs, right at the spot where her coat's inside pocket had been.

She cupped the glasses in her hand and held them at her side. She glanced back at the house. Grandma was watching her, eyes shaded against the setting sun.

Julie in the cemetery grove, her golden hair in the sun, already prepared to die, she had handed the photograph to Sorrow and she had said: *They don't realize that what they're hiding from isn't as bad as what they're doing to themselves by hiding.*

Sorrow had assumed she'd been talking about Verity and Hannah. She had been tracing lines between their families since that day, weaving a spiderweb of gossamer-fine relationships. Verity and Hannah. Patience and Julie. Devotion and Perseverance. Mothers and daughters, sisters and friends, neighbors and enemies, women alone and women surviving. Julie and herself.

She had forgotten about Cassie. Cassie, who had accused Patience of setting the fires even when nobody else believed it. Cassie, who had confronted Sorrow not once but twice, flinging insults and challenges in her face, in public where anybody could hear.

Cassie, who had been alone since her sister's suicide, and was now missing.

"I'm going to look for her," Sorrow said.

Grandma nodded.

Sorrow walked past the chicken coop, down the hill, around the field below the house. She touched her grandfather's pickup as she passed; the metal was warm, gritty, solid.

She stopped at the edge of the apple trees. Ahead the dirt road headed west into the shadows. A chorus of insects sang. The orchard in evening was breathtakingly beautiful: shades of green shivering to silver when the air stirred, golden light touching the highest treetops and the hills beyond, the velvet sky clear, cloudless, magnificent.

She rubbed at her arms. She looked back at the house. Grandma was still standing on the porch, her face alight. A small woman and a small house, old mountains and old trees, all of it so warm and familiar it made her heart ache. Sorrow pressed her fingers briefly to the skin at the base of her neck, tried to steady her breath, to calm her nerves. She didn't know where to go. She didn't know where Cassie would run to hide from her family and herself.

The apple trees were a wall of green and brown, a border between daylight and darkness, with roots that had been clinging for centuries and branches so entangled the canopy itself had forgotten where one tree ended and another began. There might be diseases lurking in the trunks and leaves, there might be blights and bacteria, fungus and rot, but hidden, gnawing from the inside, easily missed if you didn't know how to look, and there were so many different ways to look. Sorrow had been turning and turning in her mind, grasping for memories unreachable through a thicket of snapping branches and rustling leaves, but her past had never been lost. Her memories had never been unreachable. They had been here all along, waiting for her to see not a barrier of shadows but a living thing, a breathing thing, a land that shuddered when her heart beat, that rose and fell with every breath, that gathered grief and pain and tears and held them close, intimate as secrets, and did not forget.

She stepped from the field into the orchard. The sun was sinking behind the mountains, the sky a searing blaze of gold. She took another step, and the deep green shadows surrounded her. A soft breeze pushed through the trees, and it was cold, a startling bite, raising goose bumps on her arms.

There, at the base of the first tree in the row, was a small bead on a leather string. She leaned to pick it up. It was as round and red as a white rabbit's eye. She rolled it between her thumb and forefinger, then tucked it into her pocket.

Three rows into the orchard she found a filigree lady's fan open against the base of a tree. She picked it up, eased it closed, coaxed it open again. She had never known who it belonged to; she had never thought to ask. When she was a child the favors were gifts from the orchard to her, nothing more and nothing less. She tapped the fan closed, slid it into her pocket, and kept walking.

Barely fifty feet along she found a pocket watch dangling from the low branch of an apple tree. *To George, Love Forever, From Catherine.* She had read those names a hundred times as a child, tracing the engraving, admiring her treasure. She wondered now how Catherine had mourned her husband when he disappeared. How long she had remained hopeful that he would one day return.

"Okay," Sorrow said.

She reached up to untangle the chain; her hands were shaking. When she held the watch she felt cool water dribble onto her fingers. She opened the clasp and shook it slightly, heard the patter of droplets on the ground. The face was cracked, both of the hands pointing toward midnight. A dank, mossy smell rose.

The cider brewers of Abrams Valley liked to talk about the different qualities of apples grown in different parts of the valley—more sour from the northern end, more bitter from the Lovegood end—endless arguments around and around about the terroir of every orchard, that unique combination of soil and geology and human care that made even apples of the same variety noticeably different. Perhaps the same could be said of girls growing up in the same place at different times, if the landscape beneath their feet and the world around them was changing. A mother's illness growing stronger. A family's isolation drawing in on itself. Dreams of escape washing away. Patience had always been trying to get Sorrow to listen to the orchard, to hear the memories that vibrated in its stones and trees. Sorrow had never been able to hear those echoes. The orchard spoke to her in a different way.

"Okay," Sorrow said again. Her heart was thudding in her throat. "You have my attention. Show me where to go."

She was whispering, her words barely more than the faintest exhale of breath, but as she spoke, the trees around her stirred in a sudden lift of breeze. The leaves rustled and turned, the grass rasped and swayed, and a shiver crept over her skin.

33

EIGHT YEARS AGO

OUTSIDE, THE WINTER day was bitter and gray. Icy snow scraped on the windows, and the wind worried and whined in the chimney. All the color had been sapped out of the world. When Sorrow looked over the barren soil of Grandma's garden, the snow-covered lawn and field, the naked brown apple trees, she worried that she might forget how to see green, that her eyes wouldn't even know what they were looking at when the first shoots pushed through the dirt and the first leaves unfurled.

Outside, the orchard had become another world, one crueler and less welcoming. Even though it was only March, Sorrow very much believed winter had long outstayed its welcome.

Inside, the house was warm and bright, and everything was normal until Patience asked about school.

"It's okay if I just go by and talk to the high school, isn't it?" she said.

Sorrow froze with a spoonful of soup halfway to her mouth. They were sitting at the table, her and Patience, a lunch of grilled cheese and tomato soup before them. Grandma had finished her own soup and gone to her room for a nap. Mom was at the sink, washing dishes. Steam from the running water fogged the window.

"Just to get some information?" Patience added.

Mom was rigid as a tree trunk from head to toe, betrayed only by the faint tremble in her hands. Sorrow looked nervously between them. The soup churned unpleasantly in her stomach.

"I said we would talk about it," Mom said.

Patience stood to lean against the counter with her arms crossed over her chest. She was as tall as Mom now, and they could have been two sides of a mirror, except that Patience was fully dressed and had combed her hair sleekly over her shoulders, whereas Mom was still wearing her flannel nightshirt, and her hair was a bird's nest tangle of brown and gray.

"We are talking about it," Patience said.

"Later," Mom said. "We'll talk about it later."

"How much later?" Patience demanded, and Sorrow flinched. "Dad said if I want to enroll by fall I have to catch up—"

Mom dropped a bowl into the sink with a clatter, tossed the towel onto the counter, and walked out of the kitchen without saying a word. There was the muffled thumping of her sock-clad feet on the stairs, the snap of a door closing.

Sorrow glanced at the clock. Mom hadn't even been out of her room for a full hour.

Patience sighed and turned off the faucet. She picked up the towel Mom had discarded, set it down again. "I can't believe her."

"You shouldn't have mentioned Dad," Sorrow said.

"Oh, shut up," Patience said. "You don't even understand what's going on."

Sorrow's face burned and anger buzzed in her ears. Patience was sixteen. People in town were always telling Sorrow how beautiful her sister was, how she was growing to be such a lovely young woman. Sorrow was eight, exactly half Patience's age, and she knew she would always be exactly half of what Patience was: half as beautiful, half as beloved.

Maybe she was only half as smart too, but she wasn't *stupid*. Mom and Patience were arguing because Patience wanted to go to school—to regular school, the high school in town, after being homeschooled by Mom for her entire life. She claimed Dad agreed it was a good idea, but his last visit had been in January, which meant Patience had waited almost three months to say anything. Three months of mulling it over, forming her arguments, making a plan, and today was the day she chose to bring it up, even though it was one of Mom's bad days and she knew better.

"You could have helped, you know," Patience said.

Sorrow looked up. "Helped what?"

"Don't you want to go to school too? Meet new people? Make friends?"

Sorrow swirled her spoon angrily in her soup. "I don't know."

"I think you would like it," Patience said. "You can help me talk to her later. We can convince her if we do it together."

It didn't sound all bad, having a chance to go to school in Abrams Valley and learn things Mom didn't teach them, to talk to girls her own age and maybe even play with them. But Sorrow couldn't think about what she might like about school without thinking about all the things she knew she would hate. She didn't even like to go into town, where everybody knew about their family and made jokes about the weirdo Lovegood girls. Last week two boys about Sorrow's age had followed her and Mom all the way from the grocery store to the post office and back, muttering about crazies and psychos when their backs were turned, bursting into fits of laughter when Sorrow glared at them. Mom had pretended not to hear anything, but when they got back to the car she had sat for a long time without turning the key, not looking at Sorrow, not doing anything except staring through the windshield and breathing.

"I don't know," Sorrow said again.

Patience rolled her eyes. "Fine, whatever. I don't need your help."

She stomped out of the kitchen. More footsteps on the stairs, another door slamming shut, and Sorrow was alone.

She poked at her soup, but it was cold and filmy and she wasn't hungry anymore. She had been hoping to convince Patience to play a game or go for a walk. She was tired of being stuck inside through the gray days and cold nights. She was tired of cold, tired of snow, tired of mud, tired of wind and ice. Their farmhouse felt small and isolated in this gray tail end of winter in Vermont. The orchard was only a few miles from town, but nobody came to visit, not unless there was trouble.

She didn't need Patience. She would be fine on her own. She bundled up against the cold and went outside.

Sorrow followed the path around the barren garden, past the chicken coop, down to the old dirt road. Her boots crunched through the crusty top layer of snow to the hard ice below. The pickup at the edge of a fallow field was a soft white lump.

She knew winter couldn't last forever, however much it felt like it would. Spring was coming. She could feel it in her bones, in the light flutter beneath her lungs, even if she couldn't yet smell it in the air.

And when spring came to the orchard, the favors would return.

Last spring she had found the very first favor of the year by the pond in the northwest corner of the property, in the branches of a crooked old beech tree leaning over the water. She wanted to look there again, just in case there was a sign of spring waiting to be found. She followed the dirt road around the hill and stomped down the slope, slipping and sliding in the deep snow, toward the boundary with the Abrams land. When she reached the meadow, cold wind whipped around her, stinging her face and making her eyes water. The stone well at one end of the meadow was a fat hump beneath a snowdrift, the wire fence a sketched black line. At the other end of the meadow was the cider house.

The cider house door was open.

Sorrow's heart thumped in surprise. The weathered two-by-six that normally barred the door was lying on the ground, and all along the front of the building the snow was trampled. A line of footprints led to the fence and through the field on the Abrams side.

The Abramses weren't allowed on Lovegood land, no more than the Lovegoods were allowed on Abrams land. The sheriff had made both families promise to keep to their own property after the last time Mr. Abrams had called the police and said Mom was cutting down trees on his side of the fence, and Mom had called the police when Mr. Abrams and his brother were hunting in the orchard.

Sorrow crept forward to approach the door from the side. Her mouth was dry and her heart was racing so fast she could feel it in her throat. She had to say something. She wasn't a baby. She was eight years old, and she was a Lovegood. She wasn't going to let an Abrams scare her away.

She leaned into the open doorway. "Hello?"

Her voice echoed dully. It was so dark inside it took her eyes several seconds to adjust.

"Hello! Who's in there?"

All she could hear was the wind and the rattle of icy snow on naked branches. She eased one boot forward, stretching over the slick of ice to step inside. The floor creaked and she held her breath, trying to make herself as light as possible. There were piles of apple crates in the corners, stacks of orchard ladders against the wall, barrels and buckets and all kinds of junk, but no person that Sorrow could see. Long ago the old cider press had smashed through the rotten floorboards to the muddy cellar below, leaving a gaping hole in the floor.

Sorrow leaned forward to peer into the cellar. It was so dark it could have been a bottomless pit. There was no ladder; if somebody fell through the floor, they wouldn't have any way to get out.

"Are you down there?" Her voice, now, little more than a whisper. "Hello?"

"I didn't even know you could talk."

Sorrow spun around, her heart jumping.

Cassie Abrams stood in the doorway. She cocked her head to one side, considering Sorrow with an unimpressed expression. "I thought you were mute like your grandma."

Cassie's blond hair curled in pigtails beneath her red knit hat, and her round cheeks were pink with cold. Her coat was red too, a deep crimson velvet with shiny silver buttons marching down the front, and her puffy snow boots were bright pink.

"Or can you only talk to empty rooms, not people?" Cassie said.

"I can talk," Sorrow said, bewildered. She blushed when Cassie laughed.

"I bet my friend Madison I could make you talk," Cassie said. "Now she has to kiss Jemma's brother Hunter on the playground tomorrow. Maybe she won't believe me but I'm going to make her anyway. You *can* talk like a normal person, can't you? Say something else."

Sorrow didn't know Madison or Jemma or Hunter. She barely even knew Cassie. She and Patience weren't allowed to talk to the Abramses or make friends with their daughters. Mom said that making friends with an Abrams would only lead to heartache.

"What are you doing here?" she asked.

Cassie kicked a clump of icy snow; it slid past Sorrow's boots and dropped into the cellar. "Nothing. I was bored."

"You're not supposed to be here."

"I thought this building would be cooler on the inside, but it's just a bunch of junk. My playhouse is way better." Cassie pointed across the snow-covered field toward her house. "It's in the barn. I get to have the whole hayloft just for myself, and it's not gross and dirty like this."

Sorrow bristled, even though Cassie was right. "If you think it's gross, maybe you should leave."

"Maybe I don't want to," Cassie said.

"You have to. You're not supposed to be here."

"Says who?"

"Says my mom, and your mom, and your dad," Sorrow said. "The sheriff said we have to stay on our side of the fence so everybody stops bothering him." Those had been his exact words, in fact, and Mom hadn't been at all pleased to hear it.

Cassie snorted. "I don't care what the dumb old sheriff says. Let's do something fun. Can we climb that big tree on the hill? I've always wanted to climb it."

Sorrow stared. It was a trick. It had to be a trick. No Abrams would invite her to play for no reason.

Even so, a part of her wanted to say yes. This lonely gray day would be more interesting if she could stomp through the orchard and climb the black oak with Cassie, breaking the rules their parents had set.

But she couldn't. She couldn't risk Mom finding out, not when she was having a bad day. Patience had already pushed Mom too far by asking about school. Getting caught playing with Cassie Abrams would be so much worse.

"I don't want to play with you," Sorrow said. "I want you to leave."

"I don't want to leave."

"You have to," Sorrow said, her worry turning into a desperate kind of fear. "You *have* to. You have to go before somebody sees you."

Cassie's eyes narrowed. "I'll just tell them you made me come over here. I'll tell them it's all your fault."

Something hot and angry was building in Sorrow's chest, a bright painful ember pushing out into the cold. "That's not true."

"So? They'll believe me more than you. Everybody knows you're just as crazy as your mom."

Sorrow lunged forward and shoved Cassie backward through the door. "Shut up!" she shouted. "You shut up about my mom!"

Cassie stumbled in the deep snow and fell. She struggled to her feet, and her cheeks were even pinker now. There was snow stuck all over her mittens and red coat. "I knew you were crazy. Your whole family is crazy."

"Shut up!" Sorrow stepped toward Cassie again, but her boot slipped on the ice just inside the door. She grabbed for the door-frame to catch herself.

Cassie slammed into her before she was steady on her feet, and Sorrow's feet skidded out from under her. She fell, hard, right onto her back. The jolt knocked the breath out of her, made her vision blur, and everything went dark with a thunderous thump. There was another thump—the walls shook—and a noisy clatter.

Cassie had shut the door.

"Hey!" Sorrow yelled. "Hey, what are you doing!"

She climbed to her feet and tumbled against the door, but it didn't budge. Cassie had barred it from the outside.

"Let me out!" Sorrow hit the door hard enough to make the whole wall shake. "What are you doing? Let me out!"

"No," Cassie said. Her voice was muffled through the door. "No way. No way. You're crazy. You'll kill me or something. Your whole family is insane."

Her footsteps crunched through the snow.

"Cassie! Wait! Come back! Please come back!"

The footsteps paused.

"Please come back," Sorrow said, more quietly. "Let me out. Please?"

Cassie started moving again, but now she was running. Her footsteps faded, and faded, and there was silence.

Sorrow turned in a slow circle, trying to breathe normally. All she could see was the faint gray light around the edges of the door. Everything else was darkness. Tears stung her eyes and scalded her cheeks. She scrubbed at her face; her mittens were cold and rough and dirty. She was trapped. She didn't know what to do. Her breath was shallow, her heart racing so fast she felt it in her ears. She couldn't get enough air. She couldn't see. She was between the door and the hole in the floor, but she couldn't see it, and what if she was closer to the hole than she thought? If she moved the wrong way she would tumble into the cellar and break her arms or legs or even her neck.

"Help!" Sorrow shouted, her voice choked with tears. "Help me! Can anybody hear me?"

She could scream all day and all night and nobody would hear. She was too far from the house. It might be dinnertime, or even bedtime, before Patience or Mom or Grandma noticed she wasn't in the house. They might not find her until morning, and by then she would be frozen solid.

"Cassie!" She slammed her hands into the door, rattling it against the bar. "Cassie, please, let me out!"

It was no use. Cassie wasn't there. Nobody was there.

Sorrow let out a choked sob, swallowed it back quickly. She wasn't going to panic. Panicking was what Mom did, and Sorrow and Patience were the ones who soothed her. They calmed her down and they worked around whatever problem she had, even if it seemed to them more imaginary than real. That was what they did. Mom said they were good at it. They were her rock, she said, for when everything else was unsteady.

This wasn't an imaginary problem. Maybe Sorrow was alone, without her older sister to help her, but she could still be the person who fixed things, who made something scary into something manageable. She could do that. She put her mittened hand over her mouth to keep the cries inside, pushed down deep until they didn't matter anymore, and she made herself think.

The door was blocked from the outside. She had to find a way to unblock it. She had to do it in the dark. She had to do it without falling into the cellar, which she couldn't even see, which could be right next to her, it could be that shadow *right there*, and she was all confused again, confused about which way to turn, terrified of taking the wrong step, making a wrong move, and the cold was so sharp it felt like a living thing clawing its way into her skin—

Cold with teeth. That was what Patience called it, and she would bare her teeth and raise her hands like claws and pretend to be a winter monster chasing Sorrow all over the house. She used to, anyway, but it felt like a long time since Patience had played with her. Now when Sorrow suggested a game Patience would roll her eyes and say she was busy. She didn't want to play Pioneers any-more, or Explorers, or even Traitors and Spies, which used to be her favorite. Patience had always made Sorrow be the nasty old preacher Clement Abrams so she could be their ancestor Rejoice Lovegood, who had been locked up after the townspeople accused her of being a witch. But she had broken out of their makeshift jail, not using magic as the men later claimed, but only a whalebone stay she tore from her corset.

Sorrow didn't have whalebone stays beneath her dress. She had to find something else. It was too dark. She couldn't see anything. She needed to *see*.

She lowered herself to the floor. She took off her mittens and began to search the space around her. When her fingers curled over the end of a broken board, she snatched her hand back.

That was the hole in the floor. She could feel the cellar breath-ing. In her mind the broken floorboards took on the shape of a great mouth rimmed with jagged wooden fangs.

Sorrow squeezed her eyes shut. She had to stay calm. She was good at that. Mrs. Roche from down the road said she was *eerily calm*. Sorrow hadn't known what that meant, so she'd asked Patience, and Patience had said Mrs. Roche was only admiring how Sorrow didn't throw tantrums or make a fuss like other kids her age.

She wasn't making a fuss. There were sobs trapped in her throat and her breath was rasping and fast, but she was okay. She was okay. She wasn't afraid of the dark. She wasn't. She *wasn't*. She just needed to see. She searched the area around her, and when she didn't find anything she crawled a few feet and kept searching. Her fingers brushed over a curve of metal—the iron ring on the bottom of a barrel. Sorrow tugged at it, but she couldn't break it free. She moved on, still searching. The metal head of a shovel. A couple of bottles that rolled and clinked when she touched them. More barrels. A scattering of short metal nails. A crusty chunk of something that Sorrow hoped was mud but knew was probably the dried-up remains of some unfortunate mouse or bird.

She brushed her hand on her coat, and she reached out again, walking her fingers along a gap between the floorboards until they touched something hard and cold.

It felt like metal, but not the gritty iron of old farm tools and cider press parts. She tugged, rocking the object back and forth until it came free. She turned it over in her hands. It was a rectangle about the size of a matchbox, mostly smooth, with a small bump on one side—a hinge, she realized, and her heart jumped in excitement. She flipped it open and ran her fingers over the inside, feeling for the small, ridged wheel. She knew what it was.

It was a lighter, an old-fashioned one like Mr. Roche used for his pipe. One evening last summer he and Mrs. Roche had come over to drop off some mail that had gone to the wrong house, and Mom had been in a rare good mood, bright and bubbly and cheerful, so she had invited them to stay awhile and drink cider on the back porch. Sorrow had been fascinated by how Mr. Roche had packed the tobacco into his pipe, the careful way he held the flame to the bowl and puffed and puffed. He had caught her staring and handed her the lighter, showed her how to use it, and he had chuckled when Mrs. Roche scolded him for teaching a child to play with fire. Mom had laughed too and told Mrs. Roche not to worry.

Sorrow struck the lighter once, twice. Nothing happened. A third try, and nothing. The cold felt even deeper, the darkness more complete, than it had a moment ago. She shook the lighter near her ear, but she couldn't tell if there was any fuel inside.

"Come on," she whispered. "Come on, please, come on."

Finally: a spark.

Sorrow was so surprised she nearly dropped the lighter. When she clicked it again, she got a small flame. It wasn't very bright, but it was enough to push the darkness back, if only a bit. Finally she could see.

She scrambled to her feet and went to the door. She studied the small gap between the door and the frame. It wasn't wide, barely big enough for her to stick her little finger in. She held the light out and looked around, searching through the junk and piles of discarded tools, until the flame burned her thumb and she had to let it go out.

She stuck her thumb in her mouth to cool it before trying again. It took a few strikes to get the flame back.

The first thing she found, a long metal nail, was too fat. The second, a drill bit, was skinny enough to fit in the gap but not long enough to reach the two-by-six on the other side. She let the flame go out again, shook her hand and the lighter to cool them. The next time the flame caught on the first try.

She finally found what she was looking for in a long sliver of wood she peeled from the cracked leg of an orchard ladder. One end was thick, but the other tapered to a point, and that point was narrow enough to jam into the gap between the door and the frame. She had to let the lighter go dark and slip it into her coat pocket to get a good grip on her wooden wedge, but she didn't need to see now. She worked the wedge upward, wood scraping on wood, until it bumped into the two-by-six on the other side. She held it tight with both hands and pushed it up and up and up. The bar on the other side moved a little. It was heavier than she expected, and holding the wood hurt her hands, but inch by inch the bar rose. When she was sure she had lifted it high enough to clear the bracket, she leaned on the door.

One end of the bar fell to the ground, and the door swung open. Sorrow tumbled out of the cider house.

It was colder now, the light grimmer, the wind more bitter. She ran back to the house as fast as she could, slipping and sliding through the snow. She couldn't wait to tell Patience and Mom how she had escaped the pitch-black cider house using Rejoice Lovegood's trick, and she had done it with the help of the first favor of the year. She had desperately wished for a light, and the orchard had given her one, and that meant the land was waking from its long winter hibernation.

Her excitement lasted right up until she burst through the door to find the kitchen empty. The soup pot was still on the stove, the bowls still in the sink. The only sound Sorrow could hear was the gentle *chug-chug* of Grandma's sewing machine in the living room.

She shut the door. The sewing machine fell quiet, and Grandma appeared in the doorway. She tilted her head to the side in question.

"I was only taking a walk," Sorrow said.

Grandma looked at her for a long moment, then nodded and went back to her sewing.

Sorrow was left alone in the kitchen. The lighter was a hard lump in her pocket.

Nobody had even noticed she was gone. She had been trapped in the cider house and she might have been trapped there forever, but nobody had noticed.

34

THE LONG WHITE whalebone stay was in her hand.

Sorrow knew what it was, even though she had never seen one before.

She had stopped walking. Before her the dirt road curved to the right, to the north, to skirt the base of the hill before dropping down to the cider house meadow. To her left was the path to the cemetery where she had chased after Patience on that winter day eight years ago. The orchard was growing dark as the sun sank lower and lower. The rows of trees were more shadow than light now, murky and indistinct at the edges of her vision. A breeze turned and brought with it a breath of air cold enough to raise goose bumps on her skin.

Leaves crackled and rustled. Sorrow suppressed a shiver.

The stay wasn't a curve of bone at all, not like she had always imagined. It was more pliable than rigid, a thin, bendable finger of fiber. It was hard to imagine how it could have been used in a jail-break, but maybe Rejoice had been even more clever than the men had given her credit for. She would have been calm, unimpressed by her predicament. She wouldn't have cried and screamed for help. She wouldn't have felt the numbing deep cold of panic settle over her, not the way Sorrow had in the cider house.

Her breath was coming fast now, remembering, fast and shallow like she was eight years old again, and in the gloaming she could hear the creak of weakened boards beneath her feet, and she could see her breath misting in opaque puffs, and she was trapped again, she was trapped, she wasn't going to get out, she was trapped and she was—

She was *cold*.

Sorrow gripped the stay so tight the edges bit into her fingers. The temperature had dropped. She wasn't imagining it, the mist of her breath, she was seeing it right there in front of her face. Her arms were covered with goose bumps, her nose stinging, her ears beginning to ache. She was so cold it felt as though the blood had slowed in her veins, and her mind was creaking and groaning through an impossible crackle of ice. Frost crept over the green leaves as she watched.

It was July. This couldn't be happening again. It couldn't. Not now. If the cold was back that would mean Cassie was gone, and she couldn't be. She *couldn't* be. Sorrow was going to find her.

She closed her eyes and shook her head, and there was a voice echoing *no, no, no,* but it didn't sound like her voice, it didn't sound like a voice at all but rather footsteps rustling through dry autumn leaves, and they were her own footsteps. She had chosen the left path. As she walked the leaves frosted and crisped around her, and when she passed they thawed and steamed, and droplets of water pattered to the ground.

She was carrying it with her, the cold. She was holding on to that icy stone of grief. It had been there all along, sitting high in her chest, and with every step another fissure split through its middle—shivering over the orchard, frosting and melting, seasons flickering around her with the rhythm of her breaths, with the beat of her heart, she and the trees and the earth all part of the same creature. The ice she was carrying, the memory she had left buried in the orchard for so long, it cracked, and weakened, and woke, and by the time she reached the fence around the cemetery grove it was ready to shatter.

There, balanced on a fence post, was an engraved silver lighter.

35

EIGHT YEARS AGO

MOM AND PATIENCE both emerged from their rooms to make dinner. They ate together, the four of them. Nobody argued. Nobody stormed away. Nobody mentioned school.

And nobody asked Sorrow how she had spent her day.

It was there on the tip of her tongue, every time Mom and Patience fell silent. She nearly blurted it out half a dozen times, but each time the urge grew smaller, the words withering away, until finally she was determined to say nothing at all. Mom was out of her room and talking, Patience wasn't picking fights or bringing up things she shouldn't, and Sorrow wasn't going to be the one to change all that. She wasn't going to let Cassie Abrams ruin everything.

When it was time for bed, Mom came to tuck Sorrow in. She smoothed Sorrow's hair back from her forehead and said, "I know it's not easy being stuck inside all day. Why don't we do something fun tomorrow?"

Let's do something fun, Cassie had said. Sorrow shivered, tried to hide it, but Mom saw anyway.

"Do you need another blanket?" she asked.

"No," Sorrow said. She hadn't felt warm all evening, not even during dinner when she had been sitting right next to the woodstove, but she didn't want Mom to worry. "I'm fine."

Mom kissed her forehead. "You're always fine. It's like having another little grandmother in the house."

Sorrow wrinkled up her nose, because that was what she was supposed to do, and she was rewarded with a smile from Mom.

"How about we bake some cupcakes?" Mom said.

"It's nobody's birthday," Sorrow pointed out.

"We'll call them it's-still-winter-and-we're-sick-of-it cupcakes," Mom said. "They'll be better than birthday cupcakes."

Sorrow wanted to believe it. She wanted to trust the smile on Mom's lips, the easy way she talked about baking without needing a reason to celebrate. But she kept hearing the sound of doors slamming in her mind. Mom's, Patience's, the cider house's, one after another, each one adding to the nervous tremble in her chest. She wanted to ask Mom to promise, but she didn't ask for promises anymore. Asking only made Mom cry.

Sorrow said, "Okay," and she tried to sound like she meant it.

After Mom was gone, Sorrow shut off the light on her bedside table. She wanted to turn it on again right away, but she kept her hands fisted at her sides. She wasn't a baby. She wasn't scared of the dark.

Her lighter was tucked away in her underwear drawer. She had never kept a favor secret before, but she wanted to keep this one to herself more than she wanted to show it off. She had examined it in the light before hiding it away: it was a tarnished silver color, etched with musical notes on both sides and the words *To My Joy, With Love and Music, Rosie*. She had struck it one more time, here in her room, and her heart had raced when the little flame whipped and danced.

Hard snow skittered over the window, and the wind groaned and wailed. Sorrow closed her eyes, but as soon as she did she was back in the cider house, and the darkness was pressing all around her, and the hole in the floor was gaping, waiting.

Your whole family is crazy, Cassie had said, and the memory of the words made Sorrow's face burn. It wasn't anything she hadn't heard before, from kids in town snickering as she and Patience passed—Patience with her head held high, Sorrow scurrying like a rabbit hoping to go unnoticed by a fox. Because Grandma was mute, because Mom went days and days without leaving the house, because they all wore patched clothes and lived without phones and computers and TVs like it was a hundred years ago, because Mom didn't let Patience and Sorrow go to school or make friends in town, for all those reasons and more, they never, ever left the Lovegoods alone.

Sorrow rolled onto her side. She didn't care what Cassie said. Cassie was an Abrams. She didn't know anything. Sorrow rolled over again.

Everybody knows you're just as crazy as your mom. Cassie's voice echoed like she was right there in the room with Sorrow. Cassie had probably marched back to her big warm house on the hill and hung her fancy coat in a fancy closet and laughed to herself about Sorrow freezing to death in the cider house.

She shouldn't get away with it.

The thought crept into Sorrow's mind softly, like summer fog.

Cassie shouldn't be allowed to get away with it.

Sorrow sat up. Her heart was thumping.

Sorrow's favorite part of Rejoice Lovegood's story came after she had escaped from her jail cell. Rejoice had returned to the orchard to find that Clement Abrams and his sons had piled up logs to build a cabin on her land. That had been their plan all along, to chase her and her husband away so they could take the Lovegood farm, where the water was sweeter, the soil richer, the trees sturdier than any others in the valley. But Rejoice had escaped, and she didn't need help from anybody at all, not even her husband, to stop Clement Abrams from taking her orchard. She made a great raging bonfire of those logs the Abramses had chopped and hewn, a fire big enough to turn the night sky orange. The Abrams family never tried to build on Lovegood land again.

Sorrow slipped out of bed and dressed without turning on the light. She pulled open the drawer, hands shaking, and found the lighter. She listened before creeping out of her room, listened again as she sneaked down the steps. She took a flashlight from a kitchen drawer and held her breath to listen one more time.

There was nobody awake. Nobody to stop her.

The night was dark and blustery and so very cold. The snow had stopped. The clouds were breaking up, racing across the sky, allowing brief glimpses of the stars. The apple trees groaned in the wind. Sorrow kept to the shadows all the way to the property line, over the wire fence and on the other side too. It was longer than cutting through the meadow, but this way nobody would see her or her footprints.

There was a light on by the front door of the Abrams house, but none inside, and the barn was completely dark. Sorrow ran to the barn door and slid it open. It rattled so loudly she jumped, but she didn't hesitate before ducking through the gap.

She pulled the flashlight from her pocket and switched it on.

The Abramses didn't have any animals. All they had in their barn was a riding lawn mower, some bicycles, skis in a rack on the wall, and a workbench with tools arranged neatly on a pegboard. Sorrow cast the flashlight around until she spotted the ladder in the far corner. She bit off her mittens for better grip and climbed to the hayloft.

There, tucked away in a corner, she found Cassie's playhouse.

Two flowery sheets hung from strings like curtains, enclosing a scrap of pink carpet and piles of pillows. A stuffed purple horse with a rainbow mane was tucked into a soft blanket nest. Against one wall wooden crates were turned on their sides as shelves; they held a stack of drawing paper, a box of colored pencils, a chipped teacup and saucer, a few thin books with ratty covers and cracked spines. Above the shelves there were drawings taped to the wall—mostly horses—and a collection of postcards. Sorrow stepped closer to look at them; her boots left clumps of mud and ice on the pink carpet. The Abramses went on vacation a lot, mostly to faraway places that existed for Sorrow only as spots on maps: Paris, New York, Hawaii.

One of the cards showed a white beach and a line of palm trees. A faint roar gathered in Sorrow's ears. The print in the corner said *Florida*. That was where Dad lived. The closest Sorrow had ever been to Florida was finding it on a map at the library and poring over encyclopedia pictures of alligators and endless blue ocean. When the librarian asked if her father was going to take her to Disney World someday, Sorrow had fled without answering.

Sometimes Dad suggested Sorrow and Patience might come visit him, and Mom always said she would think about it, but after Dad left she would say something different. She would say they didn't need to go anywhere at all. They had everything they needed right here in the orchard.

Sorrow tugged the Florida postcard from the wall. She tucked her flashlight into her pocket and grabbed Paris, London, California, Hawaii, pulling the cards down one by one and crumpling the stiff paper into balls. She took Cassie's horse drawings too, tearing the pages from the taped-up corners, but it didn't help. It didn't help. She could still hear Cassie saying how much better her playhouse was than the gross old cider house, and she could still hear the door slamming shut, and there were icicles of cold deep inside her where her bones ought to be, a cold that felt like it would never thaw.

Mom said if you let an Abrams push you an inch, they would take a mile. She said it when they were painting the No Trespassing signs to nail to fence posts, fresh lettering every spring to mark the property boundary. She said it when they were walking through town and the Abramses were too and Mom refused to cross the street to avoid them. They were Lovegoods, and they belonged in this valley, and no Abrams had any right to try to intimidate them or frighten them away.

Sorrow dropped Cassie's postcards and drawings into a heap. Her hand was shaking as she took the lighter from her pocket, shaking as she flipped it open and tried once, twice, again, to raise a flame. Rejoice Lovegood wouldn't have been frightened when she set fire to the logs Clement Abrams had piled on her land. He and his family had accused her of being a witch, they had tried to steal her land, but she had never let them win.

The lighter sparked and caught. Sorrow touched the flame to the corner of the crumpled-up Florida postcard. The paper curled and smoked and flared, filling the little playhouse with dancing warm light. Sorrow bit her lip in concentration and lit a horse drawing and another postcard. She watched them burn and wither.

The rising smoke took on a bitter, acrid scent. Sorrow scrunched up her face in disgust: the scrap of pink carpet was melting.

She jumped to her feet and stomped on the burning paper, but there was too much of it, and the fire was spreading too fast. She accidentally kicked one of the postcards away from the pile; it tumbled to a stop against the flowery sheet. Sorrow kicked at it again, but the sheet had already caught, and flames were licking up the fabric. The playhouse corner was as bright as daylight now, filled with flickering yellow light, and Sorrow's shadow was a looming shape on the wall.

The smoke was thick and foul, filling her nose and mouth. She had to do something. The fire was spreading so fast, climbing up the sheet to the ceiling, but her ears were roaring and her mind was blank with panic.

It was getting so hot. She tugged desperately at the sheet, but it wasn't just hanging over the string, it was sewn in, and she couldn't pull it down. Flames whipped close to her face, snatched at her hands and the sleeves of her jacket. She jerked away and stumbled out of the playhouse corner. The fire was spreading from the post- cards to the pillows, from the sheets to the blankets. She didn't have any water. She didn't know what to do.

She ran for the ladder and climbed down as fast as she could, slipping twice as her feet missed the rungs. She dropped to the floor and ran. The barn door swung and rattled as she shoved past, and the cold outside was a shock after the heat of the fire. Sorrow stood absolutely still for a moment, her throat aching with every inhale.

There was a light on upstairs in the Abrams house.

Sorrow sprinted for the trees, skidding precariously on the snow. When she glanced back another light came on in the house, this one downstairs. Somebody was awake. She couldn't be caught. Mr. and Mrs. Abrams would tell the police and the police would tell the social worker and the social worker would visit again and Mom—Sorrow didn't even want to think about what that would do to Mom, a visit from the police and child services all at once, so many outsiders crowding into the kitchen with accusing eyes and pointing fingers, and all of it her fault.

Her breath was wheezing and rasping before she even reached the property line, and she tasted the metallic tinge of blood at the back of her throat as she slipped through the wire fence. She looked back only once to see the Abrams house alight, and then she was running again, and she didn't stop until she was in the fallow field below her own farmhouse. The house was dark, an inkblot on the night.

Sorrow doubled over at the edge of the apple trees, sucking in air like she had never breathed before. Only when she didn't feel like her heart was going to burst from her chest did she climb the rest of the way to the house. She sneaked inside as quietly as she had left. Everybody was asleep. For the second time that day nobody had even noticed she was gone.

In her room she shut the door and leaned against it. Her heartbeat slowed and the pounding in her ears softened, and she became aware of another sound, something high and muffled. She leaned over her bed to open the window. Sirens. The high, distant wail grew louder. The Abramses had called the fire department.

As she lowered the casement, a breath of wind twisted through the gap. It felt different from the snow-chasing gusts that had buffeted the house all day. Warmer, gentler. The bite was gone.

The weather was turning. Spring was on its way.

36

THE SUN HAD set, taking with it the last golden light. The orchard had sunk into a hush of green and gray. The last frost melted away, and the warmth returned.

Sorrow reached for the lighter on the fence post. Stopped with her fingers inches away. It was a small silver square, such a tiny thing; the musical notes etched on the side were barely visible in the vanishing light. She could still feel the rasp of the ridged wheel beneath her thumb. The grit and grime of the cider house floorboards. The cold, oh, the aching, bitter cold, sinking into her limbs, sapping the heat from her core, and leaving in its place a bone-deep certainty that she would, very soon, freeze to death.

When she inhaled, she remembered the smell of smoke and the fast-building crackle of heat. She picked up the lighter, and she left in its place on the fence rail the glasses, the watch, the fan, the bead, her collection laid out in a row.

She stepped over the fence, moving slowly through the cemetery rows, past the plain white headstones and towering ash trees. Ahead there was a pale smudge in the twilight: a blue T-shirt, blond hair. Cassie.

She was sitting on the ground at the foot of Patience's grave. Her legs were bent, her arms hooked around her knees. With one hand she gripped the fabric of her jeans, holding herself so tight it was as though she feared she would fly apart.

In the other hand she held a gun.

Sorrow stopped. Her throat was raw when she swallowed. Cassie didn't look up; she hadn't heard Sorrow approach. She barely seemed to be breathing. She might have been part of the orchard, as rooted and unmovable as the trees, if it weren't for the golden glimmer of her short hair, and softly, softly, the sound of her weeping.

"Cassie," Sorrow said.

Cassie's head snapped up. Her face was pale, her eyes red. Without makeup she looked years younger, and Sorrow could see the little girl she had once been, the one whose mother dressed her up in dresses and ribbons, pretty as a doll.

"What the fuck are you doing here?" Cassie's voice was hoarse; she swiped her free hand over her nose and sniffled.

"Looking for you," Sorrow said.

"Get the fuck away from me."

Sorrow took a step forward. Grass crackled under her shoe. Another. "Your family's worried about you. Everybody's looking for you."

Cassie snorted. "Yeah, right. They don't care. All they care about is how *embarrassing* I am, that's the only thing they—they're doing it again, talking about how, oh, it's so shocking, so much young life lost in such a small town. Calling them the tragic Abrams Valley girls. It's on the fucking internet. People who don't give a fuck about them and never did."

She swallowed back a sob and twisted her face into her shoulder, wiped her eyes on her sleeve. She wasn't pointing the gun at anything—where had she even gotten a gun? Had her parents noticed it was missing?—but in her hand it was a terrible black shadow, more outline than shape, and Sorrow couldn't take her eyes off it.

She sank to the ground beside the grave, and they formed a triangle, the three of them, Cassie and Sorrow and Patience's sturdy tall ash.

"I'm not as brave as Julie was. I'm sitting here, trying to convince myself I can do it. But I'm a fucking coward." Cassie scrubbed at her face again. "You know, I used to be so jealous of you."

Sorrow wasn't expecting that. "Me? Why?"

"You. Her. Both of you." She gestured toward Patience's headstone with the gun, and Sorrow flinched. "I thought you had the best life. You didn't have to go to school. You didn't have your parents freaking out over everything you did. Nobody telling you that your whole life was decided for you. It seemed so perfect. Your mom let you do anything and everybody loved your grandma and it was . . . everything we didn't get to do. Everything. My mom was always like, Oh, those Lovegood girls, look at how dirty they are, they don't even wear shoes, they're like wild animals, and the whole time I was just thinking how much I wanted to be one of you. I was so jealous. I knew your mom was crazy—sorry, *depressed*—but still I used to pretend—this is so stupid."

"It's not stupid," Sorrow said softly. She had no idea if she was saying the right thing. She only knew that talking was better than letting Cassie's confession fall into a horrible empty silence. "What did you pretend?"

"I used to pretend I was a Lovegood. A secret Lovegood, like, your long-lost sister or cousin, and my parents had stolen me away for some reason, and someday it would all come out and I would get to go back to the right family and . . . It's so fucking stupid."

"It's not," Sorrow said again.

"That's what I used to pretend when I went up to my play-house," Cassie went on. "I wanted, like, a real playhouse, or a tree house, but my dad kept promising to build one and never doing it, so I just had that stupid corner of the hayloft. And that day after the fire my parents were all, Were you playing with matches? Did you leave a candle burning? You can tell us, you can tell us, and . . . they didn't believe me. I was telling the truth, but they just looked at me like they were looking at—like they were looking at some stranger, like I was this problem they had to solve. But I wasn't lying."

"I know," Sorrow said, the words barely louder than a whisper.

Cassie looked up. Her eyes burned in the growing twilight.

"You said it wasn't your sister."

"It wasn't," Sorrow said. "It was me."

There was a long silence, as though the entire orchard was holding its breath. Cassie didn't move. She didn't sniffle. She didn't wipe her tears. In her stillness she sank into the shadows.

Then she let out a ragged breath, half laugh and half sob. She lifted her hand—the hand with the gun—to wipe at her eyes with her wrist. "Of course you did. Jesus fucking Christ. Of course it was you." She pressed the curve of her wrist against her eyes, shaking her head with her face hidden. "I should have known. You must have hated me so much."

Lovegoods hated Abramses. Abramses hated Lovegoods. That was how it had been since Clement Abrams had first come to this valley to find that a woman had already claimed the fertile land he wanted for himself. That was how it had been since Rejoice Lovegood had spilled her own blood and sweat and tears to bind these acres to herself and herself to the land, sharing her burden with the mountains and hollows when there was no one else to help her carry it. Seasons turned, apple blossoms blushed and withered, fruit swelled and dropped, snow fell and melted, and children grew to bear children of their own, to make mistakes of their own, to love and hate and fear on their own, to die by hunger, by violence, by the lure of the wider world. Promises were made, hearts were broken, and people twisted themselves around and around and around, the soft green tendrils of their dreams hardening into woody vines that could not bend but would someday break. Mounds of lush green grass erupted where bodies lay buried. Children spilled blood in a creek. A man drowned in a well. A fire burned out of control.

The lighter was warm. Sorrow's fingers ached from holding it so tight.

There might be a spark, if she struck it. It might catch still.

Sorrow opened her hand, each finger releasing like vines unwinding, and she looked at the lighter on her open palm.

You must hate me, and I you.

All she had been, in the end, was a thoughtless child with a grudge and a stupid idea.

She didn't know if this was the right way to help. She wanted to ask. She wanted to accuse. She didn't know if there was a right way. She was not going to lie.

"I don't think I hated you," Sorrow said. Carefully, so carefully, taking small steps in her mind. "I didn't even know you. I was angry and jealous and I didn't know how to put a fire out once I got it started."

Cassie's smile was a terrible, crumbling thing. She gestured with the gun—a shape in the darkness, a void—and Sorrow curled her fingers into the soft earth. But Cassie wasn't pointing the gun at her. Her finger wasn't on the trigger; she didn't even seem to remember she was holding it. She was motioning toward Patience's headstone.

"Did you know they were friends?" Cassie said.

"Not until right at the end."

"I knew all along. I used to follow Julie—" She choked on her sister's name, held her breath a moment before going on. "I used to follow her. After she came home from school that year, our parents were so pissed at her, but it was the kind of pissed that meant they obsessed over everything she did. Everything was about Julie. Get Julie a therapist, get Julie a tutor, get Julie into a summer program. Everything was about fixing Julie. And around them she acted all . . . contrite, you know, she was *so* sorry, she wouldn't mess up again, they could totally trust her. But she was still sneaking out and I thought—I thought she had a boyfriend or, like, a drug dealer. I didn't think it was just . . . a friend. How fucked up is that? Of all the stupid, pointless secrets to keep. She just had a friend."

It wasn't anything Sorrow hadn't thought to herself before, but hearing it spoken aloud in Cassie's bitter voice made the weight of those secrets press anew on her shoulders and spine. What would it have mattered, if their parents had discovered Patience and Julie were friends? Centuries of animosity and feuding, of fighting with words and violence, of glaring and scheming across a wire fence that bound their families together more than it separated them, and what were they left with? Two dead girls and eight years of secrets. A girl in a graveyard with a gun.

"I thought . . ." Cassie sniffled. "I thought maybe Julie and Patience were the ones who had—I thought they'd been in my playhouse. Maybe they'd been smoking or something. Left a candle burning. Whatever my parents thought I'd been doing. I don't even know why. I just thought, it wasn't fair, everything was all about Julie, and that one thing that was supposed to be mine, I didn't even have that anymore. So I followed her that night when she went out to meet your sister. They had this—secret meeting code, I don't know, it was stupid. I guess they had to make something up because you guys never had phones. Your sister would shine her flashlight from the meadow so Julie would know she was there."

You know how to find me, Julie had said, that day in the orchard. It had meant more to Patience than it had to Sorrow. An invitation to reconcile. Sorrow felt the nip of a mosquito on her arm, brushed it away. Somewhere in the darkness an owl hooted. Grass rustled as a field mouse scurried for its burrow.

"I didn't mean to hurt them," Cassie said. Every word sounded as though it were being torn from her throat. "I didn't mean that. I just thought—I wanted to scare them. I wanted to make Julie mad. Everybody was looking at her all the time and I just wanted, I just wanted—to ruin her secret place like, like I thought she'd ruined mine. I never meant to hurt them."

She dropped the gun and crumpled in on herself, covering her face with both hands. Her shoulders shook as the pained sobs escaped through her fingers.

Sorrow pressed her fingers into the ground, curling her fingers into the soil again, holding herself still. She wanted to grab Cassie and shake her and demand a better explanation. She wanted to jump to her feet and run, run, run, flee into the orchard and the darkness until her breath was a rasp and the sound of Cassie's agonized sobs was swallowed by the song of crickets and the stir of breeze-turned leaves. She wanted to grab Cassie's hair and pull her head back to see her face, to *look* at her, eye to eye, and command her to say it again.

There was distant thunder at the back of her mind, like a storm crawling over the ocean. She had wanted to know. She had come back to Vermont for this very moment. She had risked breaking her family apart. She had hurt her mother and grandmother. She had scraped carelessly through the scattered debris of her own memories to find this one truth, and now all she wanted was to scream and kick and wail and make Cassie take it back. She wanted to have never heard it. She wanted the soil beneath her, the trees around her, the whole of the embracing orchard to leach away that terrible knowledge, to draw it out through her grasping fingertips to take it away as it had done before, to spread the awful bleak ache she felt in her chest over acres and hollows, hills and fields, spread it as thin and fragile as the last feeble frost before winter's end.

"Why . . ." Sorrow had to stop, steady herself, swallow the bile at the back of her throat. "Why didn't you tell anyone?"

Cassie rubbed her hands over her face. "What?"

"If you didn't mean—why didn't you run for help?"

"I—but I *did*. We did. Julie came running out first, and Patience was right behind her but she—she tripped and she fell, we heard her fall. She screamed. That hole in the floor." Cassie's breath was short, shuddering. "Julie tried, she tried to get back inside—it was so fast. The roof came down so fast, but she still tried to go back in. It was so hot and so loud and—and she was shouting and screaming and—I ran up to the house. I got our parents."

The hair on Sorrow's neck prickled. "You told your parents?"

"I woke them up," Cassie said. "I was screaming my head off."

"Your parents know," Sorrow said.

"They've always known."

They had always known.

Eight years ago Paul and Hannah Abrams had not once challenged the police theory that a homeless drifter had been responsible for both fires. They had never pointed a finger, not at the Lovegoods or anybody else. The whole town had been in an uproar over Patience's shocking death, but the Abramses had never demanded a more thorough investigation into the fire on their own land. A few weeks later they had taken their daughters out of town and let the matter wither away unsolved. If the police had asked Sorrow about the barn, she would have cracked like an eggshell, and the rest of the story might have come out. She had been a child, scared and guilty and angry all at the same time. She would have confessed in a heartbeat, if anybody had asked. They could have put it together. Nobody ever did.

"They said we couldn't tell," Cassie said. "They made us promise we would never tell. Over and over again. We kept having to say it. It was a stranger. It was a homeless person. That's all we know. We had to—" Cassie's voice broke, small and wretched. "We had to promise."

Sorrow felt something splinter inside of her, with a pain like a mountain cleaving open. She wiped tears from her face, but more were falling. The darkening orchard was a blur around them.

"You were a little kid," she said. "You wouldn't have been—you said it was an accident. They shouldn't have made you do that."

Cassie was a shuddering shape in the night, pale shirt and pale hair, hunched over herself. Her breath hitched with painful cries, and a couple of times she made a terrible keening noise, so soft it was barely audible.

She inhaled tightly, let out her breath through her fingers. She said, "Julie left a note. My mom found it before the police looked."

Sorrow was afraid to ask. "You read it?"

"She said she was . . . she was sorry but she was so tired. She didn't want to keep lying. But she didn't even say it was me. I think she wanted people to think it was her. I think she knew that I was trying to . . . I don't know. That shit I said to you, about your sister, it was bullshit. I just wanted people to notice. She knew that. Julie always understood. But she never did anything wrong. It was never her fault. I don't want anybody to think it was her fault."

A breathless pause, the orchard around them quietly waiting.

Sorrow said, "We can tell them."

Cassie sniffed roughly and lifted her head. "What?"

"We can tell the truth," Sorrow said. There was an ache at the back of her throat. She felt like she had been screaming. "Both of us."

Cassie shook her head, but she said nothing.

"I'll tell them about the barn fire," Sorrow said, "and you tell them what happened after. It was an accident. You were only a little kid. Tell them about Julie's note. Can I—" Her voice caught. She breathed a moment, cleared her throat. "Can I tell you what she said to me? The day before she died? She came over here to talk to me, and she said—she said that sometimes people don't realize that the hurt they're causing themselves by keeping a secret can be worse than the secret itself. I thought she was talking about something else, but she was—I think she was talking about you. She knew how much it was hurting you."

"Nobody will believe me that it was an accident. My parents didn't even believe me."

Sorrow's heart broke again. "Your parents aren't thinking clearly. They weren't then and they aren't now. They should never have made you lie."

"What will happen to them?"

"I don't know."

"And me?"

"I don't know."

"Why do you even care? You must hate me. How can you not hate me?"

"I don't know," Sorrow said. "Maybe I do. I don't know what else to do."

Cassie didn't answer. She didn't answer for a long time, but Sorrow didn't push. Grandma would be worried. Ethan might have called again. The people looking for Cassie might now be looking for Sorrow too. They would just have to worry a little longer. She wasn't leaving Cassie in the orchard alone.

Finally, finally, Cassie unfolded her legs. She left the gun on the ground.

"You'll come with me?" she said, her voice so small, so scared.

Sorrow stood up, felt the burn in her legs as she moved. She held out her hand.

When they left Patience's graveside they would walk together through the orchard until they heard people calling their names. They would see flashlights flicking behind trees and silhouettes moving in the distance. They wouldn't answer until they were close enough to be recognized, and when they did it would be Sorrow who spoke, who lifted her voice over the questions and demands, the exclamations and scolds, to say they needed to speak to the sheriff. They needed their parents. They needed help. They had a story to tell, and they would tell it even if nobody wanted to hear. They would tell it together. There would be whispers—the Lovegood girl, the Abrams girl, did you hear? How terrible—but they would say what needed to be said, and unearth the long-buried secrets, and weather what followed.

When they left the graveside, the world would crash around them again, but for a moment, this last moment, they were only two girls who might have been friends, had never wanted to be enemies, and a grove of ash trees bending protectively around them. Cassie took Sorrow's hand and held on tight.

37

PERSEVERANCE LOVEGOOD

1947–

IT WAS ONLY a single shoot, thin as yarn, but it was green.

The ground was soft and muddy, sinking into soggy craters beneath her feet. It had rained steadily through the night, a cold stinging downpour that drummed on the roof and rattled through the naked trees. She had sat up listening to it, alone in the kitchen, letting cup after cup of tea cool by her elbow. When gray morning light crept through the window and the rain softened to a drizzle, she stood—knees cracking, joints creaking—to go outside.

The clouds had broken apart after dawn, and in a fleeting patch of sunlight she found a green stem emerging from the ground. She knelt beside it; her knees pressed into the earth. With a trembling hand she cleared a tangle of rotted leaves and winter debris. The little shoot looked like a single green matchstick separated from its bundle, but she recognized it as the beginnings of a crocus, the first flower of spring. Two months late and so fragile a misplaced step would crush it.

And she thought, for one wild moment: she would hurry back to the house with the news. Spring had come after all, finally, finally there was life in the orchard, and the girls would whoop and laugh with joy and—

They were gone.

Her girls were gone. The house was empty. There was nobody waiting for her return, nobody to celebrate this one bold flower-to-be. A thousand flowers could have bloomed overnight and she would remain the only one to see them. Even the little Abrams boy, the one who looked so much like Henry—like the child they might have had, if everything had been different—he was nowhere to be seen. She was rather afraid she had scared him away for good, when they had surprised each other a few days ago. She had been without her notebook and unable to tell him he was allowed to stay, she wasn't a wicked witch who gobbled up little boys for supper, she wasn't going to hurt him like whoever had given him that bruise on his wrist.

She could show him the crocus if he appeared again. Enlist his small hands to search for other shoots, to clear the dead leaves and let them breathe. There was too much quiet now that she was alone. A child could be trusted with a flower.

Her knees ached. Her eyes remained fixed on the crocus shoot, but her thoughts turned and stretched, traveled through the muddy gray orchard and over the brown fields, up to the house now echoing and empty, and she imagined herself walking back slowly, grass and flowers springing from the earth with every footstep like she was a crone from a fairy tale, not a selfish hag but a generous queen. Overhead the apple trees would blossom pink and white, a blush spreading over every leafless branch, and by the time she reached the house, spring would have come, and as flowers bloomed in a riot of color and the garden grew heavy with bounty, Verity would return from the hospital, Sorrow from her father's home, and together in the orchard, in the embrace of their living mountains, they would be a family again, and begin to heal their broken hearts.

It was only a single shoot, one shy crocus not yet formed, but it was green.

38

HEAVY GRAY CLOUDS were gathering over Abrams Valley again. The air was humid and warm, but there was a breeze kicking up. This was the promise of a summer storm, not an aberration. Those few tourists still wandering around town were eyeing the sky warily.

Verity held the door of the sheriff's department open for Sorrow, and they walked down the sidewalk toward the car parked half a block away.

"It'll rain soon," Verity said.

Sorrow looked up, and with the motion a wave of dizziness passed over her. Her eyes were hot with exhaustion, her blood buzzing with too much caffeine. It felt as though the hours since she'd found Cassie in the cemetery grove had passed in the bewildering whirl of a dream. She had called Dr. Parker to get through to Verity. She had called her father. She had gone to the police station as soon as Verity came home in the morning. She had given her statement, she had told the truth, she had answered all of the sheriff's questions. Her part in it was supposed to be over now. She had been eight and Cassie nine; under Vermont law neither of them was criminally liable for the fires they had set.

But Mr. and Mrs. Abrams had known exactly what they were doing when they'd covered up Cassie's role in Patience's death. There would be consequences for them, although nobody seemed to know yet what they would be. Sorrow knew the whole town would already be talking about it—the tragic Abrams Valley girls, those who were lost and those who remained—but for once the prospect didn't anger her. She only felt tired and sad, and a pang of something almost like sympathy, that this little mountain town had to figure out, once again, how to deal with such terrible things happening to its girls.

"I hope it does," she said. Verity was looking at her across the car. "Rain," Sorrow clarified. "I hope it rains."

"Let's go home," Verity said.

Sorrow leaned her head against the seat as Verity drove them out of town. She closed her eyes, lulled by the quiet rumble of the car. When she opened her eyes again, they were passing the Abrams house. Sorrow wondered if she should say something, if she had to be the first to break the silence. Then they were passing the cider house, passing the hill, and before she could decide what to say her phone rang.

She was expecting Dad, but the name on the screen was Sonia.

"Oh. I should . . . Oh. Can you let me off at the bottom of the driveway?"

Verity was already slowing to make the turn. She let Sorrow out by the mailbox and headed up to the house, and Sorrow answered the call. "Hello?"

There was a pause, then Sonia's voice, surprised: "Sorrow! Hello. I thought you—"

Sorrow felt a tired pang of guilt. Sonia had thought she wouldn't answer, and Sorrow couldn't even blame her. "We just got home," she said. "From the police station."

"Oh, Sorrow. That must have been hard. How are you doing?"

"I don't know," Sorrow said. "I'm tired. I don't know what else to . . . I don't know."

"Your mother is home with you?" Sonia asked, and she sounded so hesitant, so unsure, like she didn't even have the right to ask that question. Sorrow hated hearing that uncertainty in her voice. She hated knowing she was responsible for putting it there.

"Yeah. She's home now."

"That's good," Sonia said.

They fell into an awkward silence. A few cool drops of rain tapped Sorrow's face. She brushed them away. She couldn't think of a single thing to say. She was too worn down, too wrung out. But she didn't want to hang up either. She leaned against the wooden fence and held out her hand to catch the raindrops.

"Sorrow." Sonia's voice was soft, almost pleading. "Why didn't you call? Why didn't you tell us what was happening? You didn't have to deal with all of that by yourself."

Sorrow's eyes stung; she squeezed them shut. "I wasn't by myself. Grandma's here."

"I know. I know she's taking care of you, but—why didn't you call?"

It was no use. The tears were going to fall no matter what she did. She was so tired of holding them in like a stone in the center of her chest. "I don't know. It just didn't seem . . . I don't know."

"Your father told me about the conversation you had yesterday."

Only yesterday she had sat in the hospital parking lot with her father on the phone, frustrated and alone and so very angry. It seemed ages ago now, but the hurt was still raw inside of her, piled up on top of everything else.

"I don't think I want to apologize to him," she said.

"I'm not asking you to," Sonia said. "I think you have a lot of reasons to be angry. I think it's good for you to be angry."

"You do?"

There was a brief pause; then Sonia went on: "You always try so hard not to be, Sorrow. You're always trying to be calm and avoid upsetting anybody and that's . . . Sometimes you're trying so hard it hurts to see."

Sorrow's face grew warm. She had never known anybody noticed. She had always hoped it looked like being relaxed, unruffled. She had never known that Sonia or anybody else might look at her and see how desperately she was trying not to fall apart.

"I didn't know a lot about your childhood until recently," Sonia said. "When I met your father, it was still so fresh and painful for you, he decided it was best to let Dr. Silva deal with it, so I tried to stay out of it. I didn't want to make things worse for you. And that's what I was thinking this year, when you were so upset after spring break. I was so used to thinking it was something that had nothing to do with me that I thought—no, I *convinced* myself I would only make it worse by sticking my nose in. You know I have a tendency to do that, and it's not always helpful."

Sorrow didn't know what to say to that. She didn't know if Sonia's interfering nature would have helped or hurt when she was trying to remember Patience, trying to decide if coming back to Vermont was the right idea, trying to find a way forward when the tangled tragedies of her past kept tugging her back. She did think she would have liked Sonia to try, but she didn't know how to say that either.

"And I was . . ." Sonia sighed. "I was reeling a little bit. I was angry at Michael. It's something of a shock to learn that you've been married for seven years to the kind of man who would have stayed away for weeks when one of his daughters had just died and the other one was all alone in such a terrible and scary situation."

"It wasn't that bad," Sorrow said weakly.

"Yes, Sorrow, it was, and you're allowed to be angry about that. You were eight years old. You never should have felt even for a second like you were responsible for your mother's well-being. And I know you love your mother and your grandmother. I know they did the best they could for you. But your father didn't. He should have been there. When he first started telling me about it back in the spring, when you were so lost and we didn't know what to do, it was—I had to figure out how to deal with it." Sonia took a breath, released it, shuddering and slow. "But I didn't want to make it harder for you, what you've been going through now. I didn't want to get between you and your father, not when you needed him. I don't think I made the right call, letting you sort it out on your own."

Sorrow couldn't help it: she let out a startled little laugh.

"What?" Sonia said. "Is that funny?"

"No. Yes. No. It's really not." But she was still laughing, trying to catch it and bottle it down, not quite succeeding. "It's just that on the scale of parents making really bad decisions I've dealt with just in the last twenty-four hours . . . that doesn't even rate. That's, like, farm-team-level parenting mistakes. You're nowhere near the big leagues."

She tried to laugh again, but it turned into a sob, and Sonia let her cry. When she felt steady enough to speak again, she said, "It's kinda starting to rain. I should get inside."

"Okay. We'll talk when we get there. Michael sent you our flight itinerary, right?"

"Yeah."

"We are going to talk. All three of us. Okay?"

"Yeah," Sorrow said.

It was what she was supposed to say, in spite of the weak nervous feeling she had inside. There had been nothing but talking around her all day. The police, Verity, the lawyers, all the murmured voices at the sheriff's department behind coffee mugs and closed doors, a constant patter of questions, and what she wanted now was quiet. But Sonia was talking about tomorrow, the next day, a promise of what was to come, and Sorrow was tired of crying, tired of shouting, tired of treating her entire life like an obstacle course riddled with traps and mistakes.

"Yeah," she said again. "Okay."

"We'll see you when we get in tomorrow afternoon," Sonia said. "I love you, Sorrow."

"Love you too."

Sorrow walked up the driveway slowly. Rain pattered on the maple trees, and the temperature was dropping, but there was no bite in it, no ominous unseasonal threat. It felt nice on her skin, soothing when she lifted her face to the sky. Soft gray curtains were drifting over the mountains, nudging the downpour closer. Everything was green and lush and summer-alive.

She went around the back of the house and into the kitchen. Grandma was chopping up vegetables and dumping them into a big pot on the stove.

"Rainy day soup?" Sorrow said, and Grandma nodded. "That'll be good. Where's Verity?"

She didn't mean to glance up at the ceiling as she asked, but she couldn't quite stop herself. Verity had been perfectly calm and controlled all day, reasonable and rational and even a bit stern when she'd met Sorrow at the sheriff's department. She had sat by Sorrow's side through the entire ordeal without once wavering.

Grandma pointed her needle toward the barn.

"What's she doing out there?"

Grandma shrugged. Sorrow went back outside and jogged across the lawn. She ducked into the barn as the rain began to fall.

At the threshold she paused to let her eyes adjust. The air was stuffy with the scents of rust and fertilizer and a faint, lingering hint of hay. Verity was sitting on the workbench with her feet propped up on the engine block of the tractor. She had cleared a space on the cluttered bench for herself and the white file box beside her; the lid was tipped off and she had a stack of papers on her legs.

"What are you doing out here?" Sorrow asked. "You've been home like five minutes."

"I was looking for some old insurance paperwork, but I got distracted." Verity fanned her face with the stack of papers. "We've been shoving stuff in here for so long I don't even know what's in half these boxes. But I'd like to get it cleared out and get rid of this thing." She kicked the tractor. "I want to park the car in here this winter. I've spent enough of my life scraping ice off the windshield."

"So you're going to start now?" Sorrow asked.

Verity glanced down at the papers, and when she looked up she was wearing a self-conscious smile. "Well, it's raining, and I don't want to be stuck in the house. I might start remodeling again just to have something to do."

Sorrow looked down uncomfortably, scraped her toe over the floor. She didn't know how to answer, not when her first impulse was to say something awful: Why did you wait until everything was ruined to start remodeling rather than sleeping all day? That wouldn't help. That wasn't the right thing to say.

But maybe there was no right thing to say. There were no magic words they could pass between them, no confessions or reassurances that would heal the wounds. Patience had figured that out too, right before the end. She had gathered her courage to push and demand, to look beyond the orchard and imagine another life for herself. For so long Sorrow had believed she'd been following Patience's lead in doing everything she could to avoid causing even the slightest ripples, but she knew now she had learned the wrong lesson. Patience would never have wanted her to make herself quiet and small. Patience would have challenged her to a race just to see how far they could go.

Sorrow's eyes were stinging again. She blinked twice, cleared her throat. "You want help?"

Verity gave her a considering look. "You don't have to. You look exhausted."

"If I nap now, I won't be able to sleep later. I can help."

"Okay. Grab a box. There's a trash bag over here, and I'm putting stuff to donate in the wheelbarrow."

Sorrow stepped over a length of dented gutter and a pile of garden stakes. There was already a pile in the wheelbarrow: mismatched tools, a painted birdhouse, an elbow of plastic piping, a pair of leather work boots. She reached for an age-softened cardboard box just inside the door, where the cool damp air stirred around her. She turned the box, and a fluttery feeling settled high in her chest, something light and a little painful. *Patience*, in Grandma's handwriting on the side. She *was* tired; she hadn't been paying attention. She withdrew her hand.

"You can go through those, if you want," Verity said.

Sorrow looked over her shoulder.

"But you don't have to."

There was a scattering of leaves and a fine layer of dust over the gray sweater at the top of the box. Below the sweater, a white dress with tiny blue flowers. A long skirt patched together from two of Verity's old dresses—Patience had made that one herself. Beneath the skirt was a sky-blue wool scarf—Grandma had knit it because Patience had fallen in love with the yarn at the store, had kept returning to brush her fingers gently over the skeins even after she had sighed at the price tag.

Sorrow tugged the scarf out, drawing it gently between her fingers. It was still as soft as a kitten; Patience had liked it too much to wear it often.

"You should take it," Verity said. "It's too nice to give away."

Sorrow didn't have any use for a thick wool scarf in Florida, but she folded it into a square and set it aside.

Under the scarf were more folded clothes, skirts and shirts with no particular sentimental meaning, and at the bottom of the box she found a journal bound in leather and tied closed with a green ribbon. It was familiar, but Sorrow couldn't recall ever seeing Patience use it. She slid the ribbon off and opened to a page in the middle.

It wasn't Patience's handwriting that filled the pages, but Grandma's.

Sorrow flipped through the book, frowning. She remembered how Grandma used to write in her journals, early in the morning before anybody else was awake, or late at night by a crackling fire, the *scratch-scratch* of her pen on paper a constant and reassuring sound, but Sorrow hadn't seen her do it once this summer.

She set the leather journal aside and lowered the box to the floor. She opened the next, dug through layers of sweaters and summer dresses until her fingers brushed over something solid. She pulled out two more of Grandma's old journals. She paged through them, one after another, her curiosity growing. She had been expecting diary entries, notes about the seasons and the orchard, thoughts and reflections. But that wasn't what Grandma had been writing at all.

"What have you got there?" Verity asked.

Sorrow slid the journals into a stack and carried them over to her. "Look."

Verity's eyes widened in recognition. "Those are Mom's."

"I know. They were in with Patience's things."

"I haven't seen these in years." Verity took the top journal, the one with the leather cover, and opened it. "I didn't even know she still had them."

"Have you ever read them? It's not a diary, not like in the normal way," Sorrow said. "They're stories. Stories about our family."

"She started writing in them when she stopped talking," Verity said quietly. "But I never knew what she was writing. I never . . . I didn't like to ask a lot from her then. Oh, I remember this story. My grandmother told this to me when I was just a little girl."

Verity paused at a page near the center of the book. At the top of the page was a name written in black ink: *Grace Lovegood.* Below, a pair of dates. *1811–1873*. Birth and death. Sorrow recognized the years from her gravestone. Silence Lovegood's one surviving daughter.

"What happened to her?" Sorrow asked. "I've always kinda wondered about that. She must've gone to live with somebody, right? After her mother was executed?"

"She did. Her father's family here in Vermont refused to have anything to do with her, so she went to stay with an aunt in Baltimore. Anne Derry. She was the only one who would take Grace in. But it turned out to be a good thing."

"It did?"

Verity's lips curved into the beginning of a smile. She turned a few pages, scanning quickly. "Anne Derry was this eccentric spinster type—not very old, maybe only thirty at the time, but a woman didn't have to be old to be considered a spinster in those days. She saw to it that Grace got a good education, learned everything a girl was supposed to learn, and all the things boys were supposed to learn too. They traveled all over together. They went to Paris, to London, eventually to India. By the time Grace was twenty she had seen half the world. She'd studied all kinds of things—math and science and law and history. She was a brilliant woman."

Sorrow had only ever known the bookends of Grace Lovegood's life: the tragic childhood, the eventual death, with the orchard always at the center.

"Why did she come back?" she asked.

"You know, I don't know," Verity said. "The way my grandmother told it, it always sounded like an inevitability, like there wasn't anything else she could have done. Something about needing to claim the land back for the family. But I was only a kid when I heard that story, and my grandmother wouldn't have bothered to explain the details to me. I do know Grace didn't come back until she had a daughter of her own. Anne, named for her aunt." Verity turned a few more pages. Her touch was gentle now, almost reverent. "There's a lot more here than I remember."

"You never knew this was what Grandma was writing down?"

"I had no idea. She must have heard a lot of this from Devotion." Verity ran her forefinger over a crease in one page. "My grandmother was a terrible person, but she had a mind like a steel trap. She remembered everything."

"She never left, did she?" Sorrow said. "She never lived anywhere else. She had no choice but to remember."

"No," Verity said. "She didn't. I don't think she ever traveled more than ten miles from this spot. She used to say—usually when she was angry about something—she used to say the land was a part of her and she was a part of the land, and anybody who wanted to separate them would have to rip up every tree in the orchard to find every piece of her."

Devotion had never ventured beyond the sloping shoulders of Abrams Valley. Every one of her days had been spent pruning Lovegood trees and tilling Lovegood land, working every season of every year until the soil was ground into the creases of her hands, until her sweat and blood flowed through the veins of the trees, and she would have remembered everything. The orchard was as much a part of their family as the mud-brown hair and hazel eyes, and it held their grief and their memories as firmly as the mountains held the roots of their apple trees.

"I thought she was just . . . well, my grandmother. I thought she was just odd," Verity said. "Until I went to college."

Sorrow studied her face for a moment, looking for signs that her question would not be welcome. "Did you start to forget?"

"It didn't feel like forgetting," Verity said. "I wasn't even gone a full year, but it felt like . . . like everything was fading. Like things that had happened to me were things I had read in a book. I began to understand why so many women in our family were so obsessive about remembering our history—including my grandmother, for all her faults."

Sorrow flipped through one of the journals, but glancing over pages of Grandma's sloping, spiky script, she felt a wormlike wriggle of discomfort. It might be their shared history on the page, but these were Grandma's words, and she had always kept them to herself. Sorrow closed the journal and smoothed her hand over the cover. It wasn't up to her to decide what Grandma ought to do with the voice she had found when she stopped speaking.

"We'll ask her what she wants to do with them," she said.

Verity looked the leather journal over one more time before handing it to Sorrow. "At the very least we should bring them inside so nothing gets into them out here. Check if there are more."

"Yeah. I'll look." Sorrow set the journals beside the blue scarf and hefted another box to the top of the stack. This one was full of

408 · THE MEMORY TREES

Patience's old schoolbooks and paperbacks; she spent a couple of minutes flipping through each notebook to see whose handwriting covered the pages.

When Verity spoke again, her voice was quiet, almost hesitant. "Are you going to go back to Florida with your father after he gets here?"

Sorrow lowered a spiral-bound notebook back into the box, but she didn't turn around. She looked instead through the open door of the barn. She had been in Vermont for just over two weeks, although it felt like a span of time impossibly longer. Half of her planned vacation. She had been so busy worrying about everything that was happening she hadn't given herself time to think about what she was going to do next.

The rain was coming down steadily now, a clean soaking shower, drumming on the apple trees, on Grandma's garden, on puddles spreading over the lawn. They still hadn't spoken to Ethan about the French drain, whatever that was. The kitchen window glowed with warm yellow light. It would smell of onions and garlic inside, chicken browning in the skillet, fresh-plucked herbs and ground pepper. There would be bread rising in a bowl on the counter. Sorrow didn't know if Verity had eaten anything today. Surely Dr. Parker would have made sure she did before they left the hospital, or on the drive down. She didn't know if she could sit at the table for dinner and not count the bites Verity took. She didn't know if she could spend another two weeks enduring whispers and glares, the rumors and questions, the way every conversation in town would turn back to Cassie, to Patience, to the Lovegoods and the Abramses and the tragedies they shared. She wanted to go home, to her family and her friends, to the ordinary life she had set aside. She wanted to let the knotted ache of grief and regret and guilt fade with distance and time, to stop feeling in every waking moment like sadness was a hole inside of her that would never go away.

But if she stayed in the orchard, to the end of her planned time or longer, the weight of its history would seep into her, and it would perhaps start to feel like her natural landscape again. She could read her grandmother's journals and meet all of the women who had come before, immerse herself in the memories until they stopped itching like skin that didn't fit right. Before she had come back, she had not considered the possibility of staying longer. One month and no more. Close the gaps in her memory, fill in the spaces where Patience was supposed to be, and leave again, mission accomplished.

It wasn't so simple, to walk away from a land that held parts of herself in its bones of wood and stone. But neither could she stand in one place and let roots anchored in centuries past push their way into her veins until she could not take a single step for fear of ripping them away.

"I don't know," she said. She could barely stand the look on Verity's face, scared and hopeful all at once, with no sign of the careful, carved mask she so often wore. "It's not really fair, is it? That I'll start to forget again if I leave."

"If you want fair, I'm afraid you're in the wrong family," Verity said. Her smile was fleeting, knowing.

Sorrow looked out through the barn door. The little farmhouse was obscured by mist and rain, and rivulets were snaking across the lawn to the edges of the garden. "I don't want to be one or the other," she said. "A different person here or there. I can't do that anymore."

The rain on the roof was so loud she thought she heard her mother say something, the beginnings of a word lost in the racket, but when she turned, Verity was looking at her, just looking, and the only answer she gave was a brief nod.

39

SORROW WOKE EARLY the next morning. Nobody else was up yet, so she left a note on the kitchen table—*went for a walk, back for breakfast*—and headed out into the orchard.

The sun was just peeking over the mountains. Another brief rainstorm had come and gone during the night. The orchard was damp, glistening with droplets still falling from the trees. The morning light was golden, the air cooler. Everything smelled fresh and clean. The ground was just muddy enough to squish beneath her shoes, but not so muddy that it stuck. Midsummer flowers were blooming under the apple trees, clustered together in splashes of color, sprinkled shyly through the shade: feathery and colorful false goat's beard, tall snapdragons in orange and pink, purple tufts of phlox, deep blue stalks of larkspur. There were mushrooms in the shadows, and Sorrow tested herself on remembering how dangerous they were and she didn't mind too much that she had forgotten most of it. She could learn it again.

She avoided the muddy road and cut through the apple trees, wandering around the base of the hill with no particular destination in mind. She stopped to examine unfamiliar shrubs and flowers, paused to listen to birdsong, breathed deeply as the light changed and the air warmed. In one spot where an apple tree had been cut down, a wild raspberry bush had taken its place, its first red fruit just beginning to swell. A few rows farther along she found a lump of rock protruding from the ground: angular Green Mountain granite softened by lichen and moss. She didn't recall having seen it before, but when she scrambled up one side and stood at the top, a memory returned, and with it a faint thrum of sadness, soft, mellowed from being held so long in a stone older than remembrance. She had climbed that boulder on a crisp, clear fall day, declared herself queen of the rock, and giggled uncontrollably as Patience tried, not very hard, to knock her from her pinnacle and tackle her into a pile of crunching golden leaves.

She balanced on the boulder's weathered edge until the ache passed and left in its wake an impression that wasn't quite pain, wasn't quite joy, but a braid of both, together bitter and sweet, like the first bite of autumn's earliest fruit.

She jumped to the ground and kept walking, meandering her way down the slope.

Dad and Sonia were flying into Burlington that afternoon. They were going to rent a car and drive themselves to Abrams Valley; they had reservations at one of the quaint historic bed-and-breakfasts in town. Verity had invited them over for supper and asked what they liked to eat. Grandma was going to give Sonia a quilt she had just finished. Gestures and overtures, rituals and manners, retreating into the familiar when there were so many things they didn't quite know how to talk about.

Sorrow had promised to sit down with them and talk, a proper talk, about what had happened and why she hadn't told them, about the questions and fears that had driven her to Vermont and the secrets she hadn't even known she had been keeping. She was going to keep her promise, but still the prospect of that conversation gave her a nervous flutter in her stomach. She had always tried so hard to keep her family in Florida separate from her family in Vermont, two worlds divided by lines in time, in geography, in sisters, in parents, past and present, forgotten and remembered. She didn't know yet how to stitch the two halves of herself together, but she knew now that those lines meant no more than wire stretched across wild mountain land: easily ducked, or clipped, or crushed by a fallen tree.

At the base of the hill she crossed from the shade to sunlight, into the meadow between the Lovegood and Abrams farms. The yellow crime scene tape was still up over the collapsed wall of the cider house, but one end had come loose to flutter lazily in the morning air. Verity had already started making arrangements to have the building torn down. Sorrow kept her distance and paced the area around the squat stone well.

When she found a flat spot, she dragged her heel through the dirt to make an X. Julie would be buried in the graveyard in town, her name carved into stone and set alongside her ancestors stretching all the way back to Clement Abrams, but she deserved to be remembered here as well. Ashes were forgiving trees, not particularly finicky about how well drained their plot of earth might be; they would grow in the damp meadow soil as well as they grew in the cemetery. The Lovegood land was the richest in Abrams Valley, with all the tragedy it had endured, giving and taking in equal measure.

Sorrow glanced at the well and, after a moment's thought, added two more marks. George Abrams would have hated it, a Lovegood daughter planting trees for him and his son, but George had died on Lovegood land, and Henry had loved a Lovegood woman. They belonged to the orchard now.

With a glance at the yellow tape and the burned ruin, Sorrow left the meadow and climbed the hill to the black oak. She walked around the perimeter of the clearing, pressing her palm to each of the children's ash trees in greeting, then circled the oak at its base until she found the protruding knot that gave her the best foot up. She climbed to a height of about twenty feet to settle on the branch Patience had always claimed was Silence Lovegood's hanging branch.

She sat on the branch with her back against the trunk, one leg drawn up and the other dangling. She wondered if she might learn to hear what Patience had heard echoing through the wood. A mother's desperation, a town's rabid terror. The chafe of a rope on bark. That could have been the end of their family, but Grace had returned to remake a home from the ruins, and they were still here.

The rising sun cast dappled patterns over Sorrow's bare arms. She felt an insect tickle her skin and brushed it away without looking. The trunk at her back was rough, almost painful, but if she didn't move, didn't shift around and fidget, she barely felt it. Here there was no decision to be made. There was no home and no away, no families split by difference and distance, no past and no present. There were no gaps in her memory anymore—the missing pieces had been here all along, cradled in the mountains and waiting—and in their absence the seams between the lonely lost child she had been and the person she was now were that much harder to find.

Nearby two birds were starting the day with an argument, and high above, a faint breeze turned the leaves of the oak. The rows of apple trees sloped into the valley, into fields and forests, hills and hollows wild and tamed, over the sharp line where the orchard ended and the preserve began, all stitched together like blocks of her grandmother's quilts in countless shades of green. In the cool morning dew everything smelled of old, old apples.

ACKNOWLEDGMENTS

Many thanks to my editor, Alexandra Arnold, without whom this book would never have evolved into anything worth reading. Thank you for your endless patience through endless revisions, and for pushing me to make the story so much more than I ever thought it could be.

And thank you to my agent, Adriann Ranta, who has yet to flinch at any of the random genre changes and wild ideas I throw her way.

A million thanks and cookies and fancy cocktails to Audrey Coulthurst, Adriana Mather, and Paula Garner. I never would have made it through the year I spent working on this novel without your friendship. (My liver, on the other hand, most adamantly does *not* thank you.)

And thank you to the members of my San Diego writing group (and our Oregon annex): Valerie Polichar, Jessica Hilt, Morgen Jahnke, James Seddon, Gary Gould, and Alex Gorman. Your beautiful stories, helpful insight, and good company were always a welcome diversion during a most difficult year.

Endless gratitude and thanks to the members of the Sweet Sixteens debut group. Through all the ups and downs of being a debut author, there is no comfort like knowing you're not alone on this wild ride. I am looking forward to cheering for every single one of you as you bring more amazing books into the world.

And thank you, as always, to my family, for your unwavering love and support.